my Dead Girlfriend ™

Vo
/

VOICES FROM THE BEYOND

"*MY DEAD GIRLFRIEND is a perfect combination of the whimsical and the morbid. It's a warped, macabre view of high school that is absolutely accurate, except for the weird fantasy element of having a girlfriend. A delight.*"

Joss Whedon, Creator/Executive Producer of
Buffy the Vampire Slayer, Angel, Firefly

"*Thrills. Chills. Romance. And laugh-out-loud humor: MY DEAD GIRLFRIEND has it all! Once you start reading it, you won't want to put it down.*"

Meg Cabot, *New York Times* Bestselling Author of
The Princess Diaries and *Avalon High*

"*Eric Wight can make anyone a fan of comics. Funny and extremely original, MY DEAD GIRLFRIEND manages to be hip and knowing, while infusing innocence and wonder. Wight's one talented guy, and with this book he finally gets the chance to prove it.*"

Josh Schwartz, Creator/Executive Producer of *The O.C.*

"*A fun, hilarious, and surprisingly touching carnival ride set in a fantastically complex world that remains grounded in very identifiable human emotion.*"

Jane Espenson, Writer/Producer of *Buffy the Vampire Slayer,
Gilmore Girls, Battlestar Galactica*

"*Poignant, funny, and terribly clever, MY DEAD GIRLFRIEND is a bold step in storytelling. Imagine Joss Whedon meets Tim Burton with a healthy dose of something entirely original and you get just to the first page of this unique and wonderful tale. The rest can only be called magical.*"

Jeph Loeb, Writer of *Superman/Batman* and *Batman: Hush*,
Writer/Producer of *Heroes, Lost, Smallville*

"*Wight has created a world ripe with humor, horror and heart that is wonderfully bizarre and yet incredibly familiar.*"

Geoff Johns, Writer of *Action Comics* and *Green Lantern*

"*MY DEAD GIRLFRIEND is like a first kiss--a little frightening, a lot fantastic, and totally unforgettable.*"

Michele Jaffe, Author of *Bad Kitty, Loverboy*

"*Whimsical, fun, heartbreaking, and tragic--man, I love this book. MY DEAD GIRLFRIEND is as original as it gets. Stop reading this blurb and buy it already.*"

Brad Meltzer, *New York Times* Bestselling Author of
The Book of Fate and *Identity Crisis*

My Dead Girlfriend™

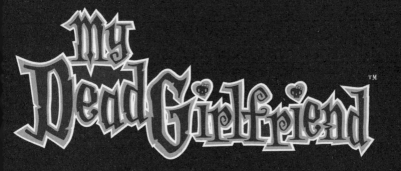

VOLUME ONE

"A TRYST OF FATE"

BY ERIC WIGHT

TOKYOPOP®

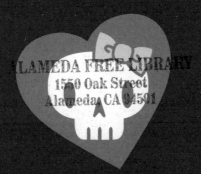

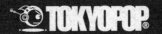

HAMBURG // LONDON // LOS ANGELES // TOKYO

My Dead Girlfriend Vol. 1
Created by Eric Wight

Additional Inks - Mike Allred
Michael Cho
Nick Derington
Tones - Mark Lewis
Additional Assistance - Lou La Palombara
Lettering - Mark Lewis and Lucas Rivera
Cover Design - Al-Insan Lashley

Editor - Julie Taylor
Digital Imaging Manager - Chris Buford
Pre-Production Supervisor - Erika Terriquez
Art Director - Anne Marie Horne
Production Manager - Elisabeth Brizzi
Managing Editor - Vy Nguyen
VP of Production - Ron Klamert
Editor-in-Chief - Rob Tokar
Publisher - Mike Kiley
President and C.O.O. - John Parker
C.E.O. and Chief Creative Officer - Stuart Levy

A  Manga

TOKYOPOP and  are trademarks or registered trademarks of TOKYOPOP Inc.

TOKYOPOP Inc.
5900 Wilshire Blvd. Suite 2000
Los Angeles, CA 90036

E-mail: info@TOKYOPOP.com
Come visit us online at www.TOKYOPOP.com

ISBN: 978-1-59816-996-6

First TOKYOPOP printing: February 2007
10 9 8 7 6 5 4 3 2 1
Printed in the USA

To Krissy -- without whom Finney could never have found his Jenny.

TABLE of CONTENTS

INTRODUCTION

It all started with the Legion of Super-Heroes.

In the fall of 2003, I picked up DC Comics' *The Legion* #25 expecting to get caught up on the comic book adventures of my favorite thirty-first century teenage super-team. Instead, I found myself transported back to the past, to the very first Legion of Super-Heroes story, where a teenaged Clark Kent met Saturn Girl, Lightning Lad, and Cosmic Boy and his life -- and mine -- were changed forever. While the original story (by Otto Binder and Al Plastino) is a classic, I found this contemporary rendering to be particularly affecting. The stark simplicity of its artwork was distinctively retro and futuristic at the same time and, in just three pages, the artist managed to capture the energy, the innocence, and the sci-fi fun of the Legion in a way I hadn't experienced since I was a kid. The issue's credits revealed that the artist's name was Eric Wight. And a subsequent Google search revealed that his Legion pages were available on eBay.

I wish I could say I am the proud owner of those pages, but, alas, I'm still bitter about having been outbid by a legion of Eric Wight fans. I am happy to report, however, that by the time Eric Wight's award-winning artwork from *The Escapist* (written by Pulitzer Prize-winning novelist Michael Chabon) hit the internet, I had stepped up my eBay game enough to become the proud owner of a page from "The Passing of the Key."

That's when Rick Cleveland, a writer/producer of HBO's *Six Feet Under*, called to ask if I knew a comic book artist who could convincingly create a fictional, golden age superhero called the Blue Twister for the show. I immediately got in touch with Eric through eBay, and our email correspondence soon became a long-distance collaboration that resulted in Eric's becoming Seth Cohen's ghost artist on FOX's *The O.C.* But by far the most impressive of Eric's achievements is the book you now hold in your hands.

MY DEAD GIRLFRIEND is a whip-smart, sweetly snarky coming-of-age tale that wittily transposes the adolescent landscape of familiar high school horrors to a cheerfully macabre world populated by brain-dead Aberzombies, blood-sucking Deadbeats, and wicked teenage Glindas. Its irreverence, humor, and heart will make instant fans of readers who are new to manga, and will remind longtime readers of why they fell in love with comics in the first place. With its compellingly original voice and visual style, *MY DEAD GIRLFRIEND* is a soulful exploration of what it means to be fully alive in a world of ghosts, where love is the most powerful force in the universe, and death is only the beginning.

ALLAN HEINBERG

Allan Heinberg is the Harvey and GLAAD Award-winning writer and co-creator of THE YOUNG AVENGERS. His television writing and producing credits include THE O.C., GILMORE GIRLS, SEX AND THE CITY, and currently GREY'S ANATOMY.

CHAPTER ONE

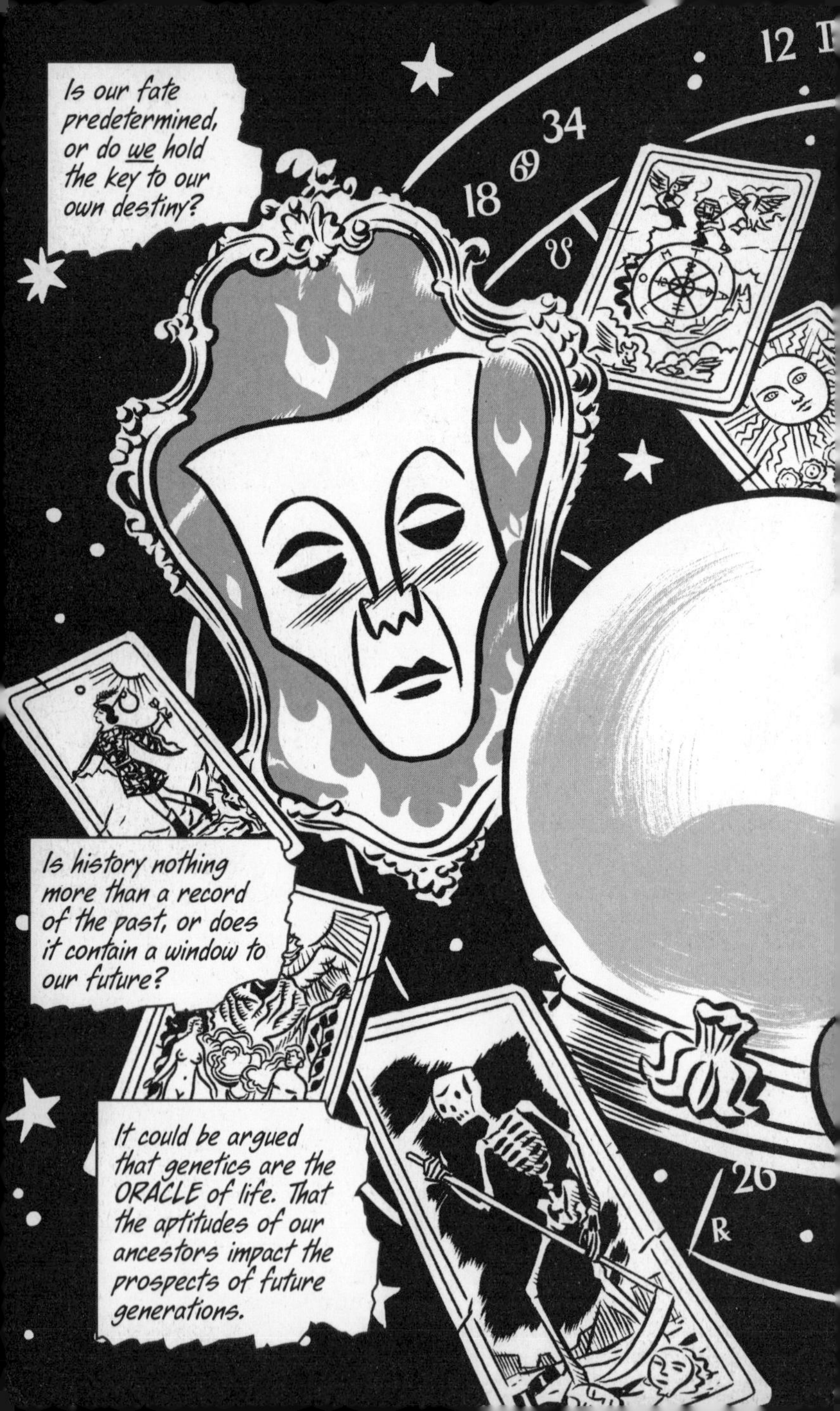
Is our fate predetermined, or do we hold the key to our own destiny?
Is history nothing more than a record of the past, or does it contain a window to our future?
It could be argued that genetics are the ORACLE of life. That the aptitudes of our ancestors impact the prospects of future generations.

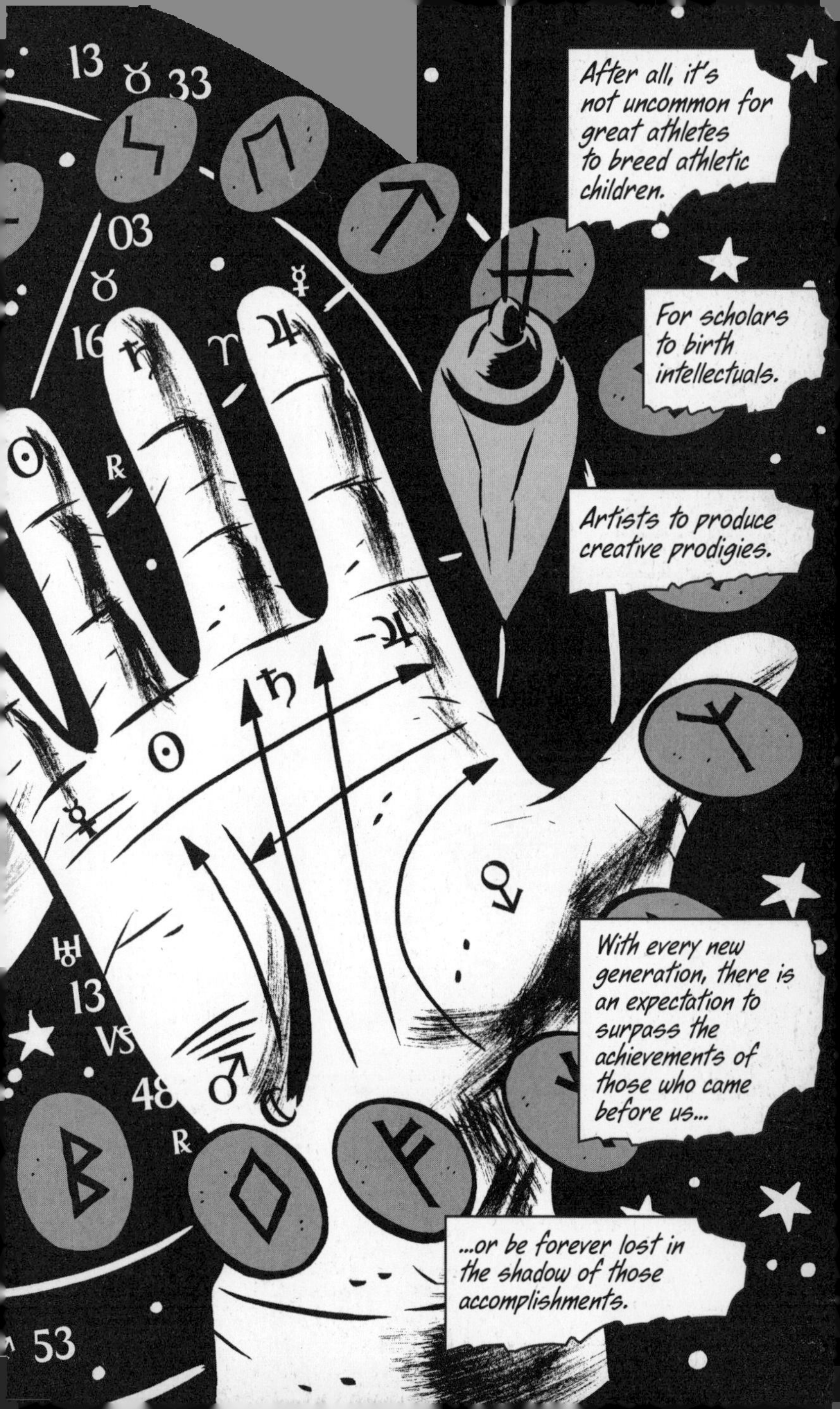
After all, it's not uncommon for great athletes to breed athletic children.
For scholars to birth intellectuals.
Artists to produce creative prodigies.
With every new generation, there is an expectation to surpass the achievements of those who came before us...
...or be forever lost in the shadow of those accomplishments.

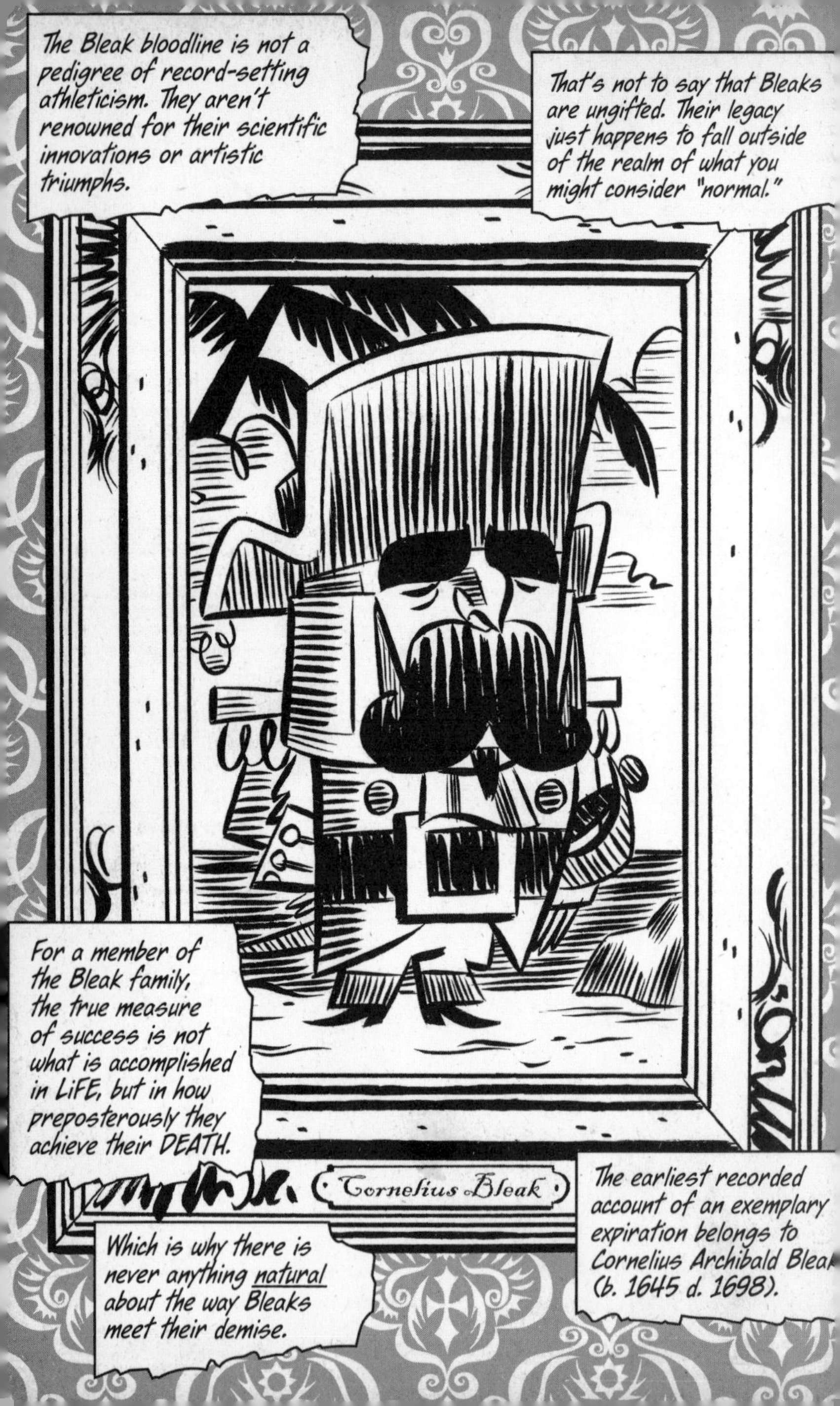

The Bleak bloodline is not a pedigree of record-setting athleticism. They aren't renowned for their scientific innovations or artistic triumphs.
That's not to say that Bleaks are ungifted. Their legacy just happens to fall outside of the realm of what you might consider "normal."
For a member of the Bleak family, the true measure of success is not what is accomplished in LIFE, but in how preposterously they achieve their DEATH.
Cornelius Bleak
Which is why there is never anything natural about the way Bleaks meet their demise.
The earliest recorded account of an exemplary expiration belongs to Cornelius Archibald Bleak (b. 1645 d. 1698).

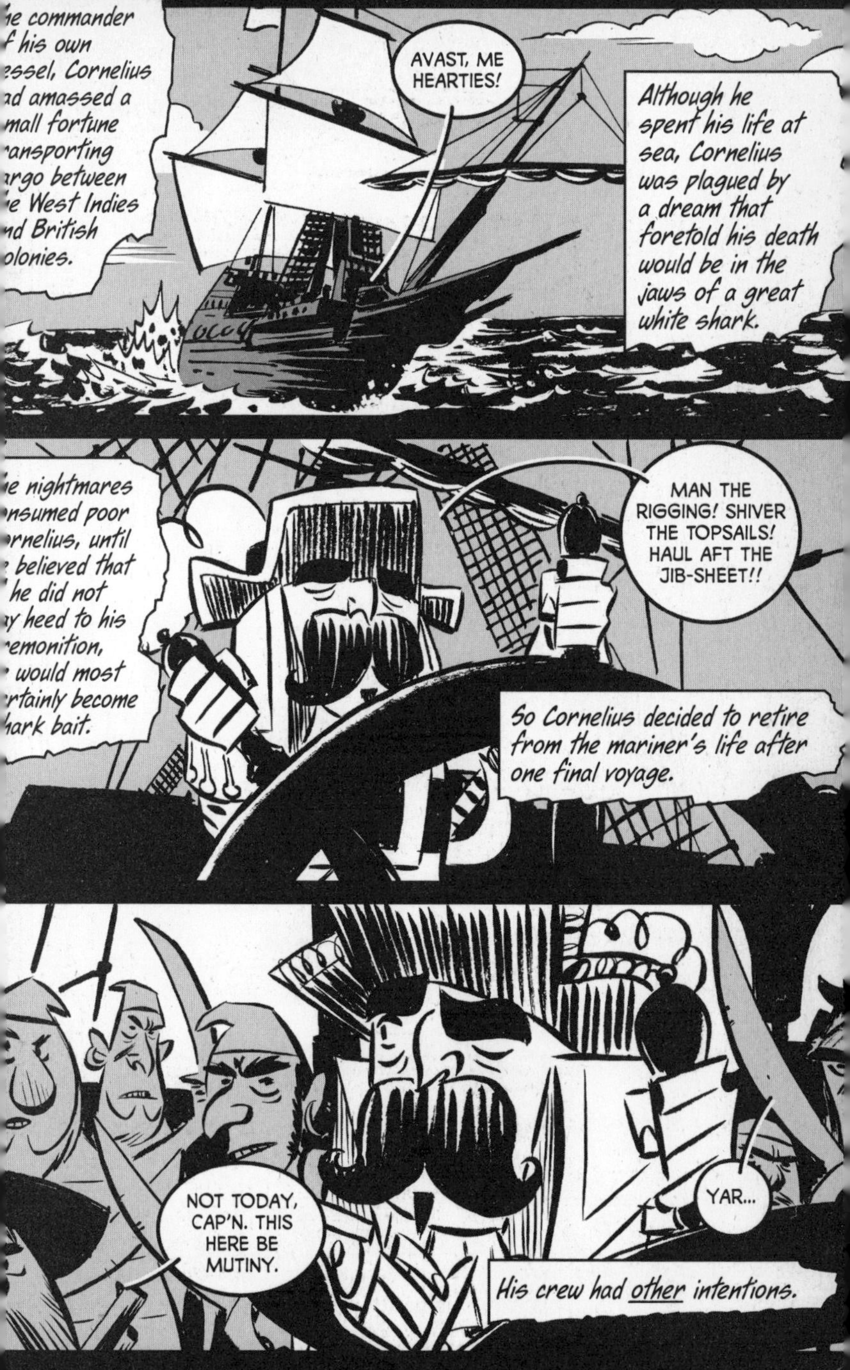

e commander f his own essel, Cornelius ad amassed a mall fortune ransporting argo between e West Indies nd British olonies.
AVAST, ME HEARTIES!
Although he spent his life at sea, Cornelius was plagued by a dream that foretold his death would be in the jaws of a great white shark.
e nightmares nsumed poor ornelius, until believed that he did not y heed to his emonition, would most rtainly become hark bait.
MAN THE RIGGING! SHIVER THE TOPSAILS! HAUL AFT THE JIB-SHEET!!
So Cornelius decided to retire from the mariner's life after one final voyage.
NOT TODAY, CAP'N. THIS HERE BE MUTINY.
YAR...
His crew had other intentions.

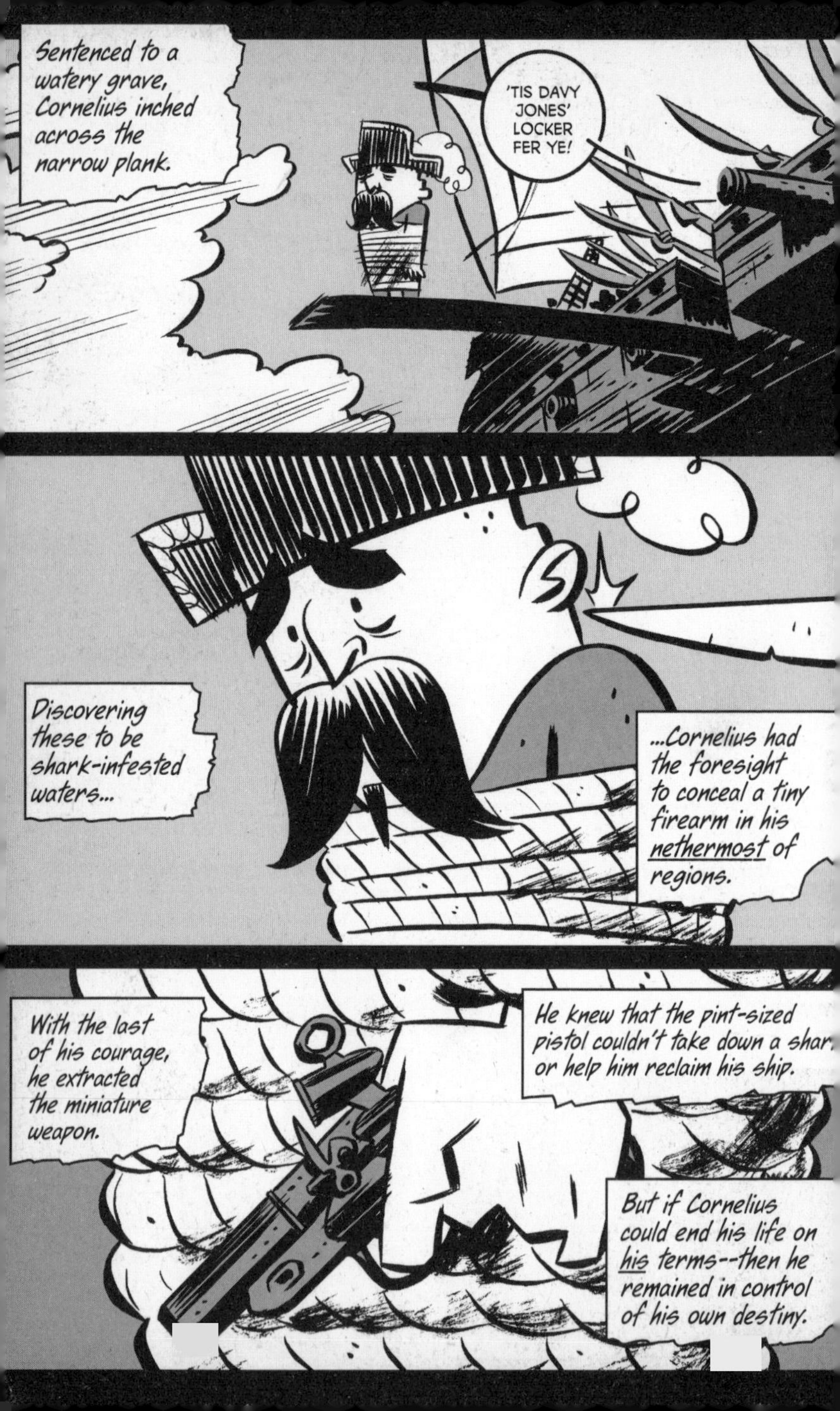
Sentenced to a watery grave, Cornelius inched across the narrow plank.
'TIS DAVY JONES' LOCKER FER YE!
Discovering these to be shark-infested waters...
...Cornelius had the foresight to conceal a tiny firearm in his nethermost of regions.
With the last of his courage, he extracted the miniature weapon.
He knew that the pint-sized pistol couldn't take down a shar or help him reclaim his ship.
But if Cornelius could end his life on his terms--then he remained in control of his own destiny.

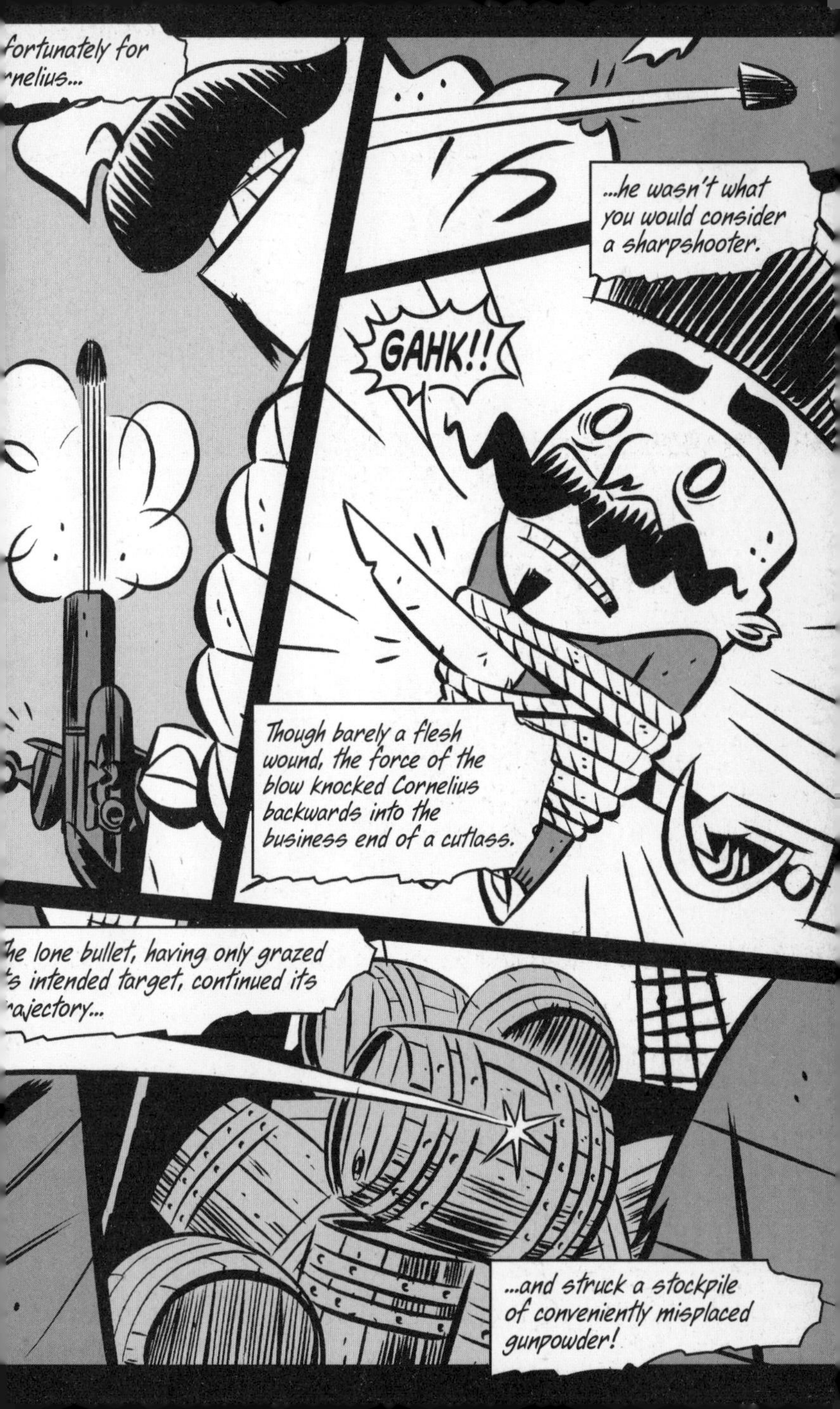
fortunately for
rnelius...
...he wasn't what
you would consider
a sharpshooter.
GAHK!!
Though barely a flesh
wound, the force of the
blow knocked Cornelius
backwards into the
business end of a cutlass.
he lone bullet, having only grazed
s intended target, continued its
rajectory...
...and struck a stockpile
of conveniently misplaced
gunpowder!

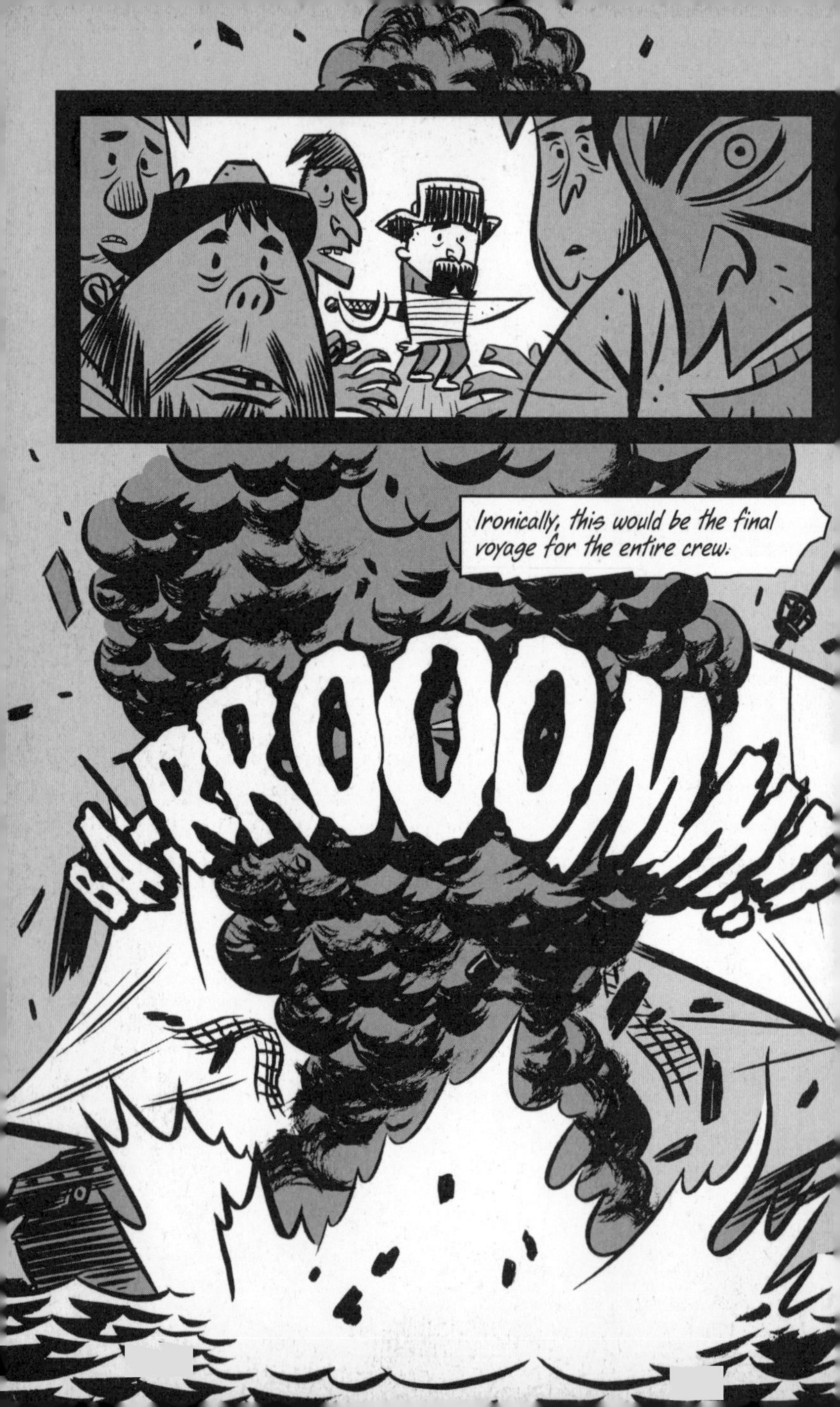
Ironically, this would be the final voyage for the entire crew.
BA-ROOOMM!!

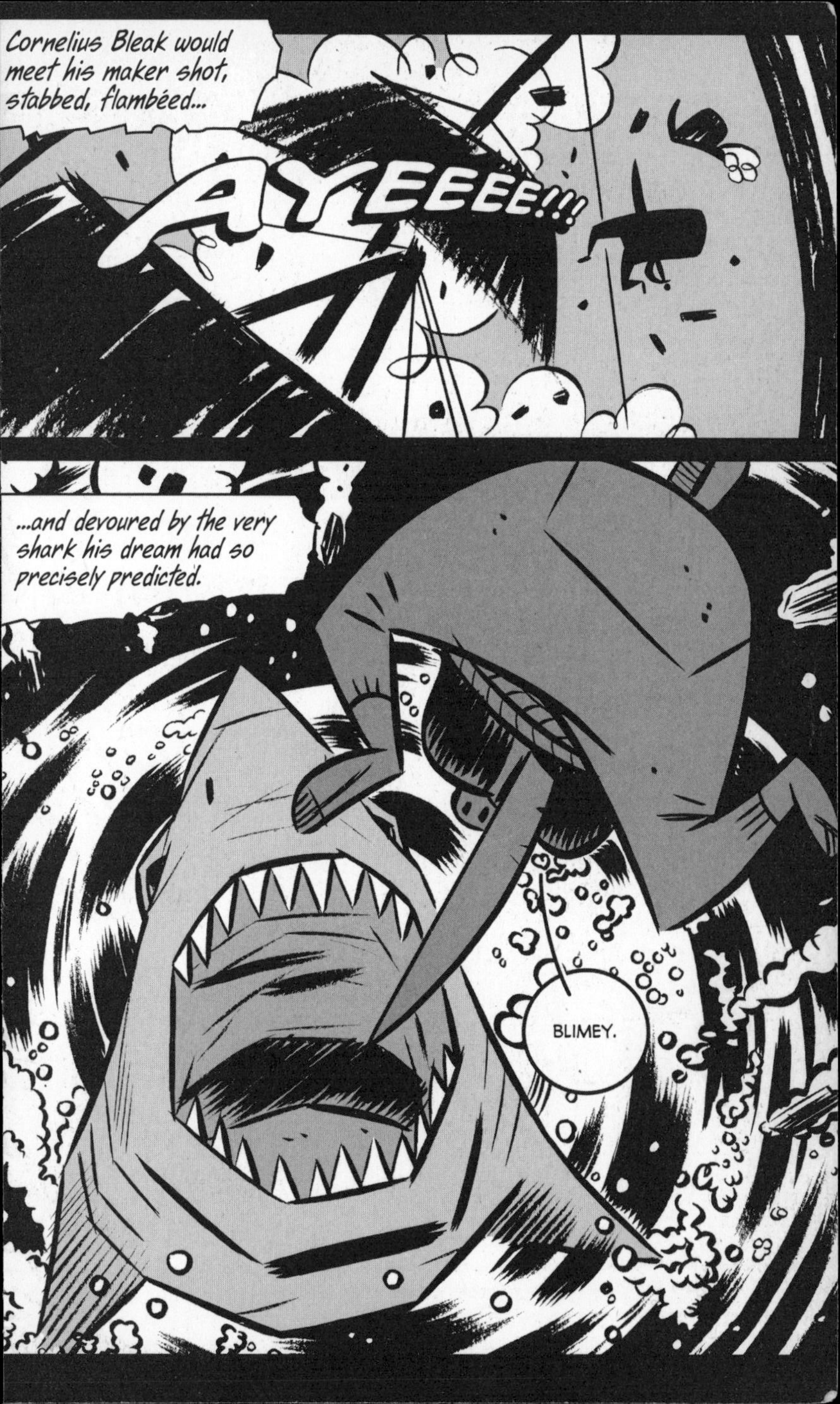
Cornelius Bleak would meet his maker shot, stabbed, flambéed...
AYEEEEE!!!
...and devoured by the very shark his dream had so precisely predicted.
BLIMEY.

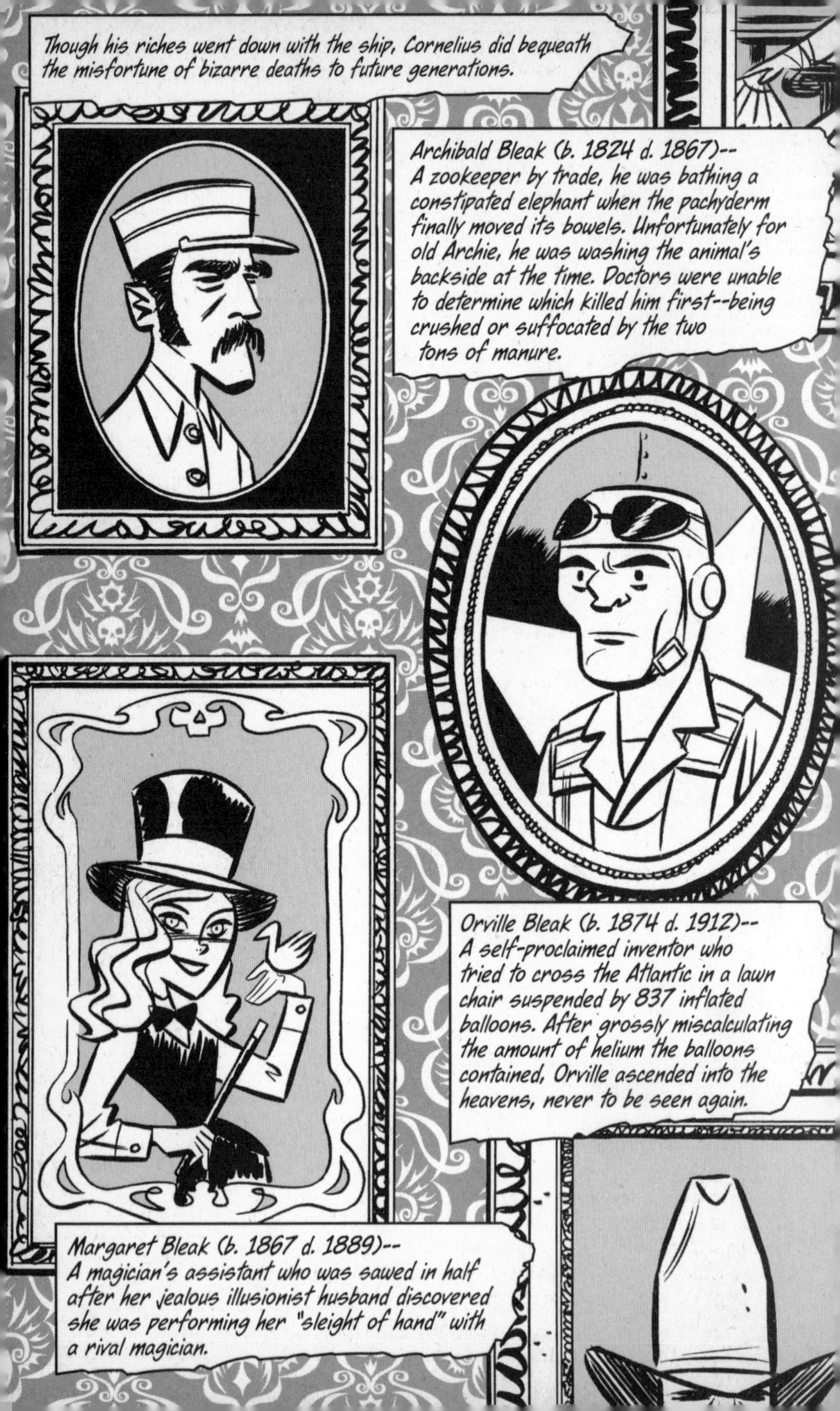
Though his riches went down with the ship, Cornelius did bequeath the misfortune of bizarre deaths to future generations.
Archibald Bleak (b. 1824 d. 1867)-- A zookeeper by trade, he was bathing a constipated elephant when the pachyderm finally moved its bowels. Unfortunately for old Archie, he was washing the animal's backside at the time. Doctors were unable to determine which killed him first--being crushed or suffocated by the two tons of manure.
Orville Bleak (b. 1874 d. 1912)-- A self-proclaimed inventor who tried to cross the Atlantic in a lawn chair suspended by 837 inflated balloons. After grossly miscalculating the amount of helium the balloons contained, Orville ascended into the heavens, never to be seen again.
Margaret Bleak (b. 1867 d. 1889)-- A magician's assistant who was sawed in half after her jealous illusionist husband discovered she was performing her "sleight of hand" with a rival magician.

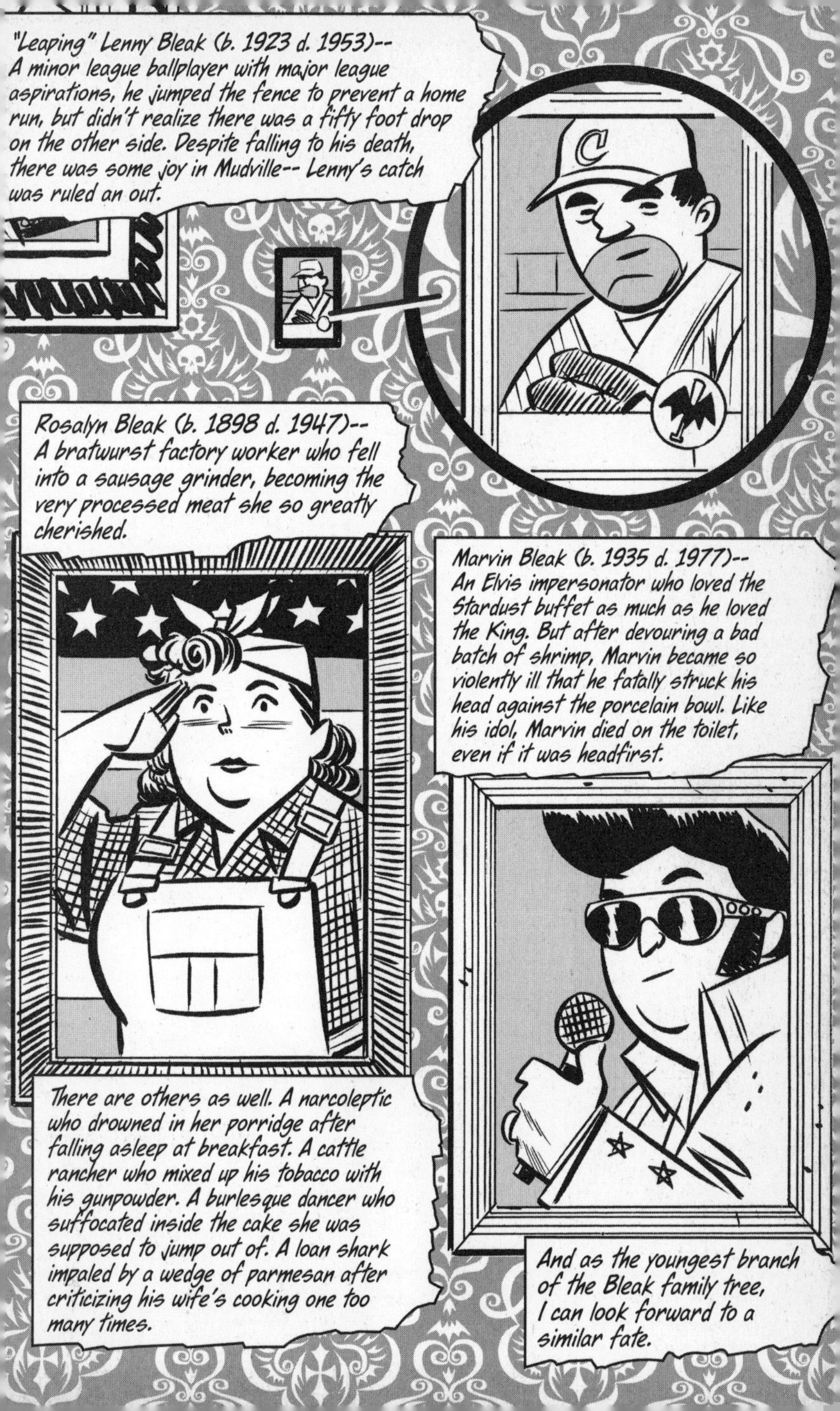
"Leaping" Lenny Bleak (b. 1923 d. 1953)-- A minor league ballplayer with major league aspirations, he jumped the fence to prevent a home run, but didn't realize there was a fifty foot drop on the other side. Despite falling to his death, there was some joy in Mudville-- Lenny's catch was ruled an out.
Rosalyn Bleak (b. 1898 d. 1947)-- A bratwurst factory worker who fell into a sausage grinder, becoming the very processed meat she so greatly cherished.
Marvin Bleak (b. 1935 d. 1977)-- An Elvis impersonator who loved the Stardust buffet as much as he loved the King. But after devouring a bad batch of shrimp, Marvin became so violently ill that he fatally struck his head against the porcelain bowl. Like his idol, Marvin died on the toilet, even if it was headfirst.
There are others as well. A narcoleptic who drowned in her porridge after falling asleep at breakfast. A cattle rancher who mixed up his tobacco with his gunpowder. A burlesque dancer who suffocated inside the cake she was supposed to jump out of. A loan shark impaled by a wedge of parmesan after criticizing his wife's cooking one too many times.
And as the youngest branch of the Bleak family tree, I can look forward to a similar fate.

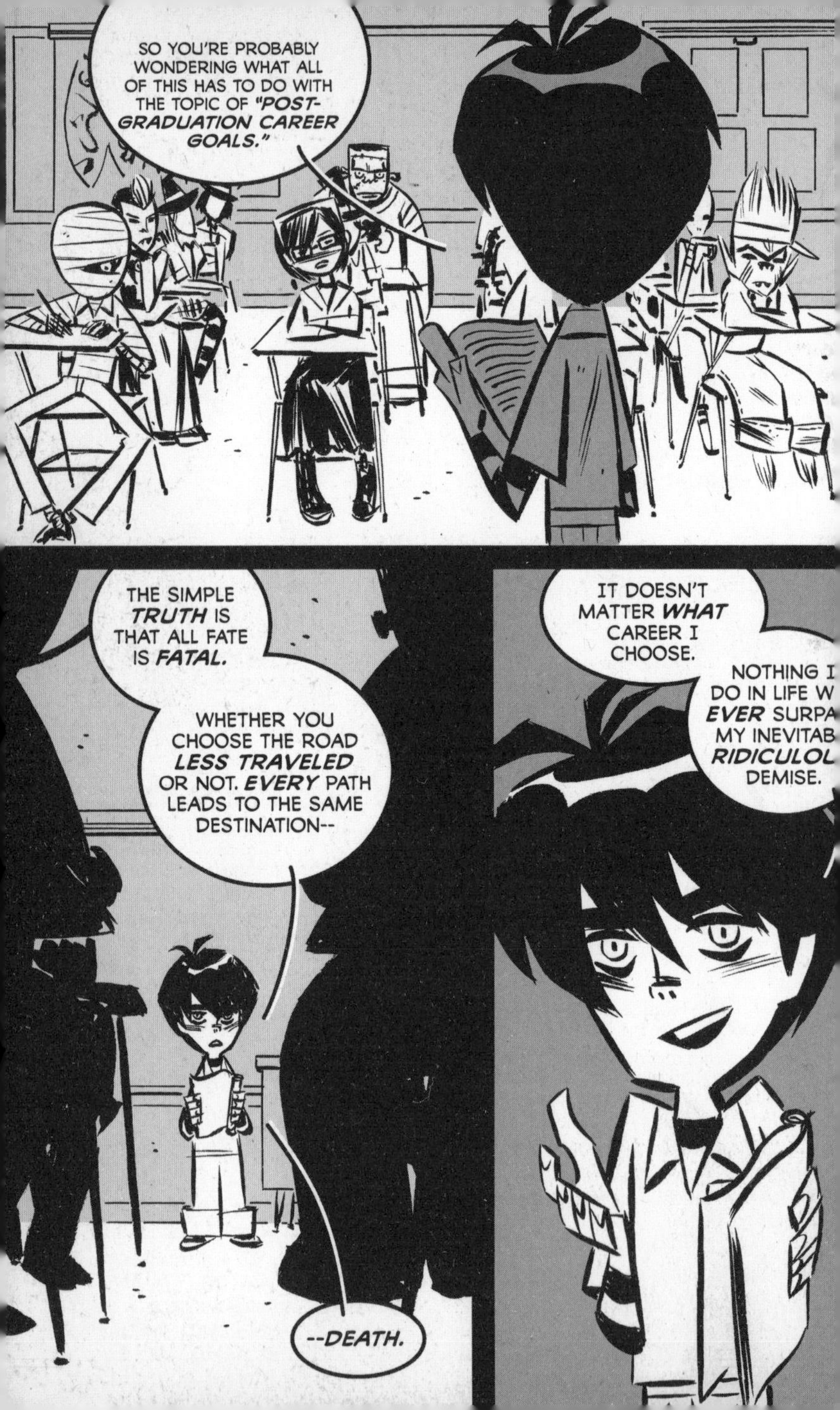

SO YOU'RE PROBABLY WONDERING WHAT ALL OF THIS HAS TO DO WITH THE TOPIC OF "POST-GRADUATION CAREER GOALS."
THE SIMPLE TRUTH IS THAT ALL FATE IS FATAL.
WHETHER YOU CHOOSE THE ROAD LESS TRAVELED OR NOT. EVERY PATH LEADS TO THE SAME DESTINATION--
--DEATH.
IT DOESN'T MATTER WHAT CAREER I CHOOSE.

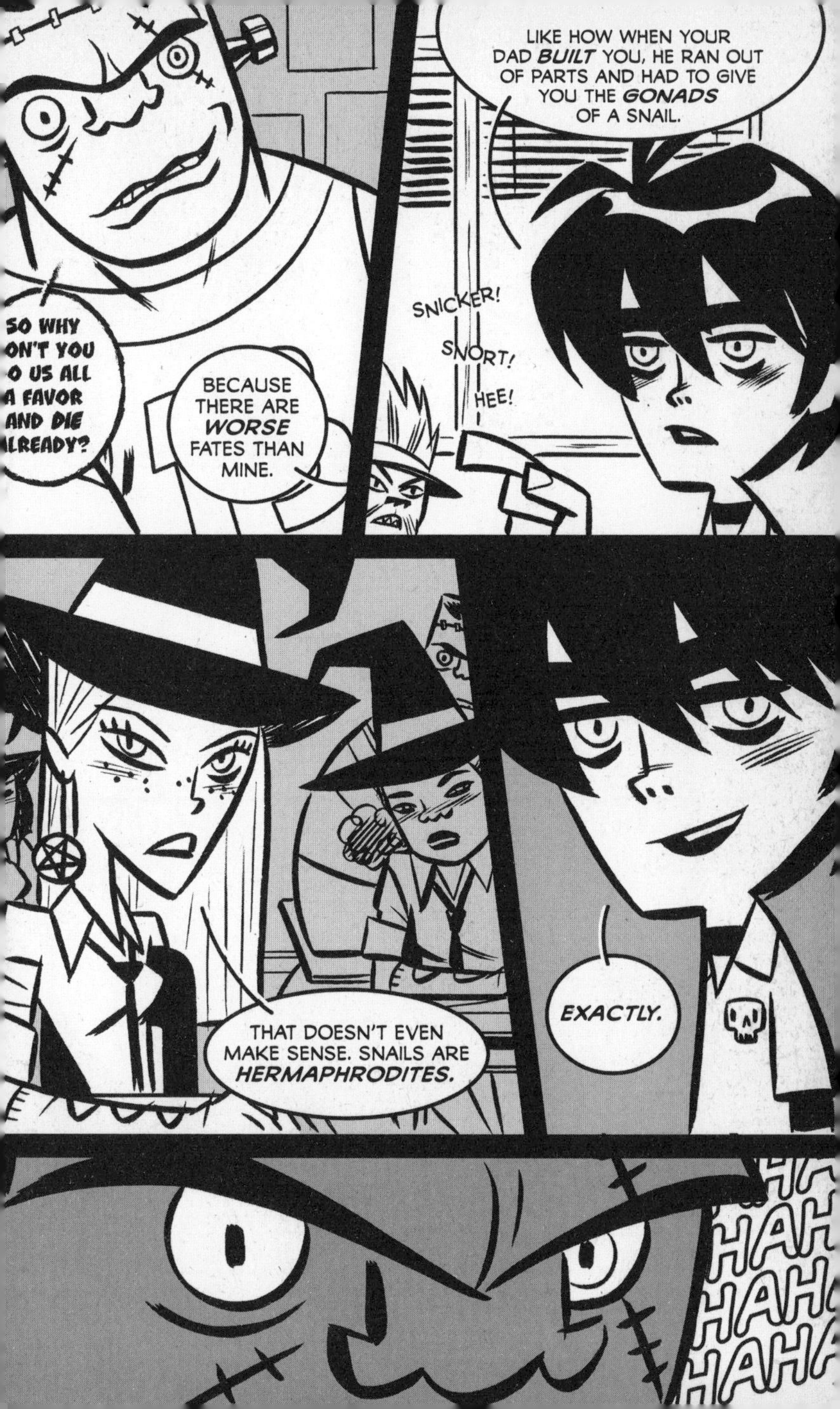
SO WHY ON'T YOU O US ALL A FAVOR AND DIE LREADY?
BECAUSE THERE ARE WORSE FATES THAN MINE.
LIKE HOW WHEN YOUR DAD BUILT YOU, HE RAN OUT OF PARTS AND HAD TO GIVE YOU THE GONADS OF A SNAIL.
SNICKER!
SNORT!
HEE!
THAT DOESN'T EVEN MAKE SENSE. SNAILS ARE HERMAPHRODITES.
EXACTLY.
HAHAHAHA

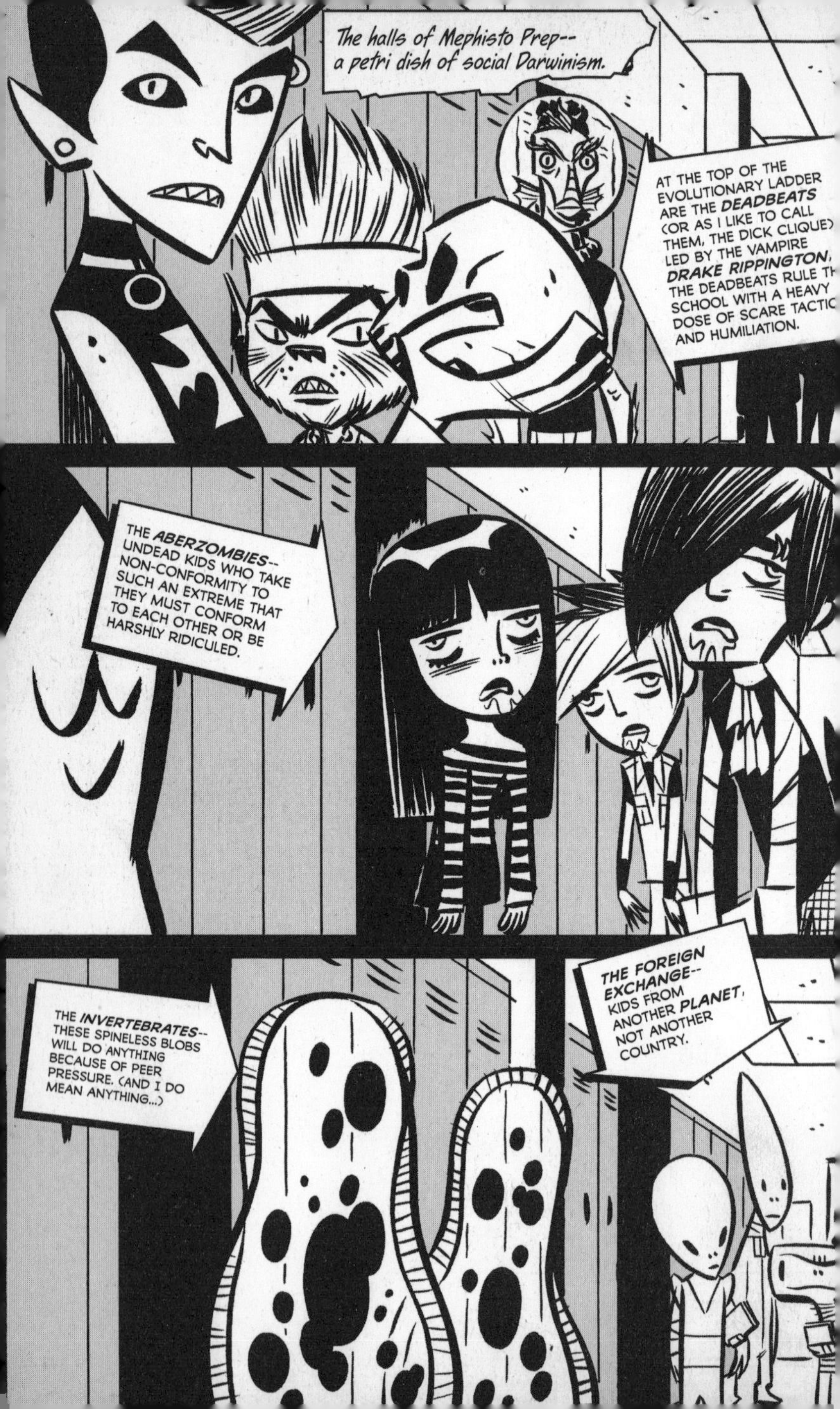
The halls of Mephisto Prep--
a petri dish of social Darwinism.
AT THE TOP OF THE EVOLUTIONARY LADDER ARE THE DEADBEATS (OR AS I LIKE TO CALL THEM, THE DICK CLIQUE) LED BY THE VAMPIRE DRAKE RIPPINGTON, THE DEADBEATS RULE TH SCHOOL WITH A HEAVY DOSE OF SCARE TACTIC AND HUMILIATION.
THE ABERZOMBIES-- UNDEAD KIDS WHO TAKE NON-CONFORMITY TO SUCH AN EXTREME THAT THEY MUST CONFORM TO EACH OTHER OR BE HARSHLY RIDICULED.
THE INVERTEBRATES-- THESE SPINELESS BLOBS WILL DO ANYTHING BECAUSE OF PEER PRESSURE. (AND I DO MEAN ANYTHING...)
THE FOREIGN EXCHANGE-- KIDS FROM ANOTHER PLANET, NOT ANOTHER COUNTRY.

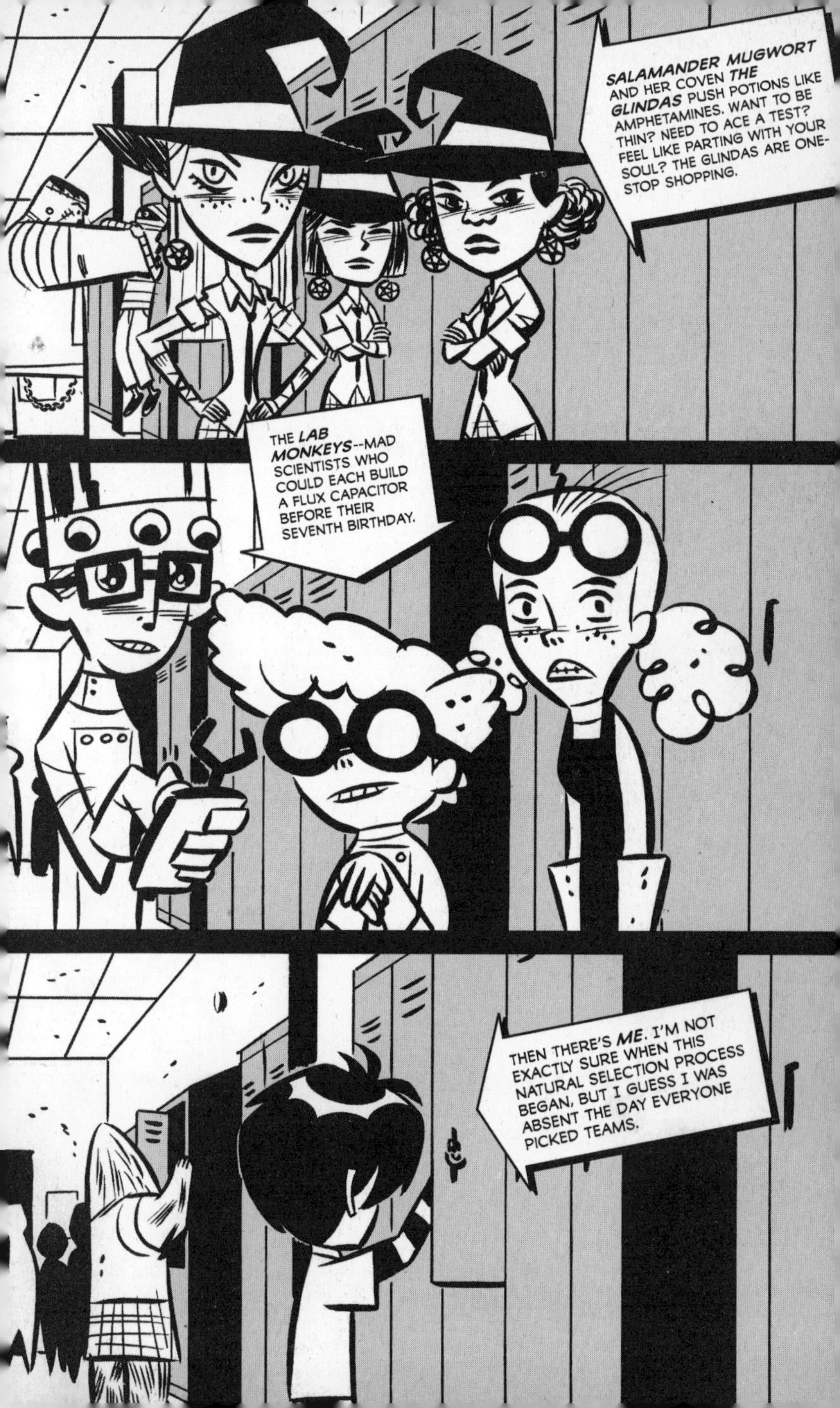
SALAMANDER MUGWORT AND HER COVEN THE GLINDAS PUSH POTIONS LIKE AMPHETAMINES. WANT TO BE THIN? NEED TO ACE A TEST? FEEL LIKE PARTING WITH YOUR SOUL? THE GLINDAS ARE ONE-STOP SHOPPING.
THE LAB MONKEYS--MAD SCIENTISTS WHO COULD EACH BUILD A FLUX CAPACITOR BEFORE THEIR SEVENTH BIRTHDAY.
THEN THERE'S ME. I'M NOT EXACTLY SURE WHEN THIS NATURAL SELECTION PROCESS BEGAN, BUT I GUESS I WAS ABSENT THE DAY EVERYONE PICKED TEAMS.

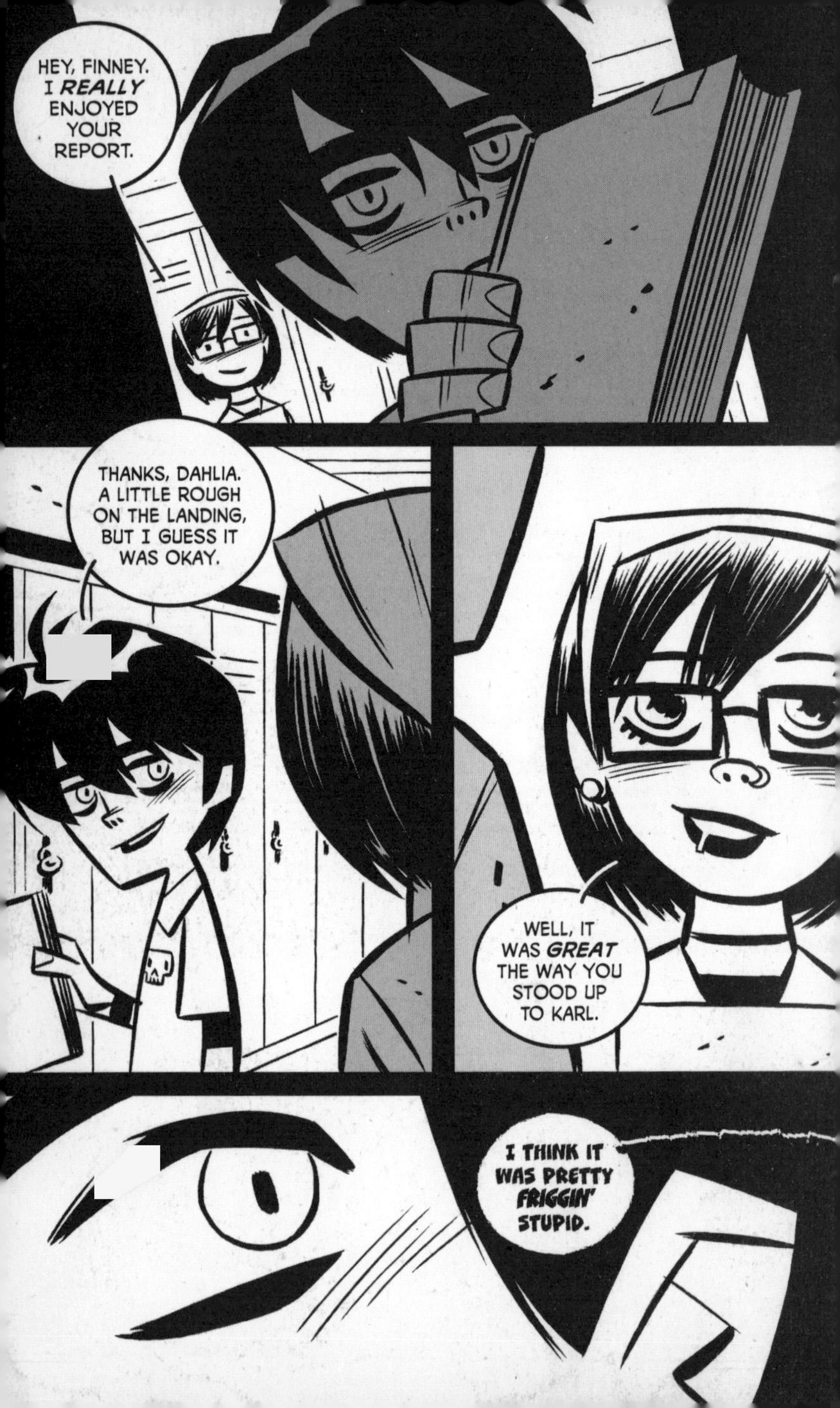
HEY, FINNEY. I REALLY ENJOYED YOUR REPORT.
THANKS, DAHLIA. A LITTLE ROUGH ON THE LANDING, BUT I GUESS IT WAS OKAY.
WELL, IT WAS GREAT THE WAY YOU STOOD UP TO KARL.
I THINK IT WAS PRETTY FRIGGIN' STUPID.

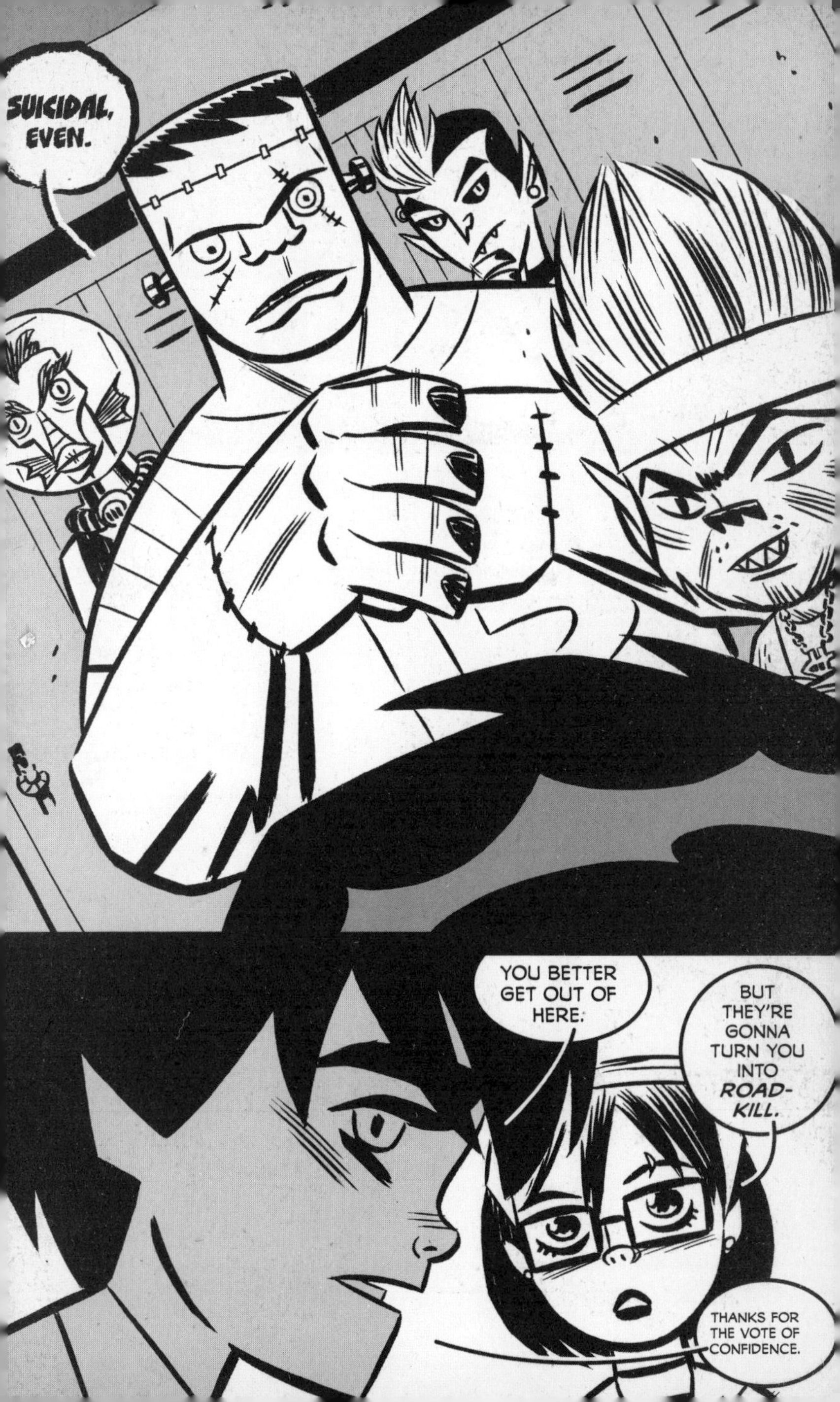
SUICIDAL, EVEN.
YOU BETTER GET OUT OF HERE.
BUT THEY'RE GONNA TURN YOU INTO ROAD-KILL.
THANKS FOR THE VOTE OF CONFIDENCE.

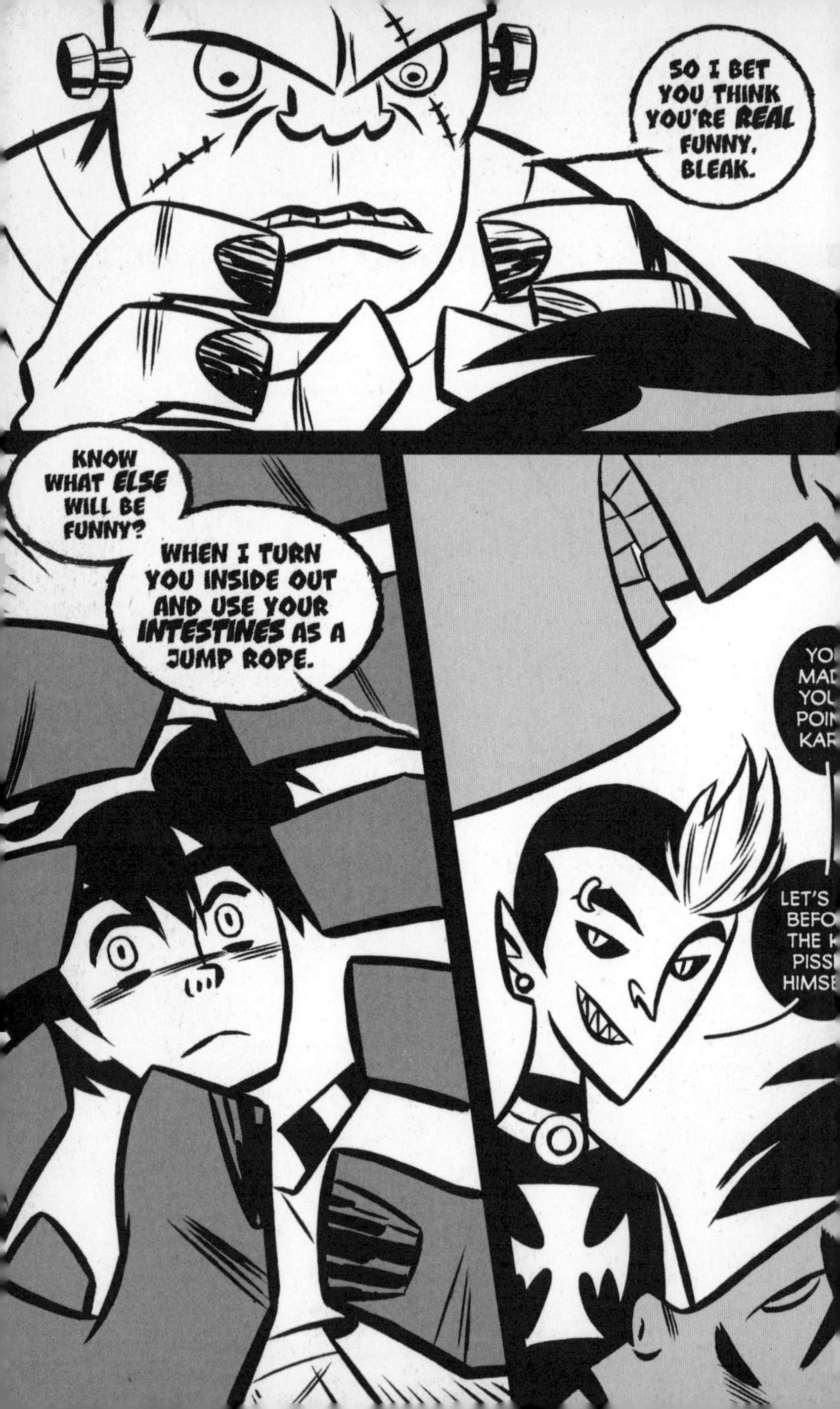
SO I BET YOU THINK YOU'RE REAL FUNNY, BLEAK.
KNOW WHAT ELSE WILL BE FUNNY?
WHEN I TURN YOU INSIDE OUT AND USE YOUR INTESTINES AS A JUMP ROPE.

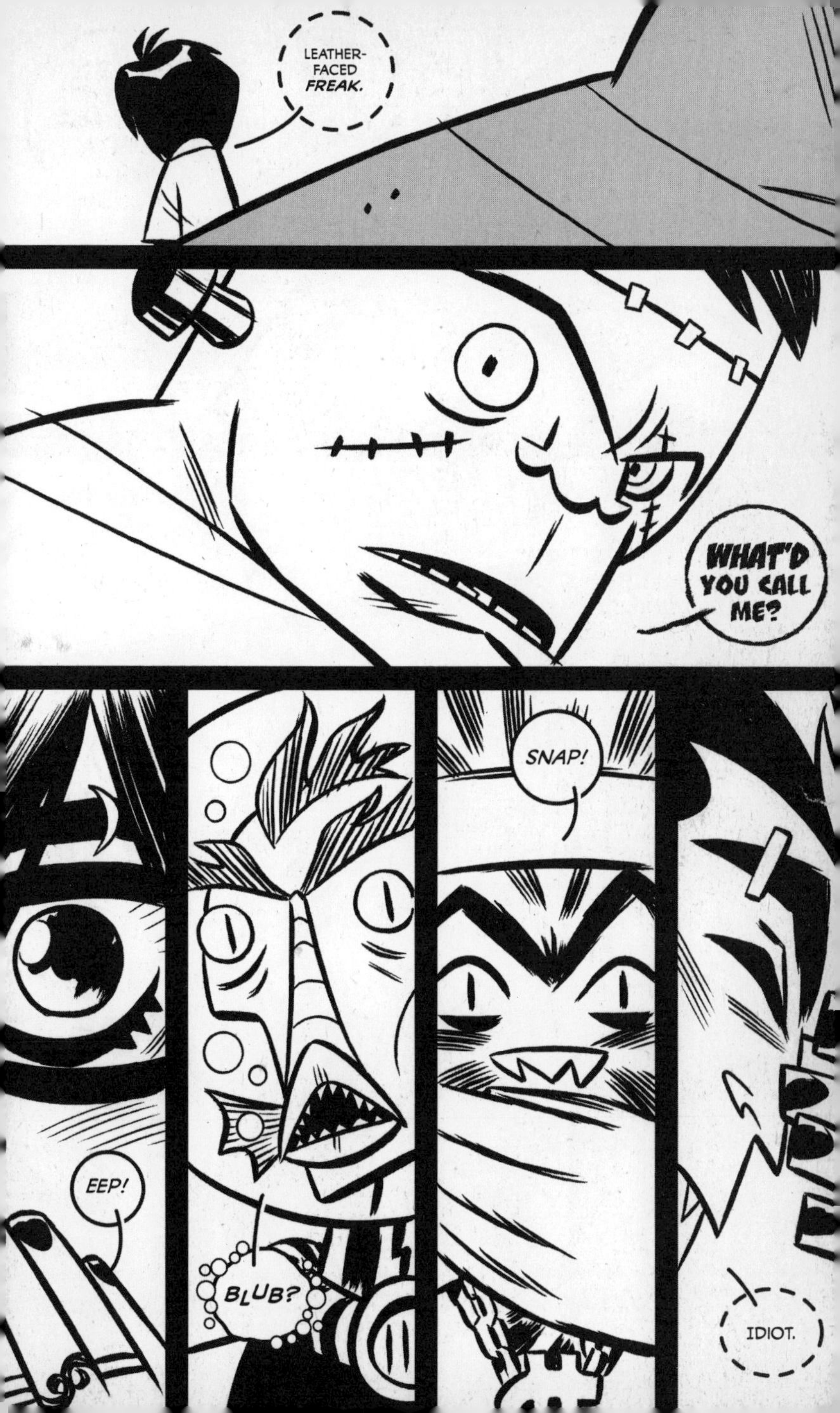
LEATHER-FACED FREAK.
WHAT'D YOU CALL ME?
EEP!
BLUB?
SNAP!
IDIOT.

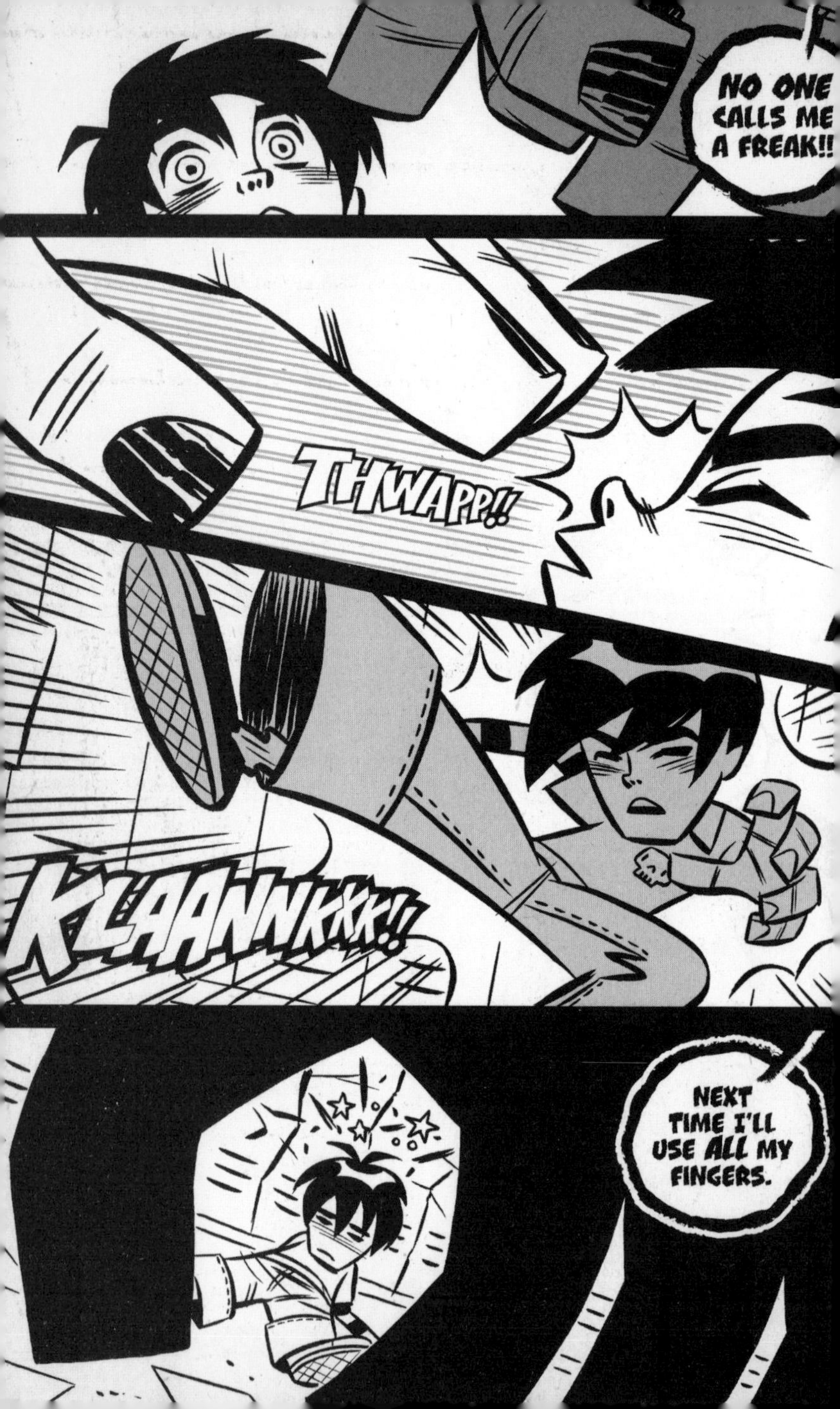
NO ONE CALLS ME A FREAK!!
THWAPP!!
KLAANNKKK!!
NEXT TIME I'LL USE *ALL* MY FINGERS.

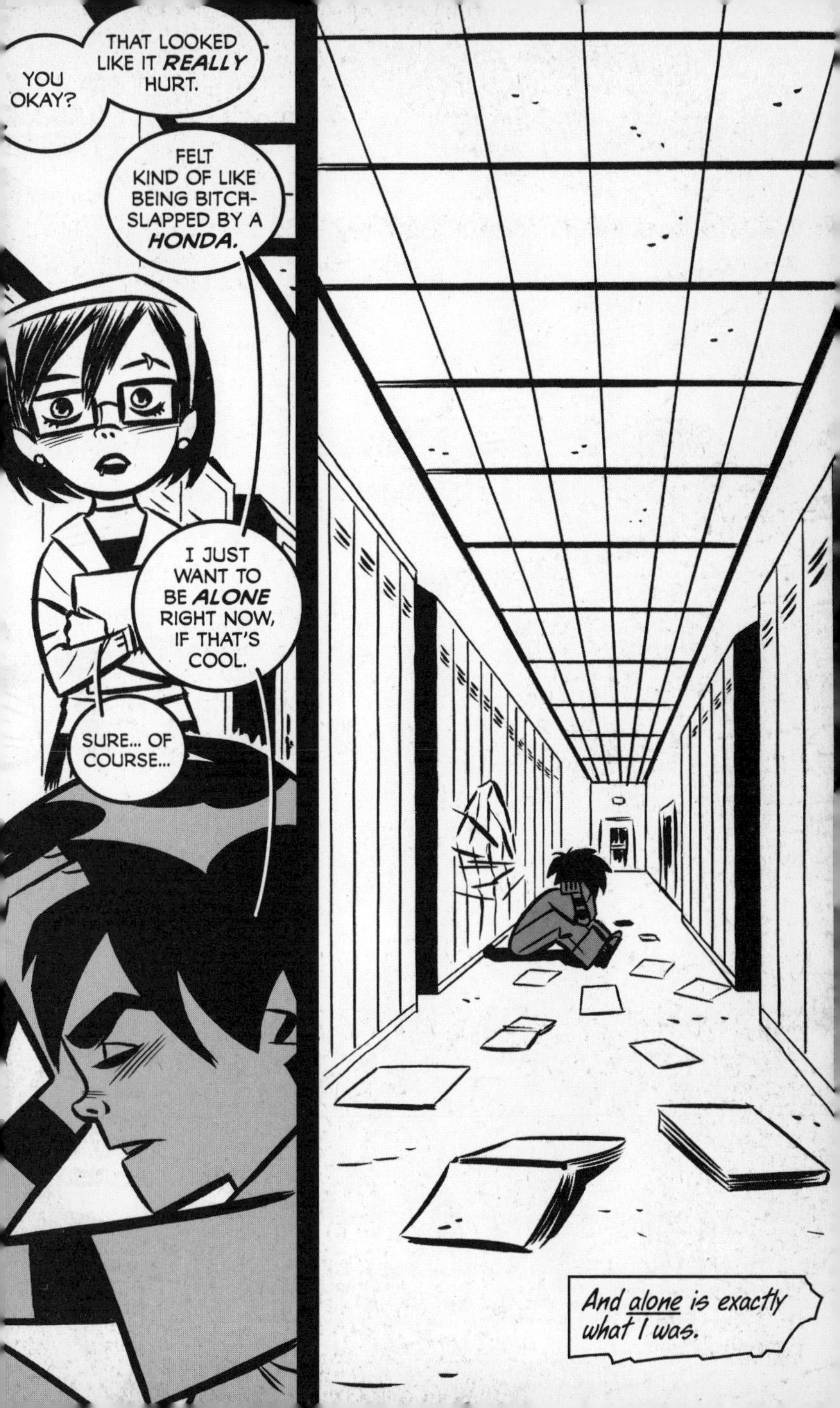
YOU OKAY?
THAT LOOKED LIKE IT REALLY HURT.
FELT KIND OF LIKE BEING BITCH-SLAPPED BY A HONDA.
I JUST WANT TO BE ALONE RIGHT NOW, IF THAT'S COOL.
SURE... OF COURSE...
And alone is exactly what I was.

CHAPTER TWO

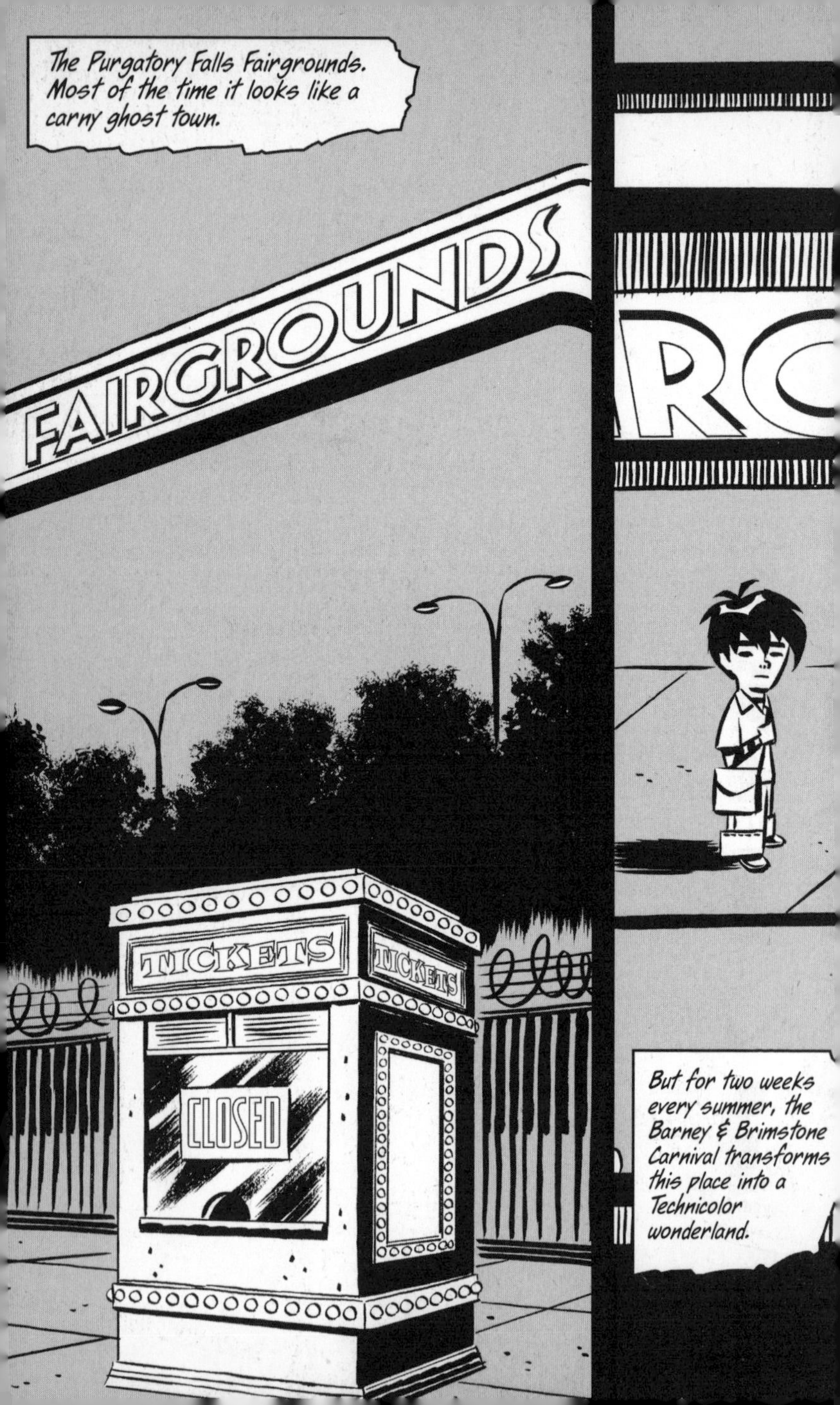
The Purgatory Falls Fairgrounds. Most of the time it looks like a carny ghost town.
FAIRGROUNDS
TICKETS
TICKETS
CLOSED
But for two weeks every summer, the Barney & Brimstone Carnival transforms this place into a Technicolor wonderland.

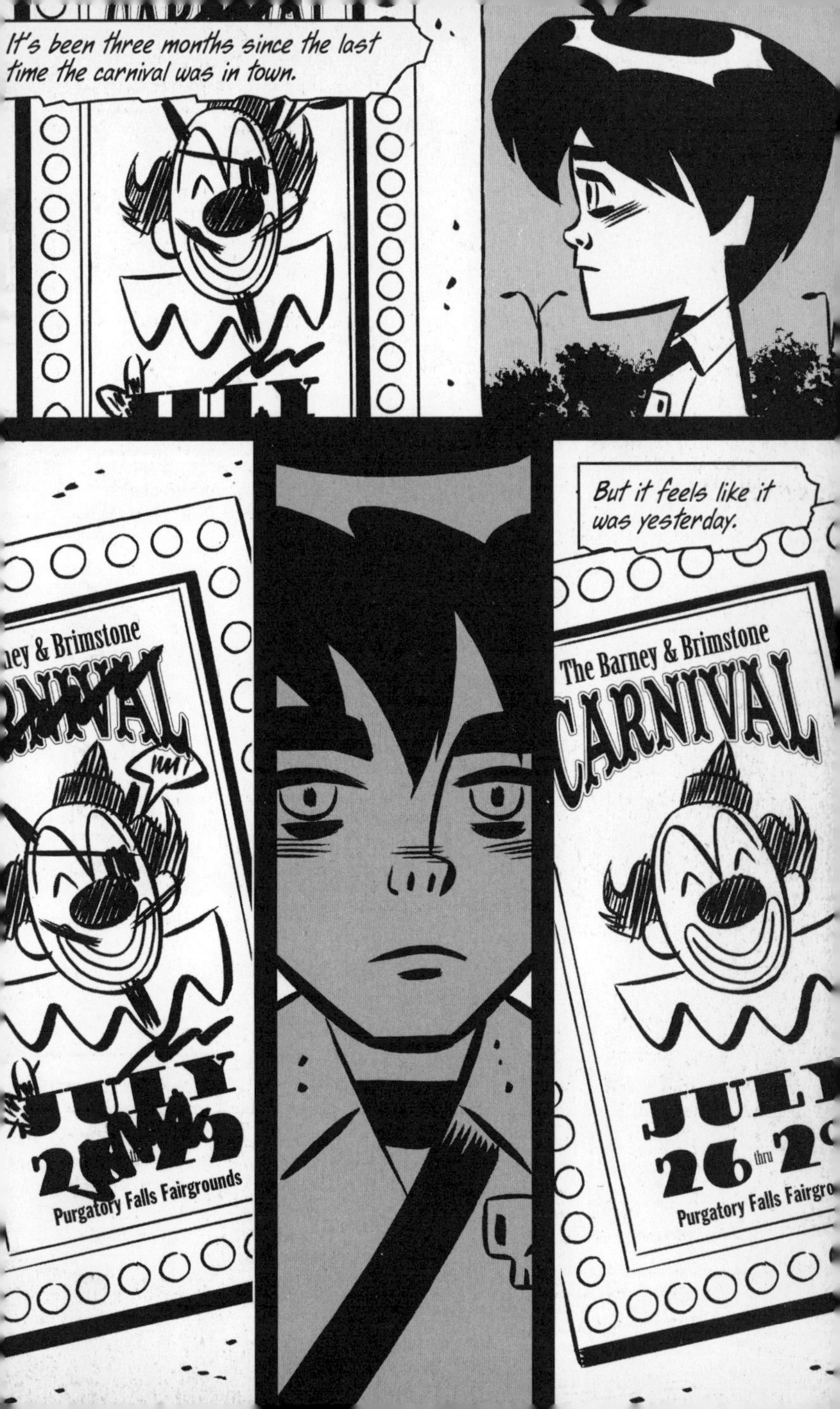
It's been three months since the last time the carnival was in town.
ney & Brimstone
Purgatory Falls Fairgrounds
But it feels like it was yesterday.
The Barney & Brimstone
CARNIVAL
JUL
26 thru 2
Purgatory Falls Fairgro

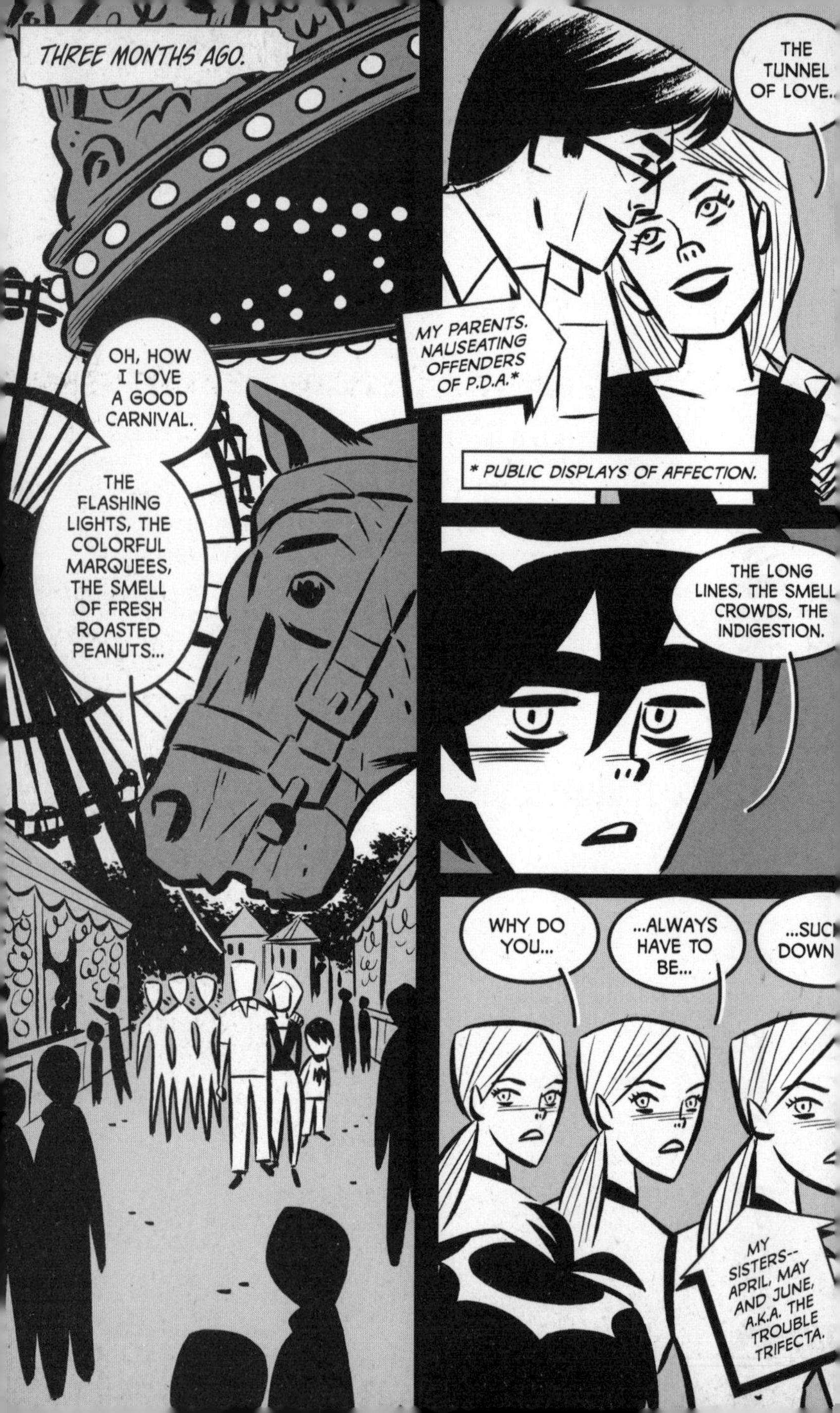
THREE MONTHS AGO.
OH, HOW I LOVE A GOOD CARNIVAL.
THE FLASHING LIGHTS, THE COLORFUL MARQUEES, THE SMELL OF FRESH ROASTED PEANUTS...
THE TUNNEL OF LOVE..
MY PARENTS. NAUSEATING OFFENDERS OF P.D.A.*
* PUBLIC DISPLAYS OF AFFECTION.
THE LONG LINES, THE SMELL CROWDS, THE INDIGESTION.
WHY DO YOU...
...ALWAYS HAVE TO BE...
...SUC DOWN
MY SISTERS-- APRIL, MAY AND JUNE, A.K.A. THE TROUBLE TRIFECTA.

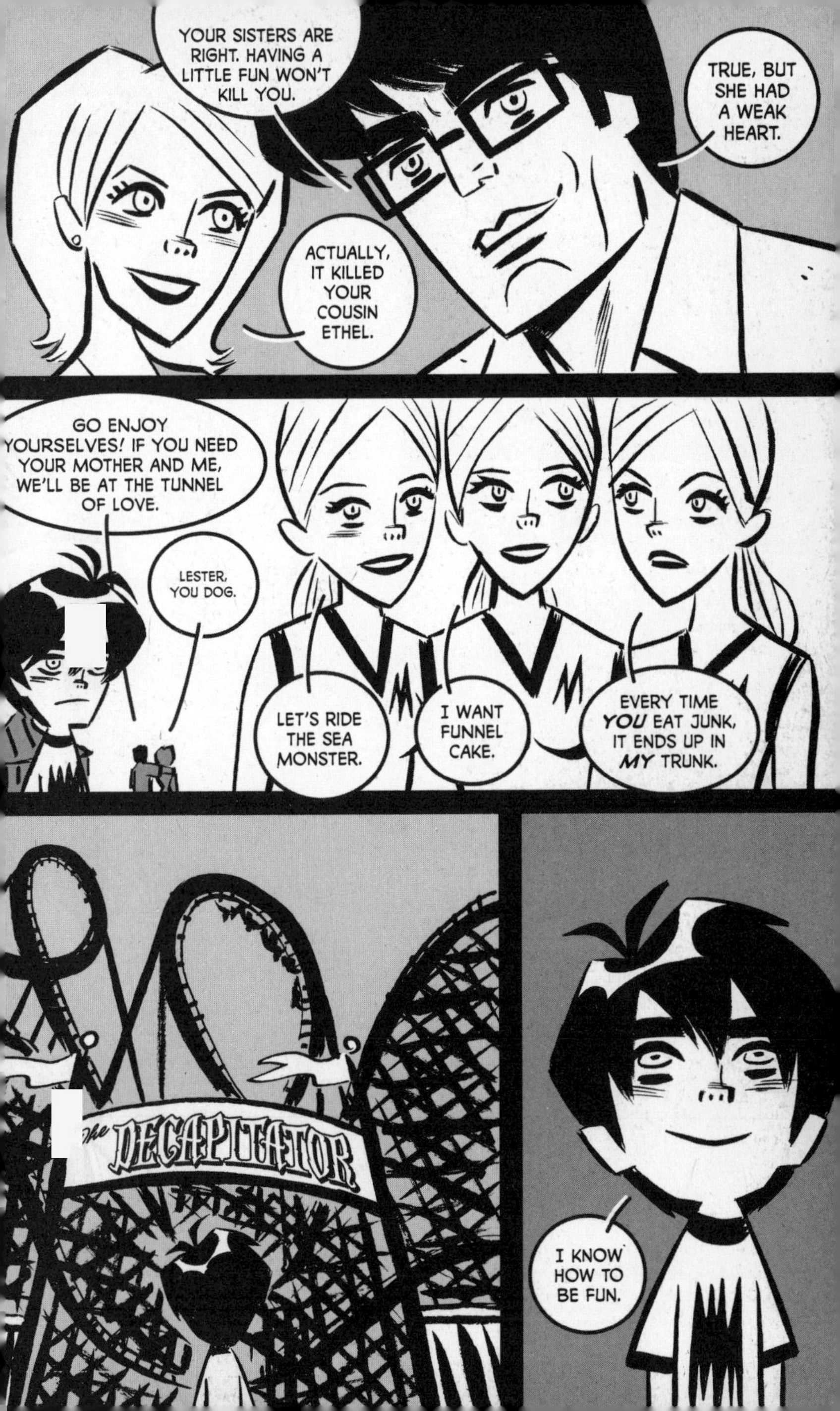
YOUR SISTERS ARE RIGHT. HAVING A LITTLE FUN WON'T KILL YOU.
ACTUALLY, IT KILLED YOUR COUSIN ETHEL.
TRUE, BUT SHE HAD A WEAK HEART.
GO ENJOY YOURSELVES! IF YOU NEED YOUR MOTHER AND ME, WE'LL BE AT THE TUNNEL OF LOVE.
LESTER, YOU DOG.
LET'S RIDE THE SEA MONSTER.
I WANT FUNNEL CAKE.
EVERY TIME *YOU* EAT JUNK, IT ENDS UP IN *MY* TRUNK.
The DECAPITATOR
I KNOW HOW TO BE FUN.

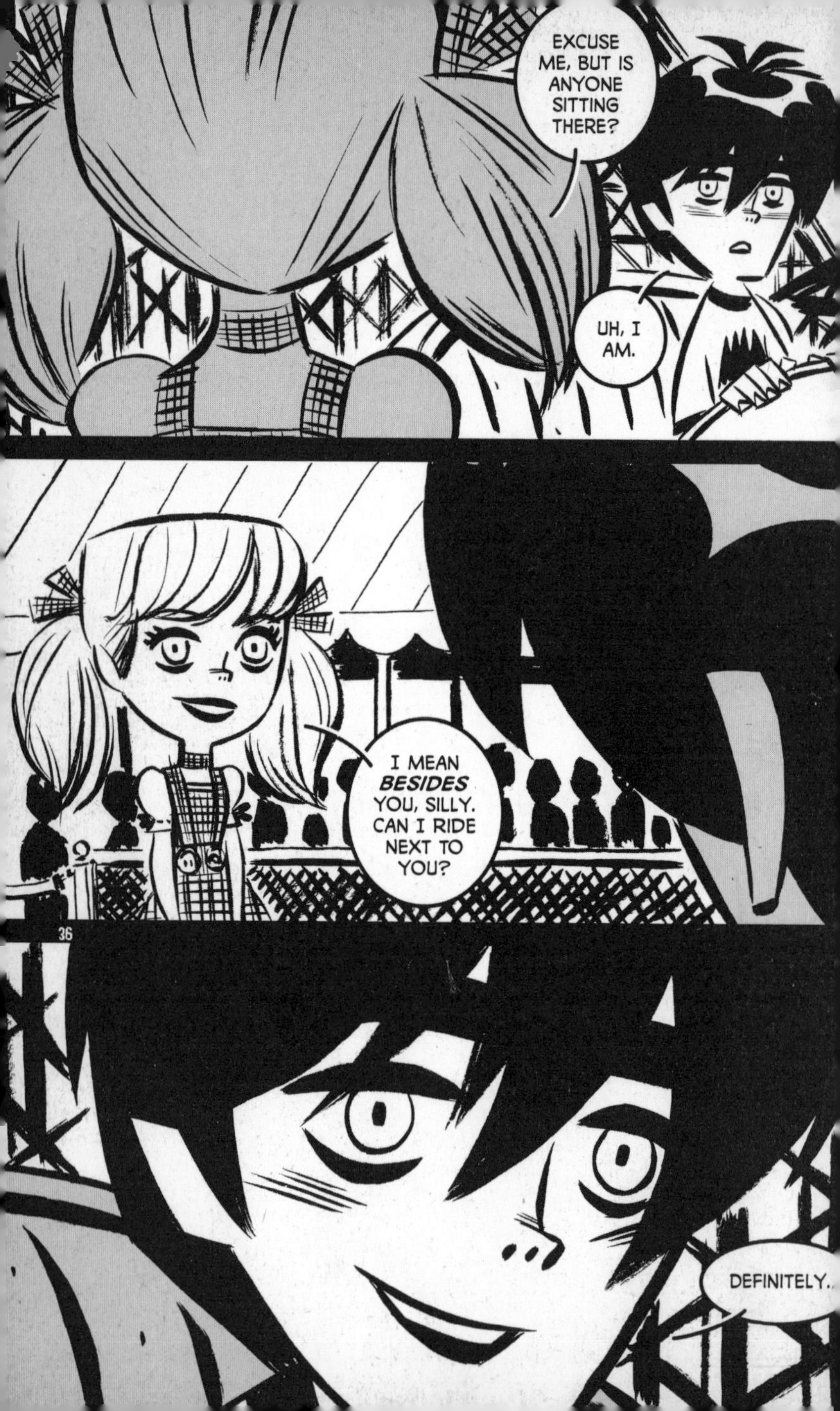
EXCUSE ME, BUT IS ANYONE SITTING THERE?
UH, I AM.
I MEAN *BESIDES* YOU, SILLY. CAN I RIDE NEXT TO YOU?
DEFINITELY.

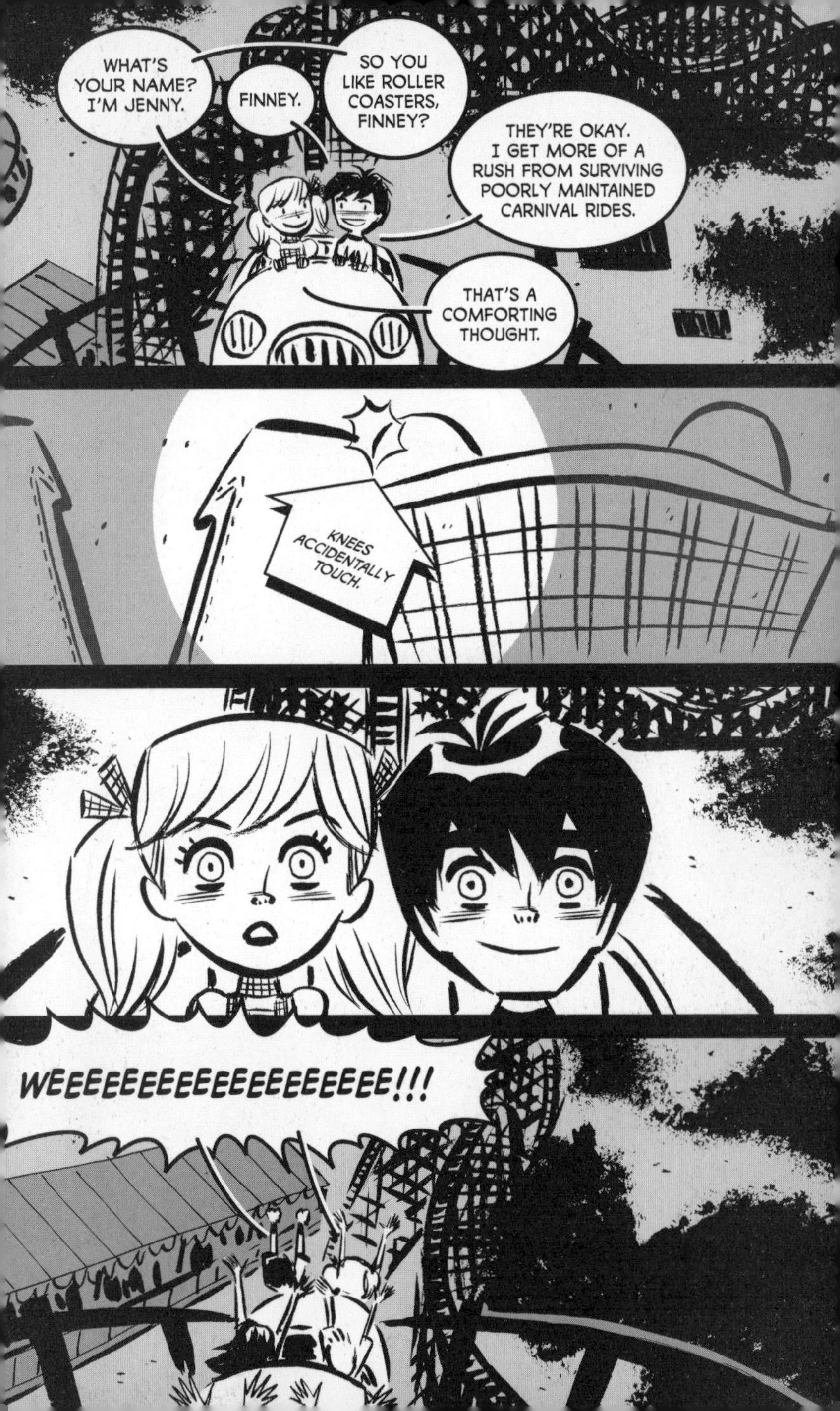
WHAT'S YOUR NAME? I'M JENNY.
FINNEY.
SO YOU LIKE ROLLER COASTERS, FINNEY?
THEY'RE OKAY. I GET MORE OF A RUSH FROM SURVIVING POORLY MAINTAINED CARNIVAL RIDES.
THAT'S A COMFORTING THOUGHT.
KNEES ACCIDENTALLY TOUCH.
WEEEEEEEEEEEEEEEEEEEEE!!!

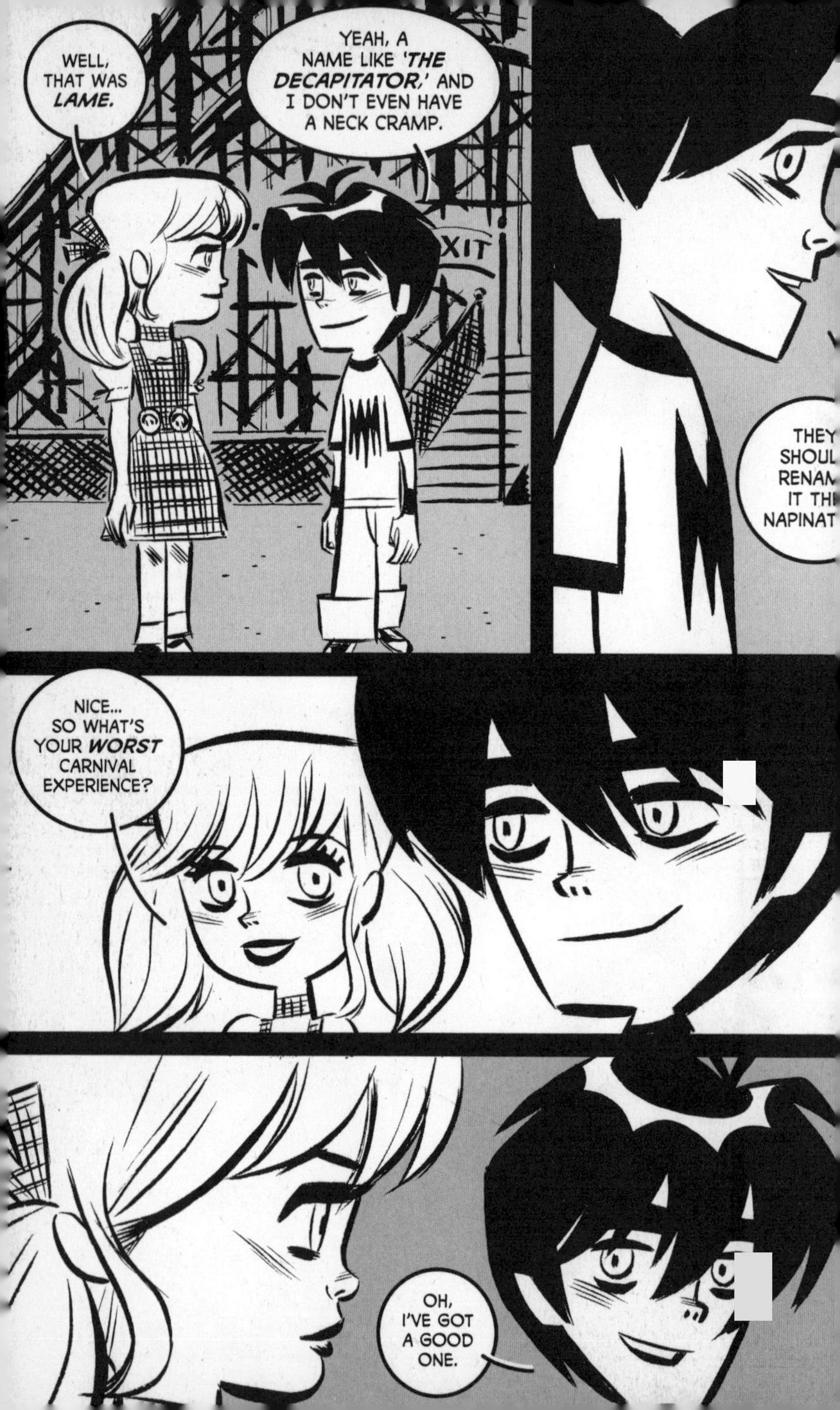
WELL, THAT WAS *LAME.*
YEAH, A NAME LIKE *'THE DECAPITATOR,'* AND I DON'T EVEN HAVE A NECK CRAMP.
XIT
THEY SHOUL RENAM IT TH NAPINAT
NICE... SO WHAT'S YOUR *WORST* CARNIVAL EXPERIENCE?
OH, I'VE GOT A GOOD ONE.

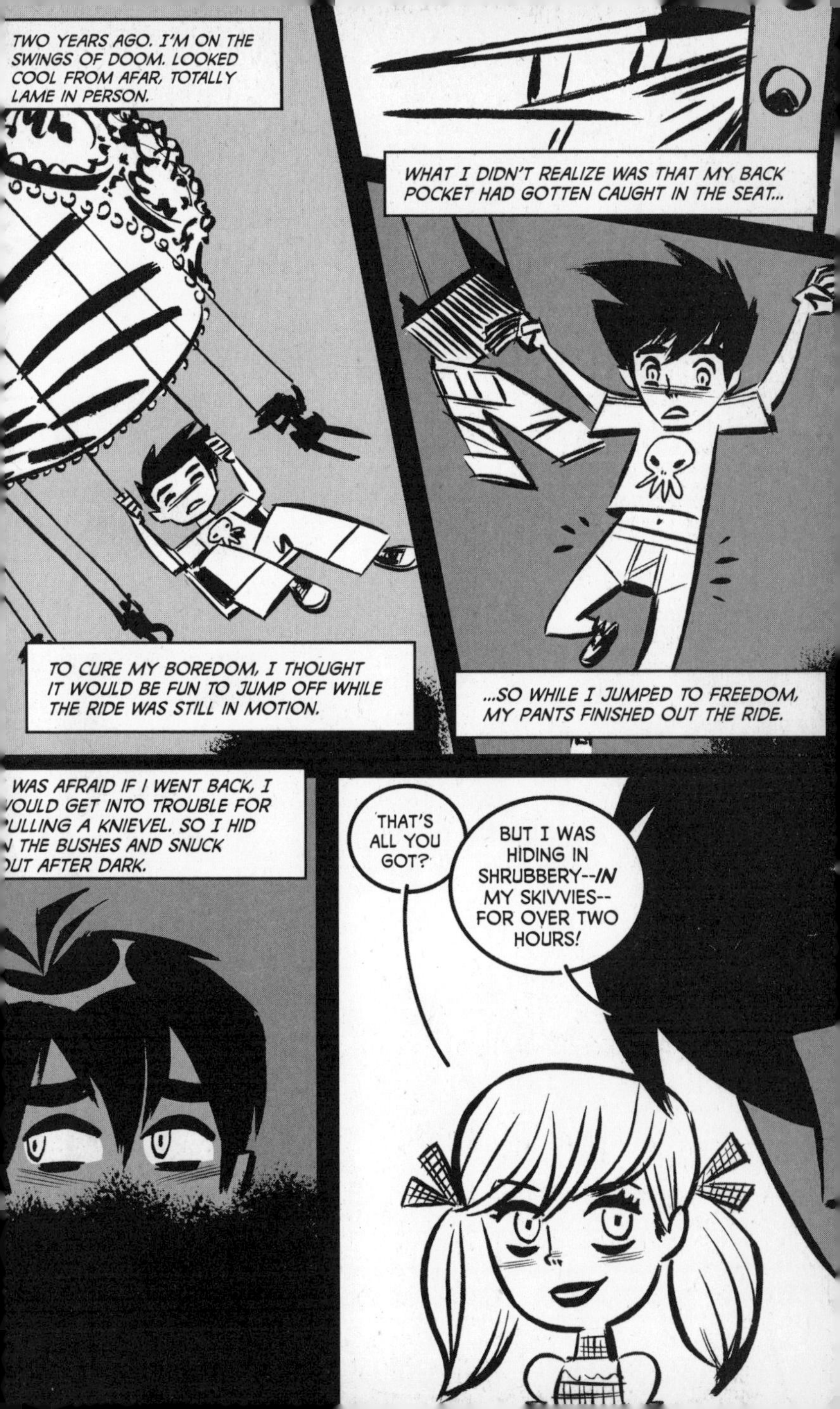
TWO YEARS AGO. I'M ON THE SWINGS OF DOOM. LOOKED COOL FROM AFAR, TOTALLY LAME IN PERSON.
TO CURE MY BOREDOM, I THOUGHT IT WOULD BE FUN TO JUMP OFF WHILE THE RIDE WAS STILL IN MOTION.
WHAT I DIDN'T REALIZE WAS THAT MY BACK POCKET HAD GOTTEN CAUGHT IN THE SEAT...
...SO WHILE I JUMPED TO FREEDOM, MY PANTS FINISHED OUT THE RIDE.
WAS AFRAID IF I WENT BACK, I OULD GET INTO TROUBLE FOR ULLING A KNIEVEL. SO I HID THE BUSHES AND SNUCK UT AFTER DARK.
BUT I WAS HIDING IN SHRUBBERY--*IN* MY SKIVVIES--FOR OVER TWO HOURS!
THAT'S ALL YOU GOT?

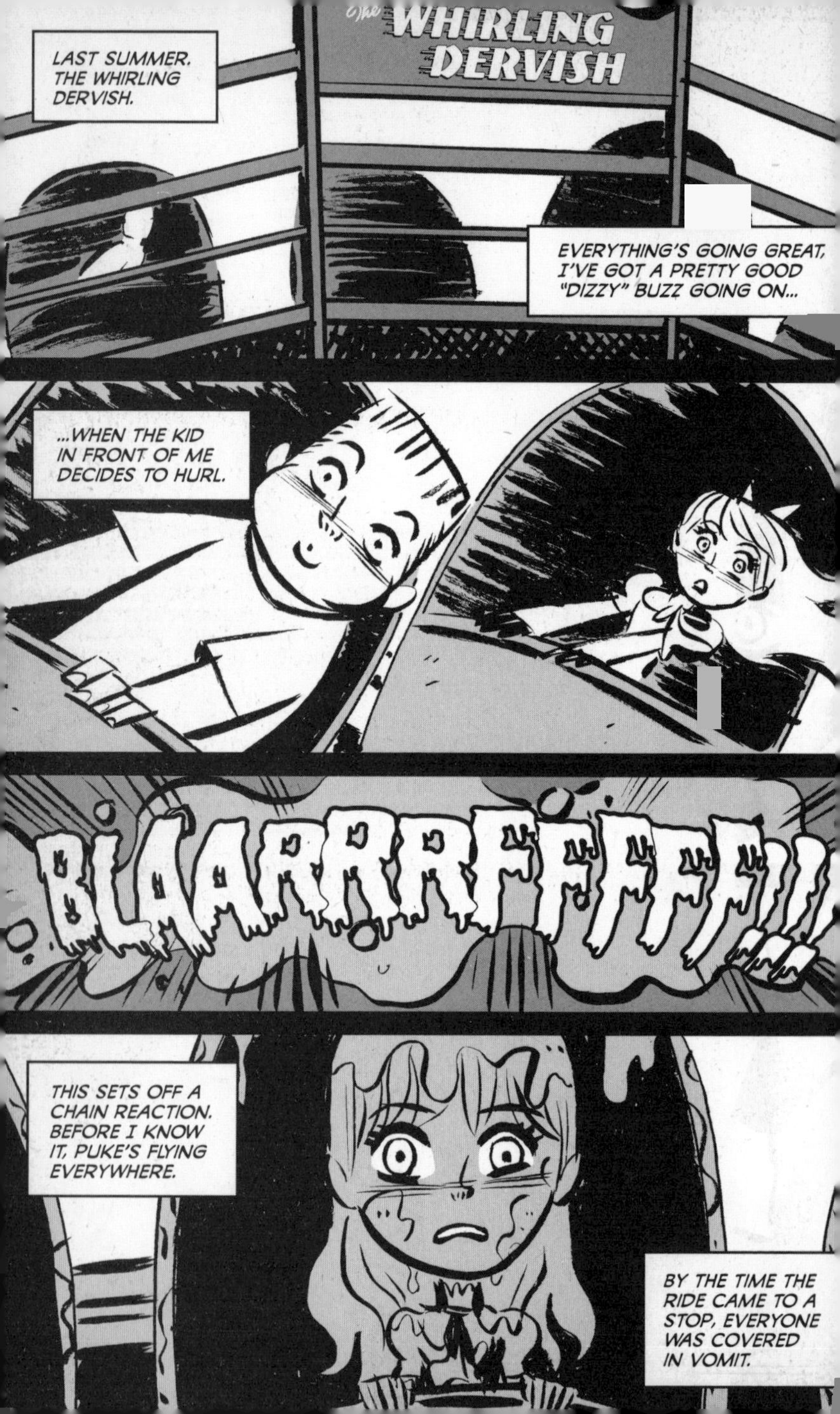

WHIRLING DERVISH
LAST SUMMER. THE WHIRLING DERVISH.
EVERYTHING'S GOING GREAT, I'VE GOT A PRETTY GOOD "DIZZY" BUZZ GOING ON...
...WHEN THE KID IN FRONT OF ME DECIDES TO HURL.
BLARRRFFFFF!!
THIS SETS OFF A CHAIN REACTION. BEFORE I KNOW IT, PUKE'S FLYING EVERYWHERE.
BY THE TIME THE RIDE CAME TO A STOP, EVERYONE WAS COVERED IN VOMIT.

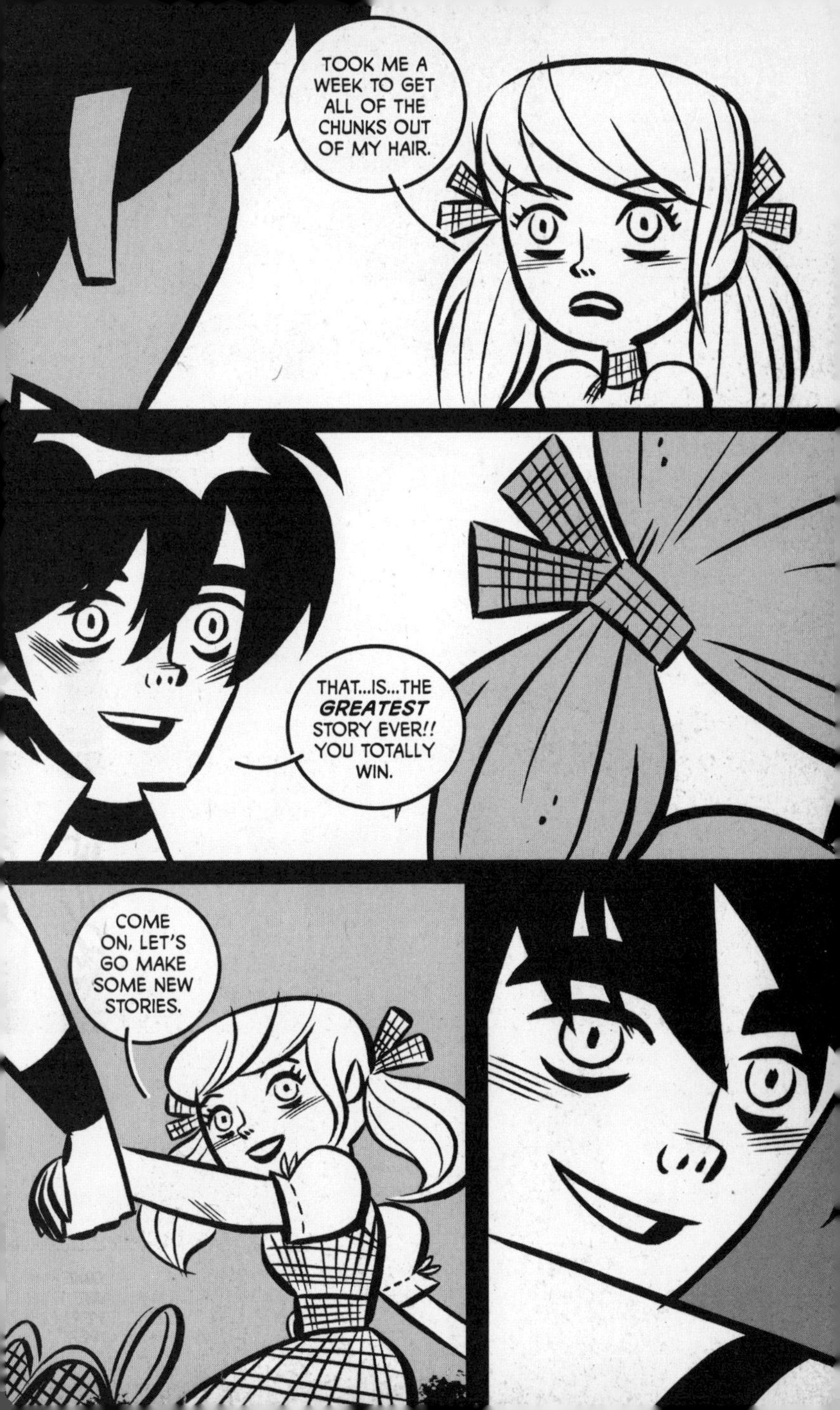
TOOK ME A WEEK TO GET ALL OF THE CHUNKS OUT OF MY HAIR.
THAT...IS...THE *GREATEST* STORY EVER!! YOU TOTALLY WIN.
COME ON, LET'S GO MAKE SOME NEW STORIES.

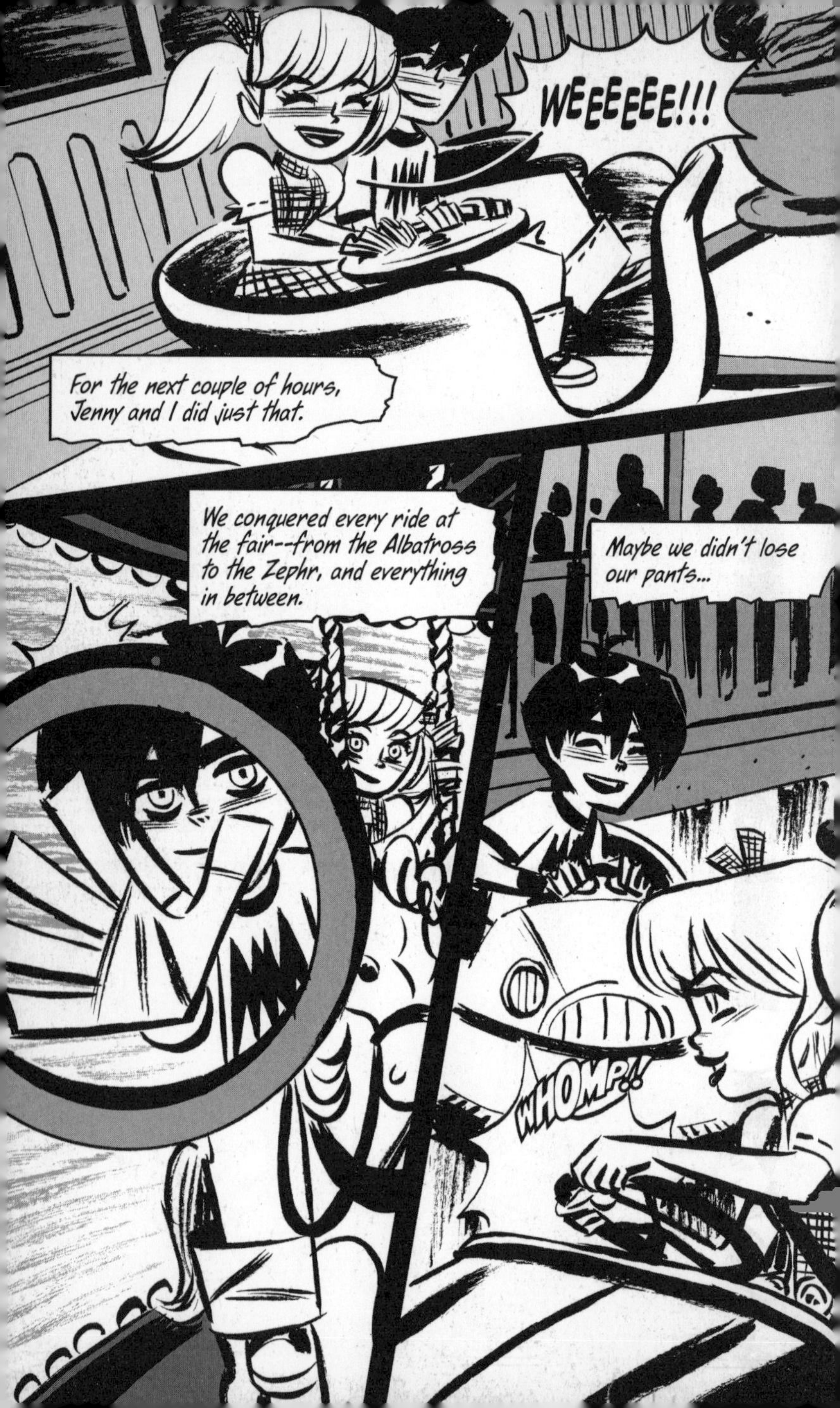

WEEEEEEE!!!
For the next couple of hours, Jenny and I did just that.
We conquered every ride at the fair--from the Albatross to the Zephr, and everything in between.
Maybe we didn't lose our pants...
WHOMP!!

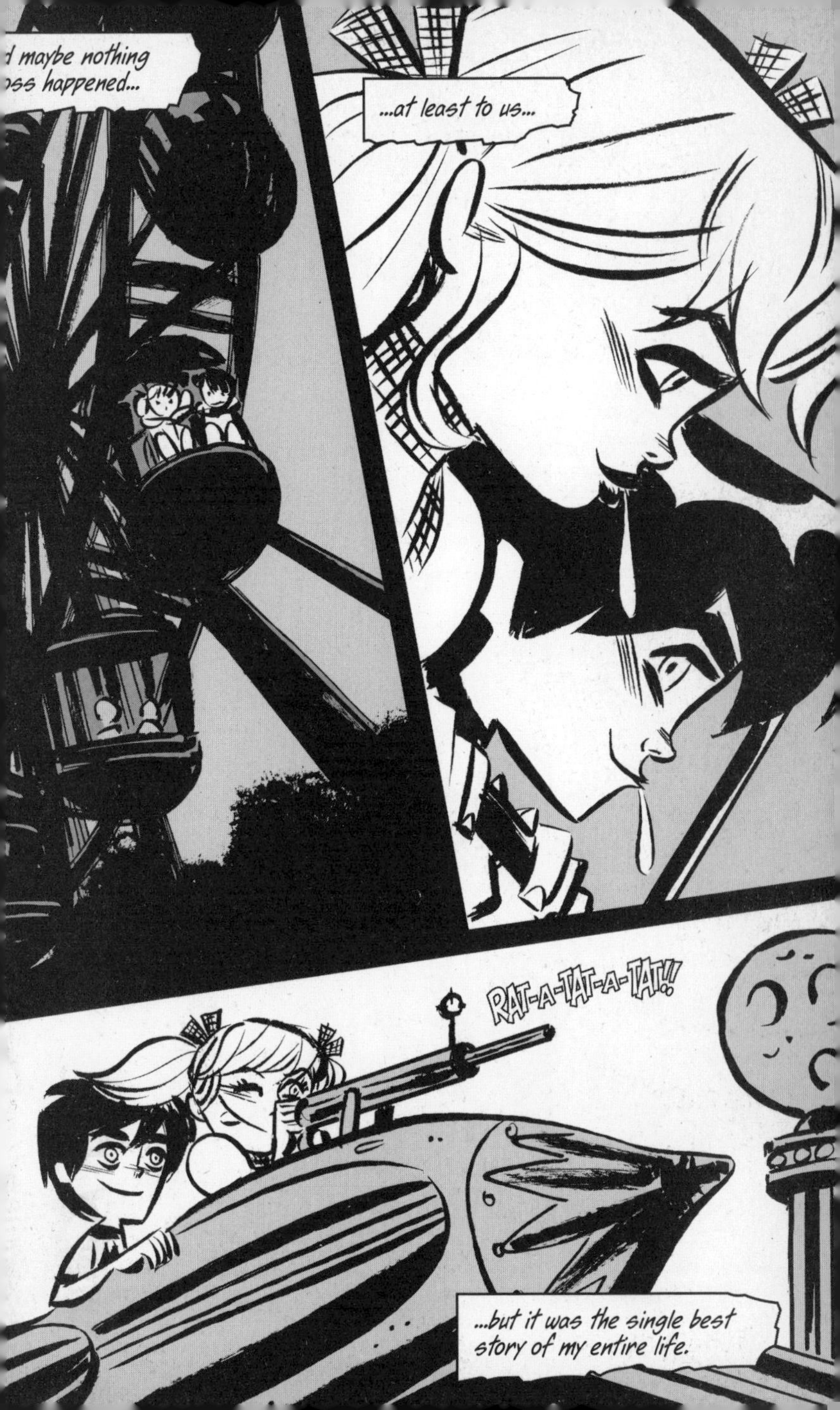
d maybe nothing
oss happened...
...at least to us...
RAT-A-TAT-A-TAT!!
...but it was the single best story of my entire life.

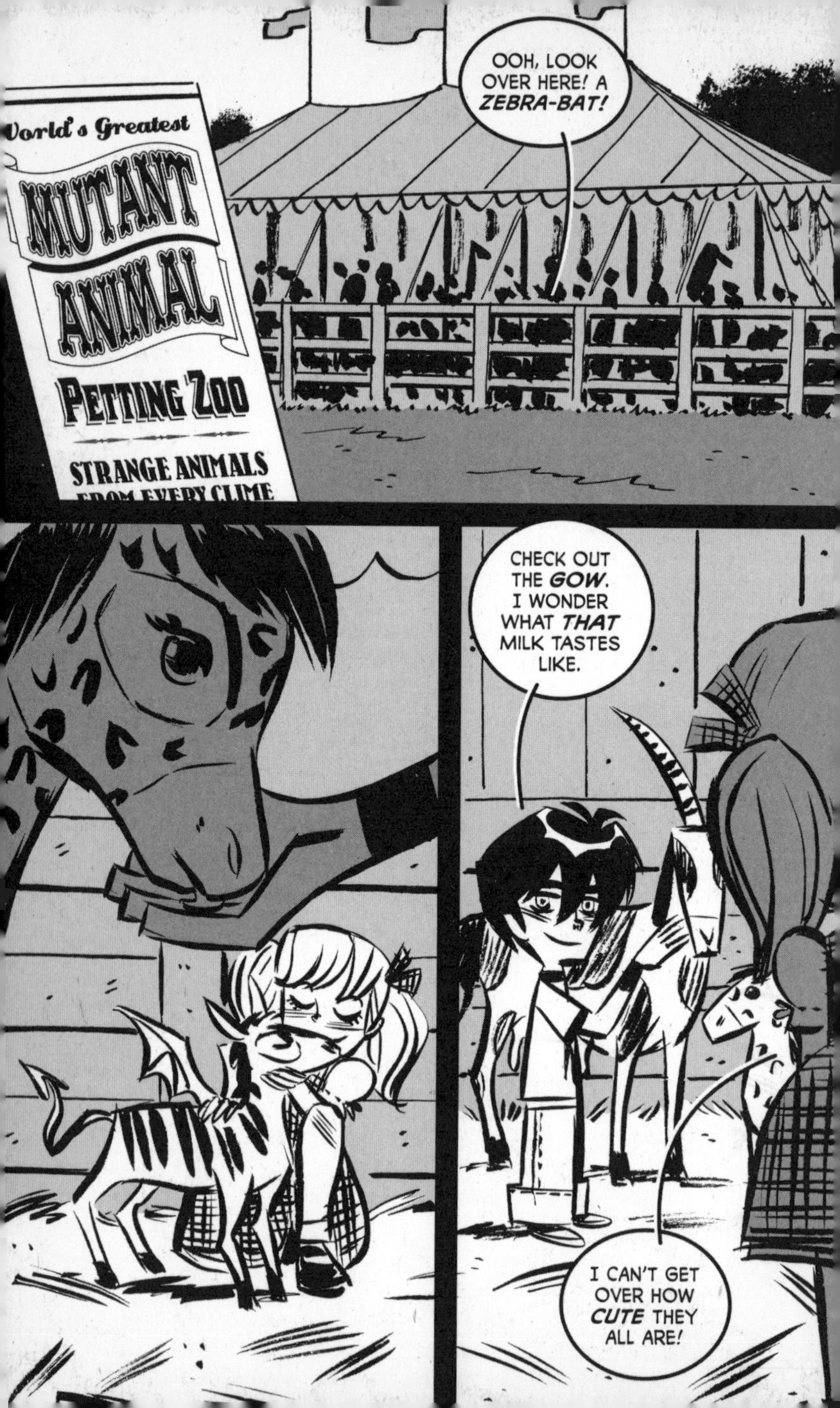
World's Greatest
MUTANT
ANIMAL
PETTING ZOO
STRANGE ANIMALS
OOH, LOOK OVER HERE! A ZEBRA-BAT!
CHECK OUT THE GOW. I WONDER WHAT THAT MILK TASTES LIKE.
I CAN'T GET OVER HOW CUTE THEY ALL ARE!

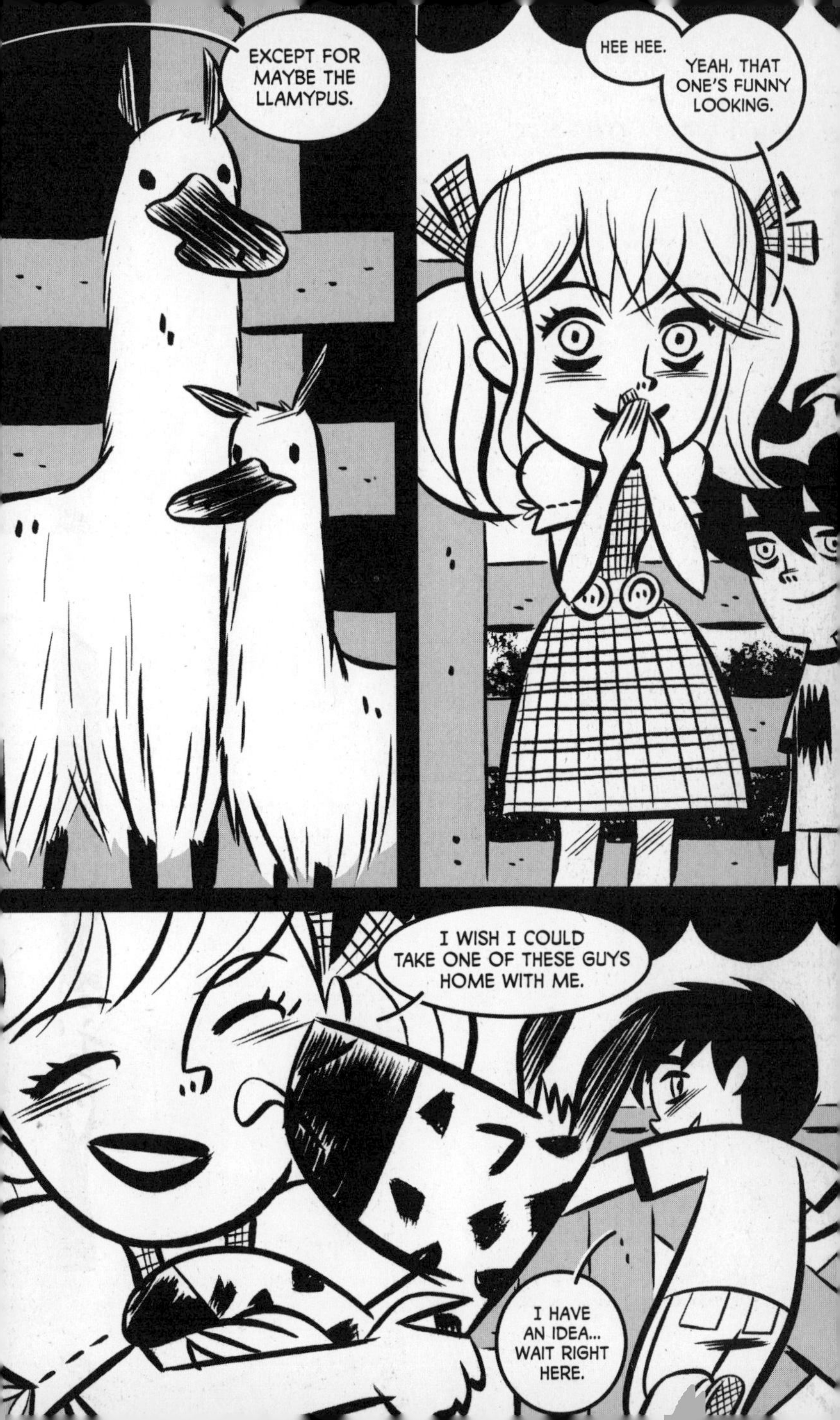
EXCEPT FOR MAYBE THE LLAMYPUS.
HEE HEE.
YEAH, THAT ONE'S FUNNY LOOKING.
I WISH I COULD TAKE ONE OF THESE GUYS HOME WITH ME.
I HAVE AN IDEA... WAIT RIGHT HERE.

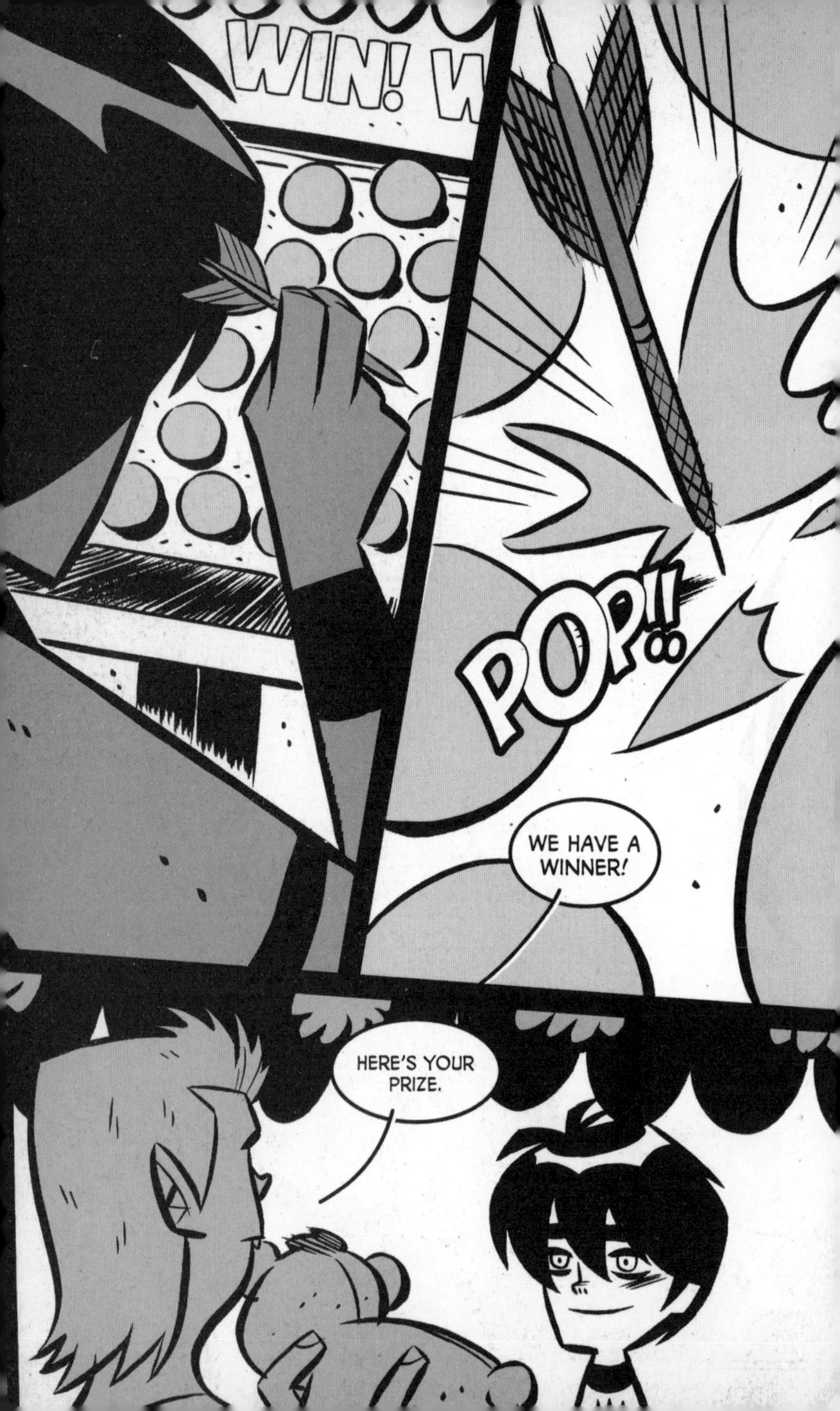

WIN! W
POP!!
WE HAVE A WINNER!
HERE'S YOUR PRIZE.

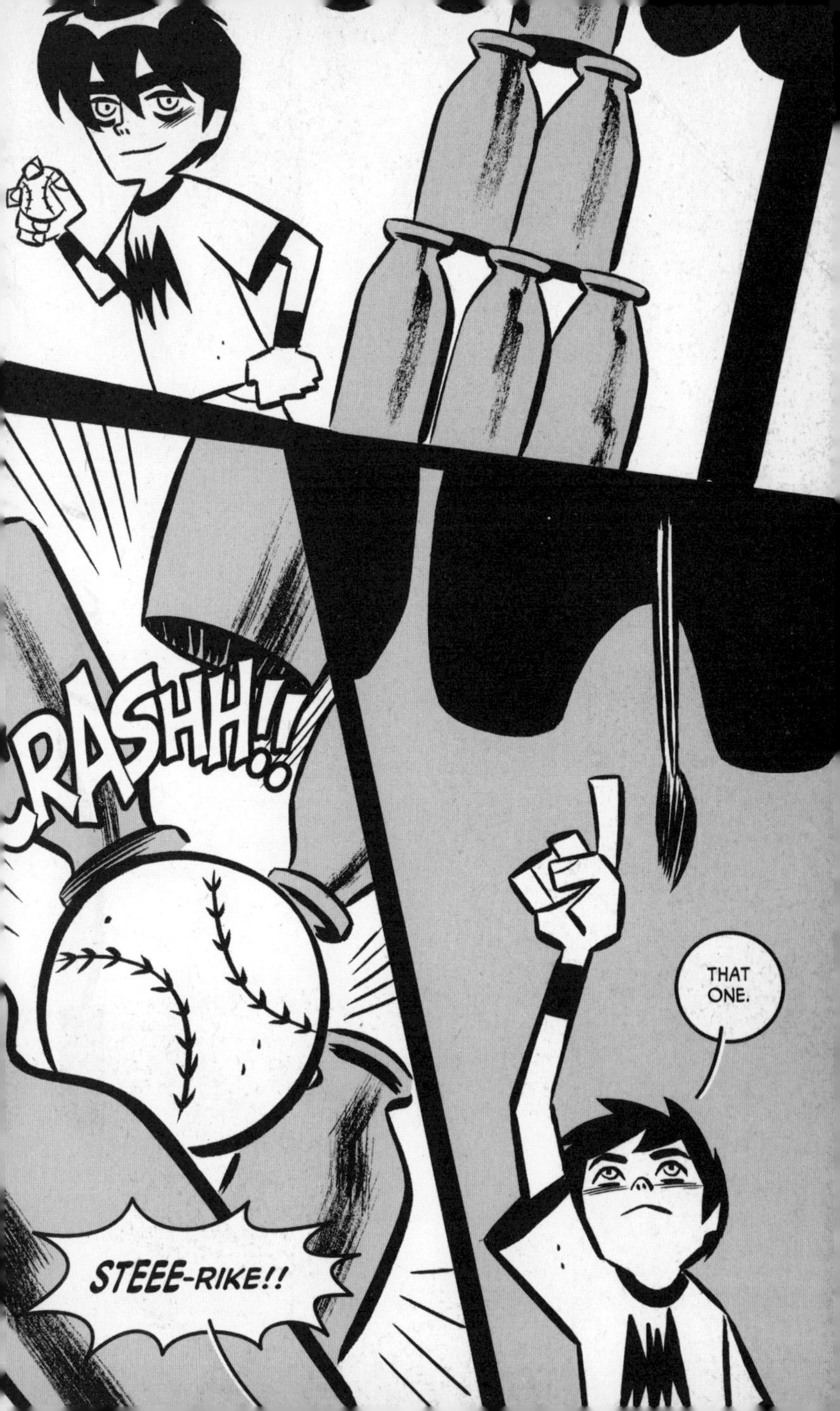
RASHH!!
STEEE-RIKE!!
THAT ONE.

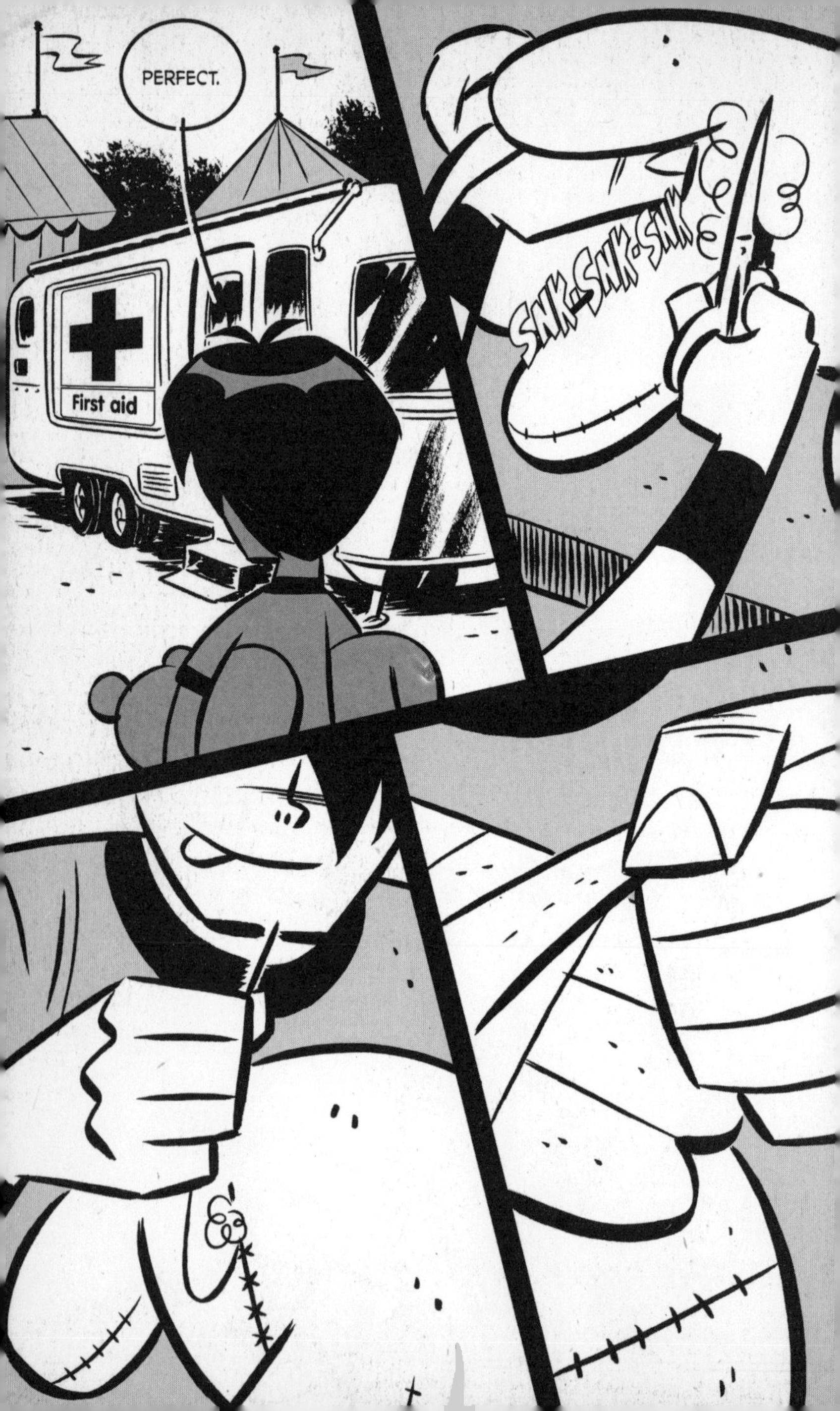
PERFECT.
First aid
SNK-SNK-SNK

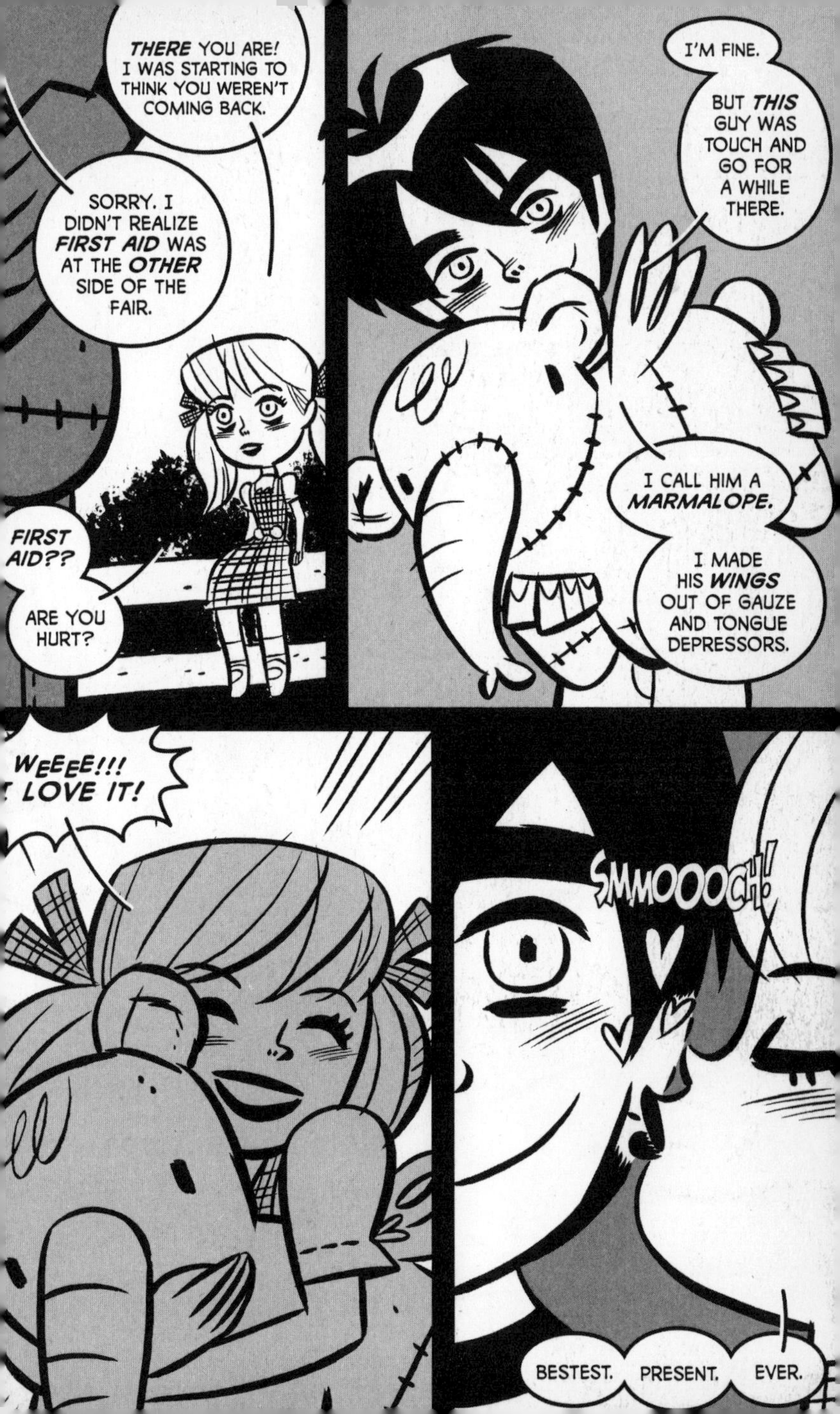
THERE YOU ARE! I WAS STARTING TO THINK YOU WEREN'T COMING BACK.
SORRY. I DIDN'T REALIZE FIRST AID WAS AT THE OTHER SIDE OF THE FAIR.
FIRST AID??
ARE YOU HURT?
I'M FINE.
BUT THIS GUY WAS TOUCH AND GO FOR A WHILE THERE.
I CALL HIM A MARMALOPE.
I MADE HIS WINGS OUT OF GAUZE AND TONGUE DEPRESSORS.
WEEEE!!! I LOVE IT!
SMMOOOCH!
BESTEST.
PRESENT.
EVER.

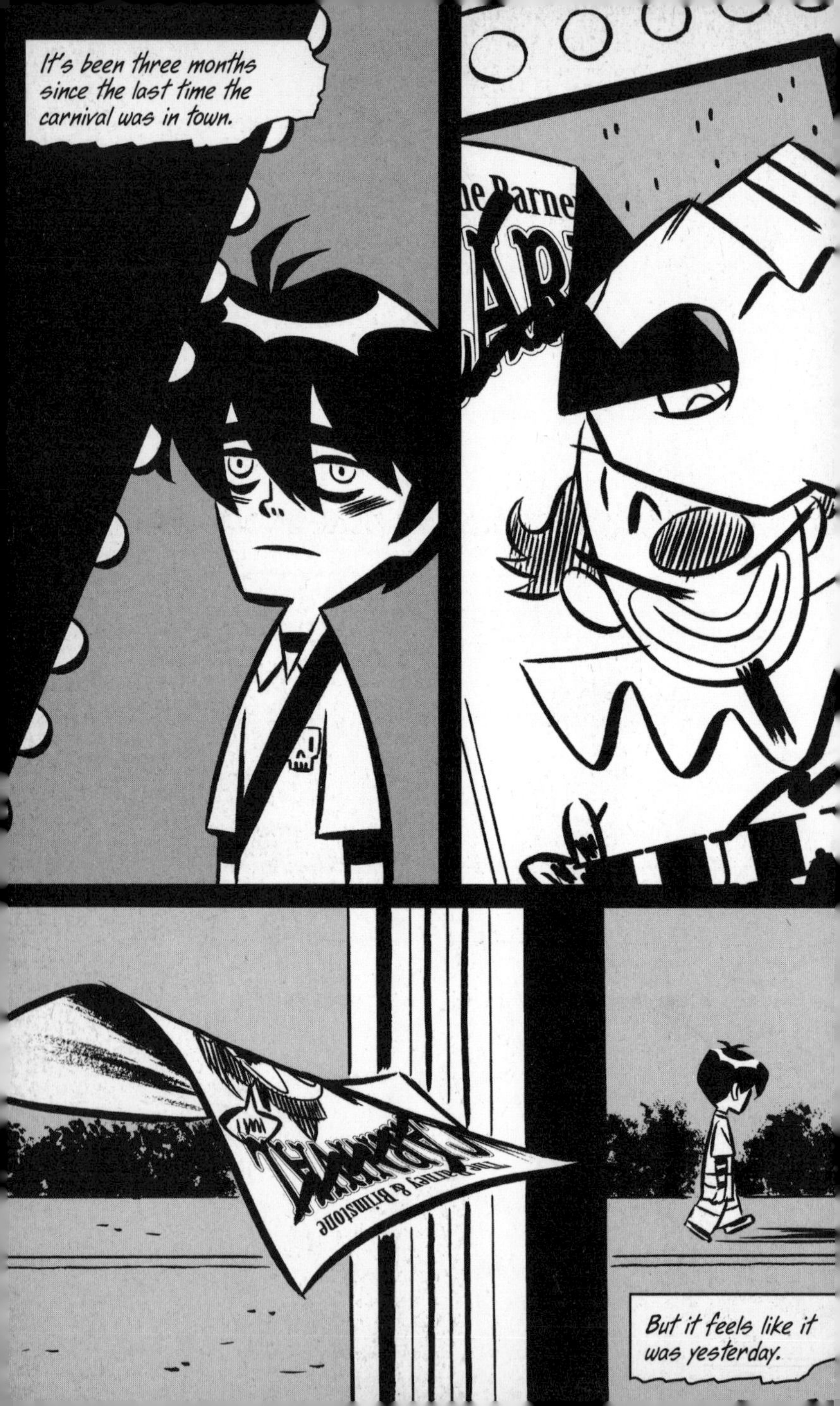
It's been three months since the last time the carnival was in town.
The Barney & Brimstone
But it feels like it was yesterday.

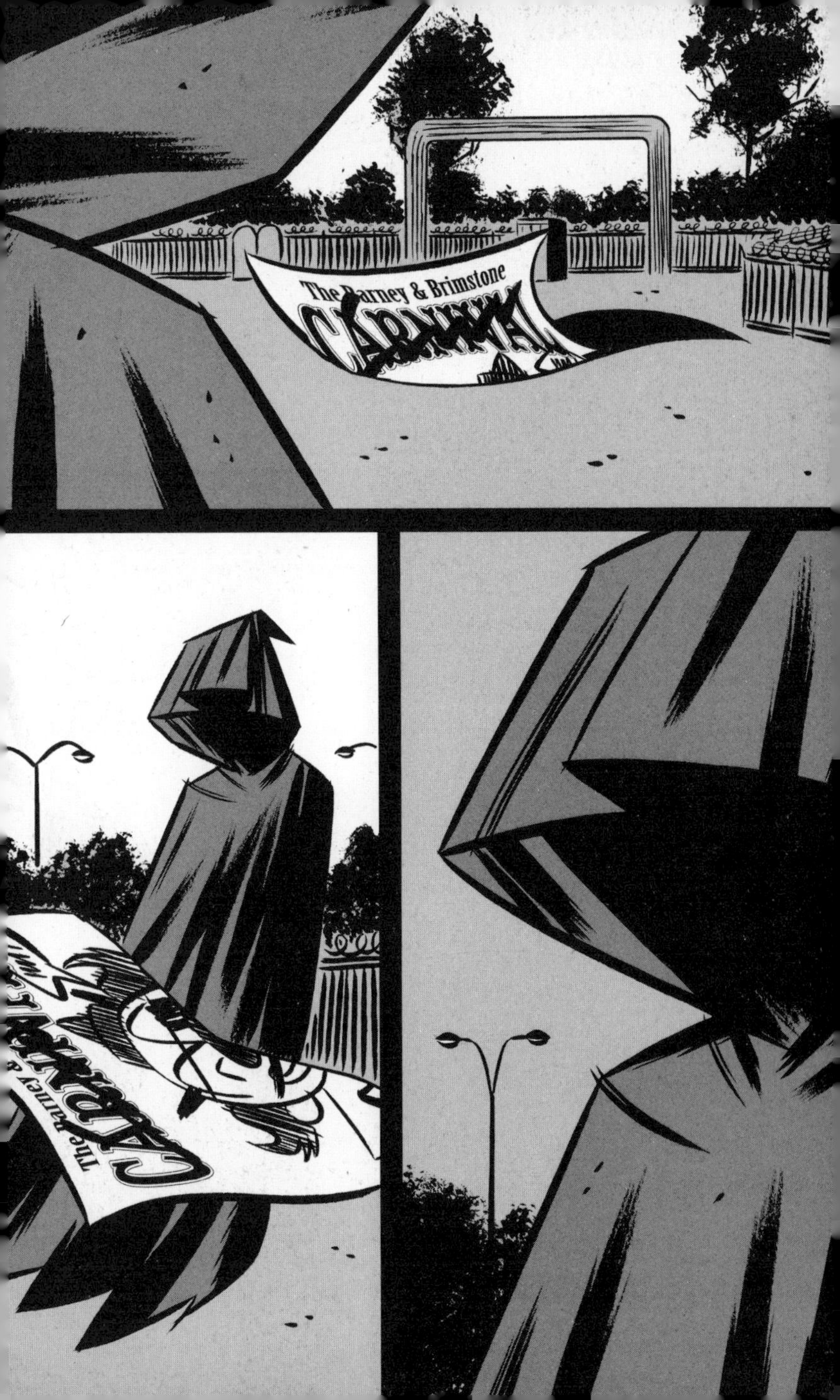
The Barney & Brimstone

CHAPTER THREE

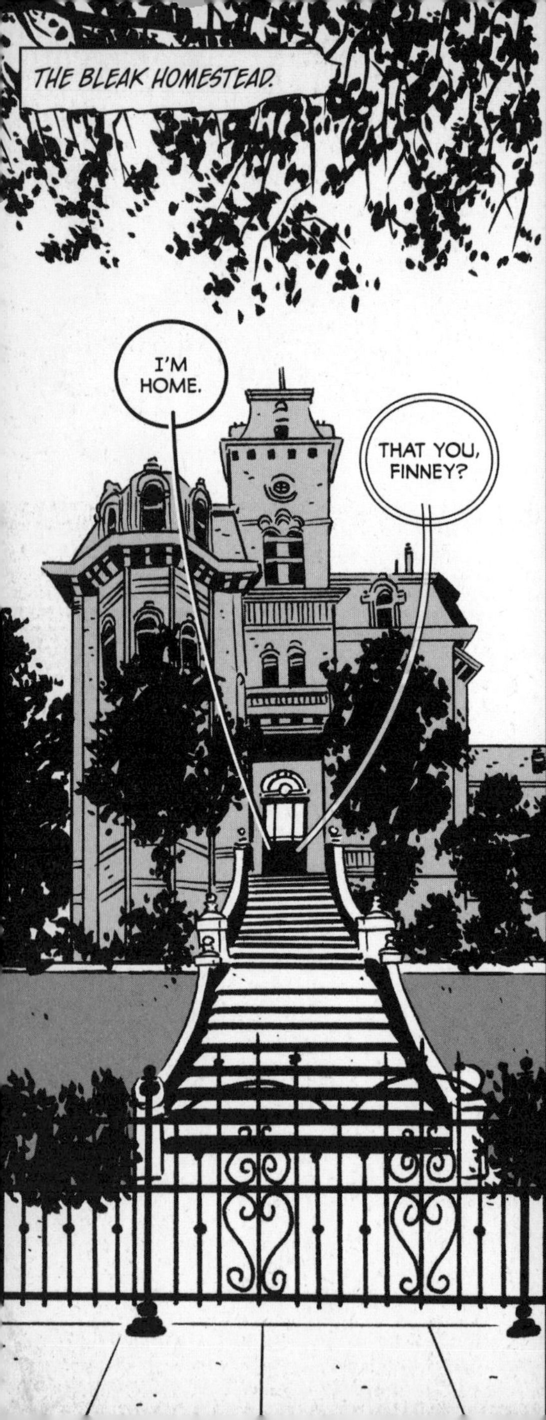
THE BLEAK HOMESTEAD.
I'M HOME.
THAT YOU, FINNEY?
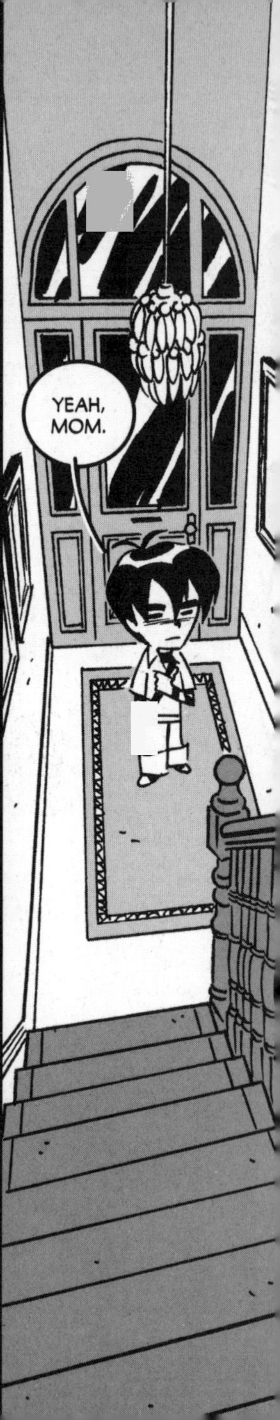
YEAH, MOM.

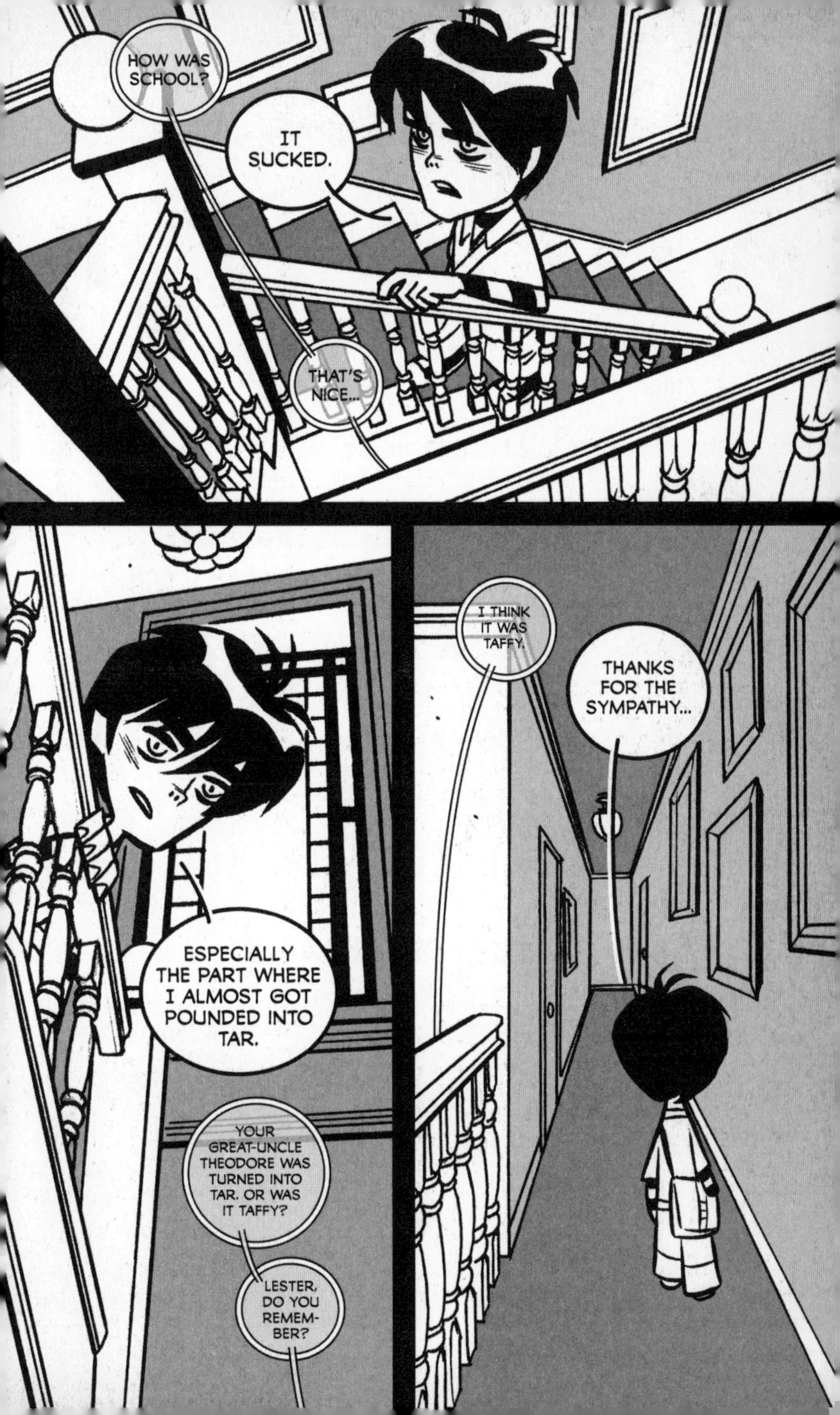
HOW WAS SCHOOL?
IT SUCKED.
THAT'S NICE...
ESPECIALLY THE PART WHERE I ALMOST GOT POUNDED INTO TAR.
YOUR GREAT-UNCLE THEODORE WAS TURNED INTO TAR. OR WAS IT TAFFY?
LESTER, DO YOU REMEMBER?
I THINK IT WAS TAFFY.
THANKS FOR THE SYMPATHY...

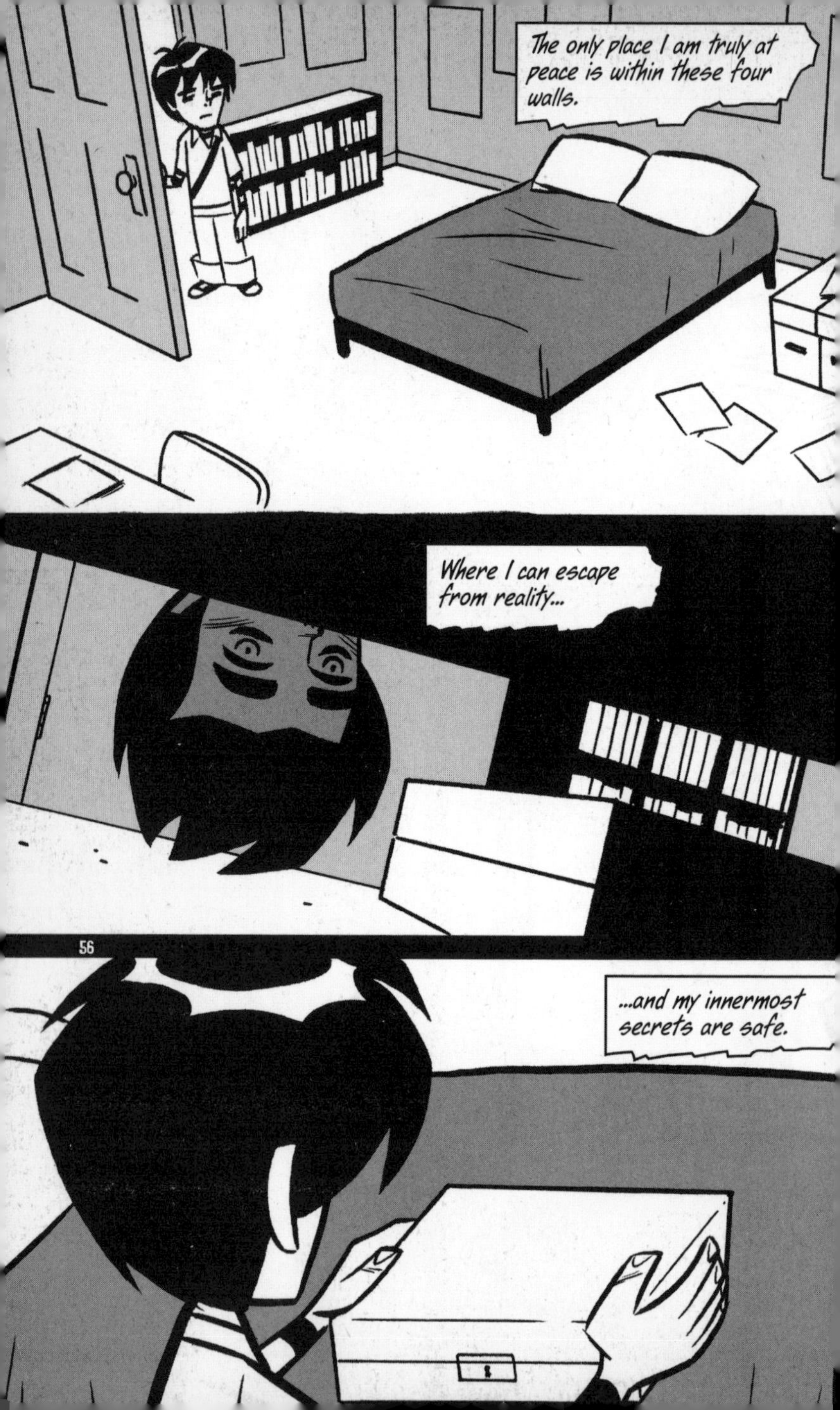
The only place I am truly at peace is within these four walls.
Where I can escape from reality...
...and my innermost secrets are safe.

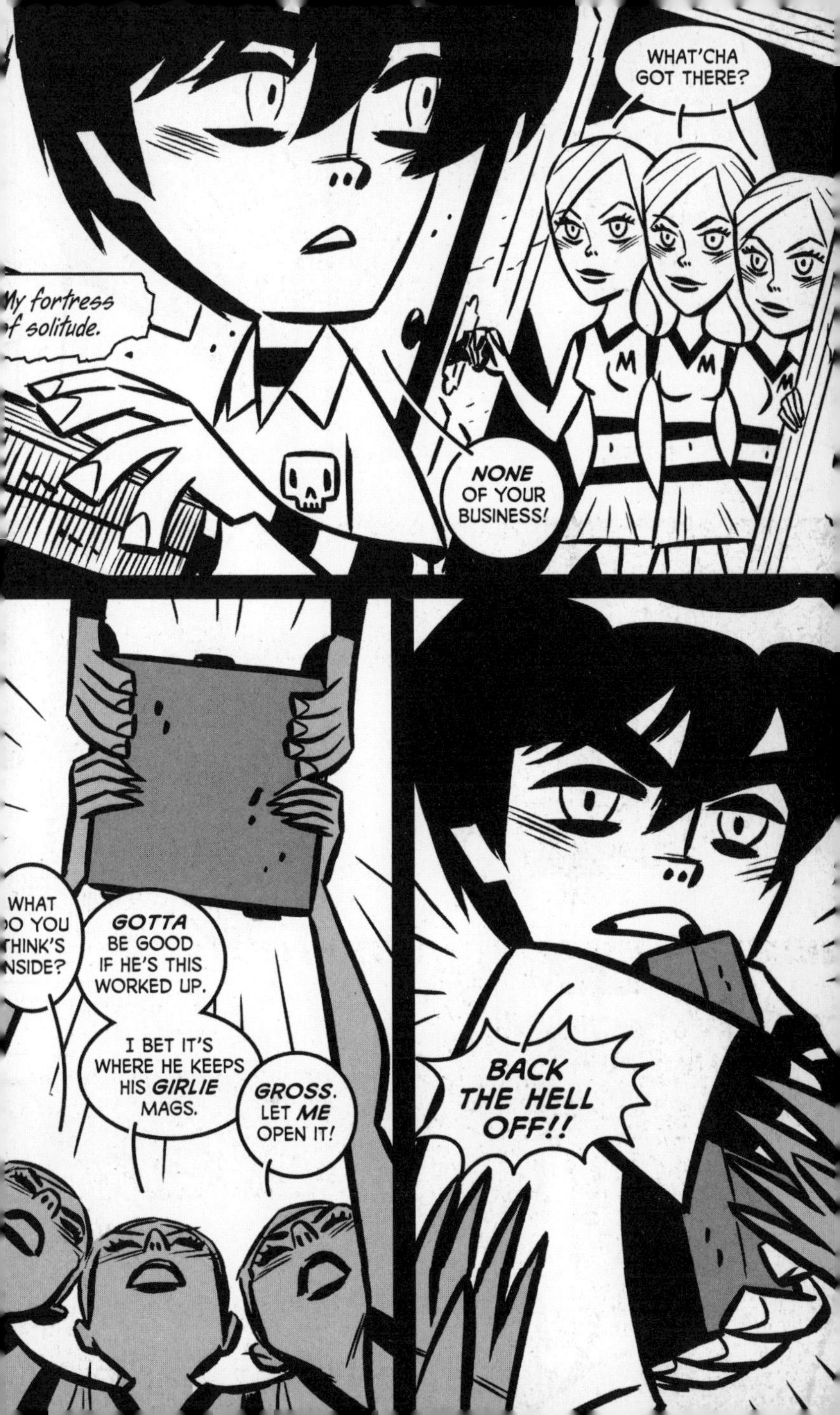

My fortress of solitude.
WHAT'CHA GOT THERE?
NONE OF YOUR BUSINESS!
WHAT DO YOU THINK'S INSIDE?
GOTTA BE GOOD IF HE'S THIS WORKED UP.
I BET IT'S WHERE HE KEEPS HIS GIRLIE MAGS.
GROSS. LET ME OPEN IT!
BACK THE HELL OFF!!

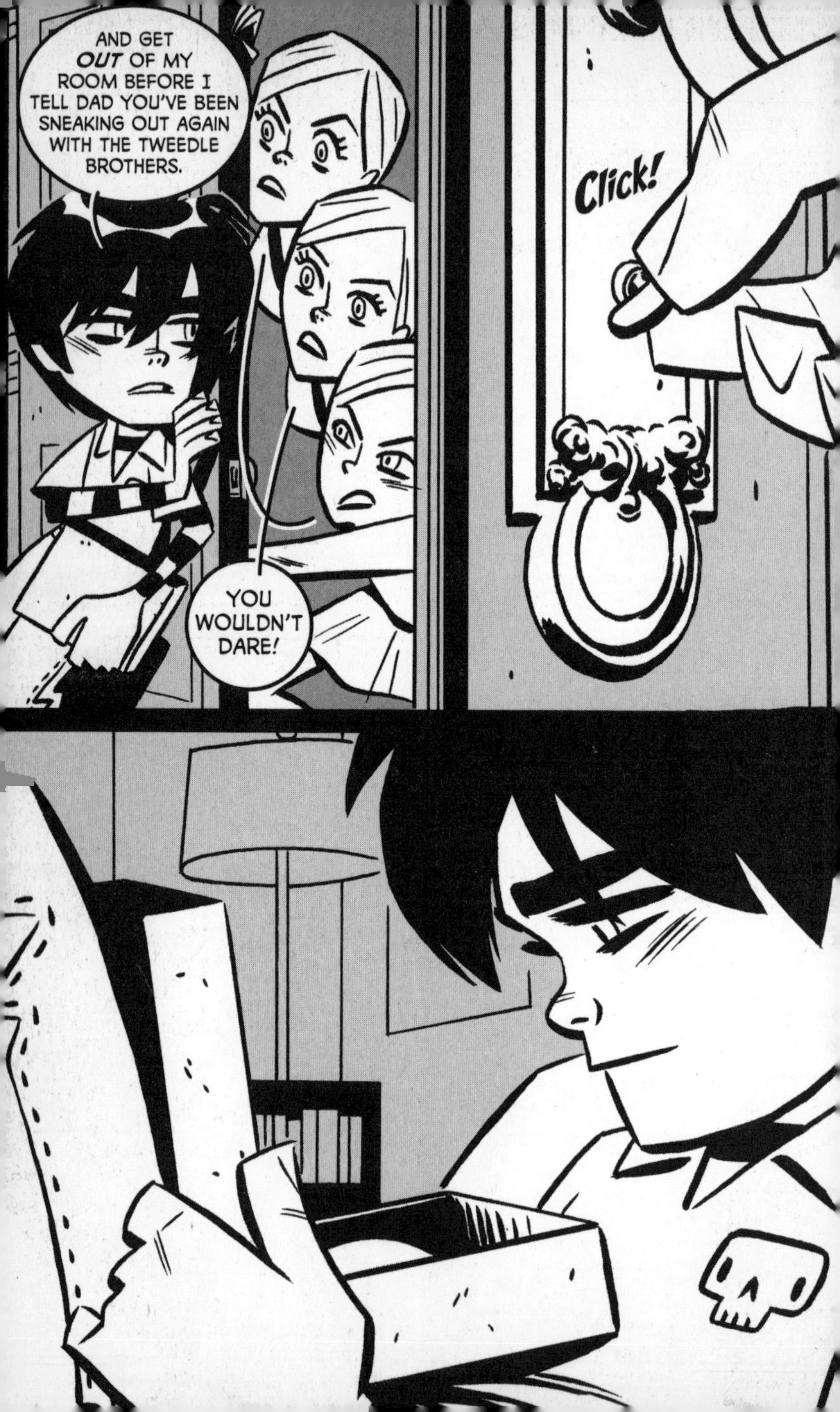
AND GET OUT OF MY ROOM BEFORE I TELL DAD YOU'VE BEEN SNEAKING OUT AGAIN WITH THE TWEEDLE BROTHERS.
YOU WOULDN'T DARE!
Click!

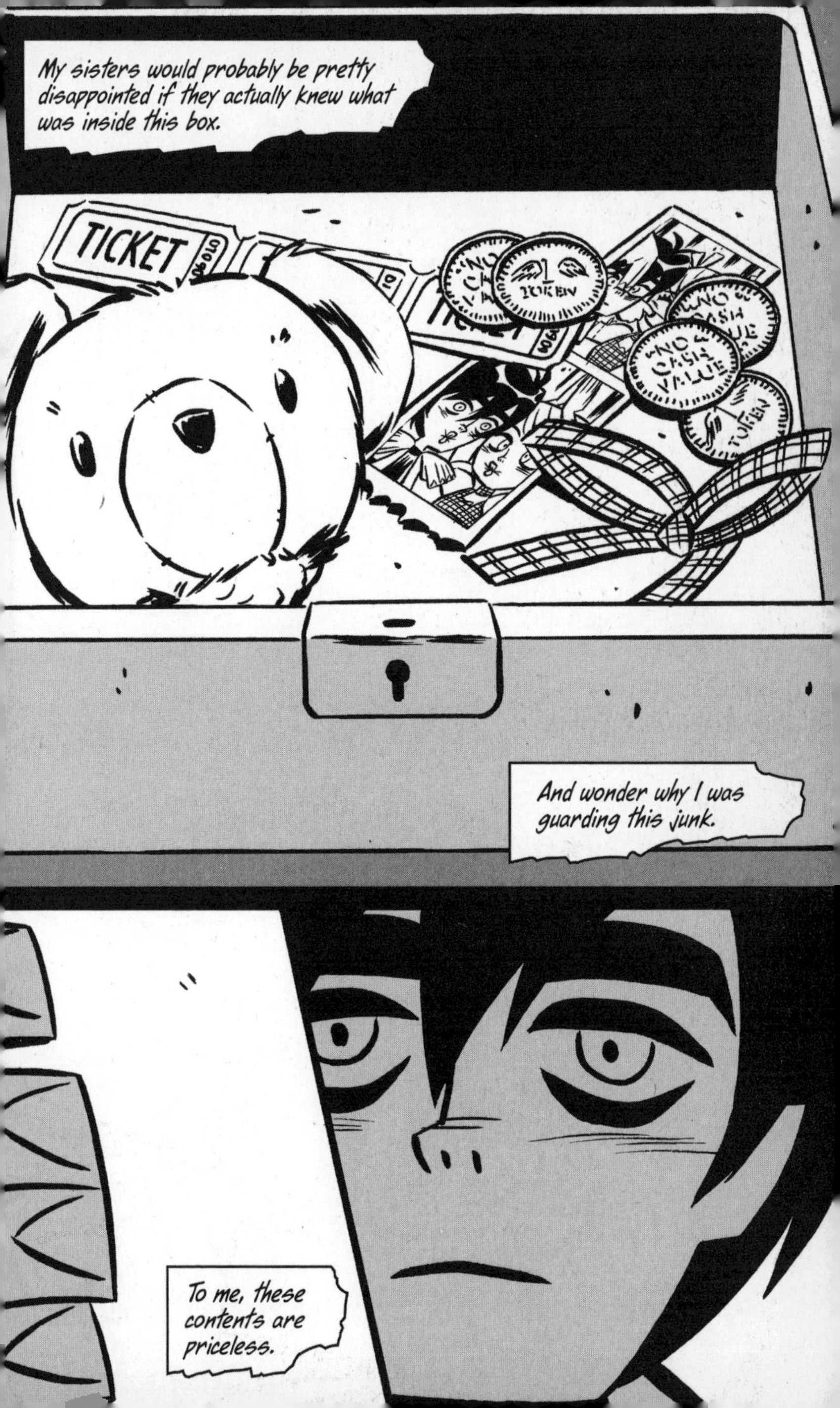
My sisters would probably be pretty disappointed if they actually knew what was inside this box.
TICKET
1 TOKEN
NO CASH VALUE
NO CASH VALUE
TOKEN
And wonder why I was guarding this junk.
To me, these contents are priceless.

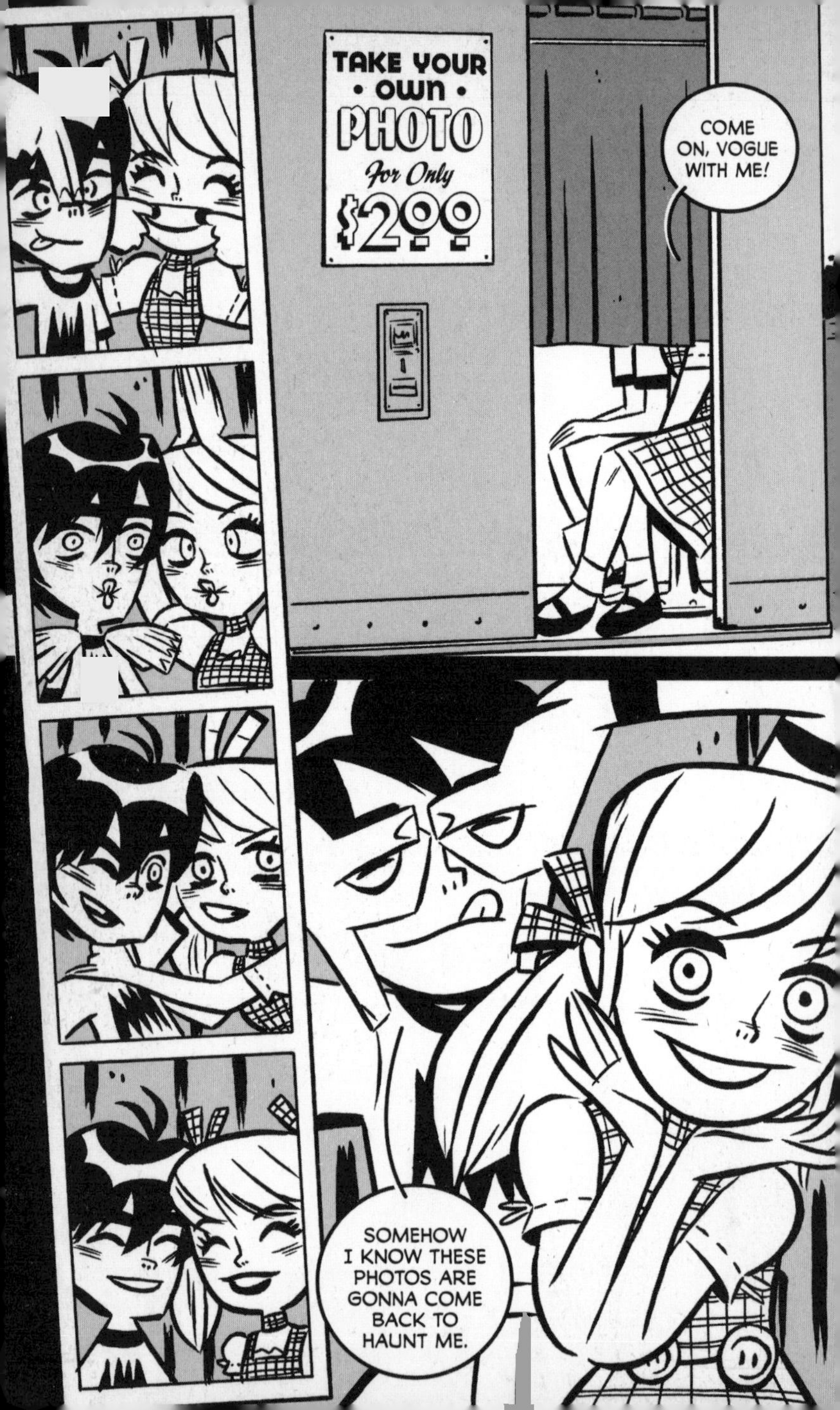
TAKE YOUR • OWN • PHOTO For Only $2.99
COME ON, VOGUE WITH ME!
SOMEHOW I KNOW THESE PHOTOS ARE GONNA COME BACK TO HAUNT ME.

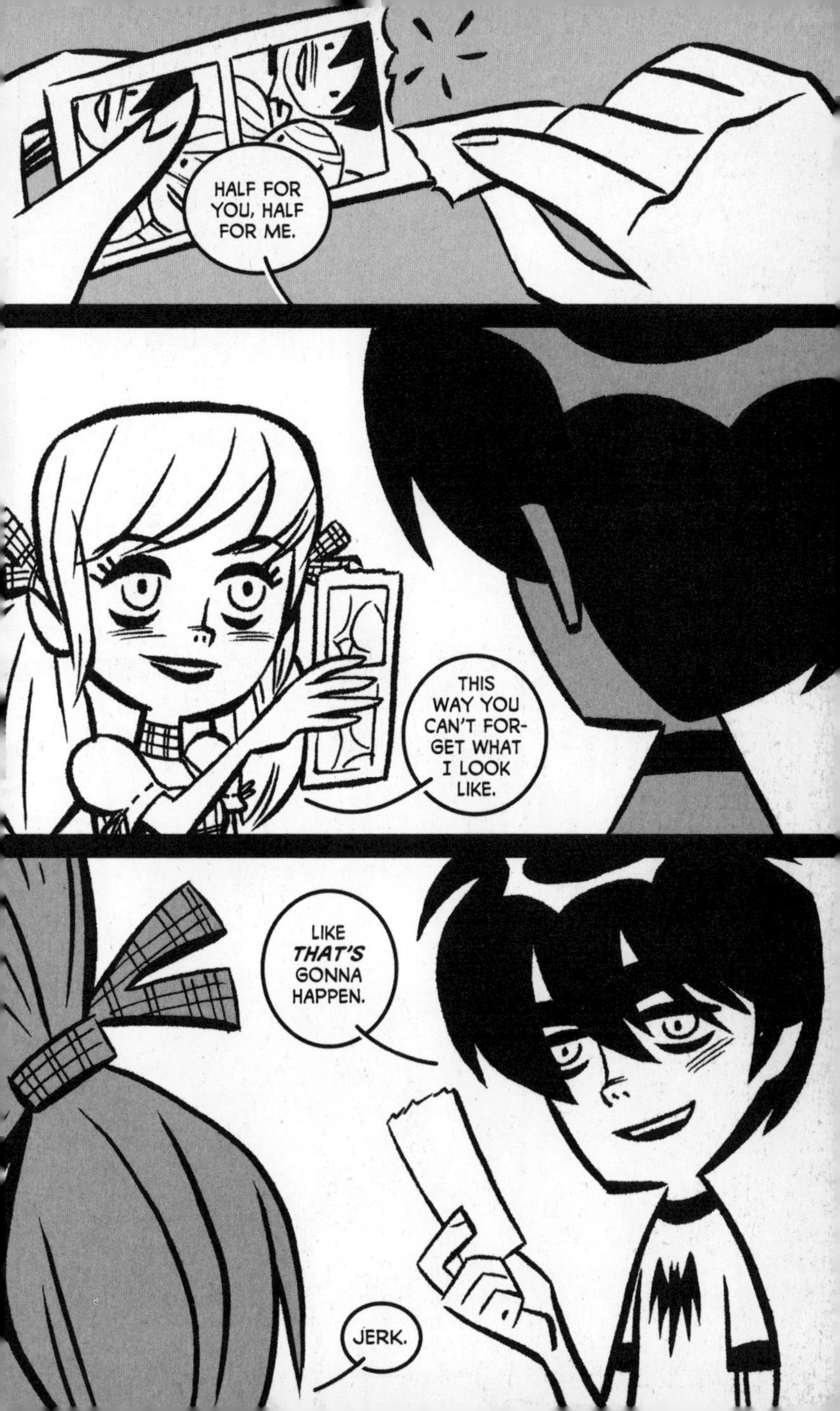
HALF FOR YOU, HALF FOR ME.
THIS WAY YOU CAN'T FOR-GET WHAT I LOOK LIKE.
LIKE ***THAT'S*** GONNA HAPPEN.
JERK.

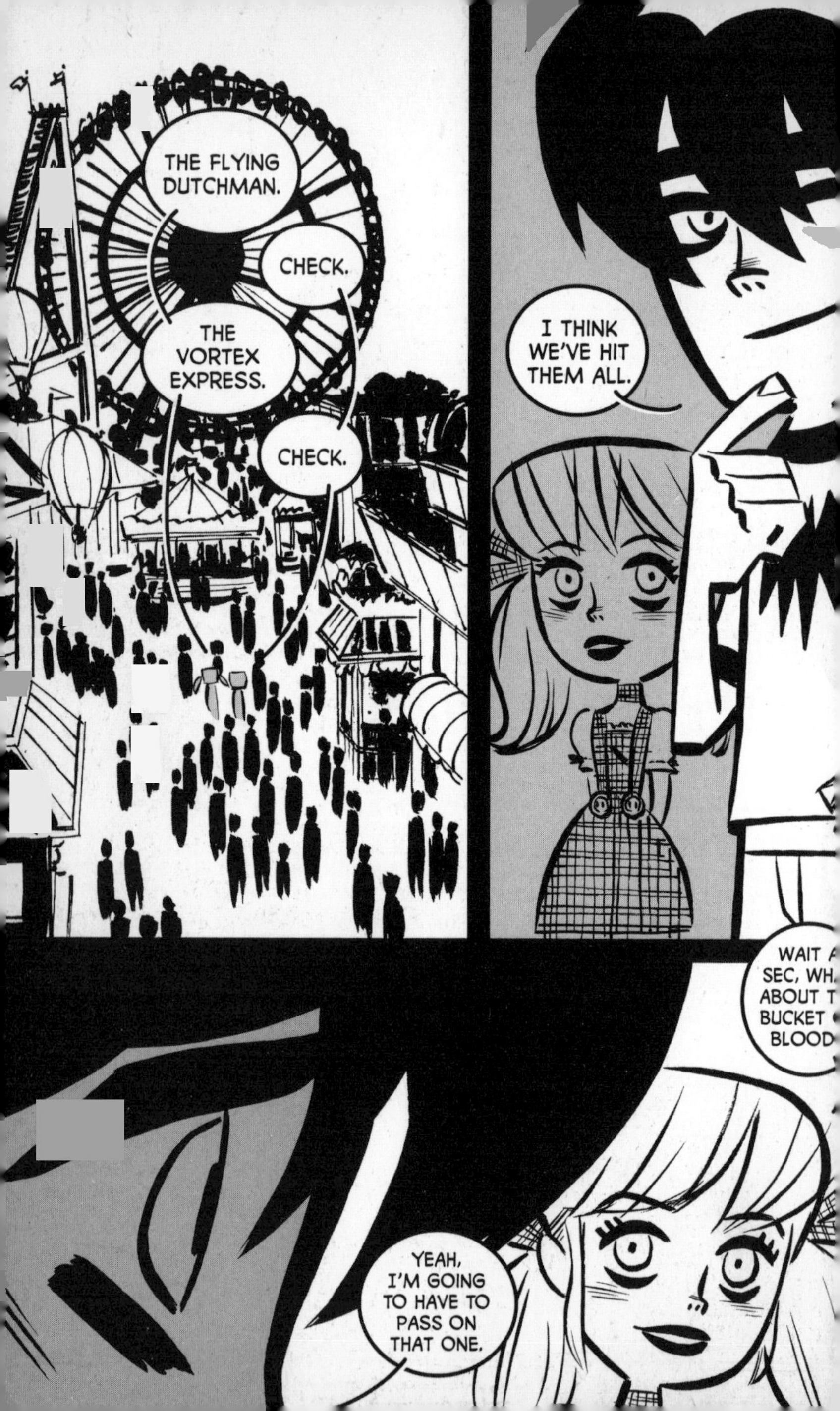
THE FLYING DUTCHMAN.
CHECK.
THE VORTEX EXPRESS.
CHECK.
I THINK WE'VE HIT THEM ALL.
WAIT A SEC, WH ABOUT T BUCKET BLOOD
YEAH, I'M GOING TO HAVE TO PASS ON THAT ONE.

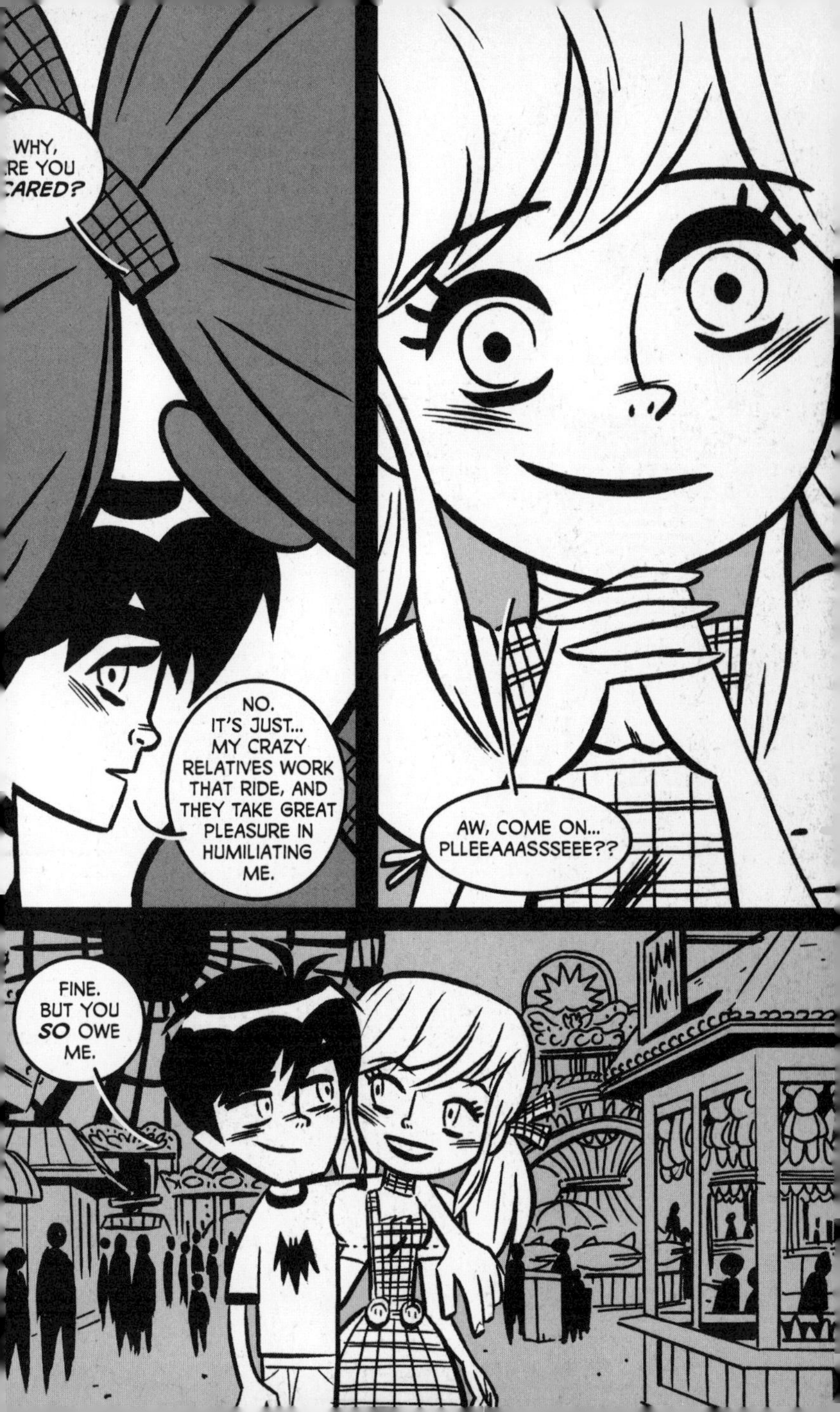
WHY, RE YOU CARED?
NO. IT'S JUST... MY CRAZY RELATIVES WORK THAT RIDE, AND THEY TAKE GREAT PLEASURE IN HUMILIATING ME.
AW, COME ON... PLLEEAAASSSEEE??
FINE. BUT YOU SO OWE ME.

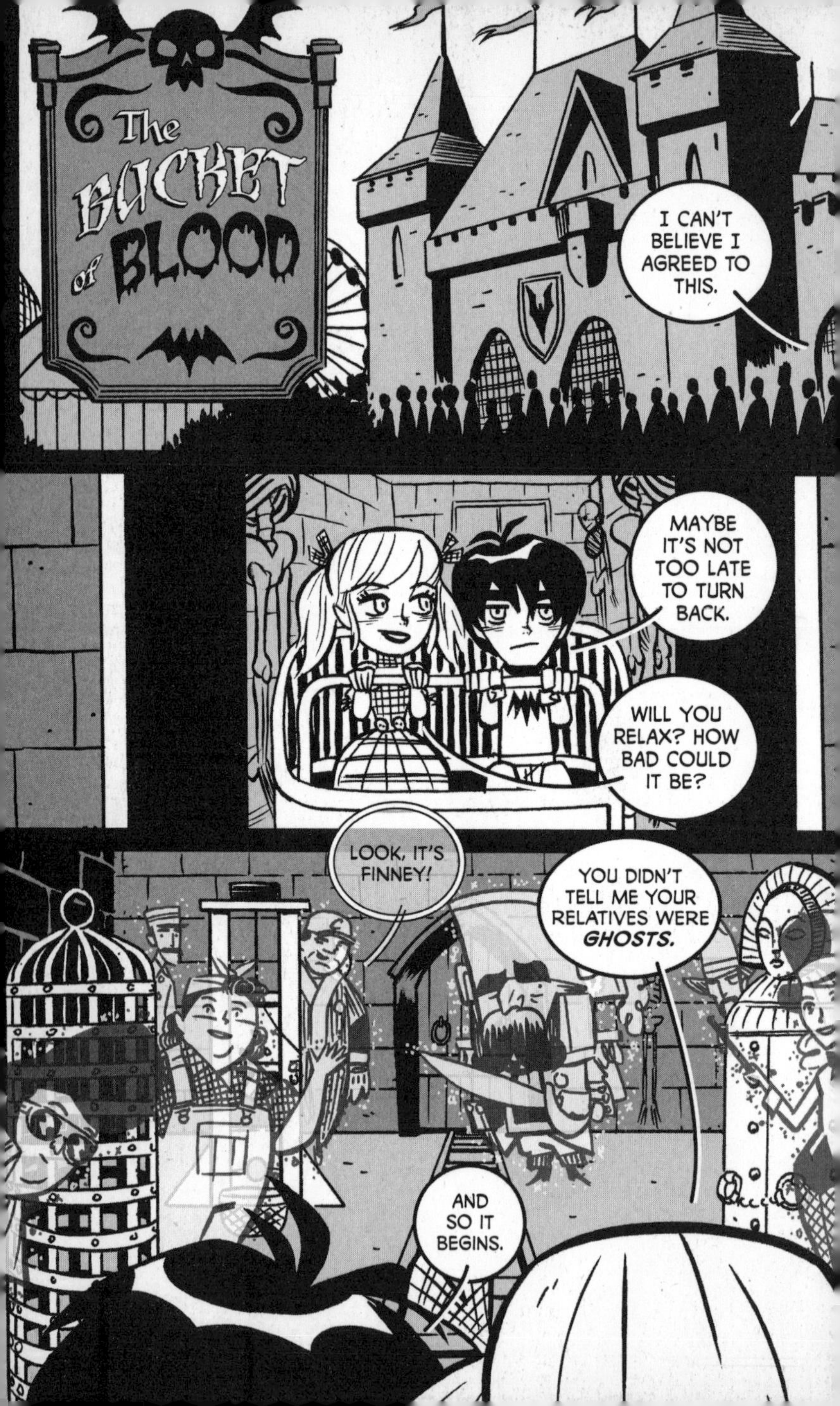
The BUCKET of BLOOD
I CAN'T BELIEVE I AGREED TO THIS.
MAYBE IT'S NOT TOO LATE TO TURN BACK.
WILL YOU RELAX? HOW BAD COULD IT BE?
LOOK, IT'S FINNEY!
YOU DIDN'T TELL ME YOUR RELATIVES WERE ***GHOSTS.***
AND SO IT BEGINS.

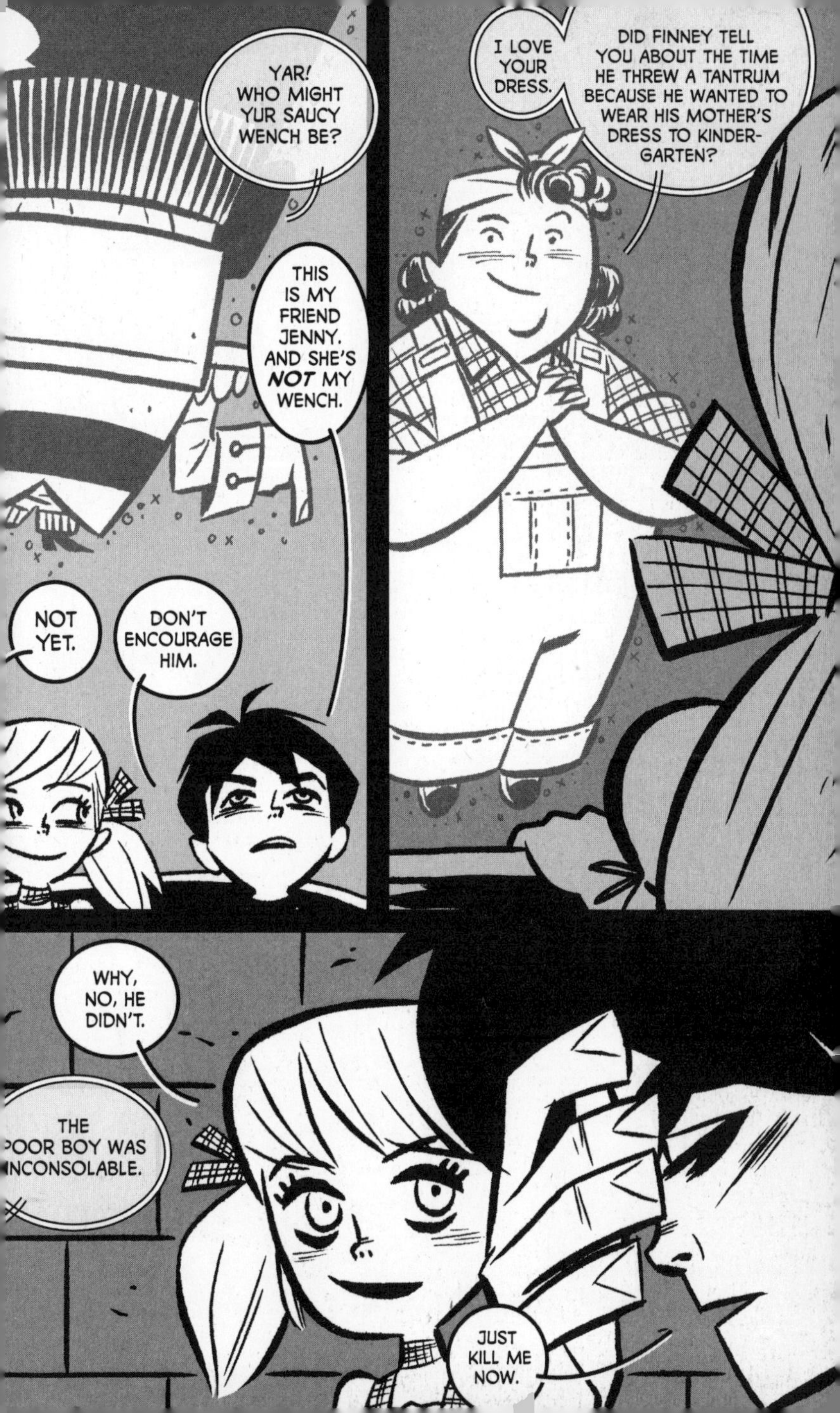
YAR! WHO MIGHT YUR SAUCY WENCH BE?
THIS IS MY FRIEND JENNY. AND SHE'S *NOT* MY WENCH.
NOT YET.
DON'T ENCOURAGE HIM.
I LOVE YOUR DRESS.
DID FINNEY TELL YOU ABOUT THE TIME HE THREW A TANTRUM BECAUSE HE WANTED TO WEAR HIS MOTHER'S DRESS TO KINDER-GARTEN?
WHY, NO, HE DIDN'T.
THE POOR BOY WAS INCONSOLABLE.
JUST KILL ME NOW.

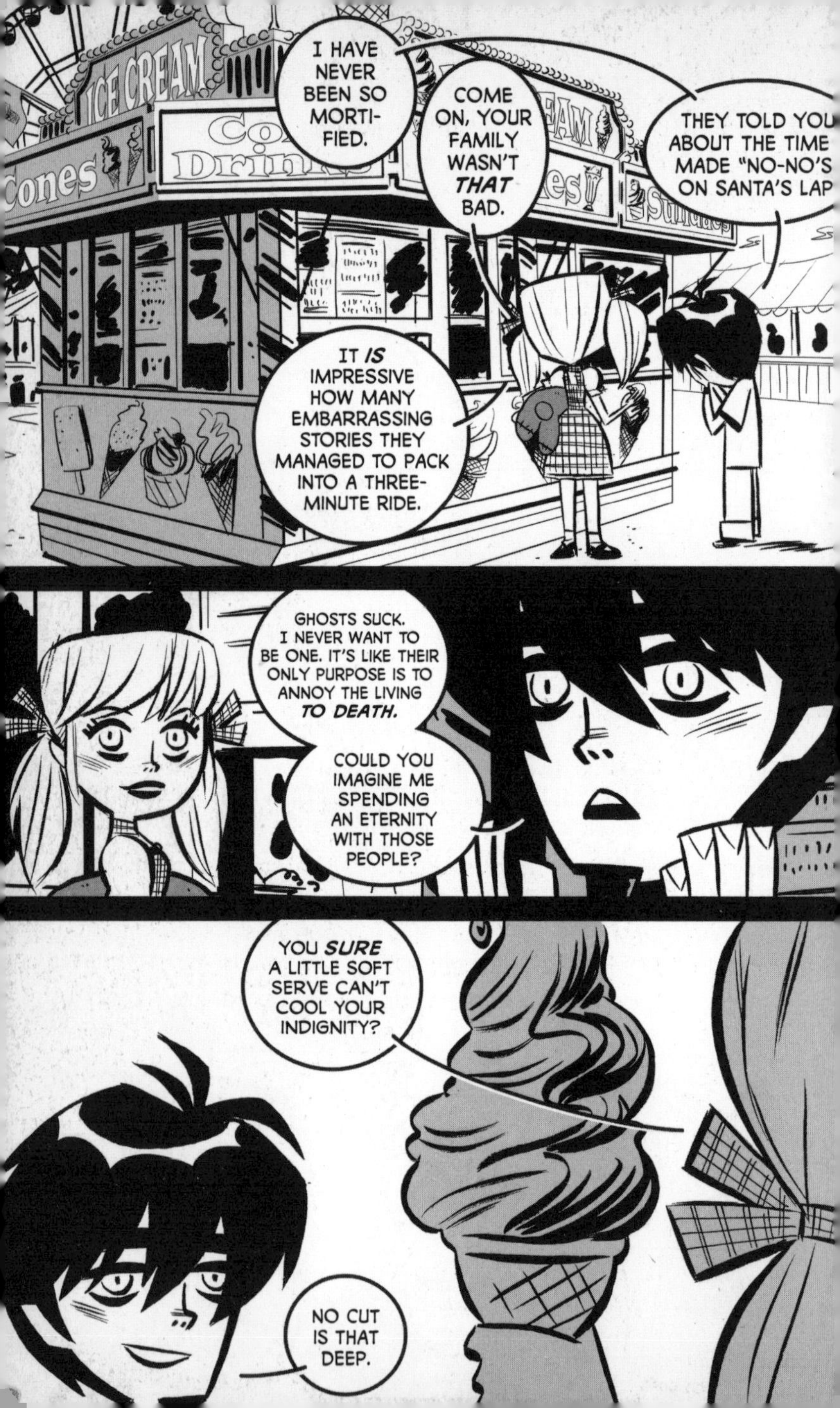
ICE CREAM
Cones
Drinks
I HAVE NEVER BEEN SO MORTIFIED.
COME ON, YOUR FAMILY WASN'T *THAT* BAD.
THEY TOLD YOU ABOUT THE TIME MADE "NO-NO'S ON SANTA'S LAP
IT *IS* IMPRESSIVE HOW MANY EMBARRASSING STORIES THEY MANAGED TO PACK INTO A THREE-MINUTE RIDE.
GHOSTS SUCK. I NEVER WANT TO BE ONE. IT'S LIKE THEIR ONLY PURPOSE IS TO ANNOY THE LIVING ***TO DEATH.***
COULD YOU IMAGINE ME SPENDING AN ETERNITY WITH THOSE PEOPLE?
YOU ***SURE*** A LITTLE SOFT SERVE CAN'T COOL YOUR INDIGNITY?
NO CUT IS THAT DEEP.

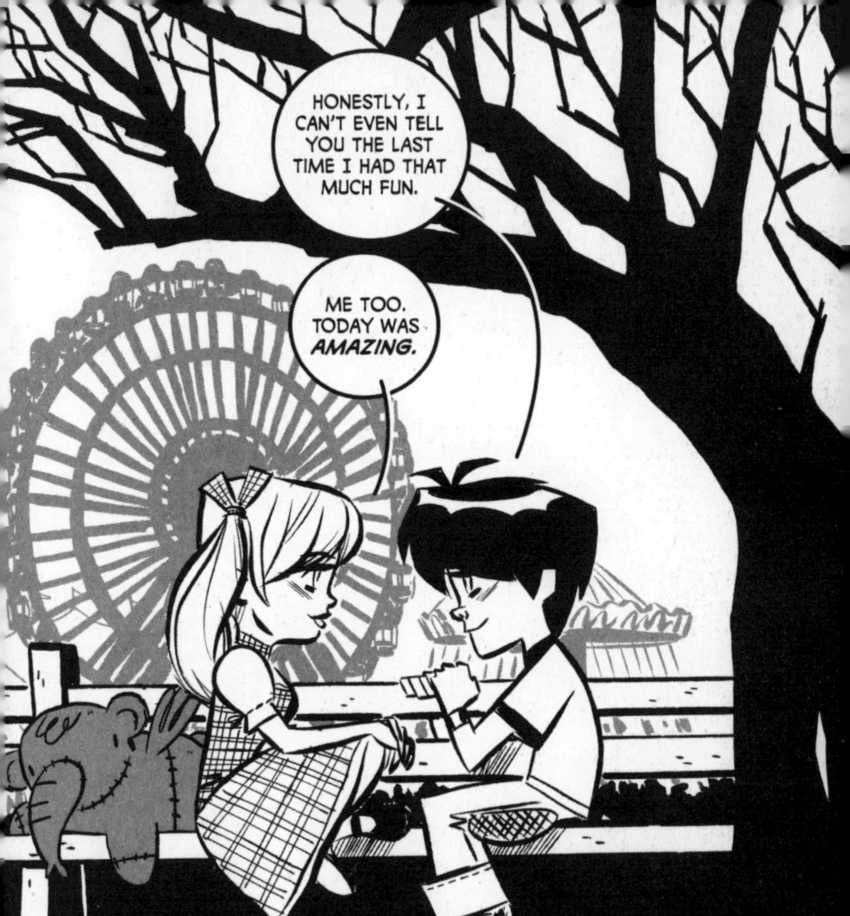
HONESTLY, I CAN'T EVEN TELL YOU THE LAST TIME I HAD THAT MUCH FUN.
ME TOO. TODAY WAS *AMAZING.*

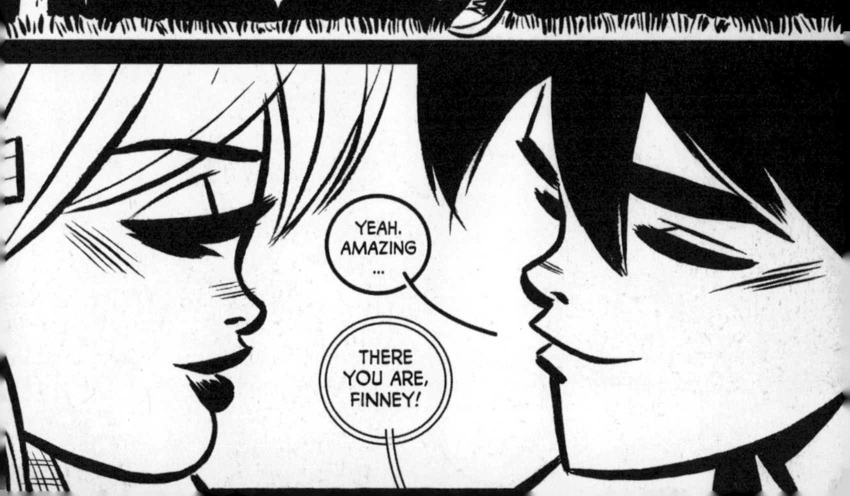
YEAH. AMAZING ...
THERE YOU ARE, FINNEY!

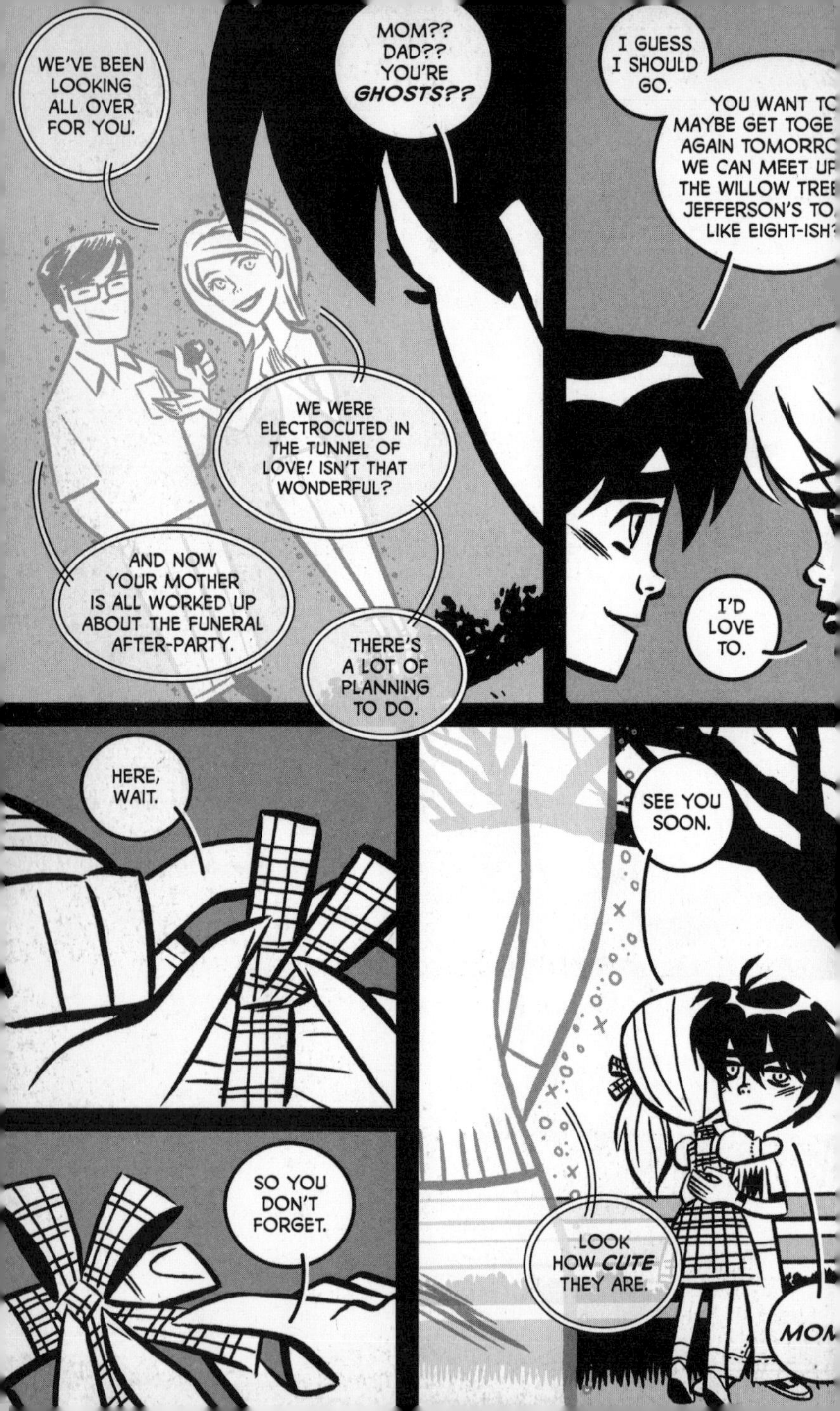

WE'VE BEEN LOOKING ALL OVER FOR YOU.
MOM?? DAD?? YOU'RE *GHOSTS??*
WE WERE ELECTROCUTED IN THE TUNNEL OF LOVE! ISN'T THAT WONDERFUL?
AND NOW YOUR MOTHER IS ALL WORKED UP ABOUT THE FUNERAL AFTER-PARTY.
THERE'S A LOT OF PLANNING TO DO.
I GUESS I SHOULD GO.
YOU WANT TO MAYBE GET TOGE AGAIN TOMORRO WE CAN MEET UP THE WILLOW TREE JEFFERSON'S TO LIKE EIGHT-ISH?
I'D LOVE TO.
HERE, WAIT.
SO YOU DON'T FORGET.
SEE YOU SOON.
LOOK HOW *CUTE* THEY ARE.
MOM

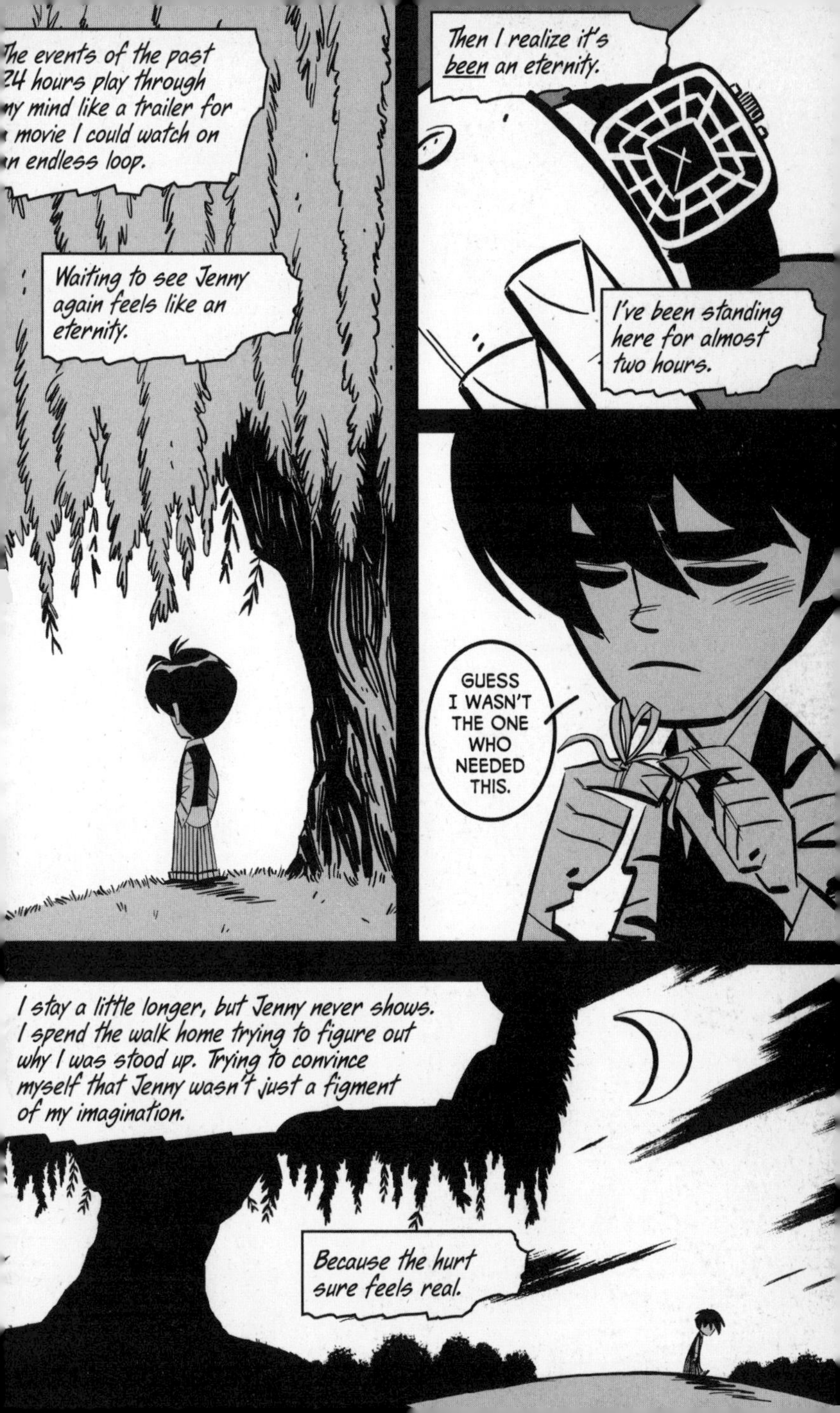
The events of the past 24 hours play through my mind like a trailer for a movie I could watch on an endless loop.
Waiting to see Jenny again feels like an eternity.
Then I realize it's been an eternity.
I've been standing here for almost two hours.
GUESS I WASN'T THE ONE WHO NEEDED THIS.
I stay a little longer, but Jenny never shows. I spend the walk home trying to figure out why I was stood up. Trying to convince myself that Jenny wasn't just a figment of my imagination.
Because the hurt sure feels real.

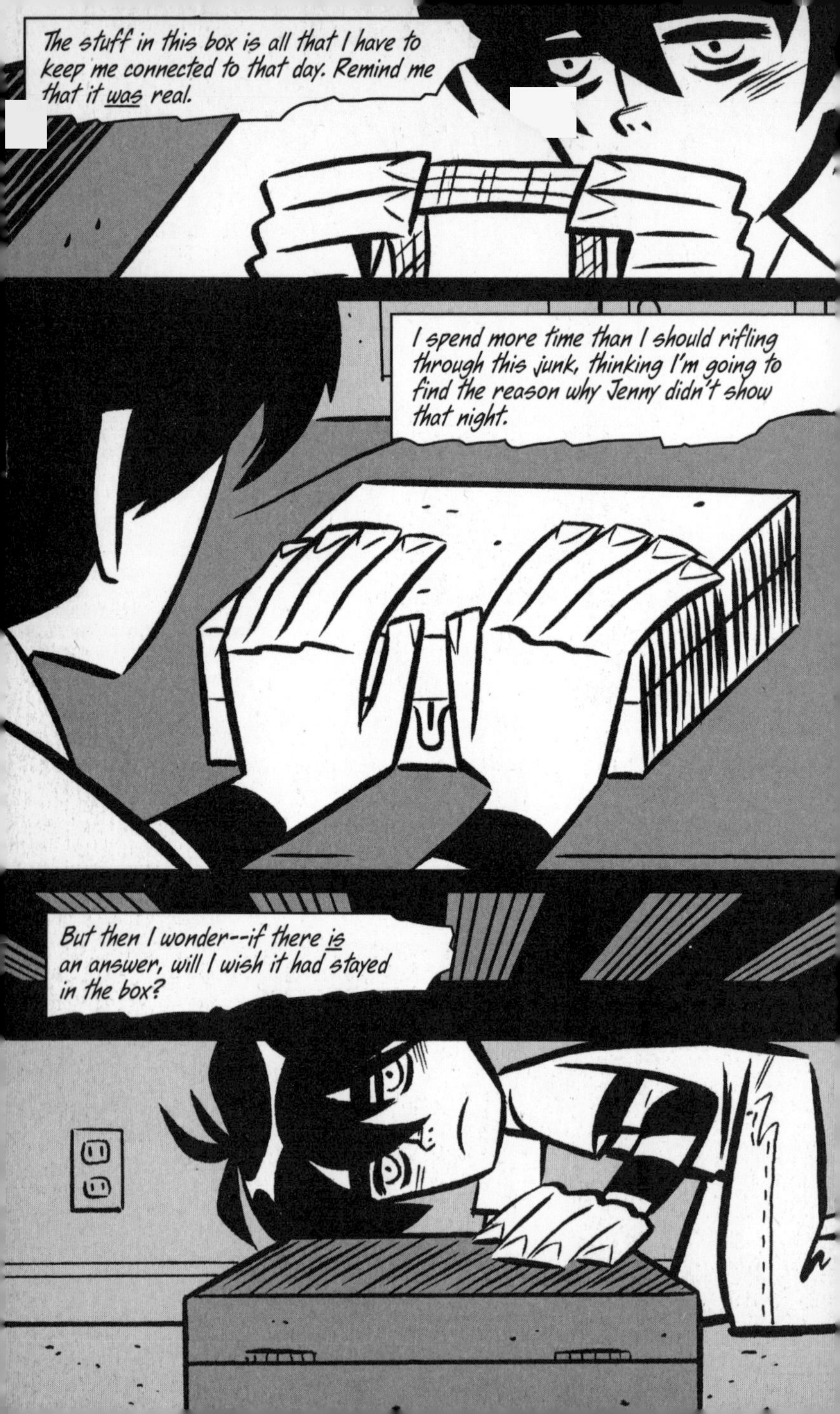
The stuff in this box is all that I have to keep me connected to that day. Remind me that it was real.
I spend more time than I should rifling through this junk, thinking I'm going to find the reason why Jenny didn't show that night.
But then I wonder--if there is an answer, will I wish it had stayed in the box?

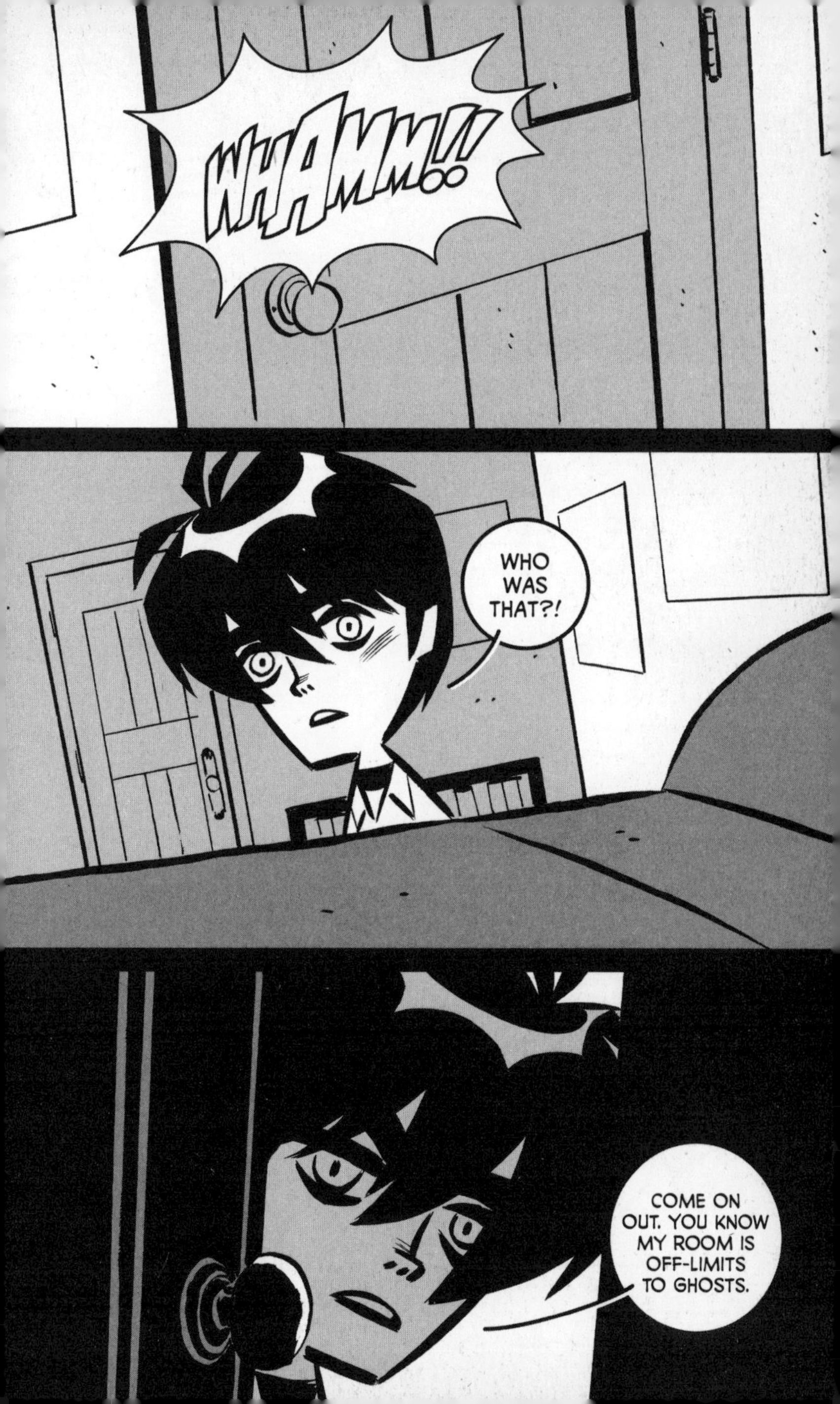
WHAMM!!
WHO WAS THAT?!
COME ON OUT. YOU KNOW MY ROOM IS OFF-LIMITS TO GHOSTS.

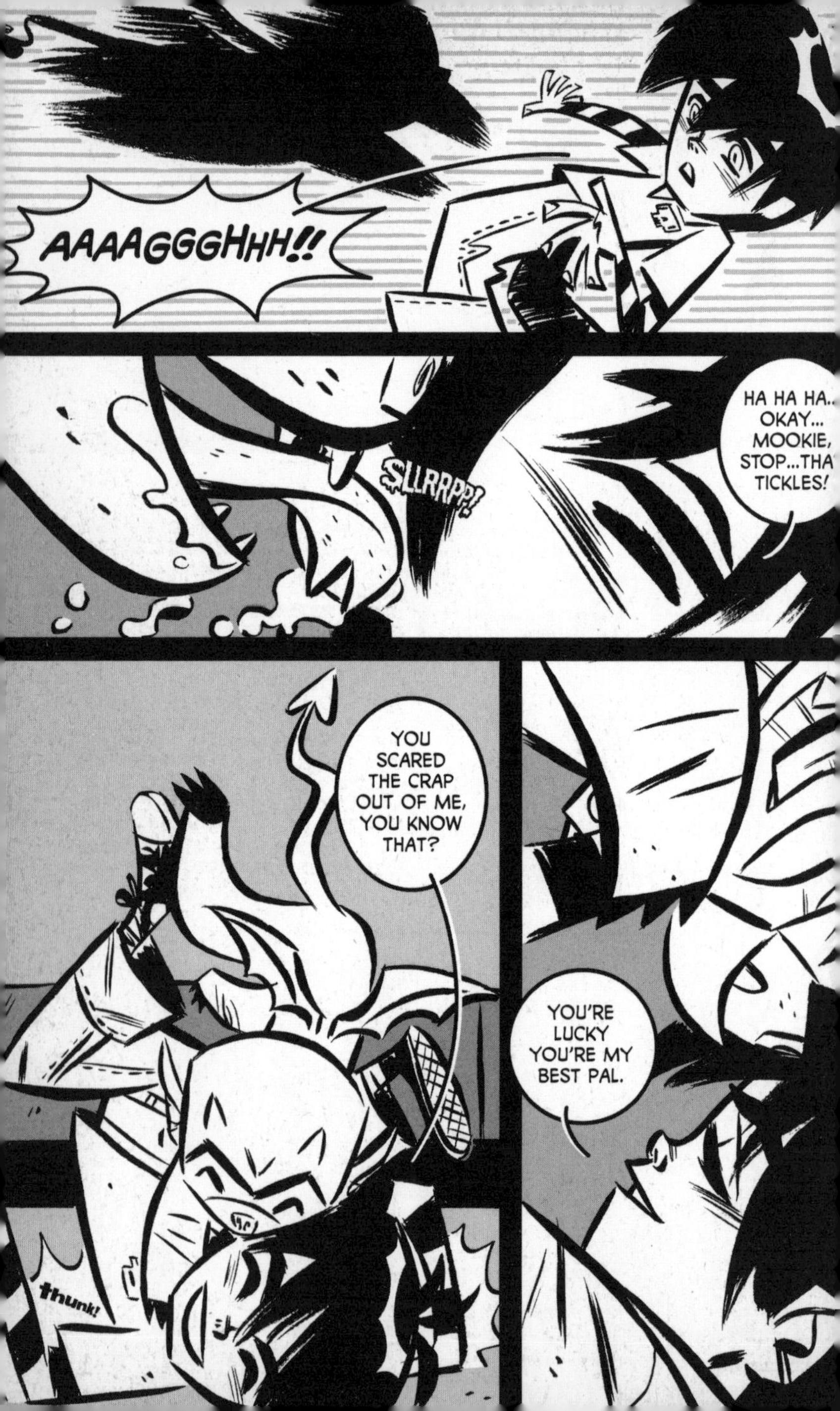

AAAAGGGHHH!!
SLLRRPP!
HA HA HA.. OKAY... MOOKIE, STOP...THA TICKLES!
YOU SCARED THE CRAP OUT OF ME, YOU KNOW THAT?
thunk!
YOU'RE LUCKY YOU'RE MY BEST PAL.

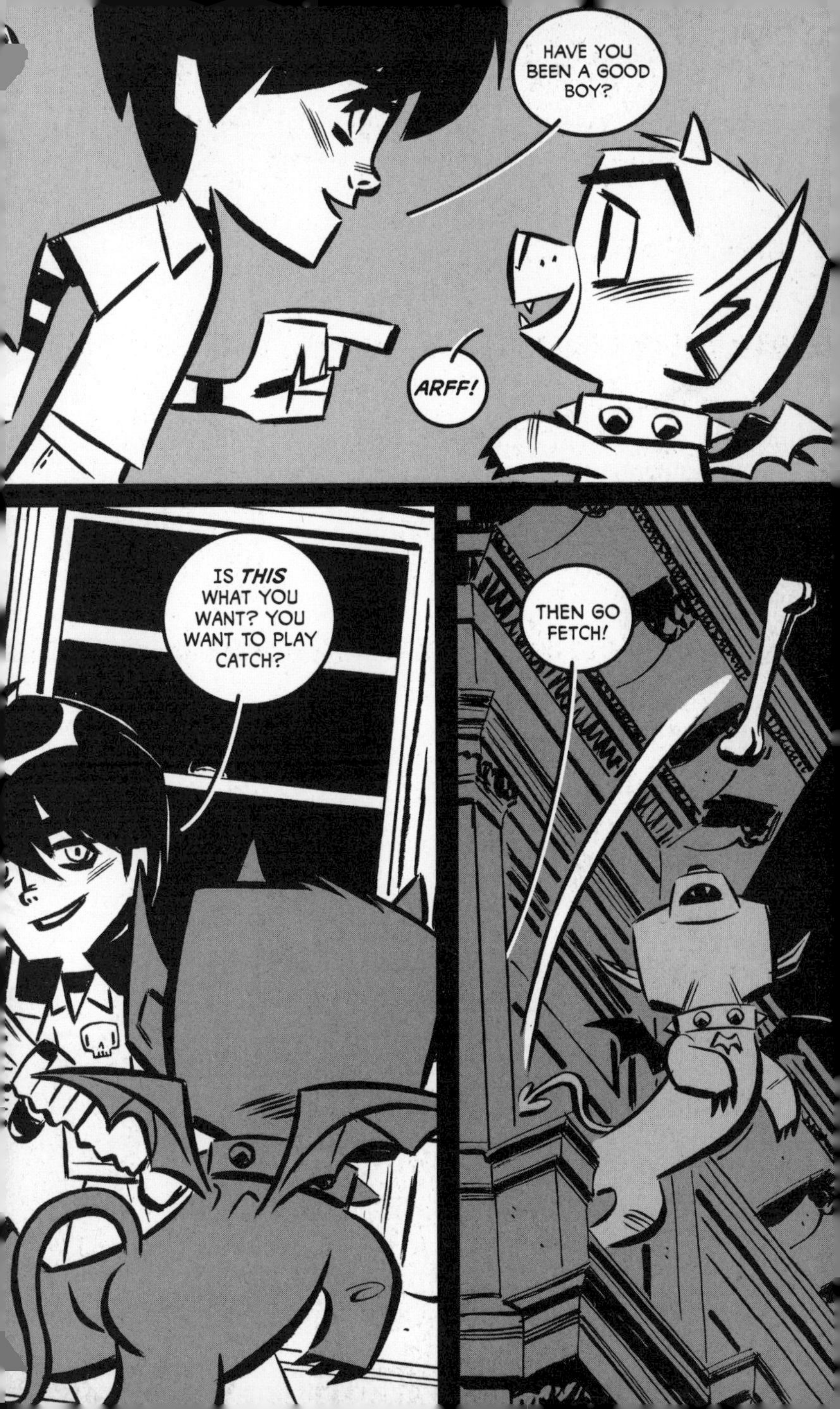
HAVE YOU BEEN A GOOD BOY?
ARFF!
IS THIS WHAT YOU WANT? YOU WANT TO PLAY CATCH?
THEN GO FETCH!

CHAPTER FOUR

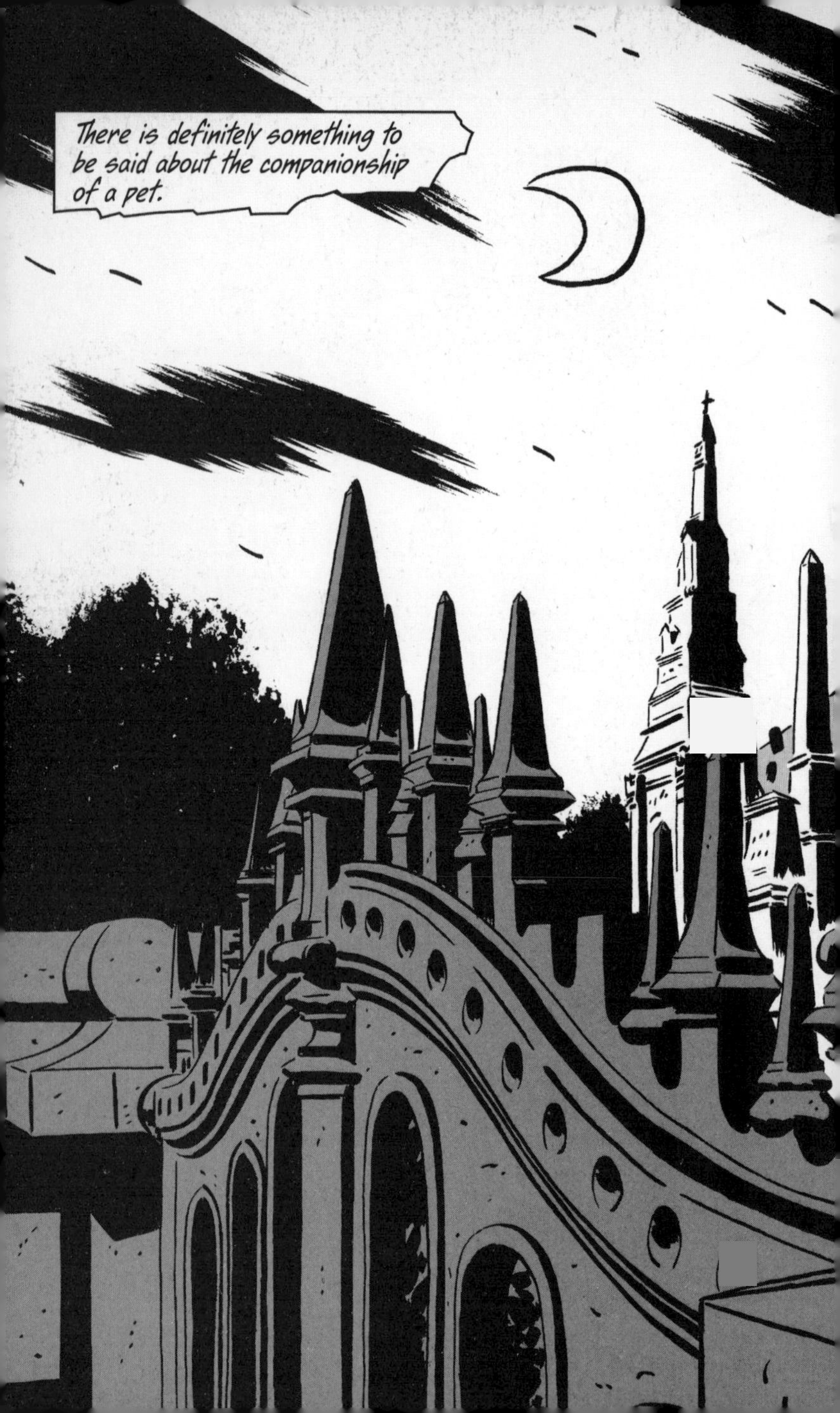
There is definitely something to be said about the companionship of a pet.

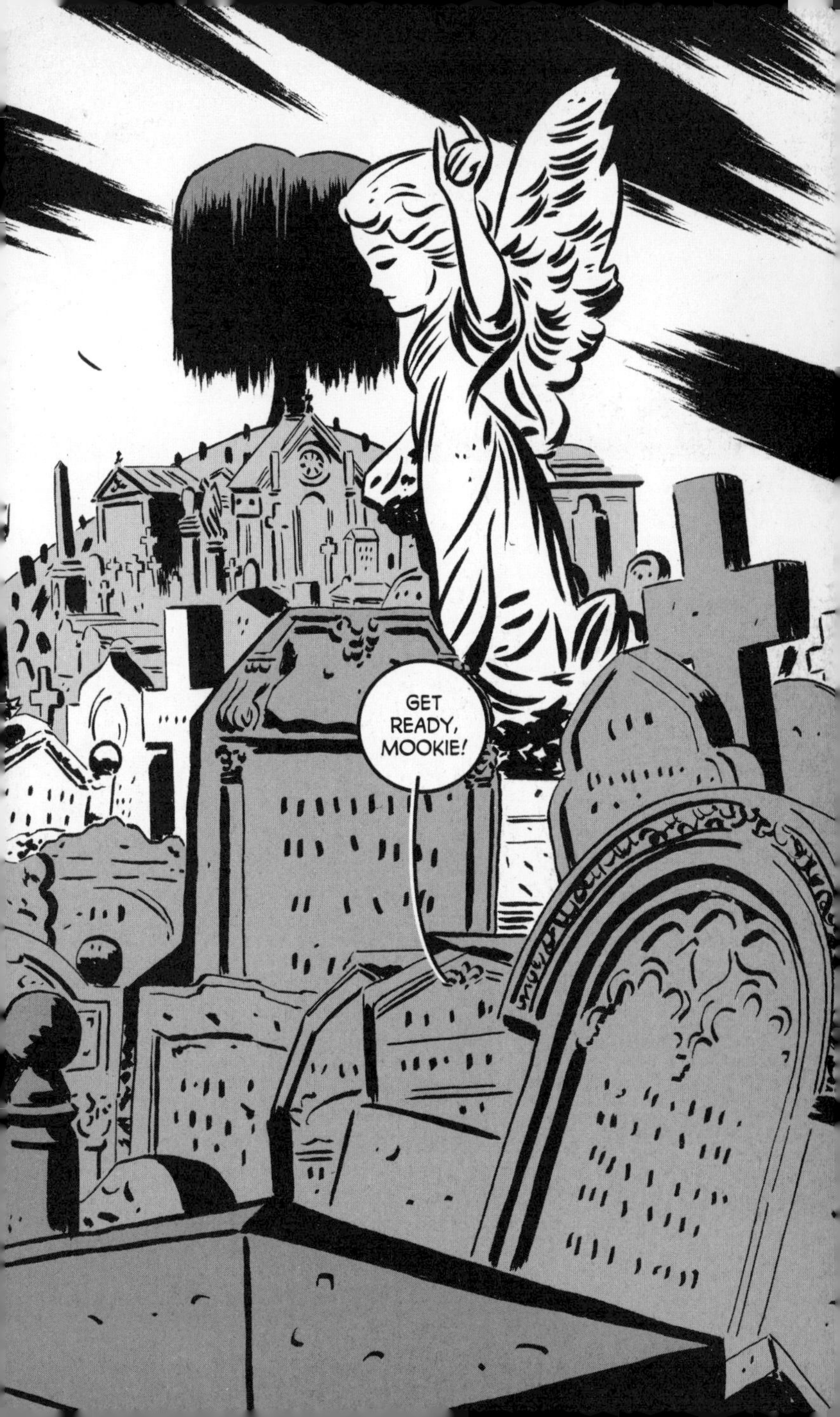
GET READY, MOOKIE!

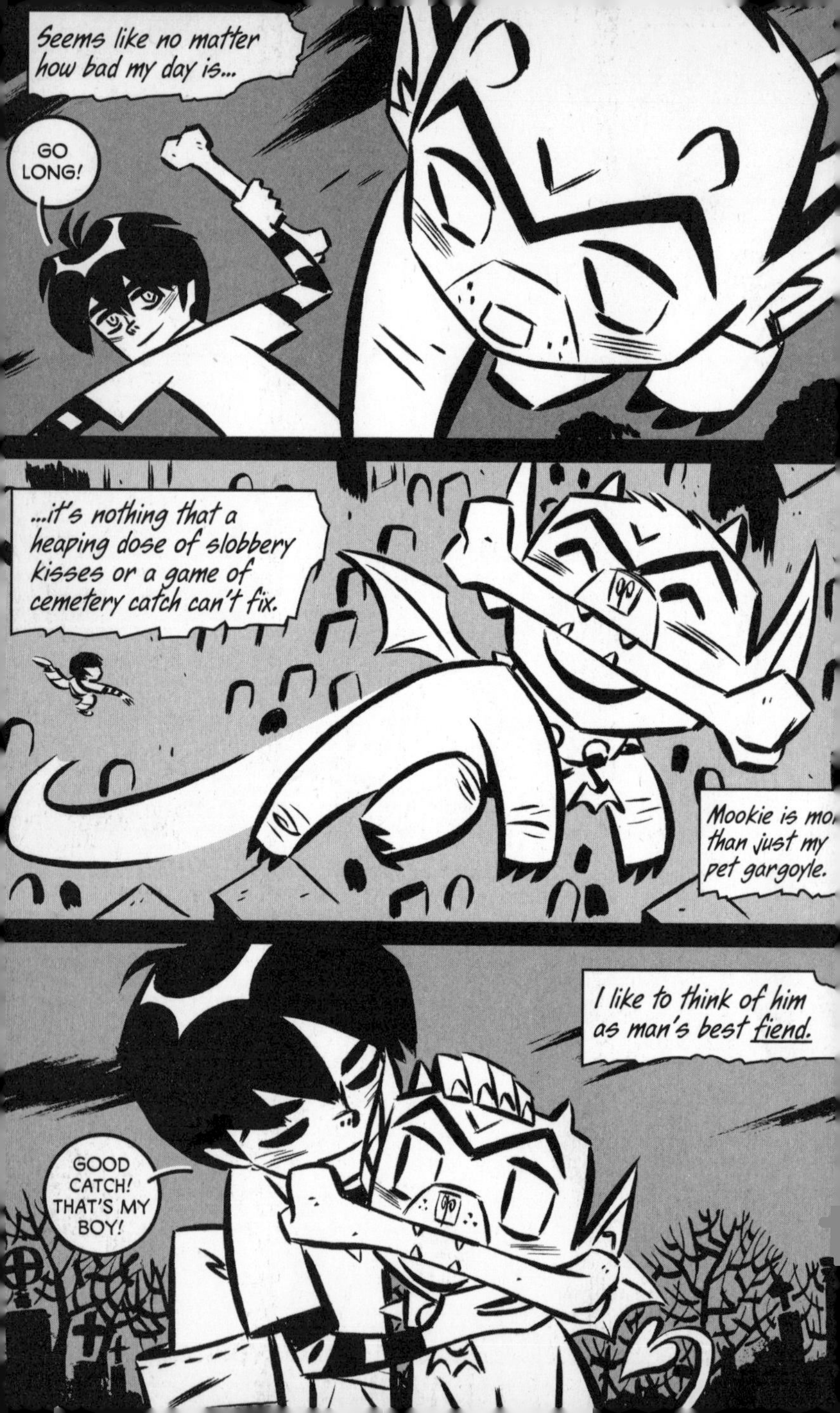
Seems like no matter how bad my day is...
GO LONG!
...it's nothing that a heaping dose of slobbery kisses or a game of cemetery catch can't fix.
Mookie is mo than just my pet gargoyle.
I like to think of him as man's best fiend.
GOOD CATCH! THAT'S MY BOY!

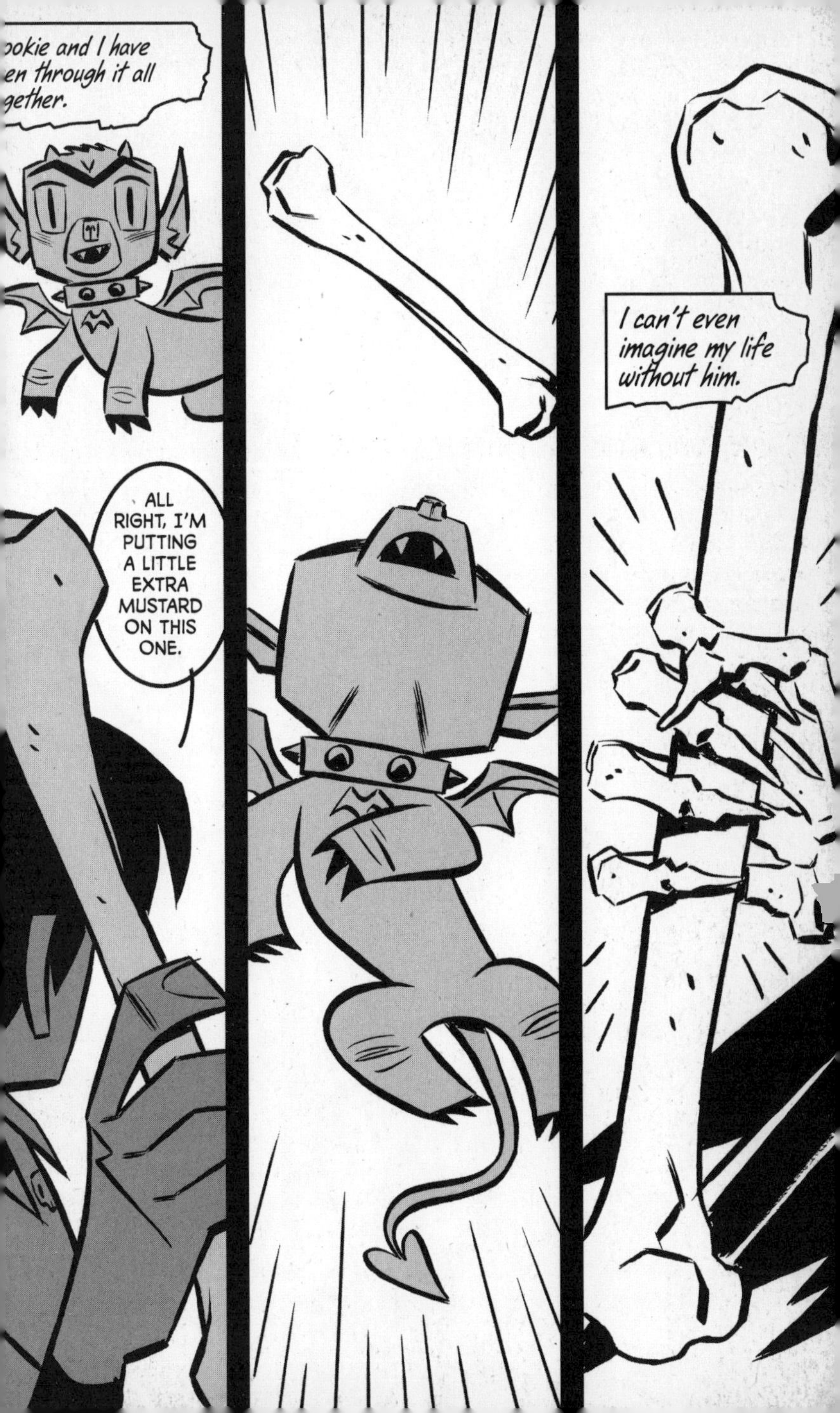
ookie and I have
en through it all
gether.
ALL RIGHT, I'M PUTTING A LITTLE EXTRA MUSTARD ON THIS ONE.
I can't even imagine my life without him.

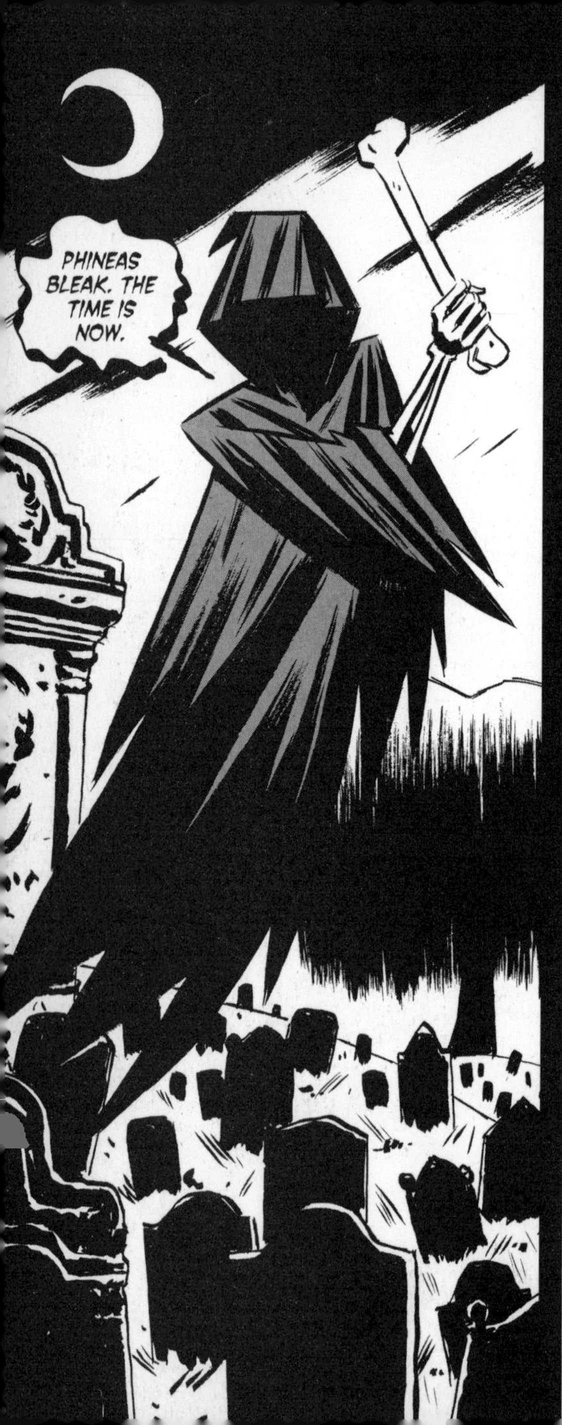
PHINEAS BLEAK. THE TIME IS NOW.
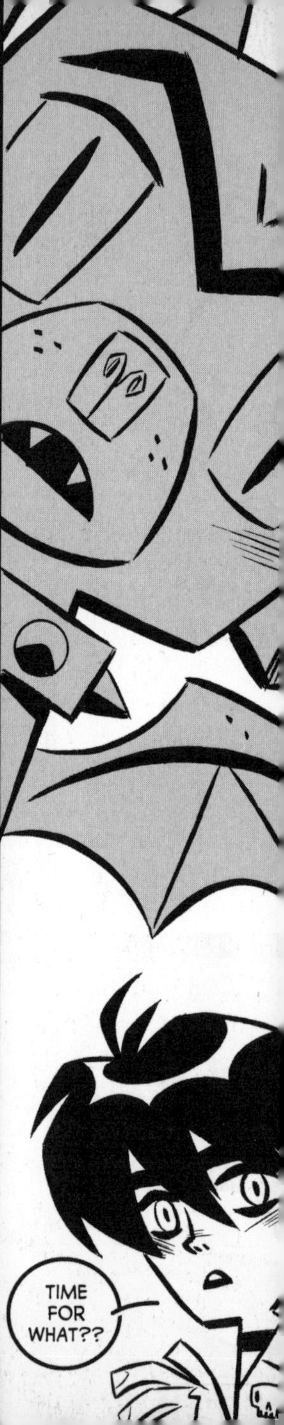
TIME FOR WHAT??

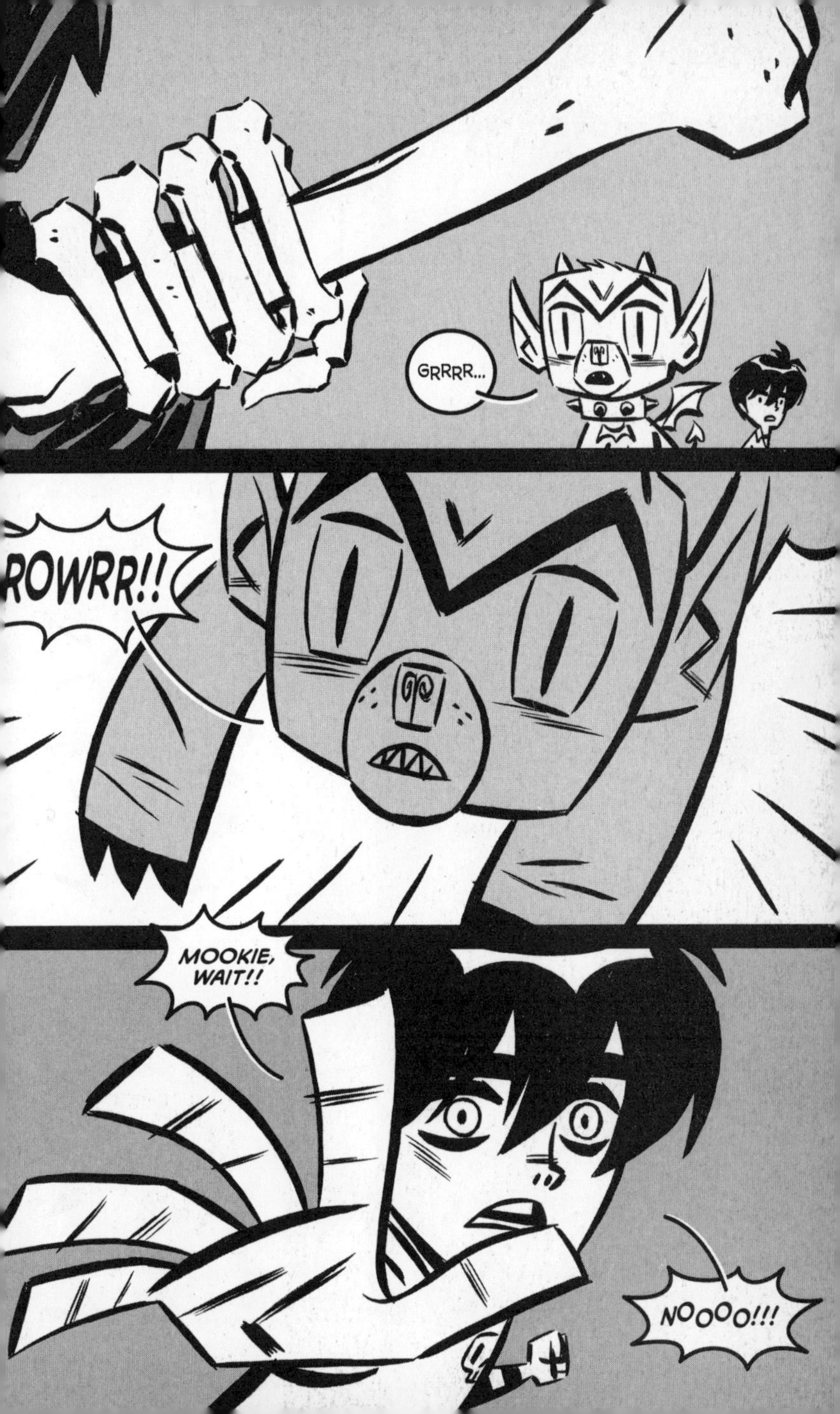
GRRRR...
ROWRR!!
MOOKIE, WAIT!!
NOOOO!!!

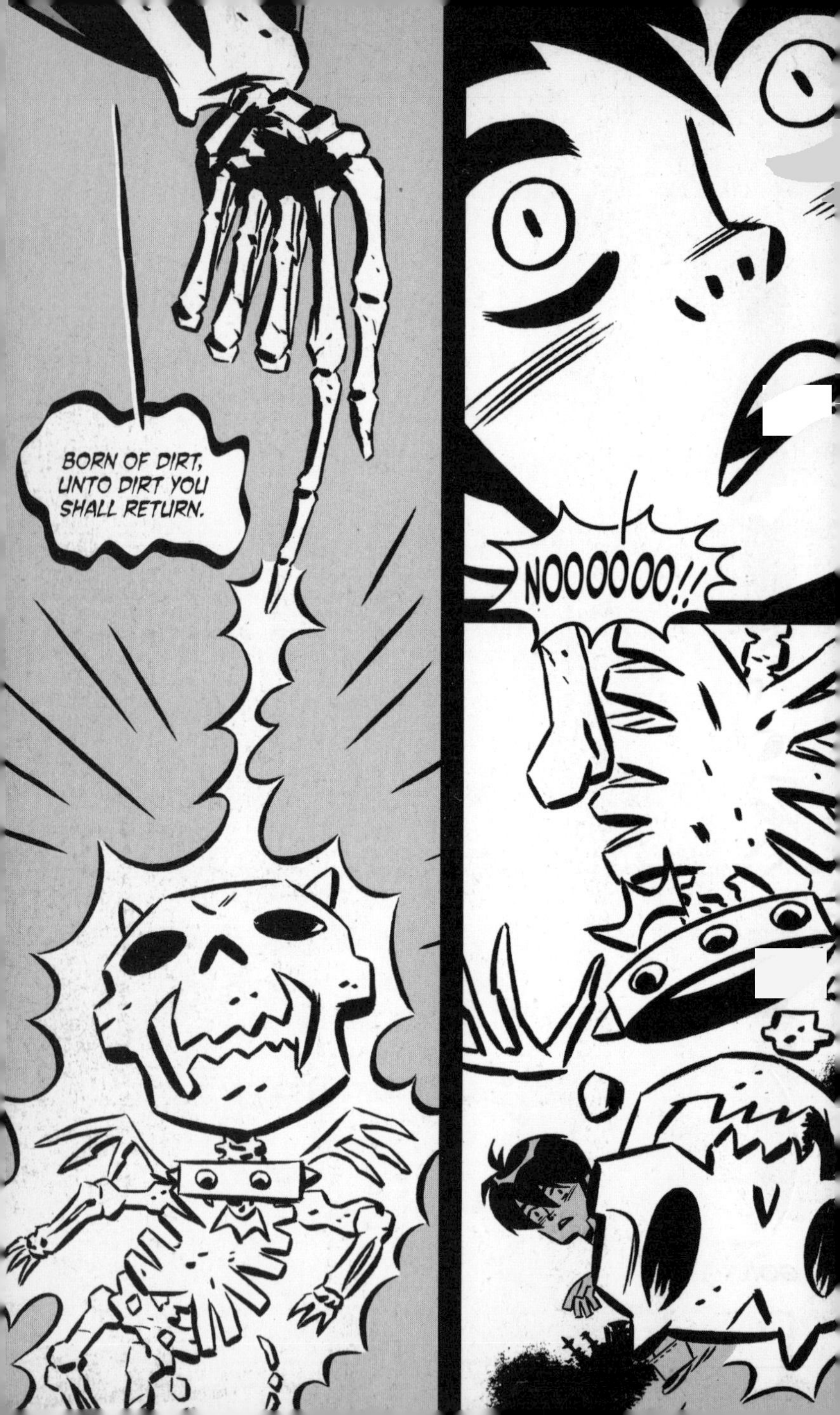
BORN OF DIRT, UNTO DIRT YOU SHALL RETURN.
NOOOOOO!!

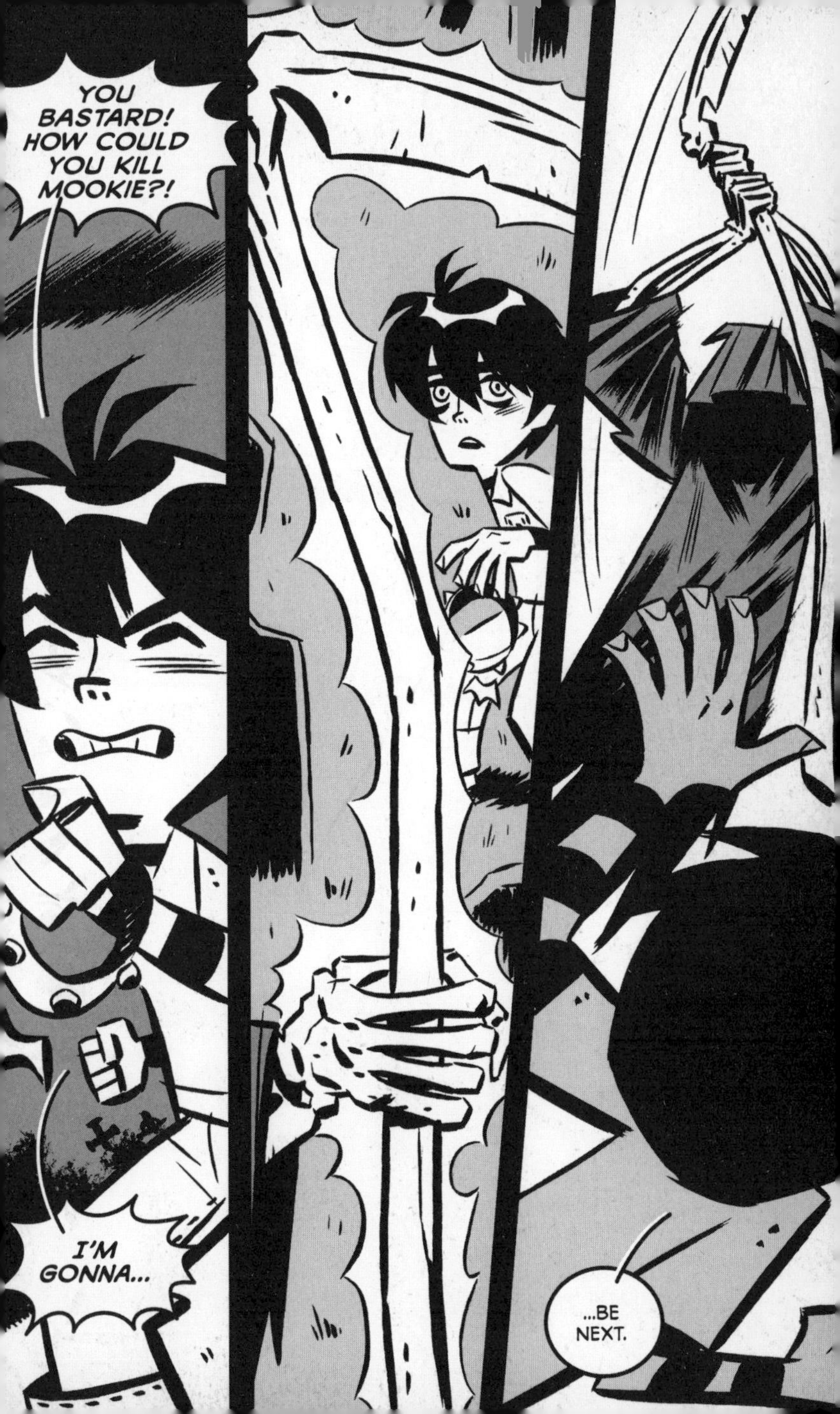
YOU BASTARD! HOW COULD YOU KILL MOOKIE?!
I'M GONNA...
...BE NEXT.

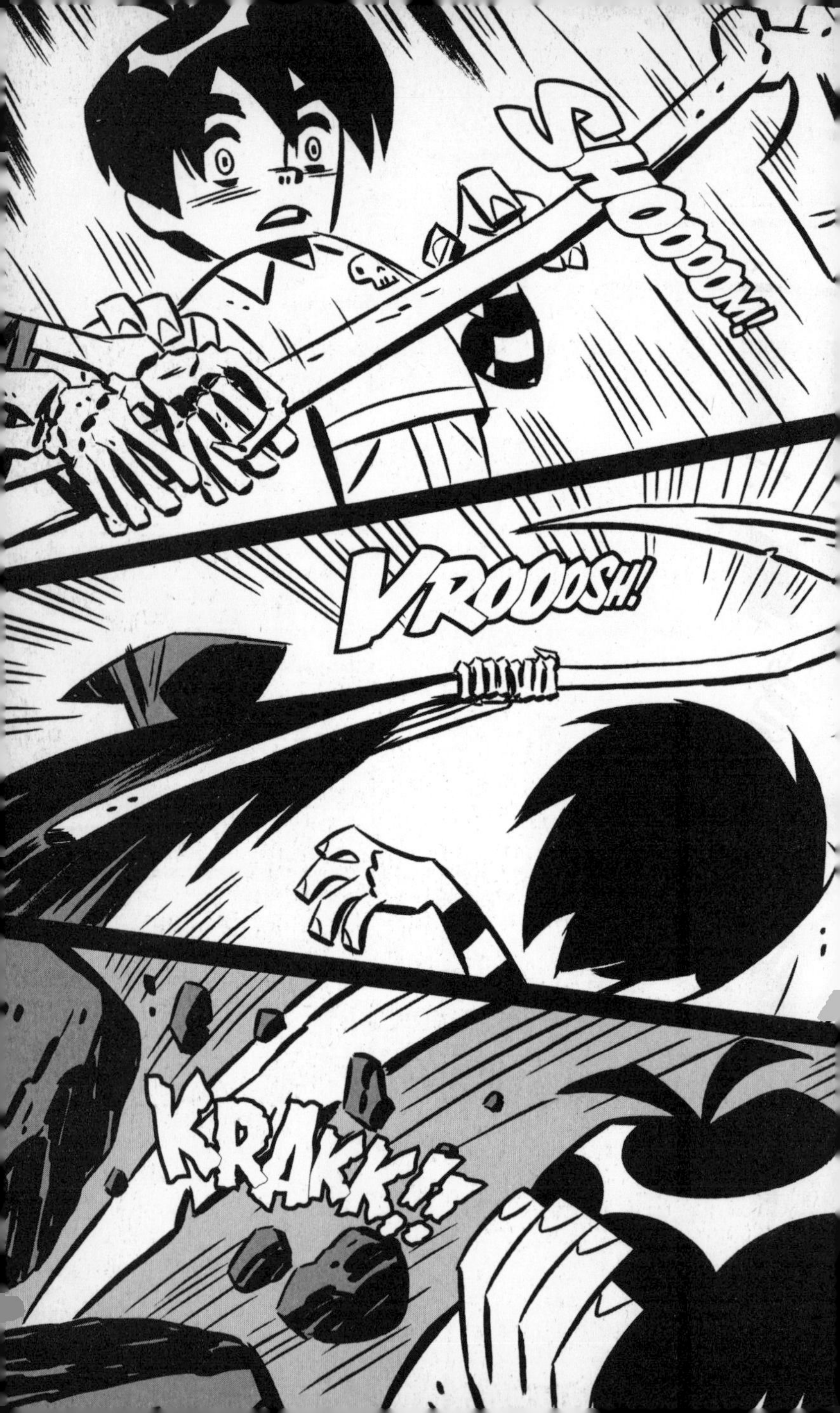
SHOOOOM!
VROOOOSH!
KRAKK!!

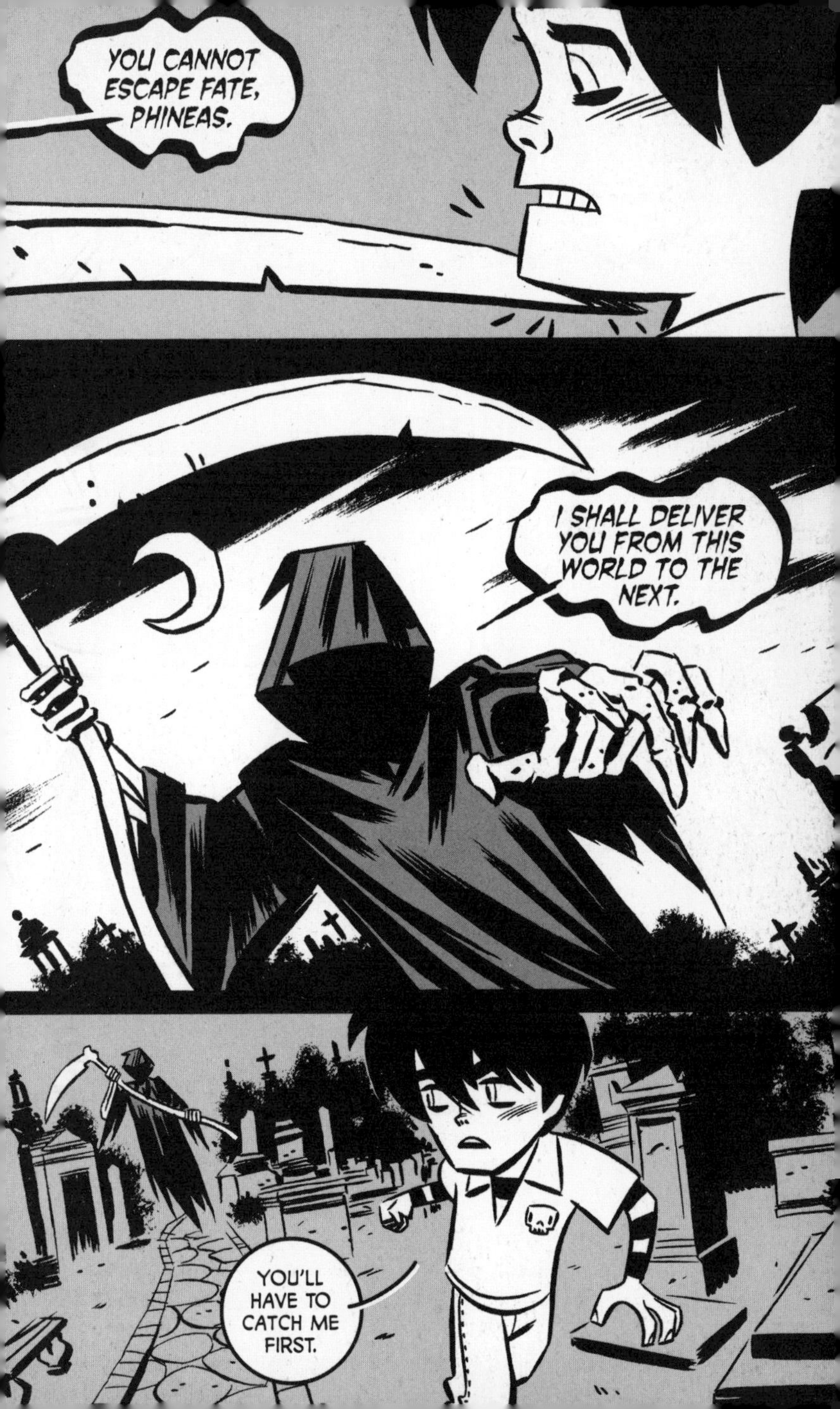
YOU CANNOT ESCAPE FATE, PHINEAS.
I SHALL DELIVER YOU FROM THIS WORLD TO THE NEXT.
YOU'LL HAVE TO CATCH ME FIRST.

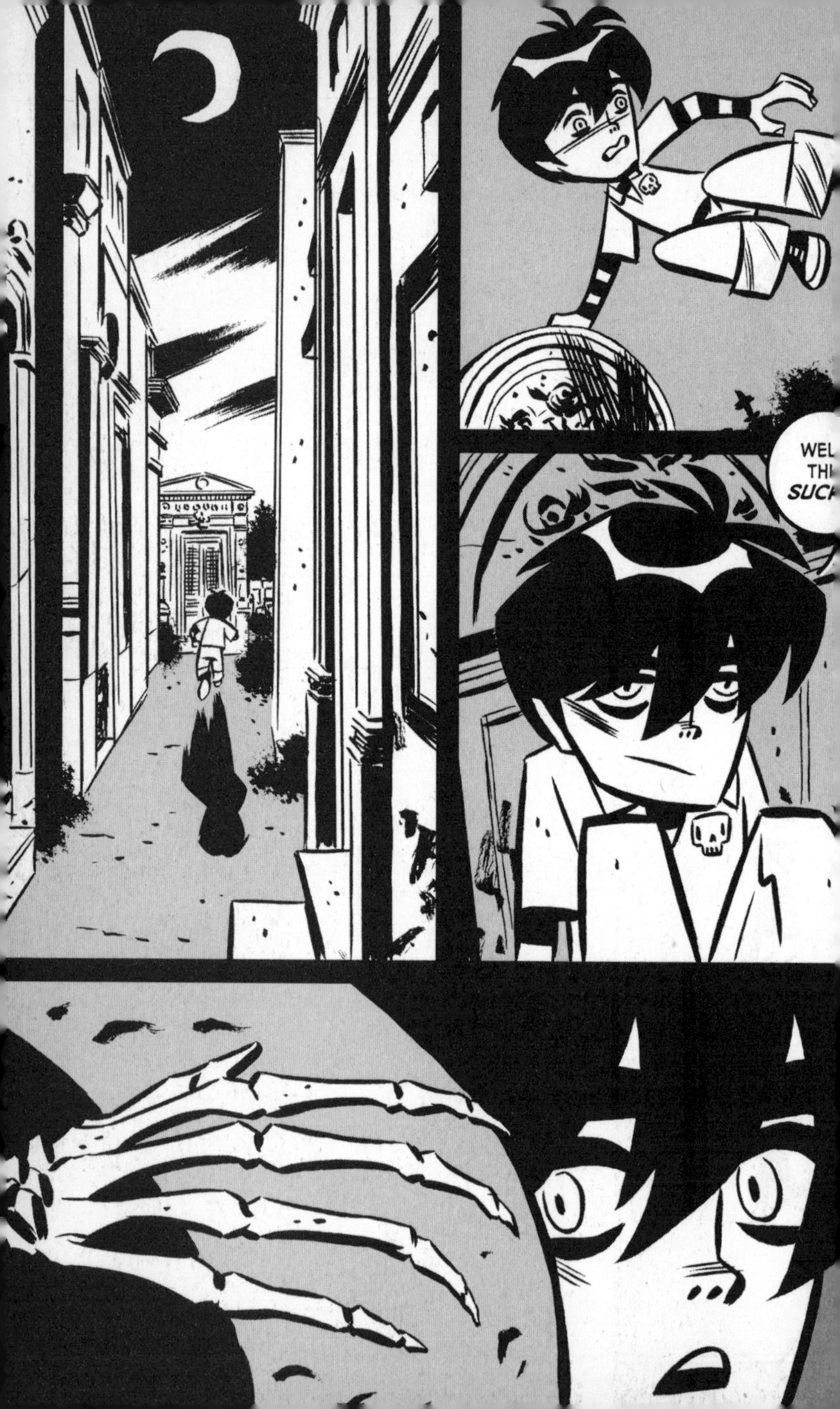
WEL
THI
SUC

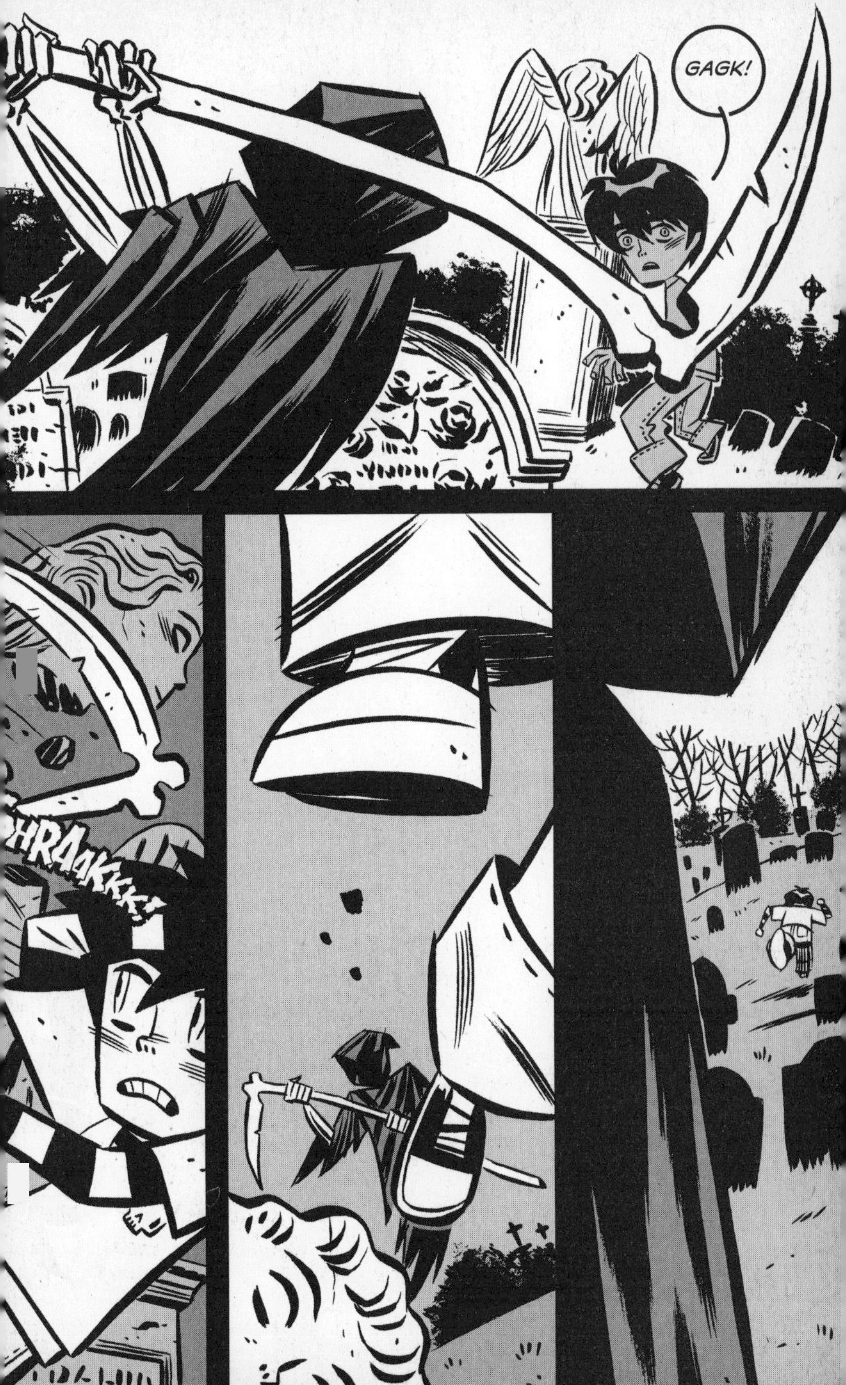
GAGK!
HRAAKKK!

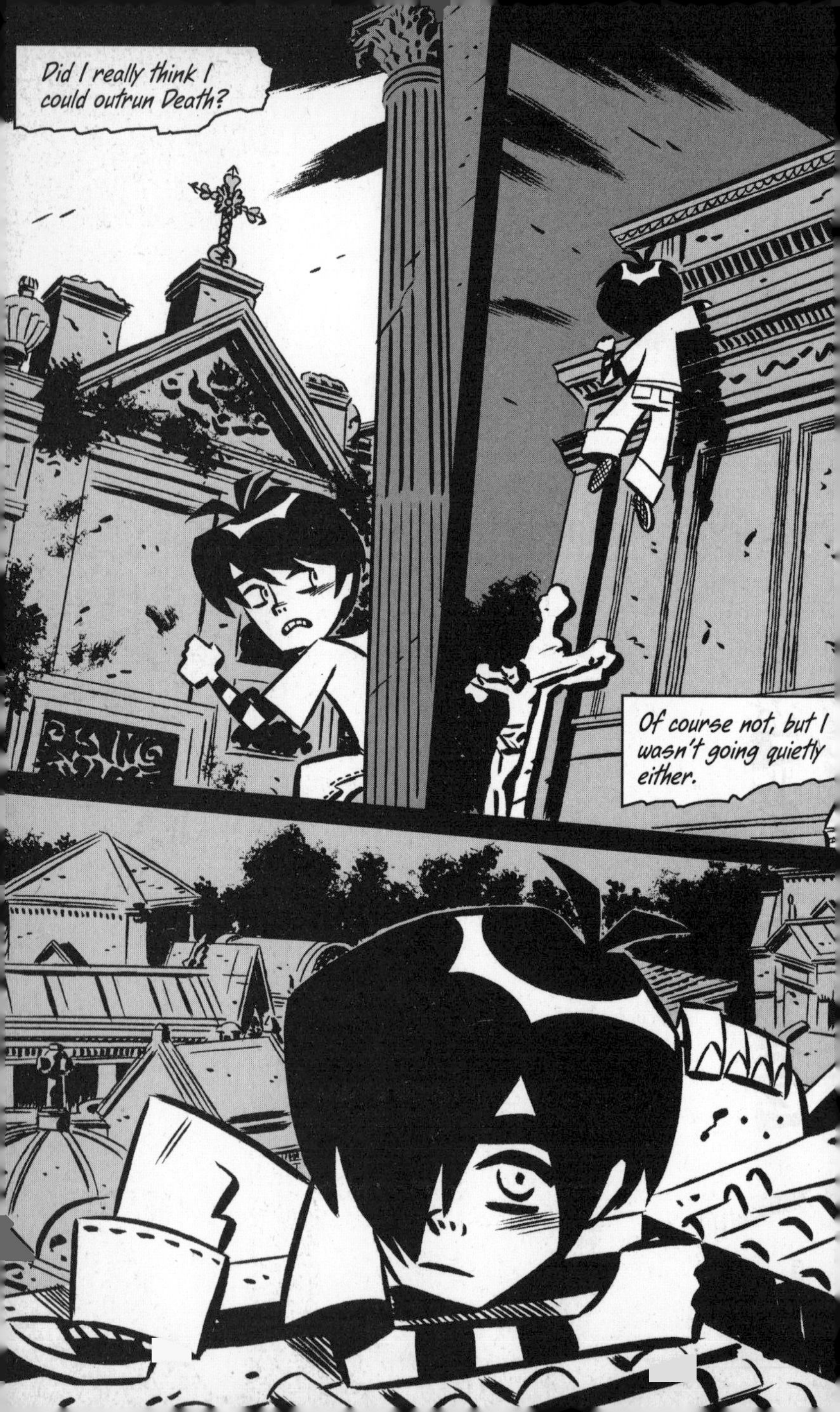
Did I really think I could outrun Death?
Of course not, but I wasn't going quietly either.

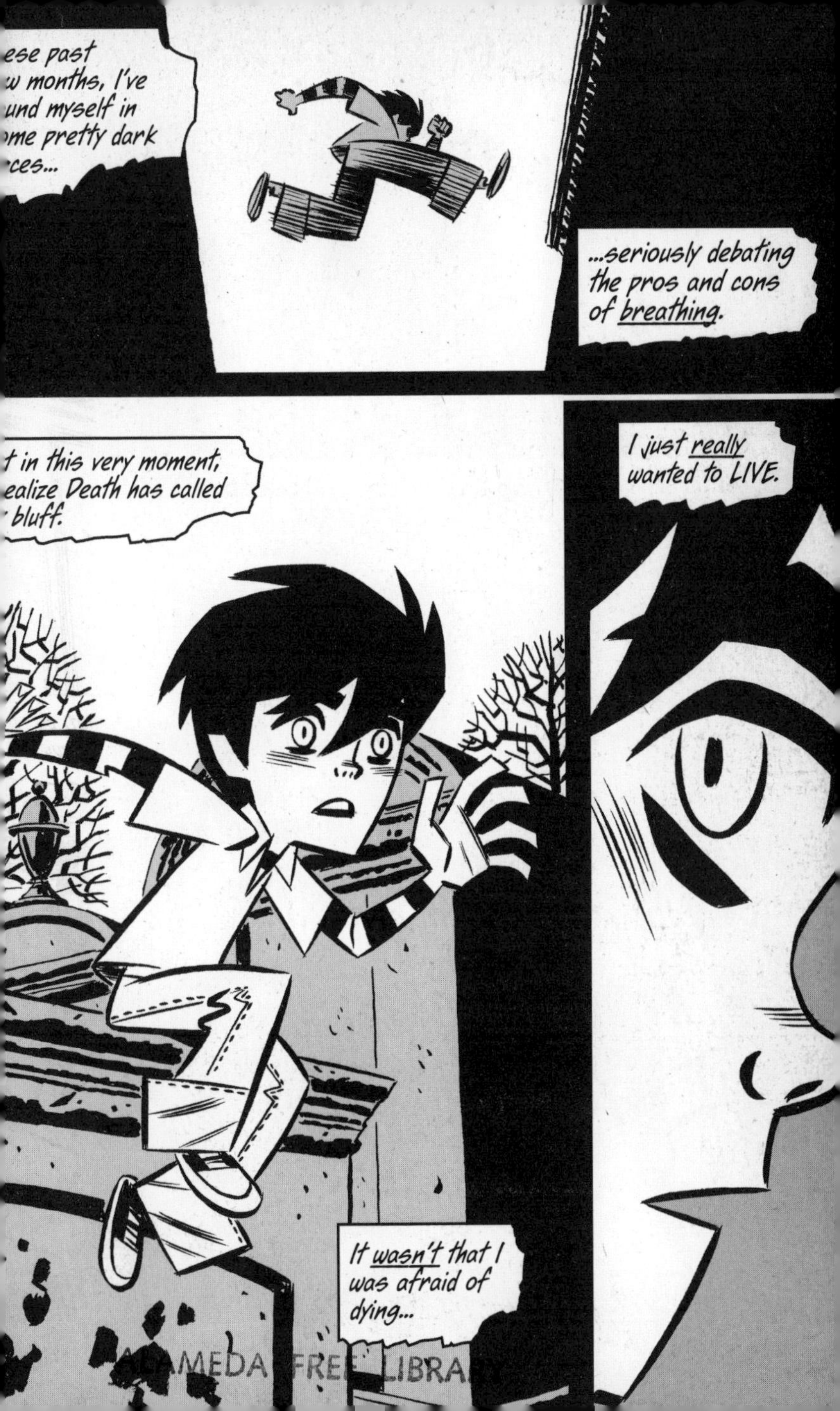
ese past
w months, I've
und myself in
me pretty dark
ces...
...seriously debating
the pros and cons
of breathing.
t in this very moment,
ealize Death has called
bluff.
It wasn't that I
was afraid of
dying...
I just really
wanted to LIVE.

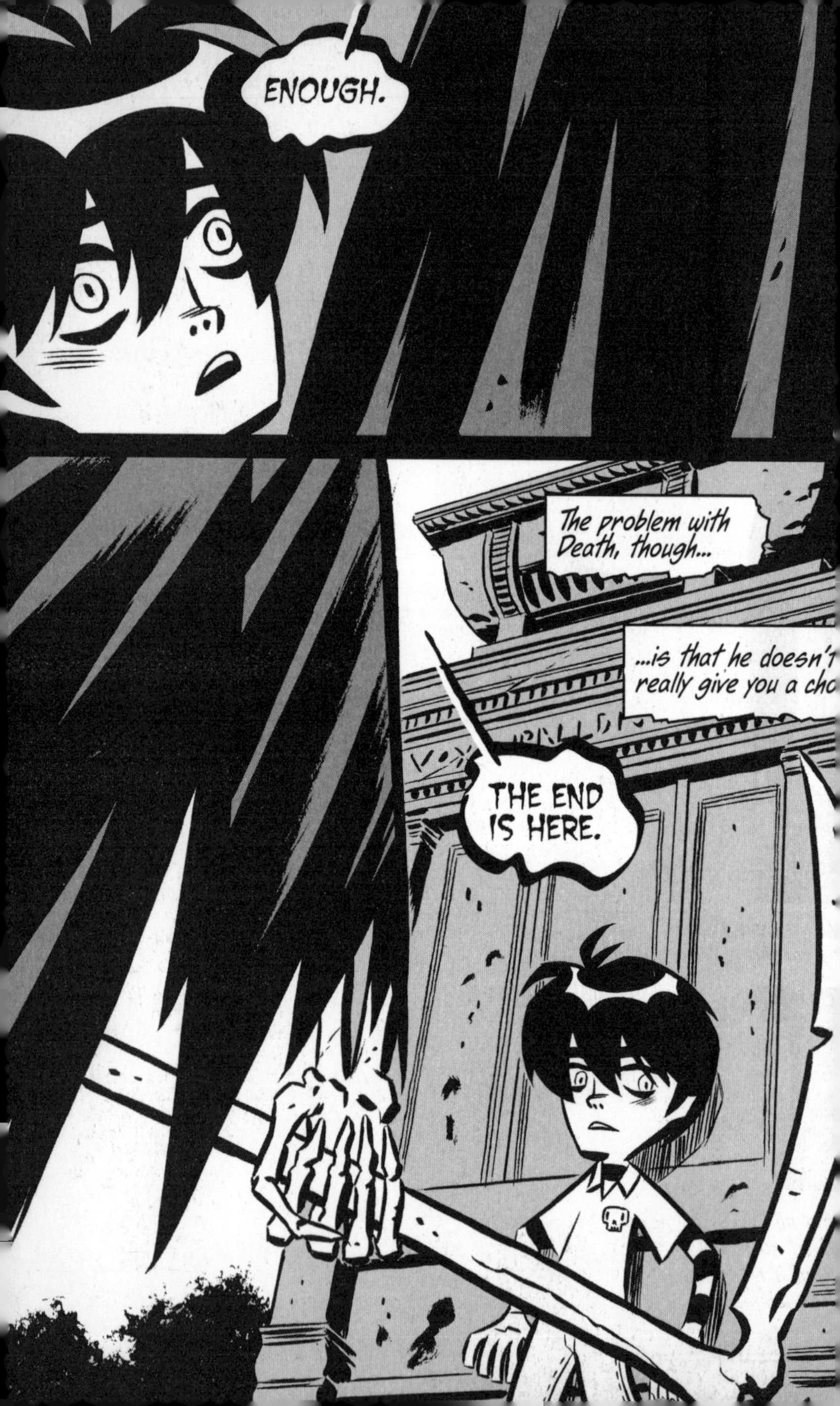
ENOUGH.
The problem with Death, though...
...is that he doesn't really give you a cho
THE END IS HERE.

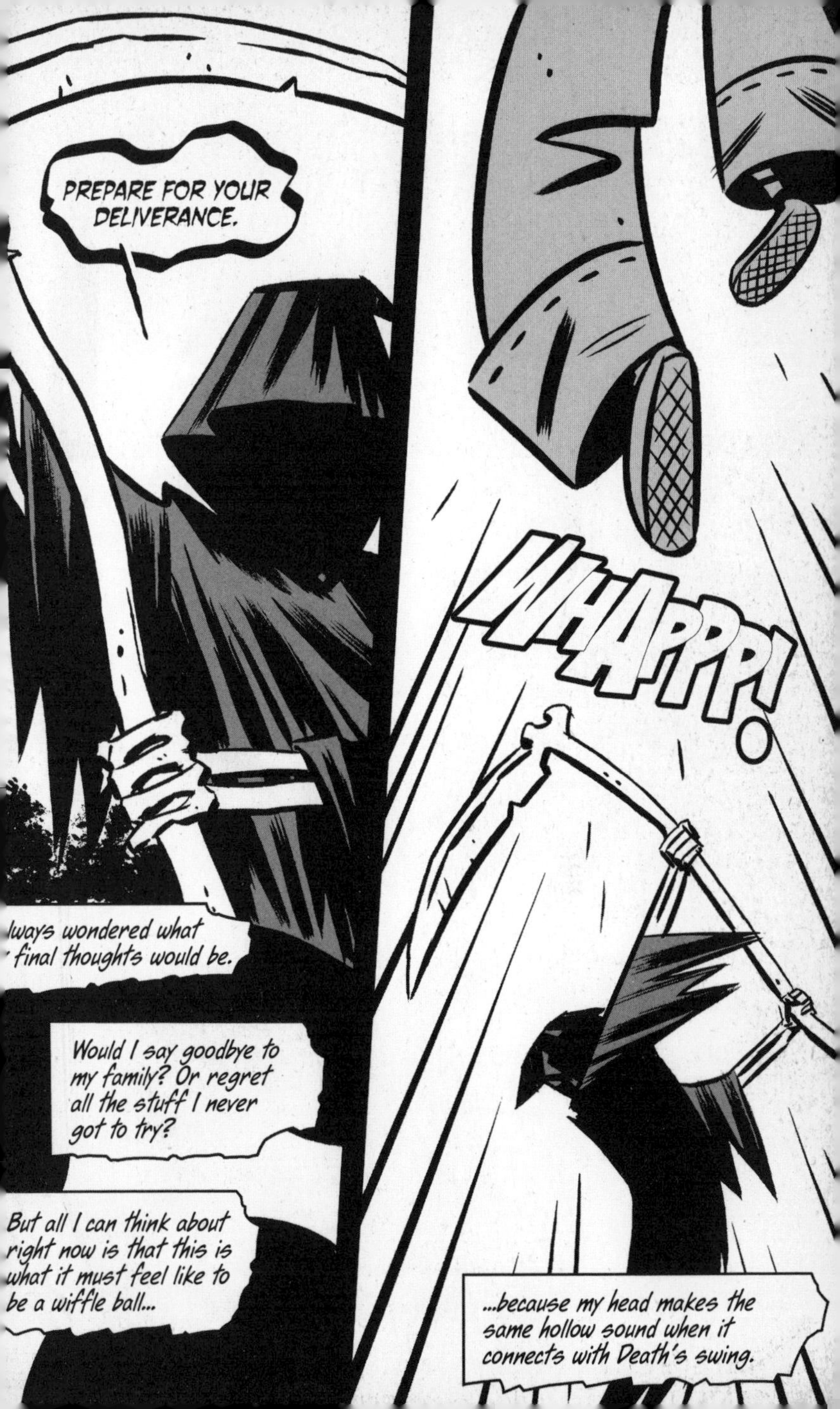
PREPARE FOR YOUR DELIVERANCE.
lways wondered what final thoughts would be.
Would I say goodbye to my family? Or regret all the stuff I never got to try?
But all I can think about right now is that this is what it must feel like to be a wiffle ball...
WHAPPP!
...because my head makes the same hollow sound when it connects with Death's swing.

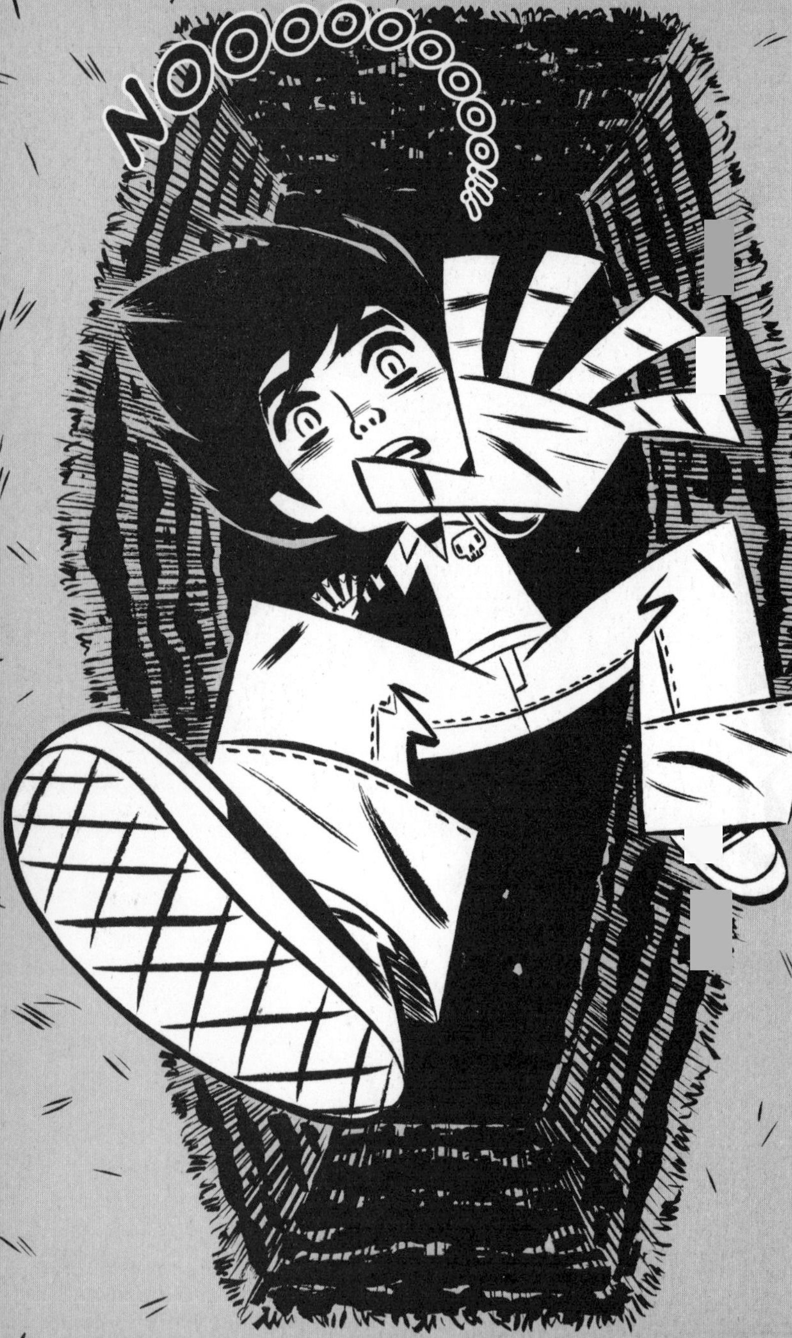
NOOOOOOOOOO!!!

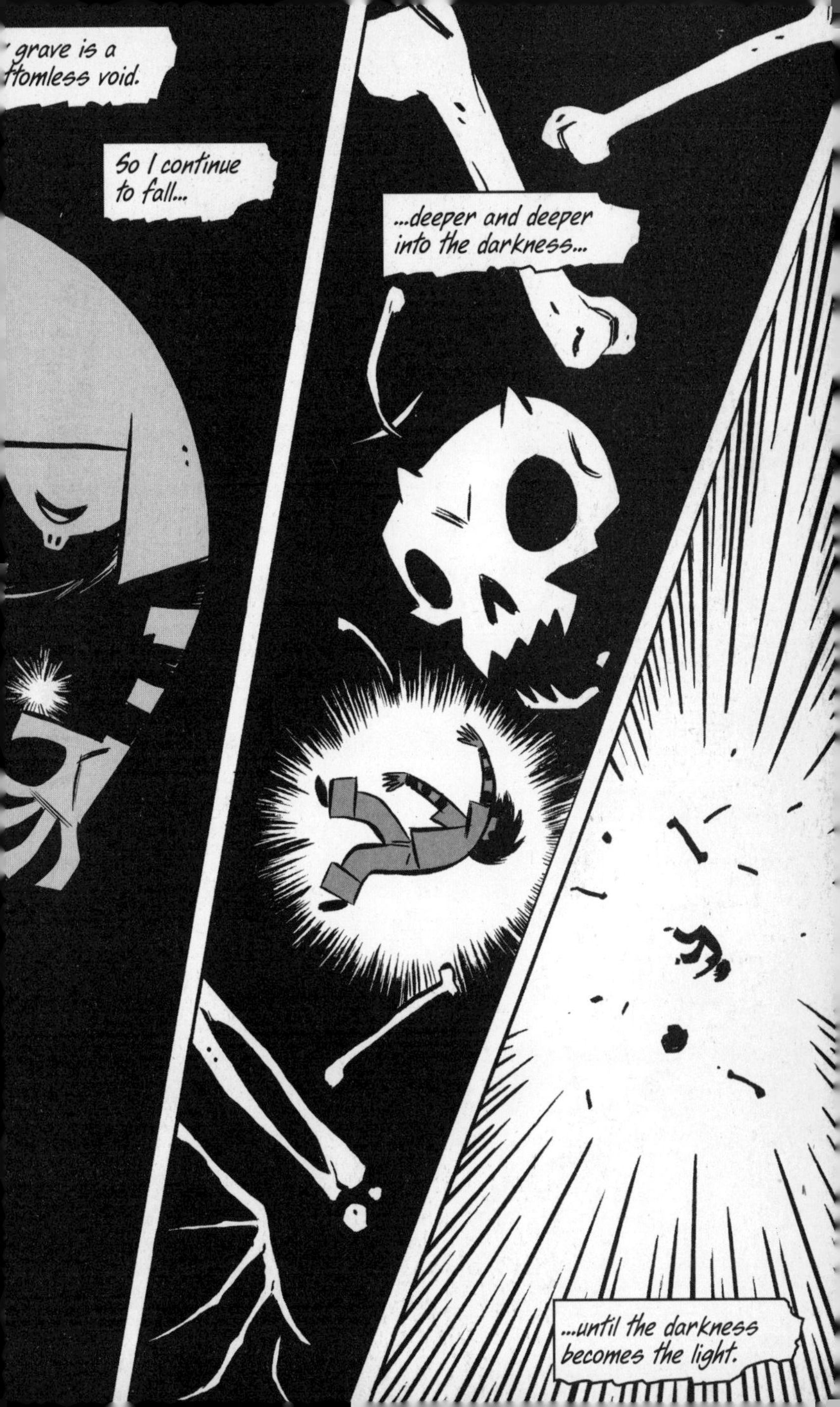
grave is a
ttomless void.
So I continue
to fall...
...deeper and deeper
into the darkness...
...until the darkness
becomes the light.

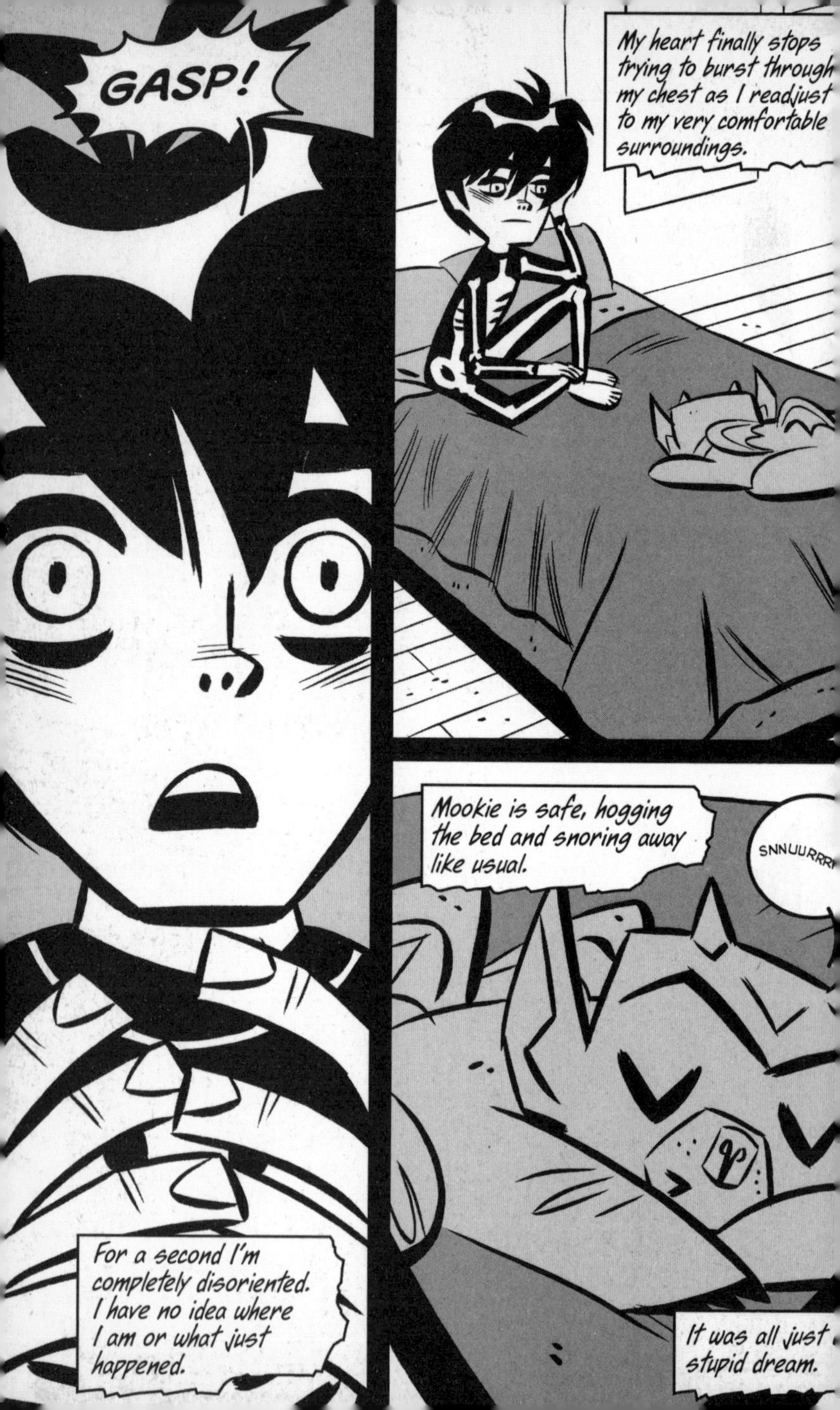
GASP!
For a second I'm completely disoriented. I have no idea where I am or what just happened.
My heart finally stops trying to burst through my chest as I readjust to my very comfortable surroundings.
Mookie is safe, hogging the bed and snoring away like usual.
SNNUURRR
It was all just stupid dream.

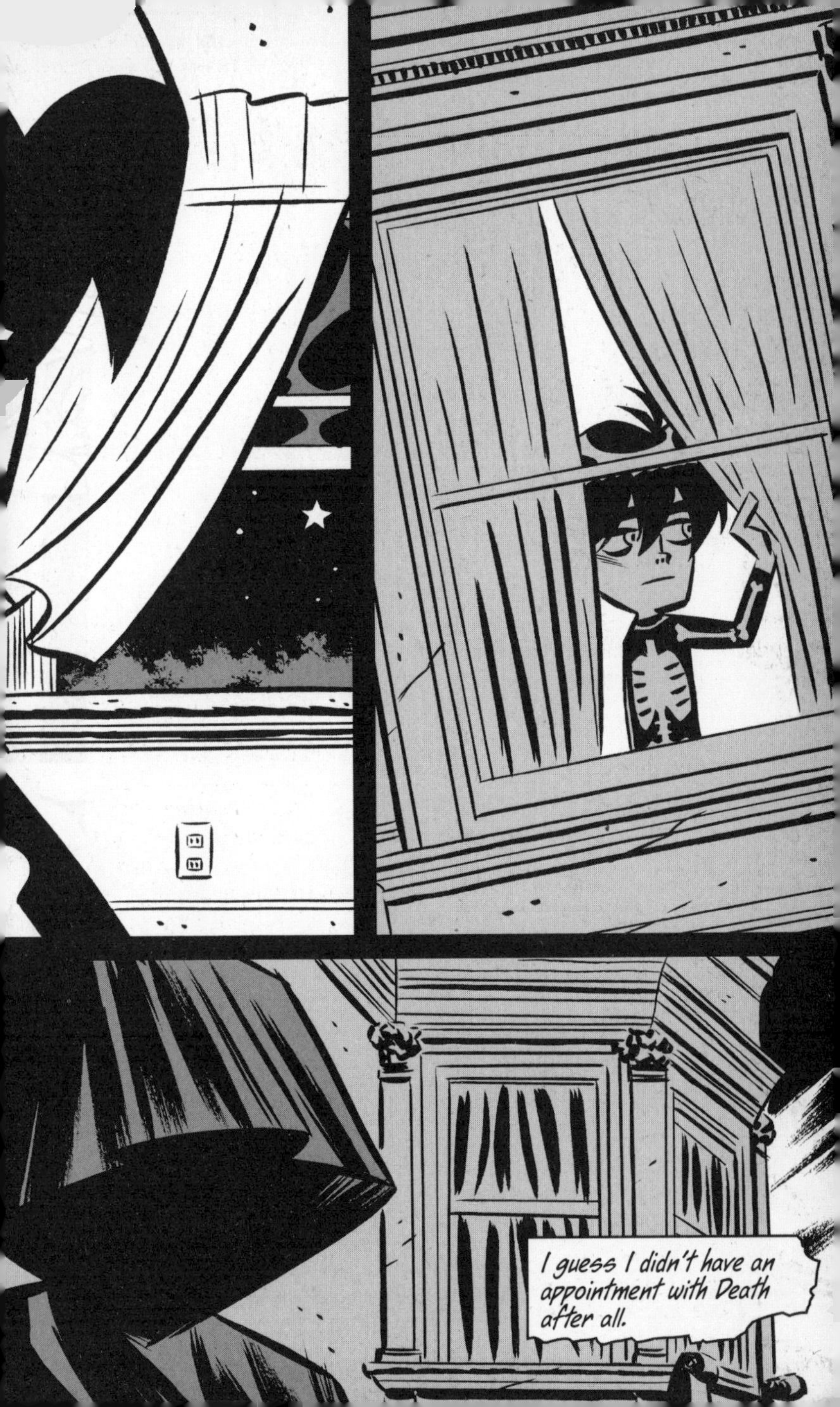
I guess I didn't have an appointment with Death after all.

CHAPTER FIVE

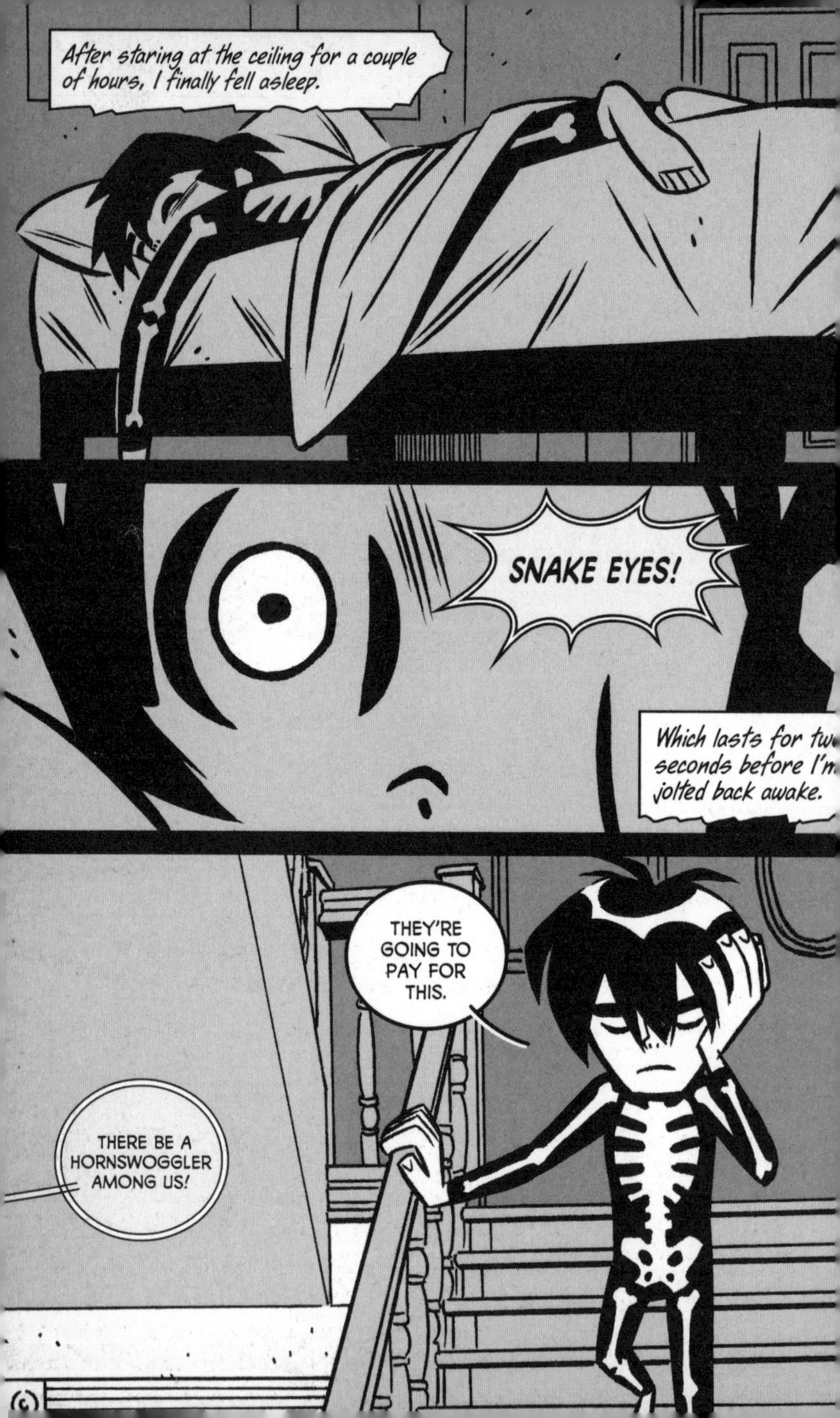
After staring at the ceiling for a couple of hours, I finally fell asleep.
SNAKE EYES!
Which lasts for tw seconds before I'm jolted back awake.
THEY'RE GOING TO PAY FOR THIS.
THERE BE A HORNSWOGGLER AMONG US!

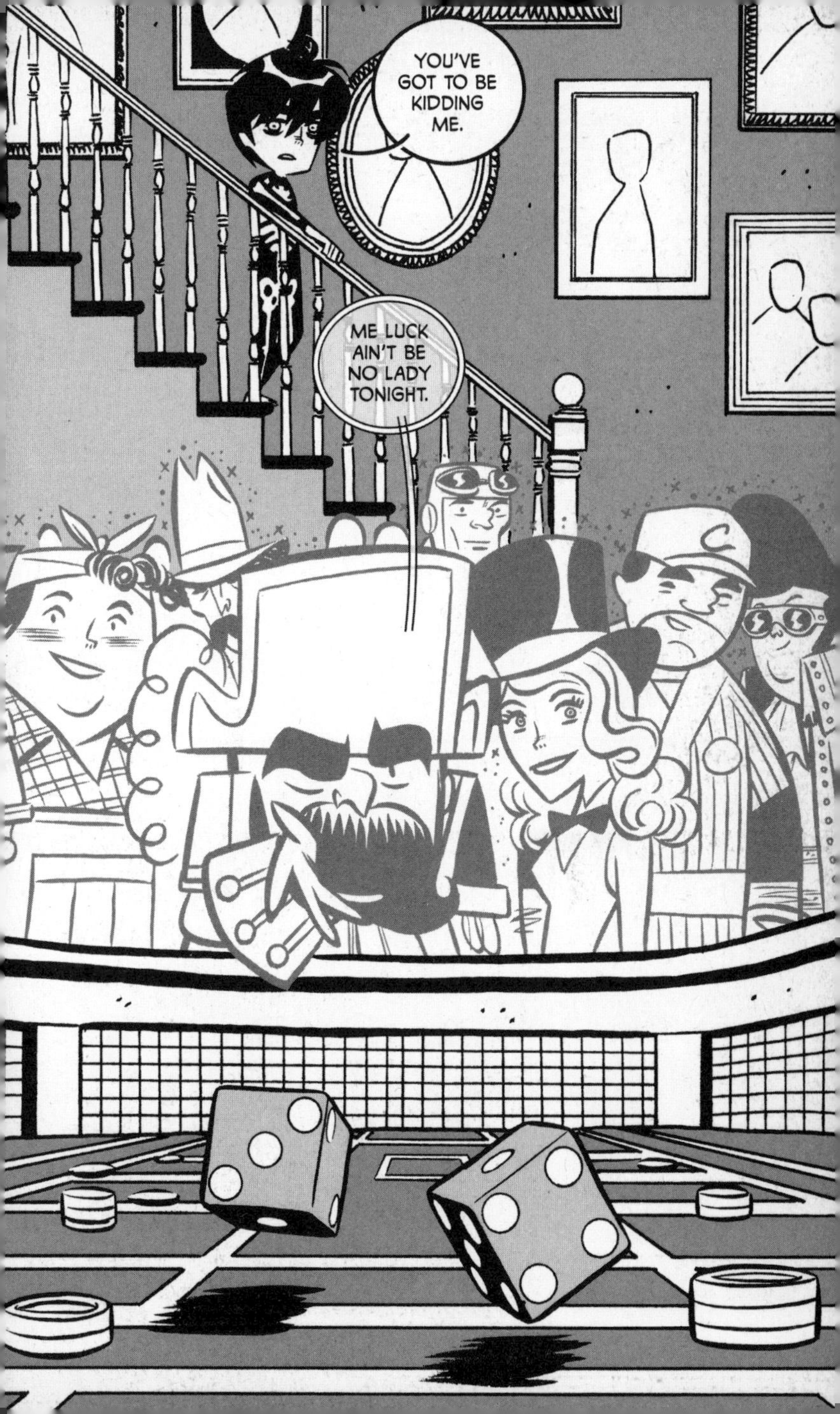
YOU'VE GOT TO BE KIDDING ME.
ME LUCK AIN'T BE NO LADY TONIGHT.

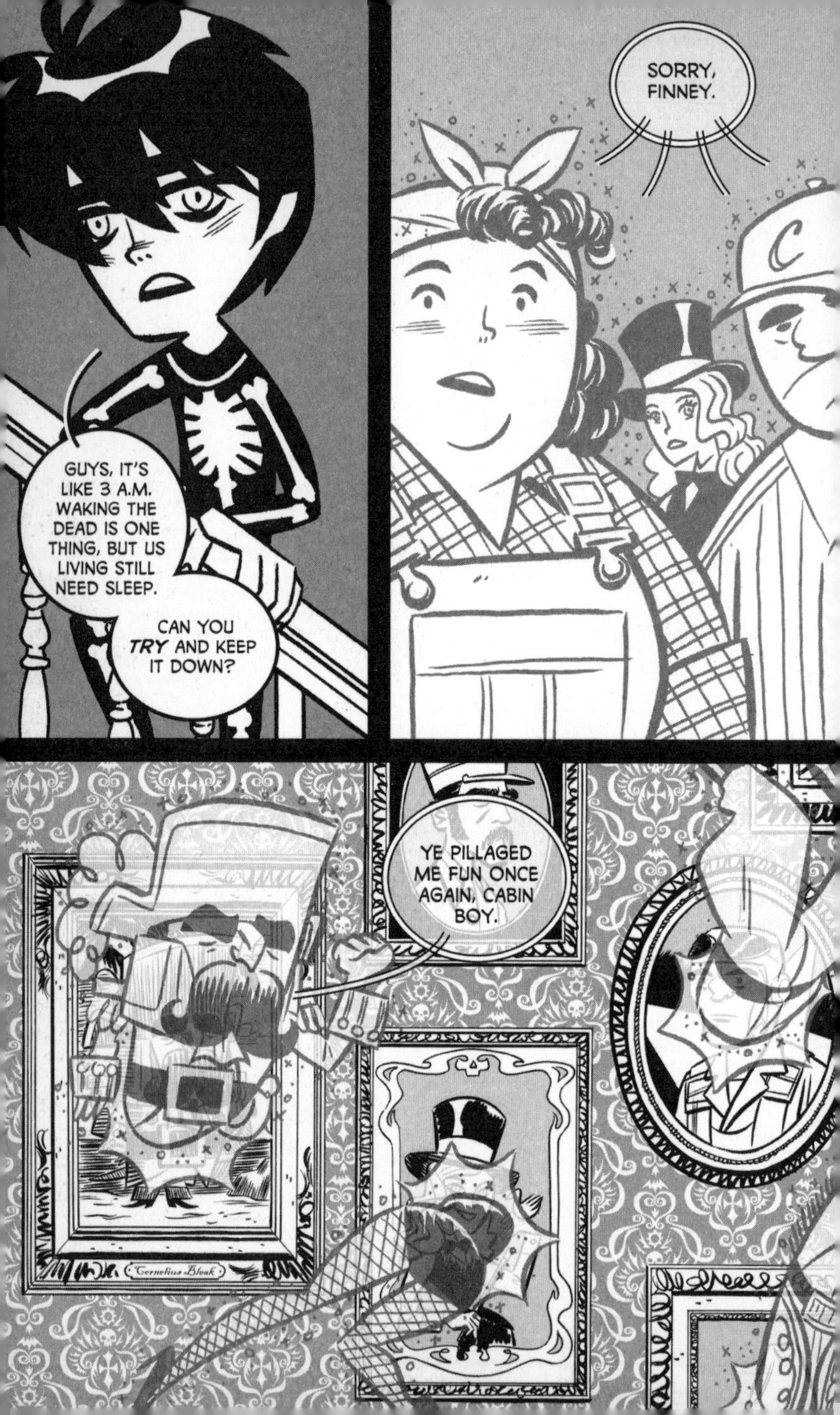
GUYS, IT'S LIKE 3 A.M. WAKING THE DEAD IS ONE THING, BUT US LIVING STILL NEED SLEEP.
CAN YOU *TRY* AND KEEP IT DOWN?
SORRY, FINNEY.
YE PILLAGED ME FUN ONCE AGAIN, CABIN BOY.
Cornelius Bleak

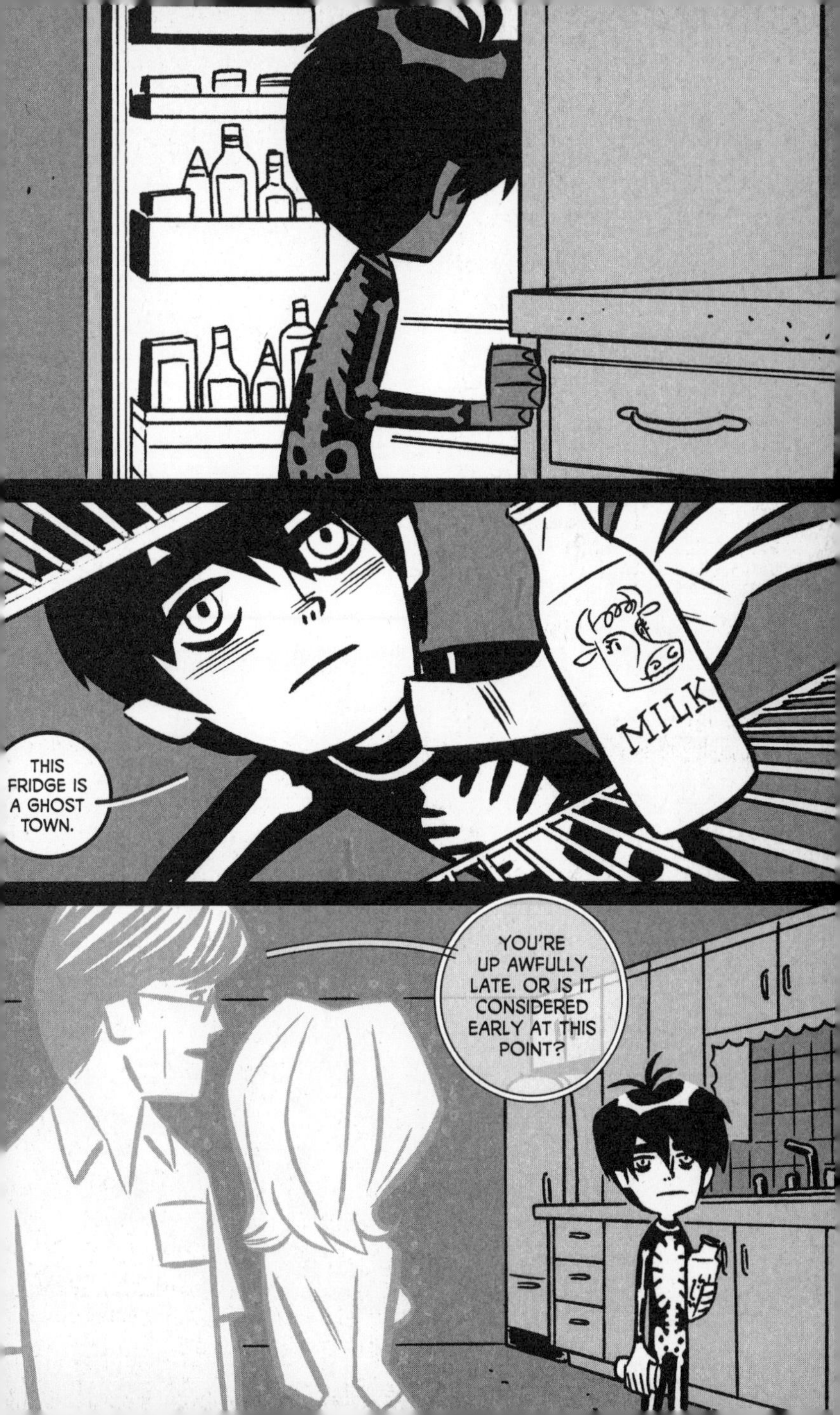
MILK
THIS FRIDGE IS A GHOST TOWN.
YOU'RE UP AWFULLY LATE. OR IS IT CONSIDERED EARLY AT THIS POINT?

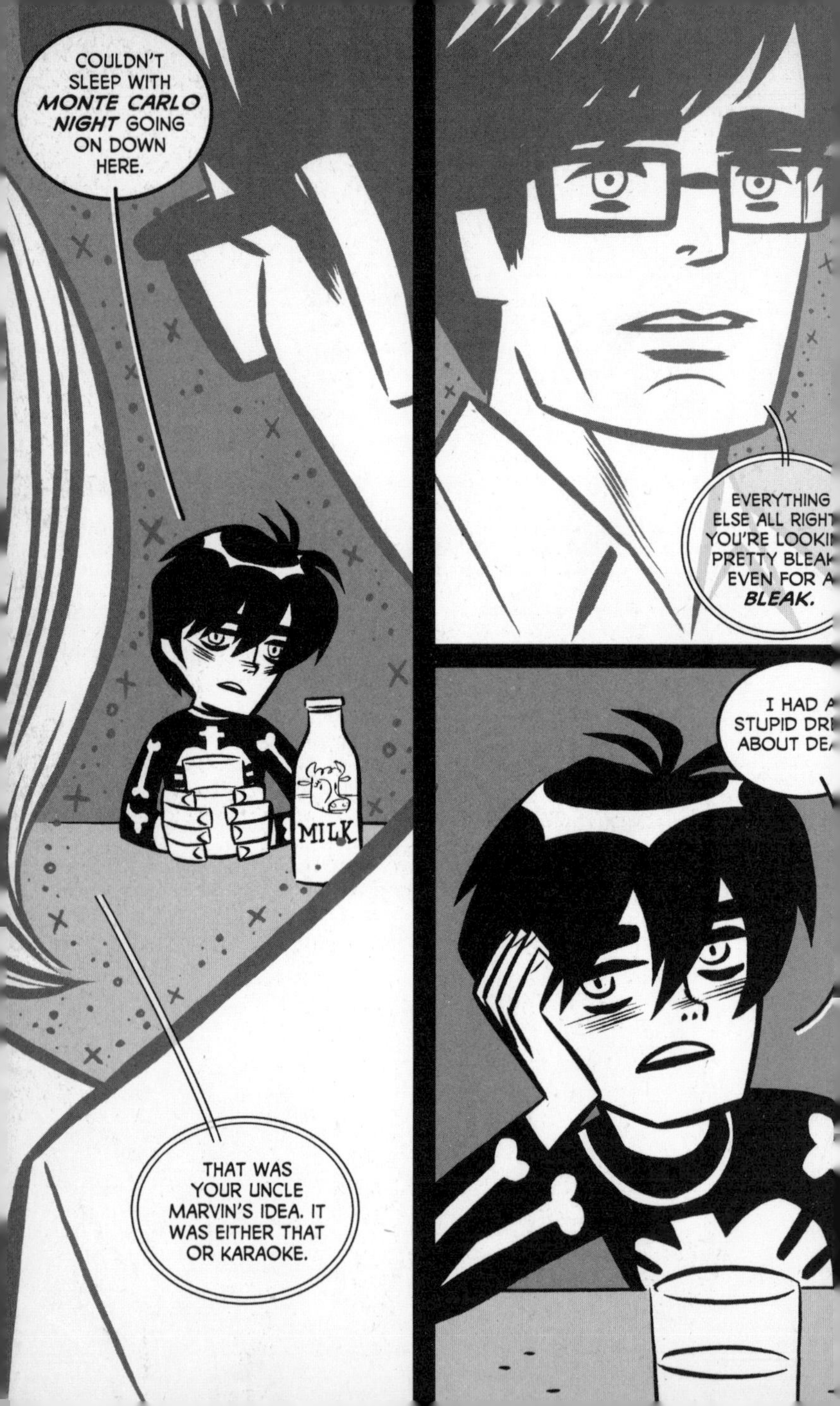
COULDN'T SLEEP WITH ***MONTE CARLO NIGHT*** GOING ON DOWN HERE.
MILK
THAT WAS YOUR UNCLE MARVIN'S IDEA. IT WAS EITHER THAT OR KARAOKE.
EVERYTHING ELSE ALL RIGHT YOU'RE LOOKI PRETTY BLEAK EVEN FOR A ***BLEAK.***
I HAD A STUPID DR ABOUT DE

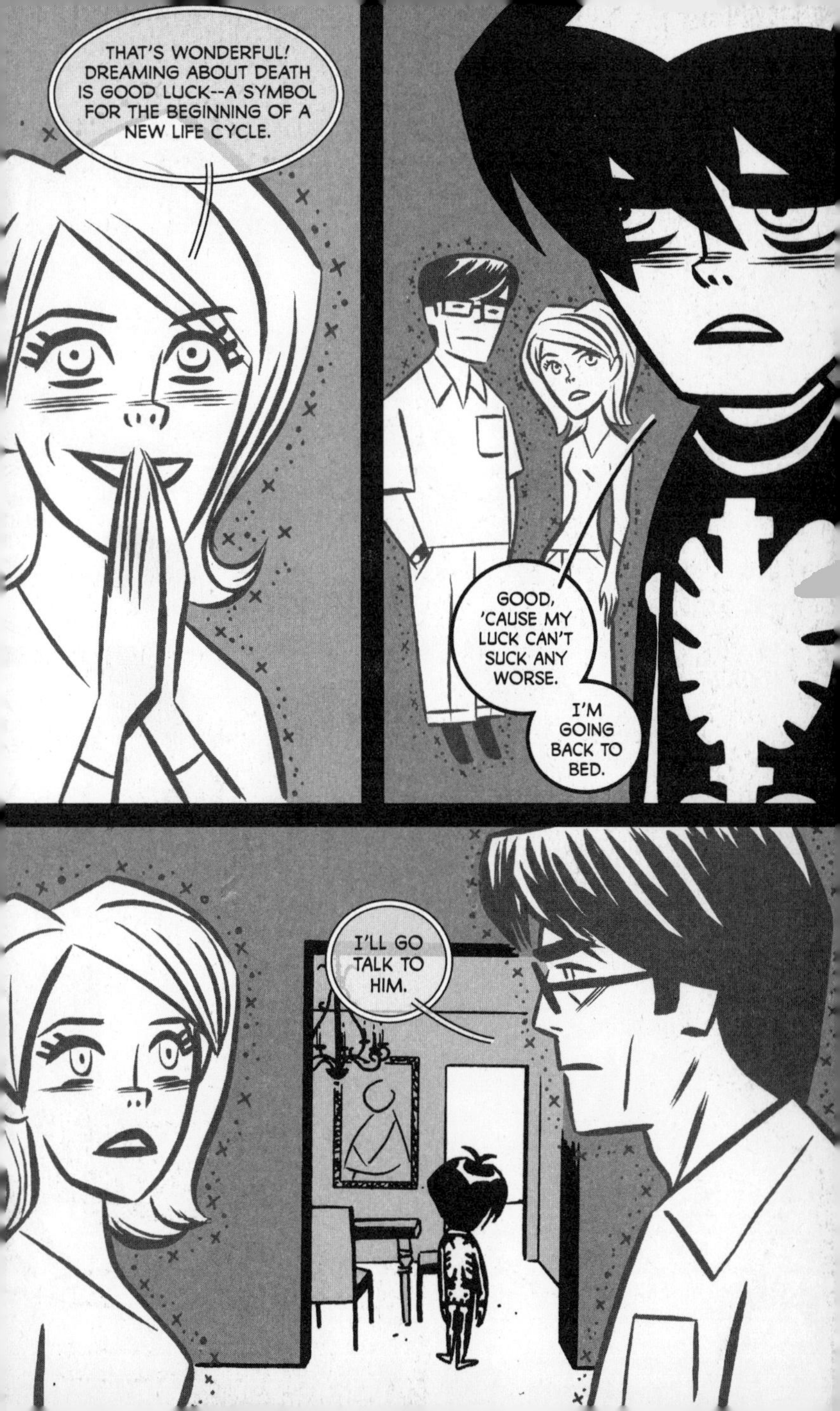
THAT'S WONDERFUL! DREAMING ABOUT DEATH IS GOOD LUCK--A SYMBOL FOR THE BEGINNING OF A NEW LIFE CYCLE.
GOOD, 'CAUSE MY LUCK CAN'T SUCK ANY WORSE.
I'M GOING BACK TO BED.
I'LL GO TALK TO HIM.

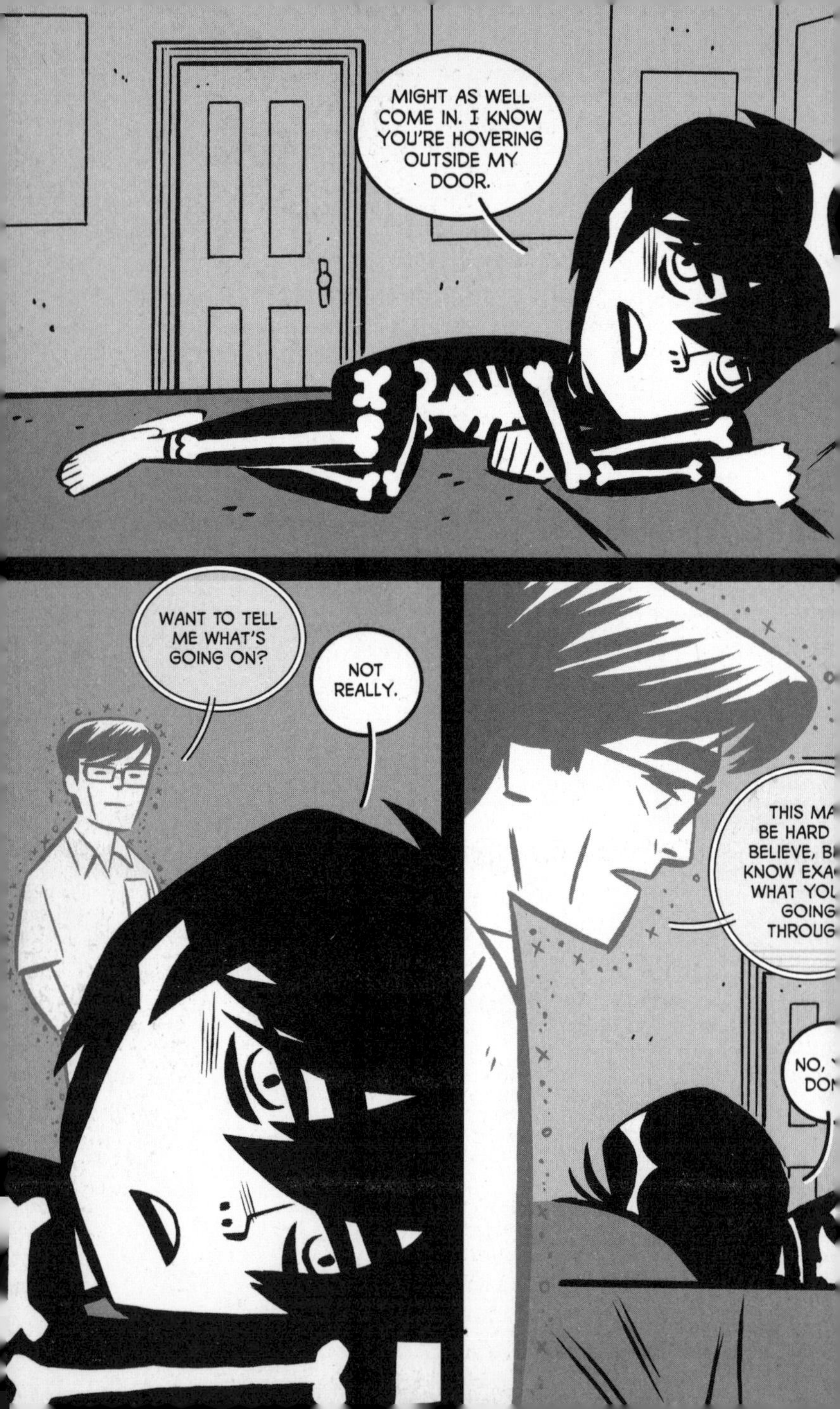
MIGHT AS WELL COME IN. I KNOW YOU'RE HOVERING OUTSIDE MY DOOR.
WANT TO TELL ME WHAT'S GOING ON?
NOT REALLY.
THIS BE HARD BELIEVE, KNOW WHAT GOING
NO,

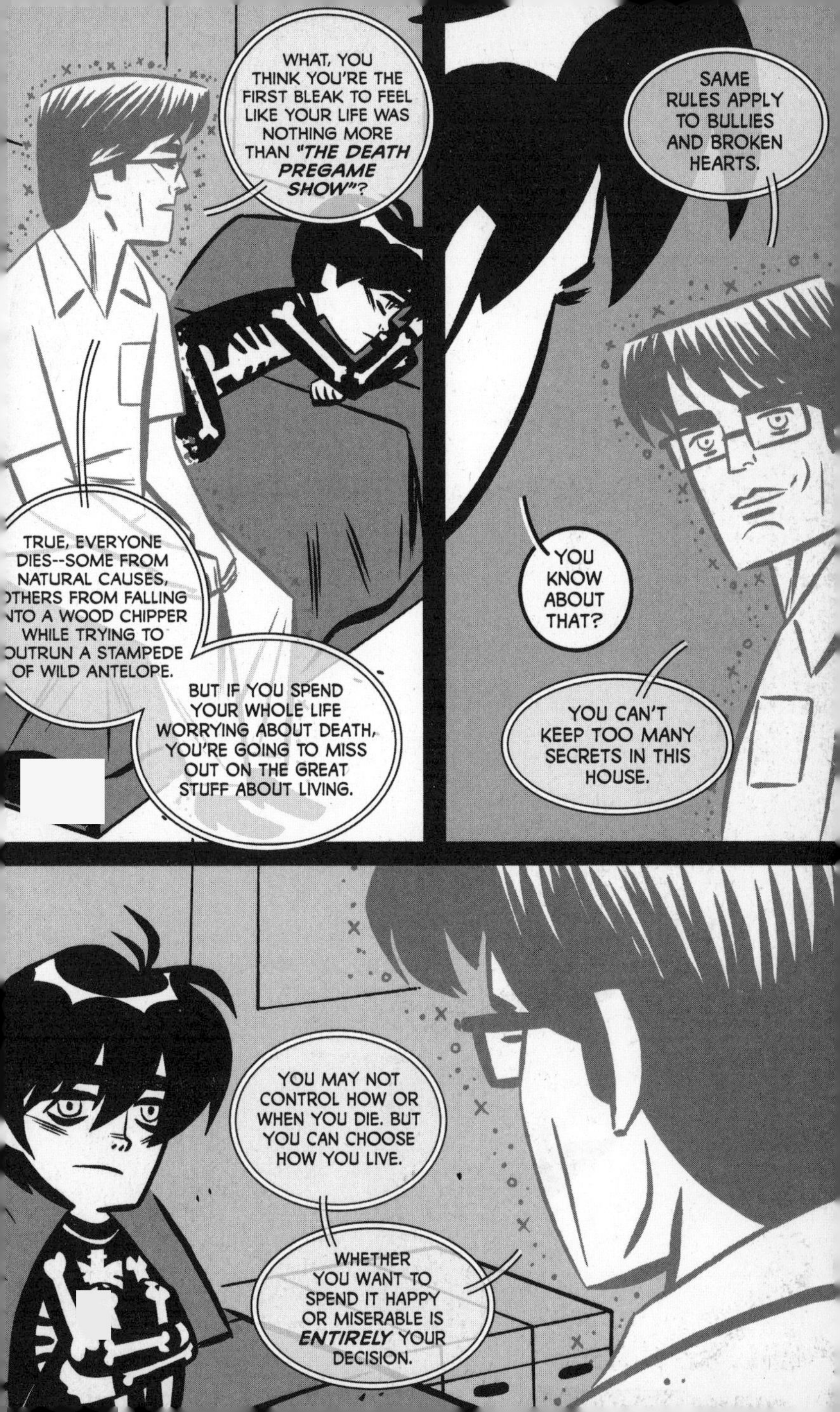
WHAT, YOU THINK YOU'RE THE FIRST BLEAK TO FEEL LIKE YOUR LIFE WAS NOTHING MORE THAN *"THE DEATH PREGAME SHOW"*?
TRUE, EVERYONE DIES--SOME FROM NATURAL CAUSES, THERS FROM FALLING NTO A WOOD CHIPPER WHILE TRYING TO UTRUN A STAMPEDE OF WILD ANTELOPE.
BUT IF YOU SPEND YOUR WHOLE LIFE WORRYING ABOUT DEATH, YOU'RE GOING TO MISS OUT ON THE GREAT STUFF ABOUT LIVING.
SAME RULES APPLY TO BULLIES AND BROKEN HEARTS.
YOU KNOW ABOUT THAT?
YOU CAN'T KEEP TOO MANY SECRETS IN THIS HOUSE.
YOU MAY NOT CONTROL HOW OR WHEN YOU DIE. BUT YOU CAN CHOOSE HOW YOU LIVE.
WHETHER YOU WANT TO SPEND IT HAPPY OR MISERABLE IS *ENTIRELY* YOUR DECISION.

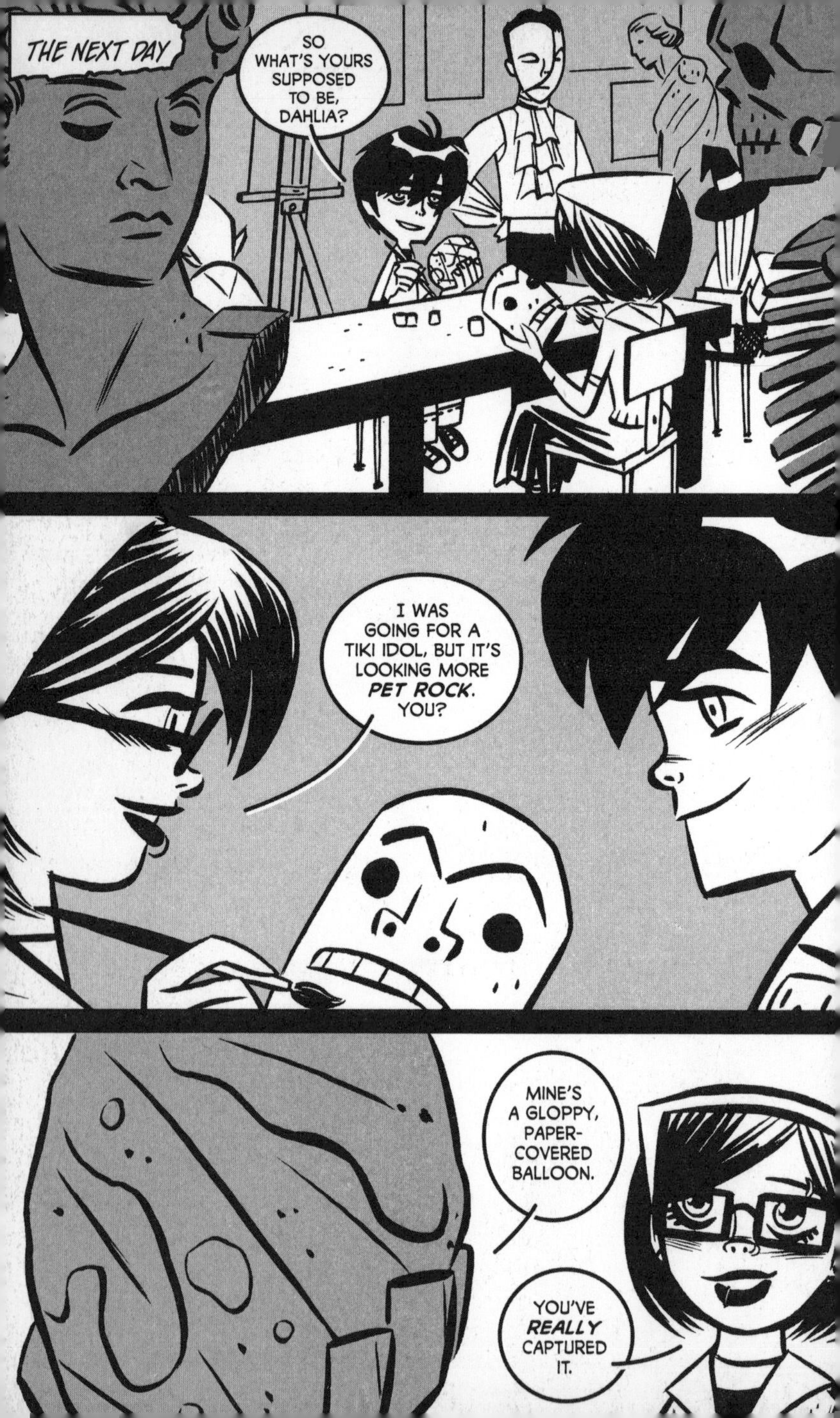
THE NEXT DAY
SO WHAT'S YOURS SUPPOSED TO BE, DAHLIA?
I WAS GOING FOR A TIKI IDOL, BUT IT'S LOOKING MORE ***PET ROCK***. YOU?
MINE'S A GLOPPY, PAPER-COVERED BALLOON.
YOU'VE ***REALLY*** CAPTURED IT.

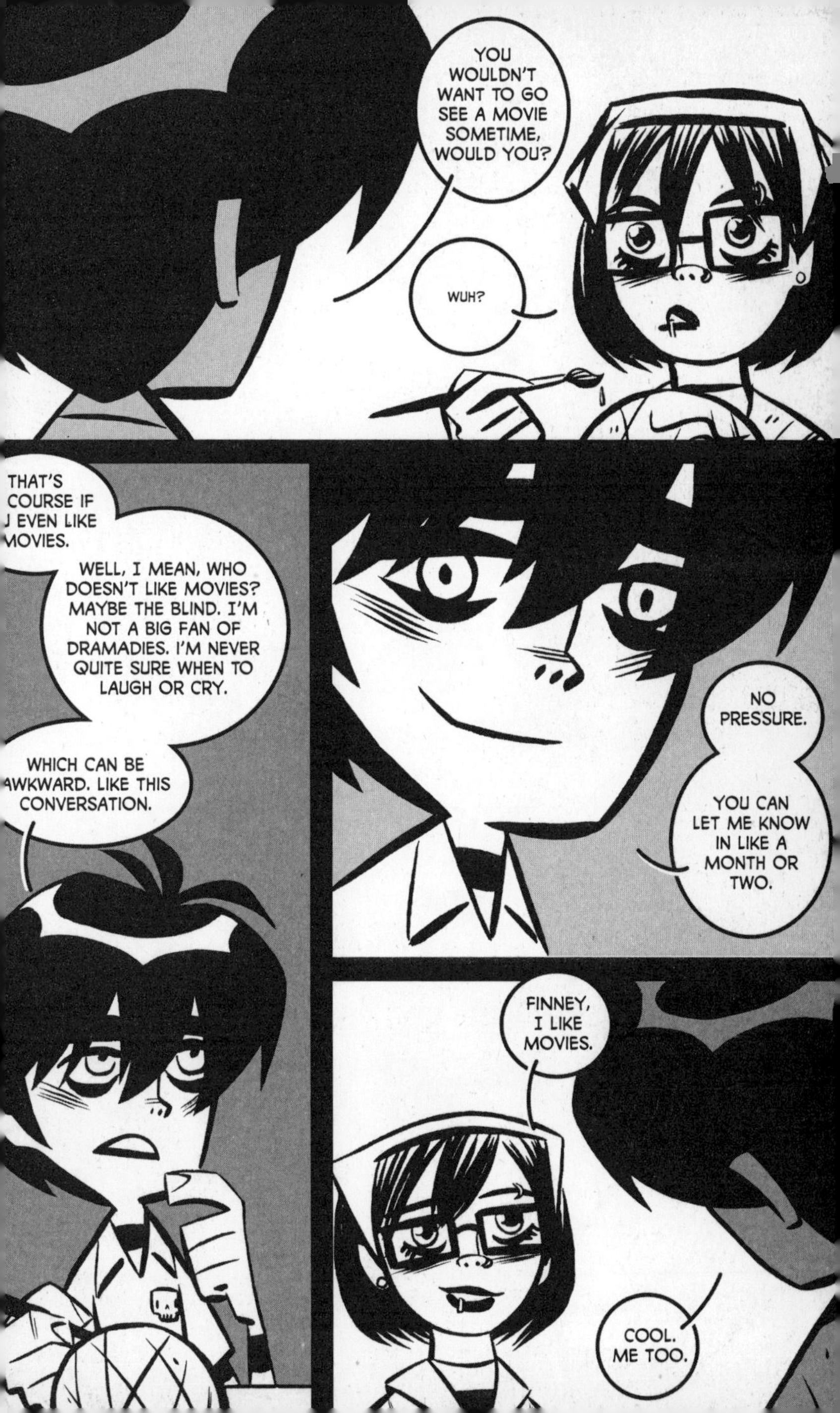
YOU WOULDN'T WANT TO GO SEE A MOVIE SOMETIME, WOULD YOU?
WUH?
THAT'S COURSE IF J EVEN LIKE MOVIES.
WELL, I MEAN, WHO DOESN'T LIKE MOVIES? MAYBE THE BLIND. I'M NOT A BIG FAN OF DRAMADIES. I'M NEVER QUITE SURE WHEN TO LAUGH OR CRY.
WHICH CAN BE AWKWARD. LIKE THIS CONVERSATION.
NO PRESSURE.
YOU CAN LET ME KNOW IN LIKE A MONTH OR TWO.
FINNEY, I LIKE MOVIES.
COOL. ME TOO.

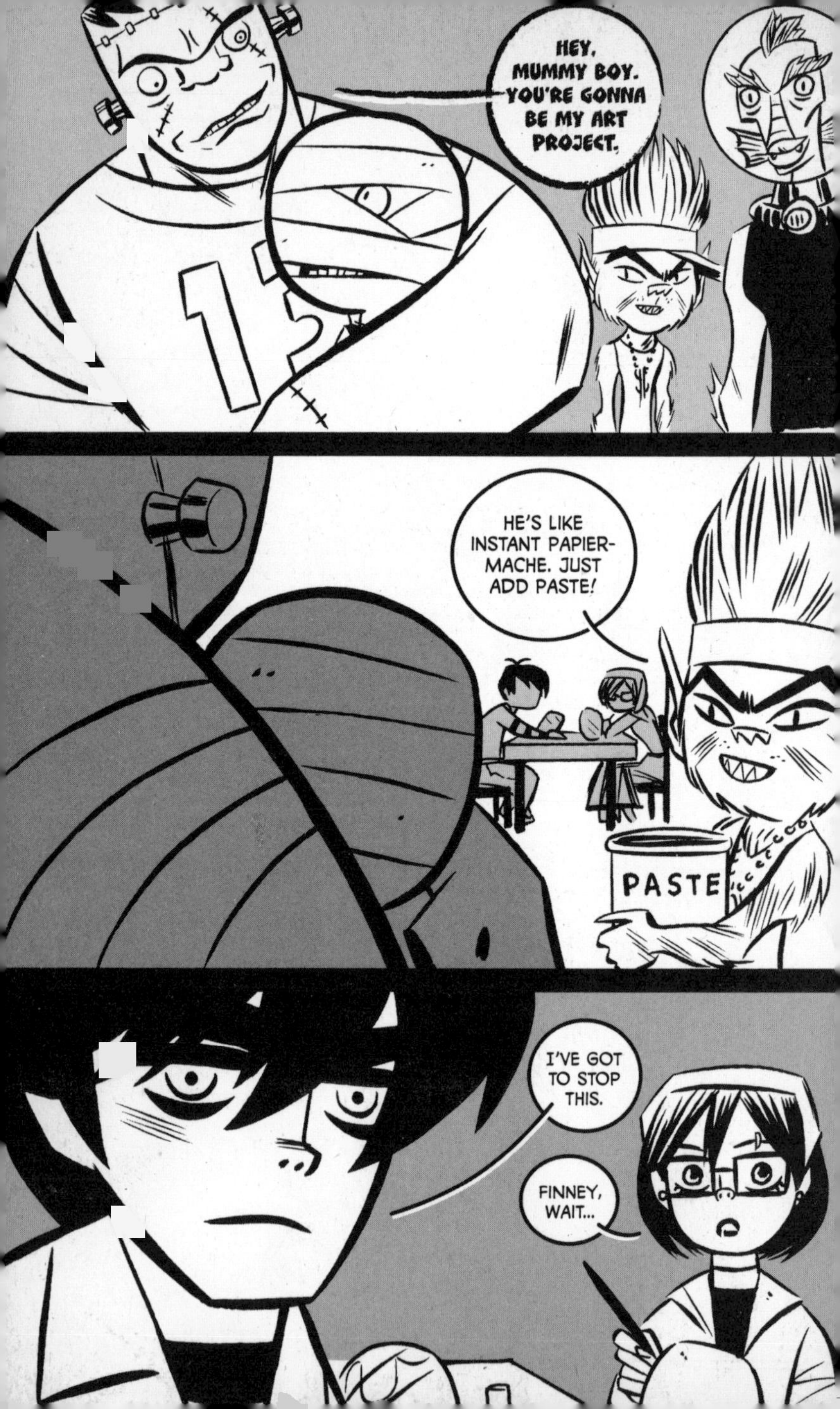
HEY, MUMMY BOY. YOU'RE GONNA BE MY ART PROJECT.
HE'S LIKE INSTANT PAPIER-MACHE. JUST ADD PASTE!
PASTE
I'VE GOT TO STOP THIS.
FINNEY, WAIT...

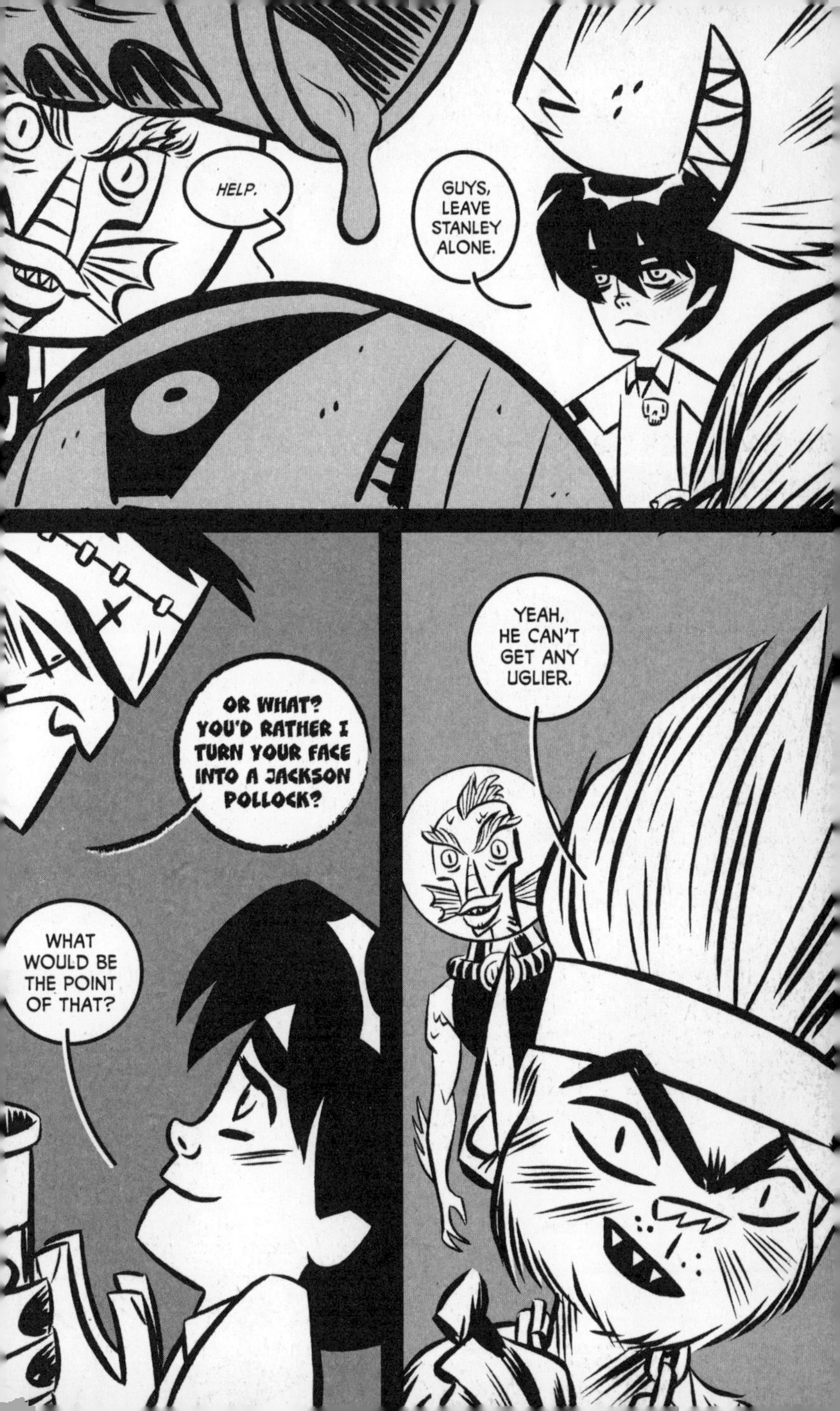
HELP.
GUYS, LEAVE STANLEY ALONE.
OR WHAT? YOU'D RATHER I TURN YOUR FACE INTO A JACKSON POLLOCK?
WHAT WOULD BE THE POINT OF THAT?
YEAH, HE CAN'T GET ANY UGLIER.

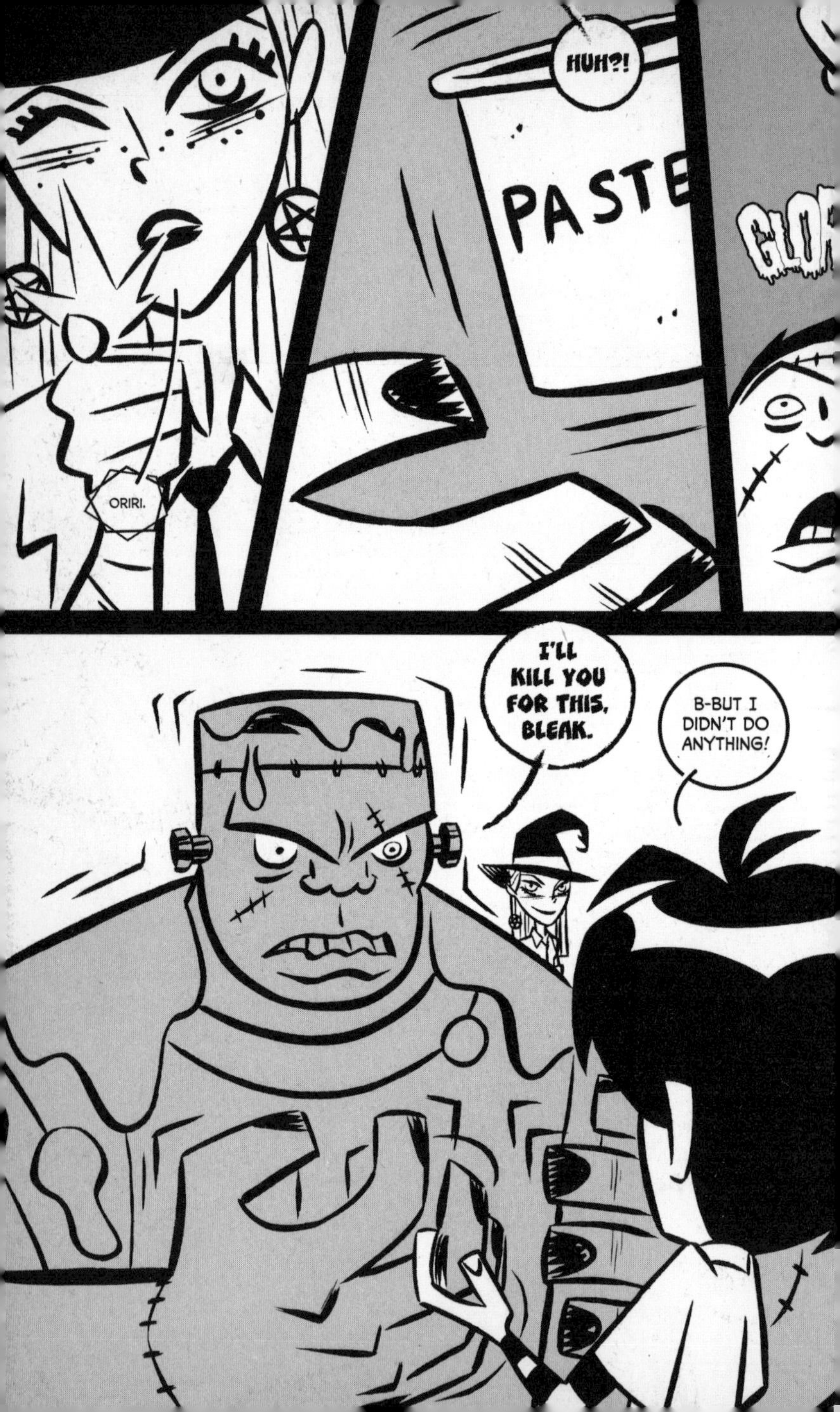
ORIRI.
HUH?!
PASTE
I'LL KILL YOU FOR THIS, BLEAK.
B-BUT I DIDN'T DO ANYTHING!

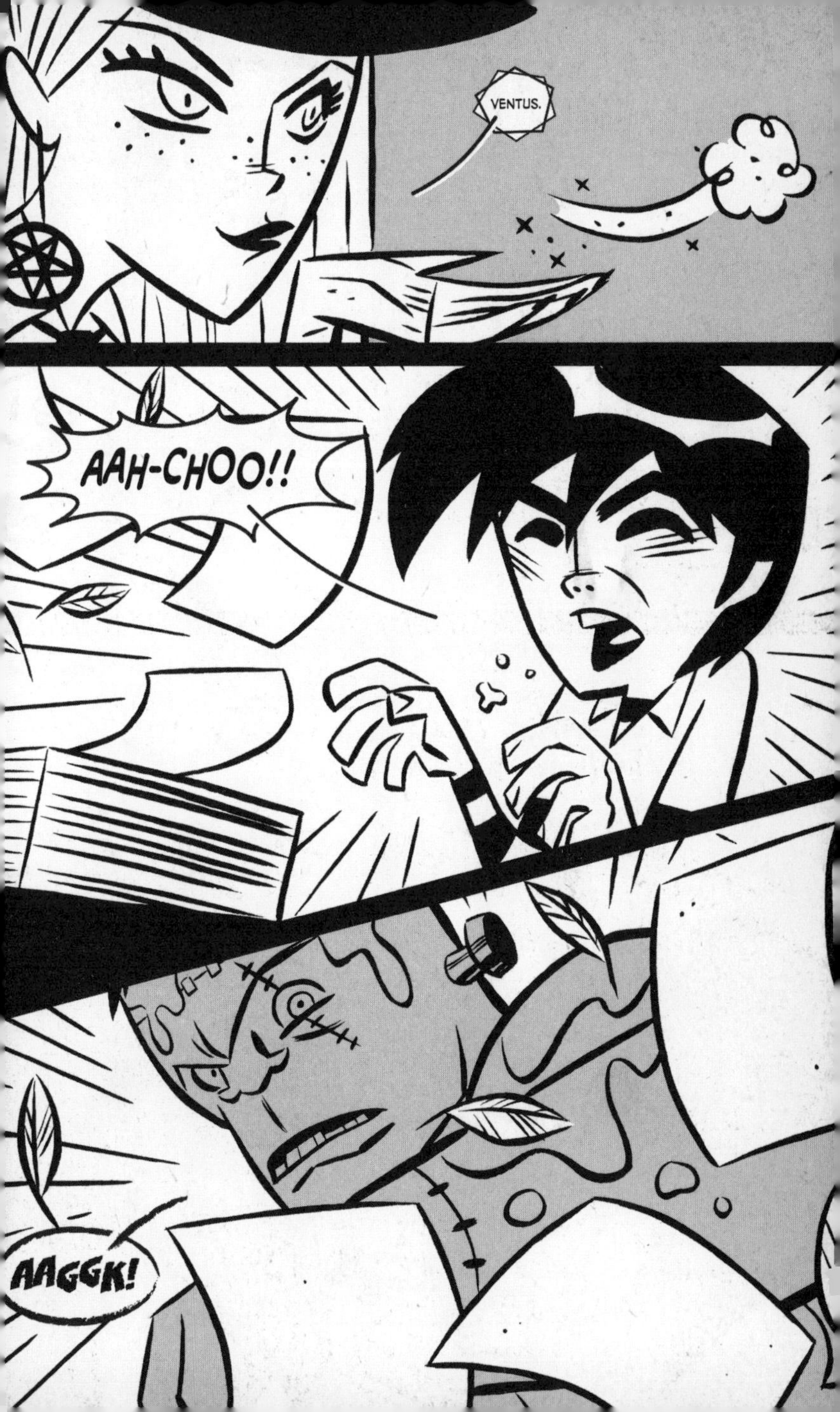
VENTUS.
AAH-CHOO!!
AAGGK!

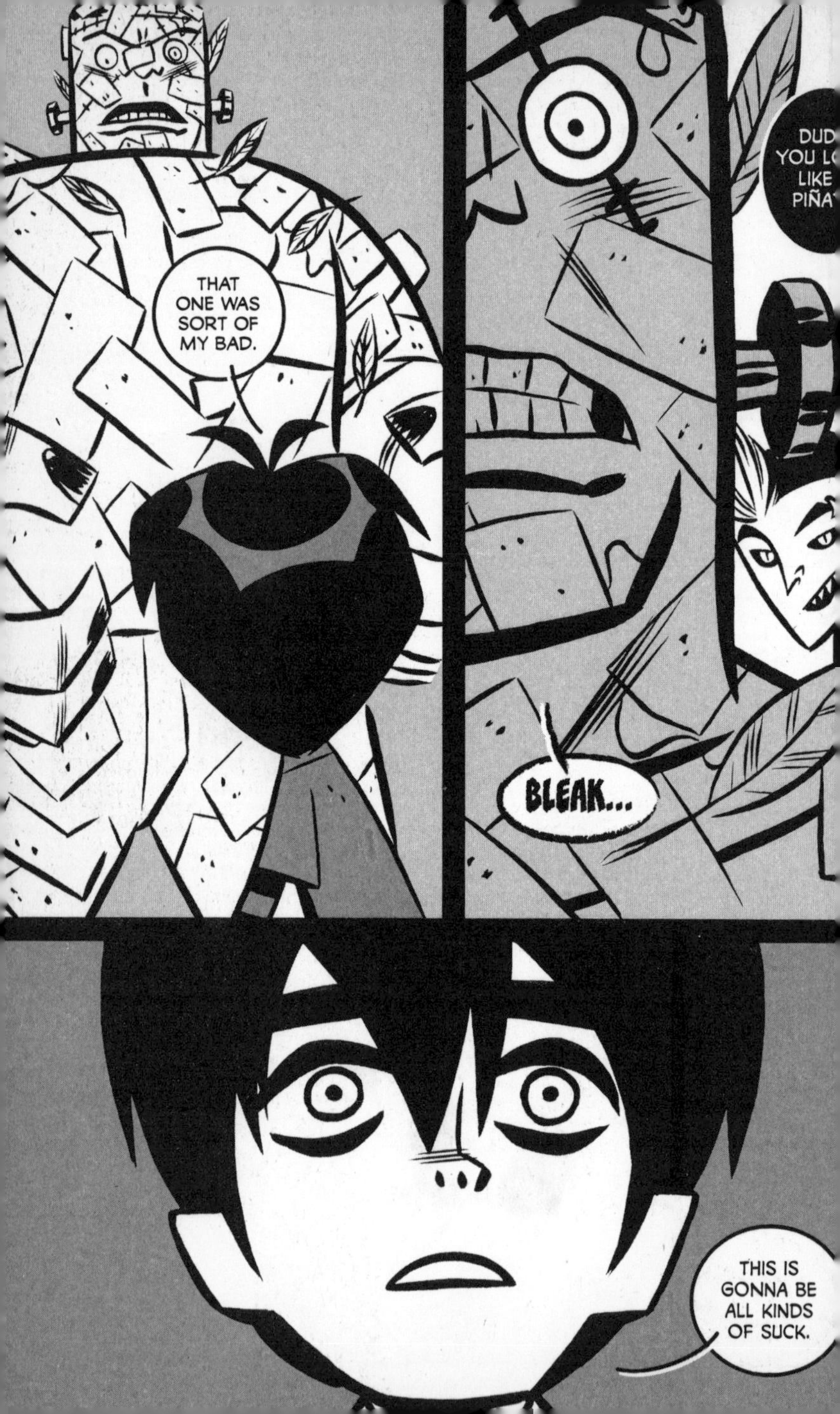
THAT ONE WAS SORT OF MY BAD.
BLEAK...
DUD YOU L LIKE PIÑA
THIS IS GONNA BE ALL KINDS OF SUCK.

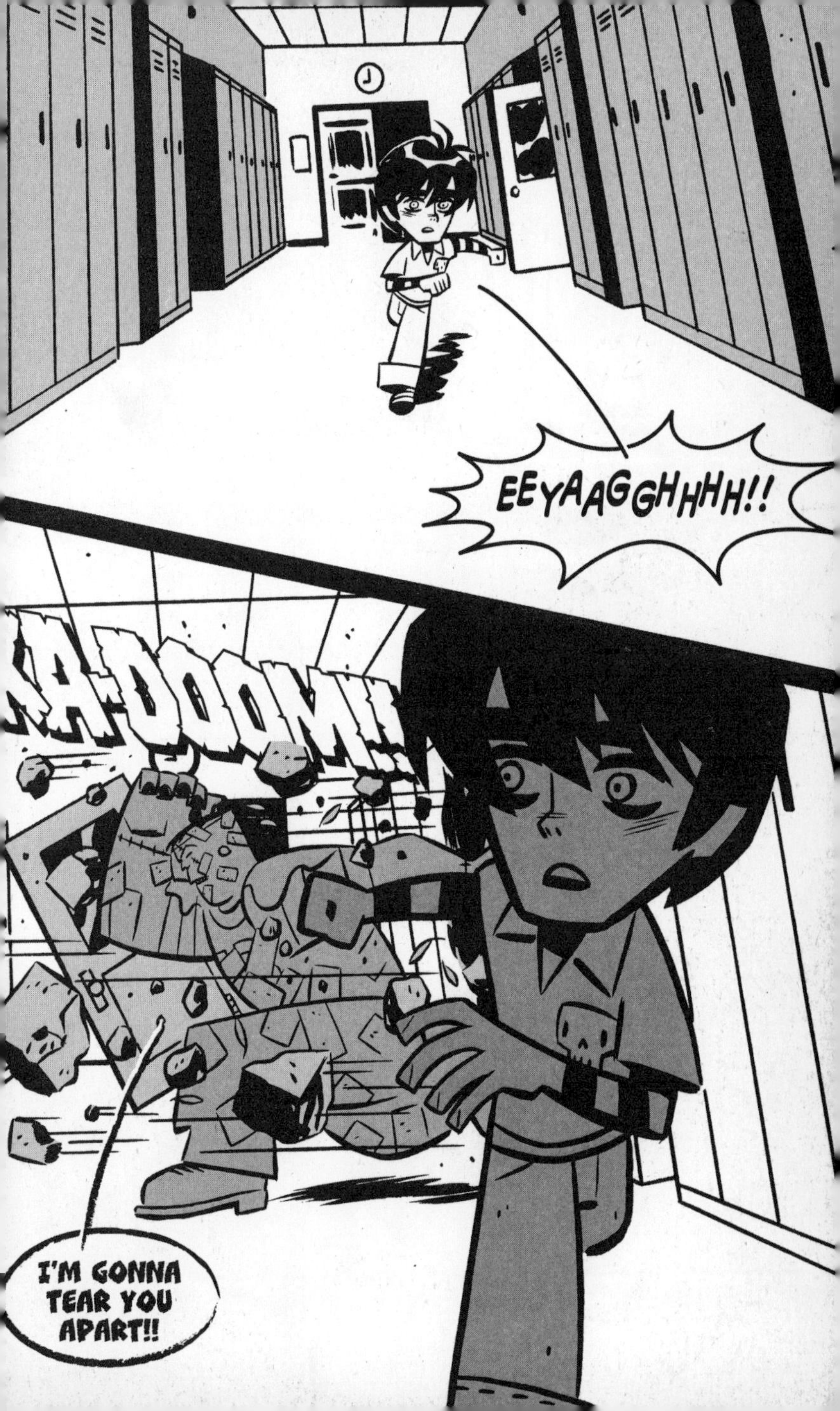
EEYAAGGHHHH!!
A-DOOM!!
I'M GONNA TEAR YOU APART!!

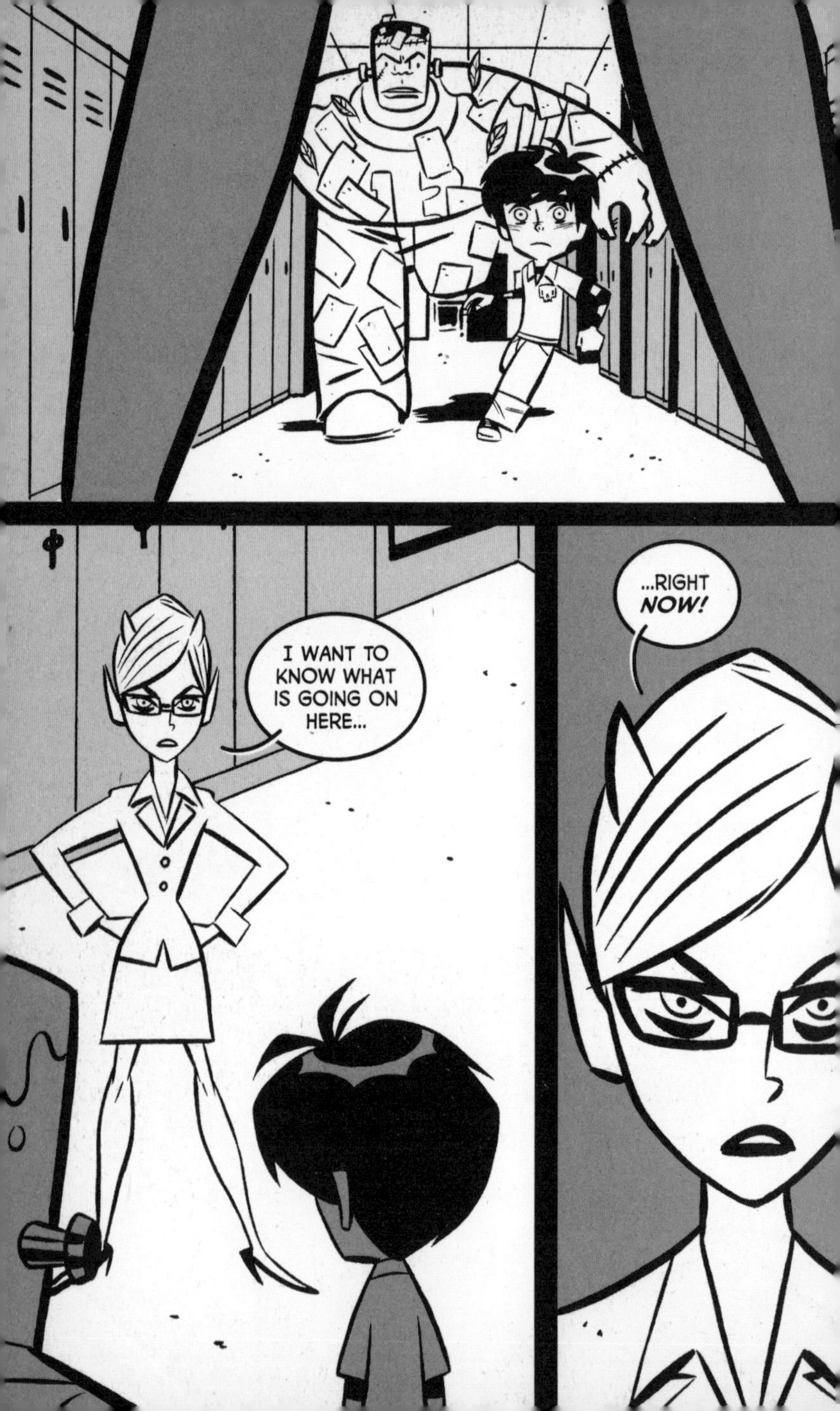
I WANT TO KNOW WHAT IS GOING ON HERE...
...RIGHT *NOW!*

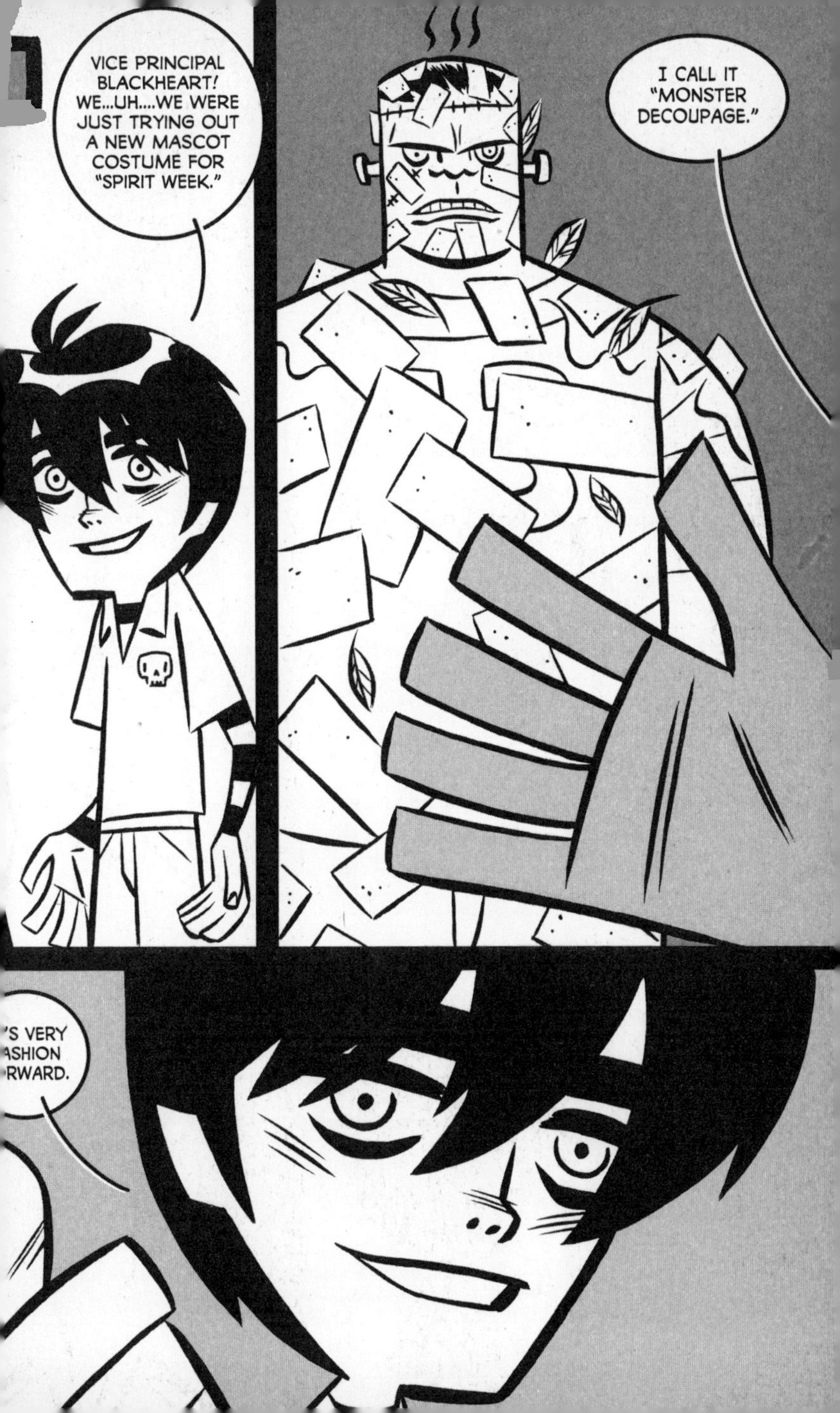
VICE PRINCIPAL BLACKHEART! WE...UH....WE WERE JUST TRYING OUT A NEW MASCOT COSTUME FOR "SPIRIT WEEK."
I CALL IT "MONSTER DECOUPAGE."
'S VERY ASHION RWARD.

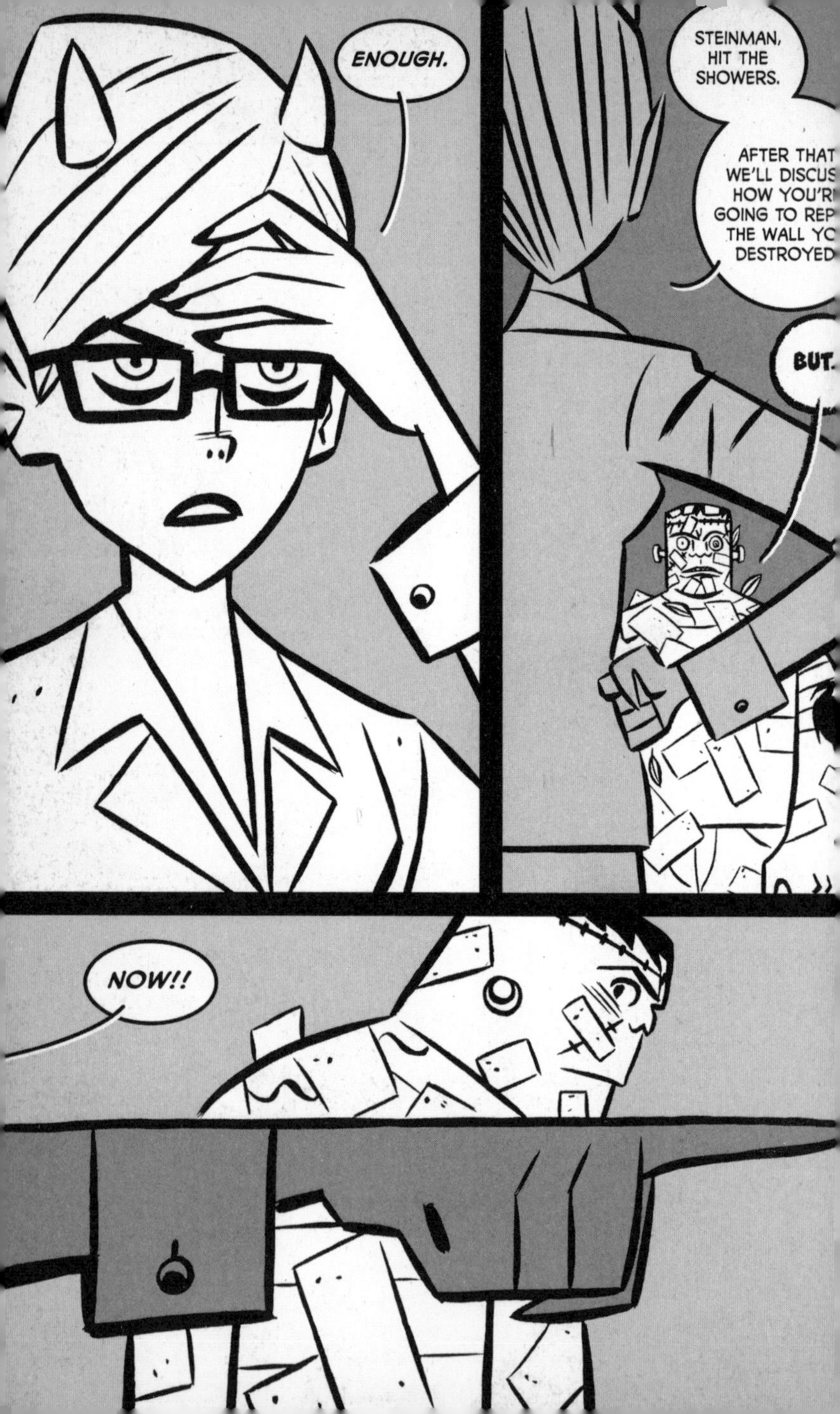
ENOUGH.
STEINMAN, HIT THE SHOWERS.
AFTER THAT WE'LL DISCUS HOW YOU'R GOING TO REP THE WALL YO DESTROYED
BUT.
NOW!!

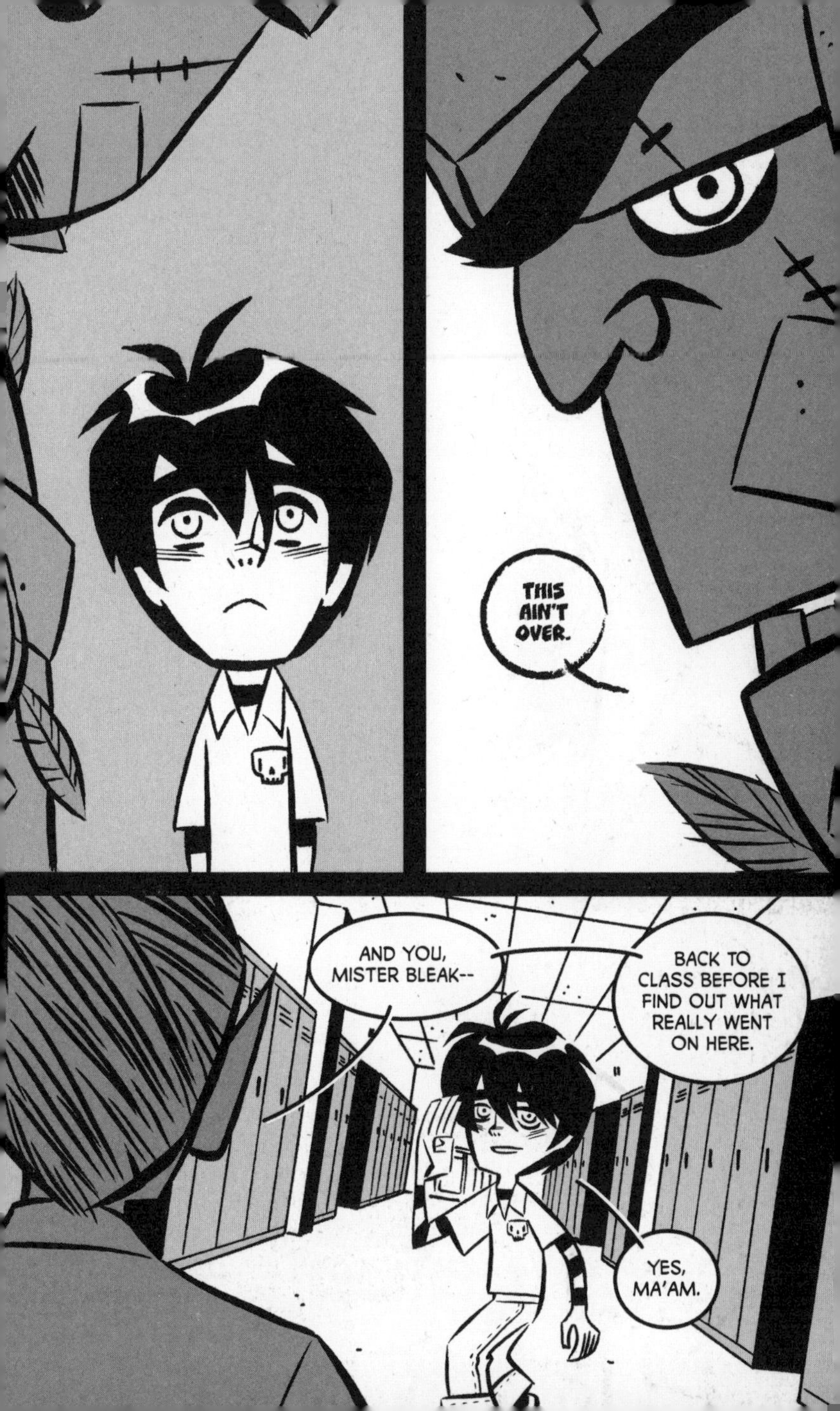
THIS AIN'T OVER.
AND YOU, MISTER BLEAK--
BACK TO CLASS BEFORE I FIND OUT WHAT REALLY WENT ON HERE.
YES, MA'AM.

CHAPTER SIX

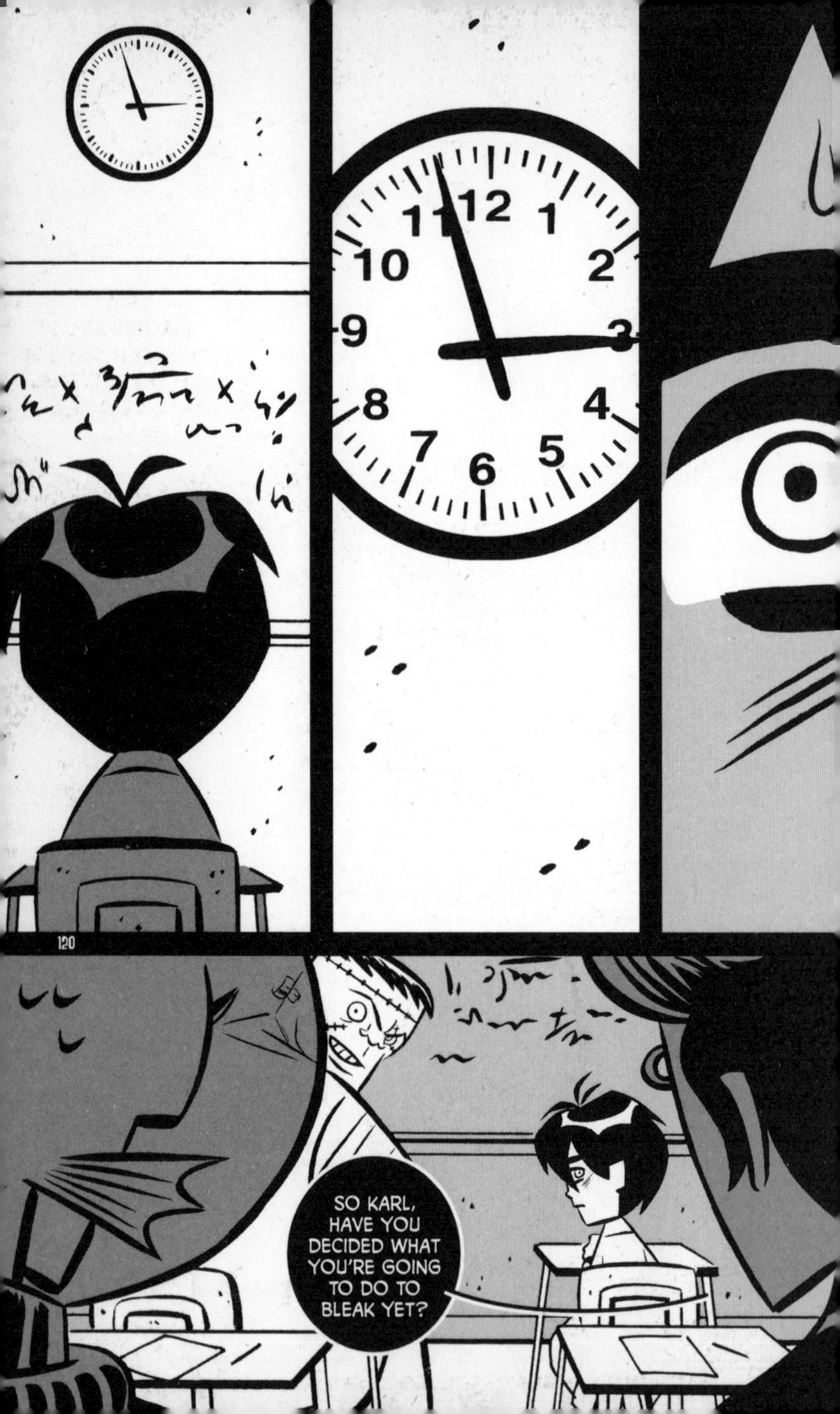
SO KARL, HAVE YOU DECIDED WHAT YOU'RE GOING TO DO TO BLEAK YET?

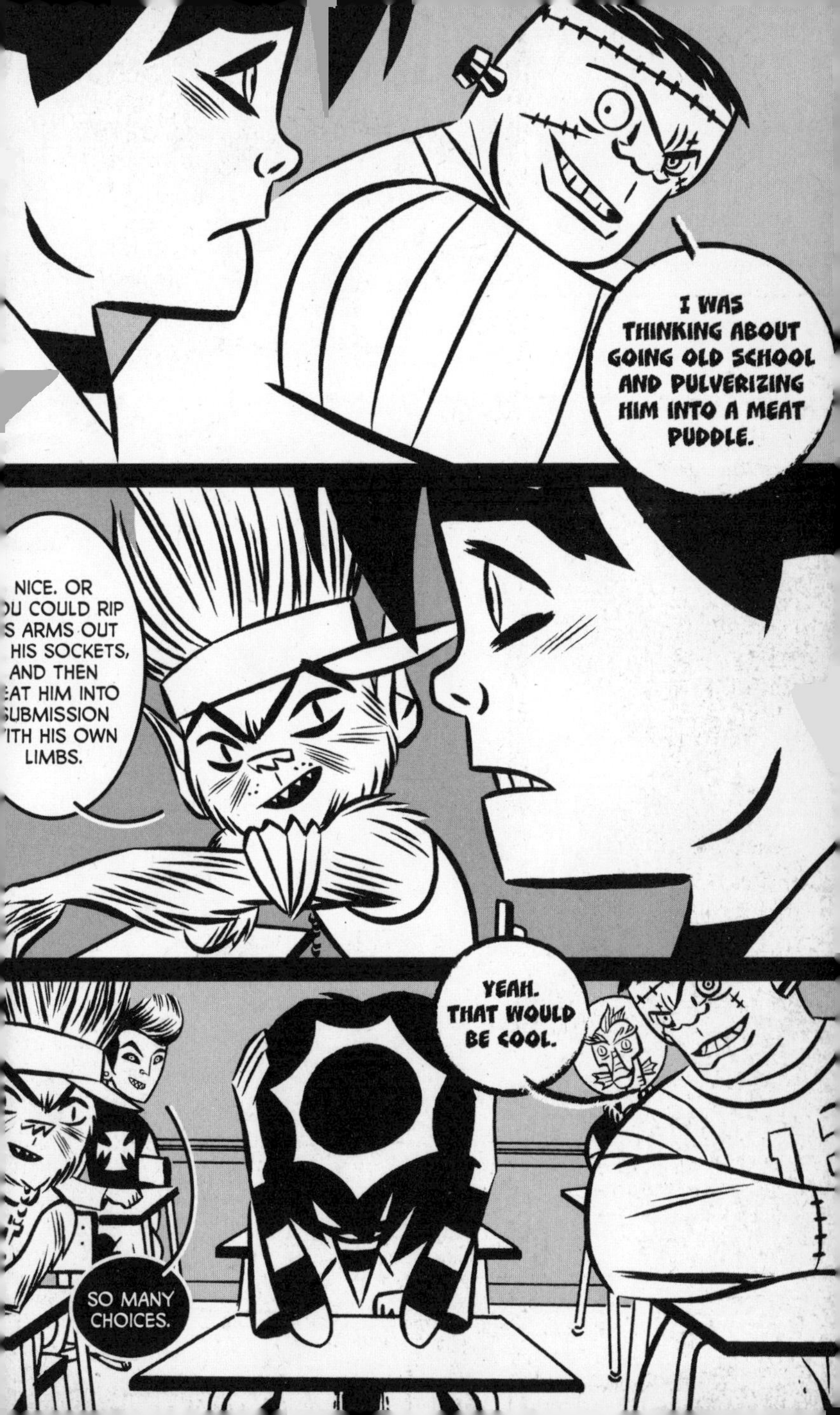
I WAS THINKING ABOUT GOING OLD SCHOOL AND PULVERIZING HIM INTO A MEAT PUDDLE.
NICE. OR OU COULD RIP S ARMS OUT HIS SOCKETS, AND THEN EAT HIM INTO UBMISSION ITH HIS OWN LIMBS.
YEAH. THAT WOULD BE COOL.
SO MANY CHOICES.

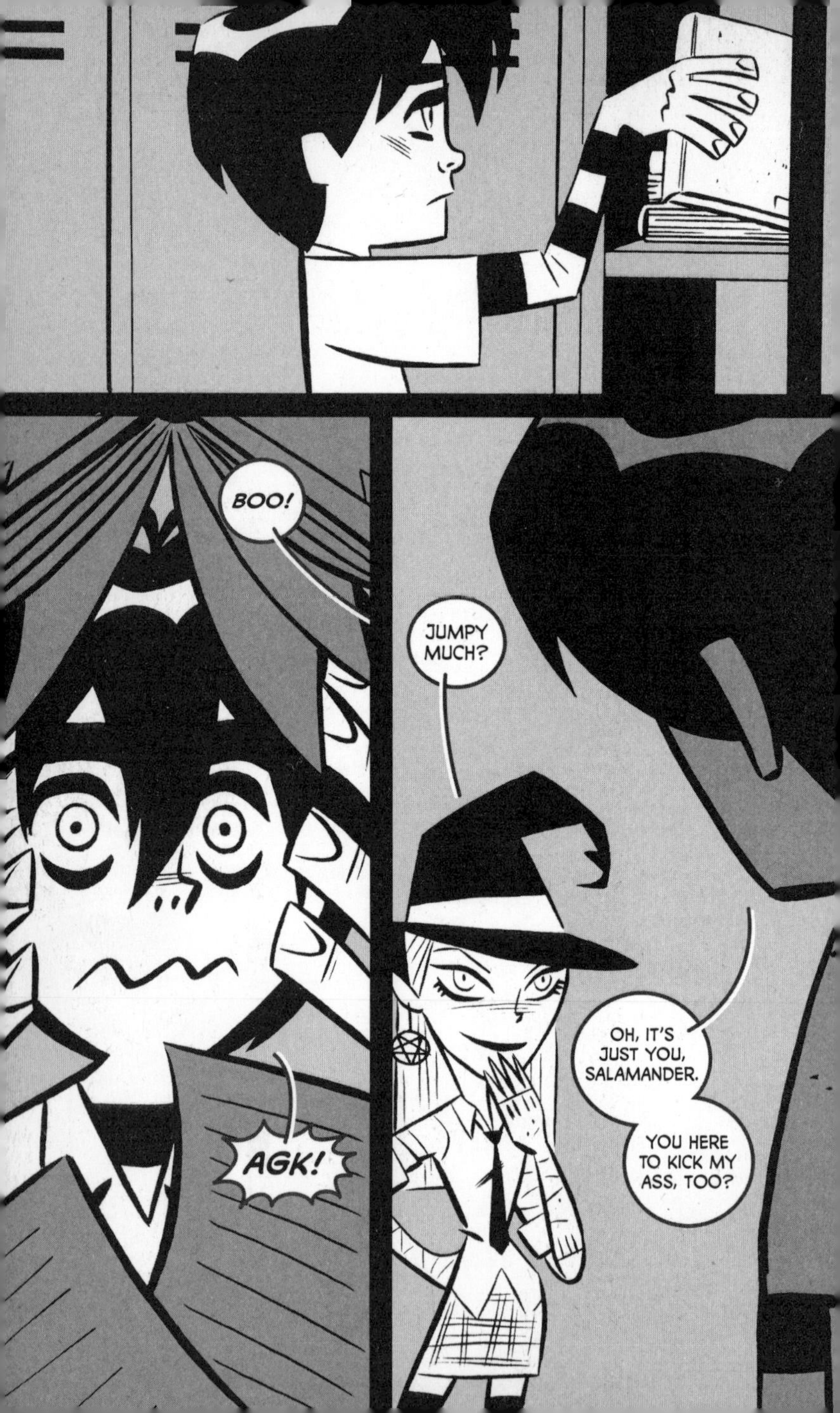
BOO!
AGK!
JUMPY MUCH?
OH, IT'S JUST YOU, SALAMANDER.
YOU HERE TO KICK MY ASS, TOO?

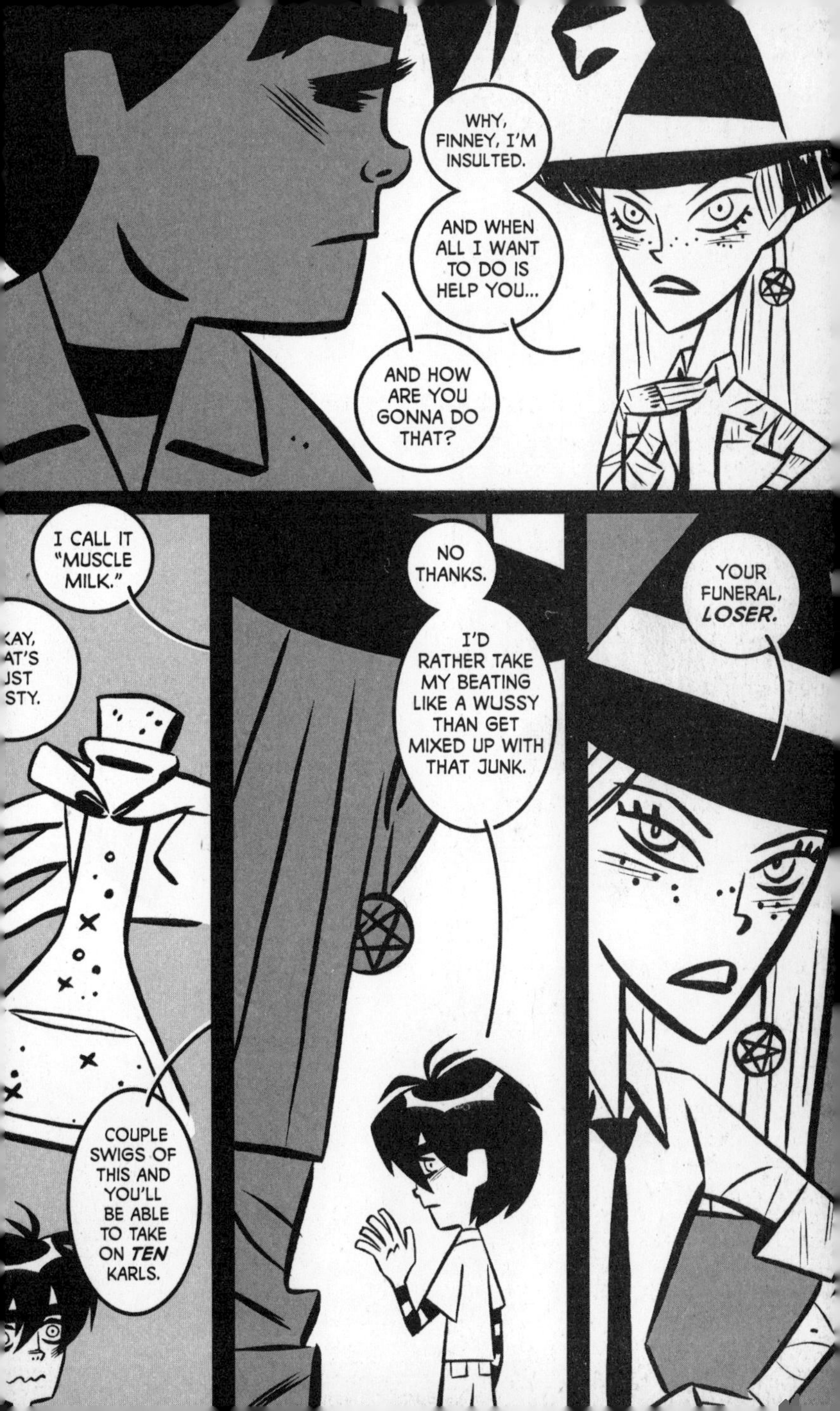
WHY, FINNEY, I'M INSULTED.
AND WHEN ALL I WANT TO DO IS HELP YOU...
AND HOW ARE YOU GONNA DO THAT?
I CALL IT "MUSCLE MILK."
COUPLE SWIGS OF THIS AND YOU'LL BE ABLE TO TAKE ON *TEN* KARLS.
NO THANKS.
I'D RATHER TAKE MY BEATING LIKE A WUSSY THAN GET MIXED UP WITH THAT JUNK.
YOUR FUNERAL, ***LOSER.***

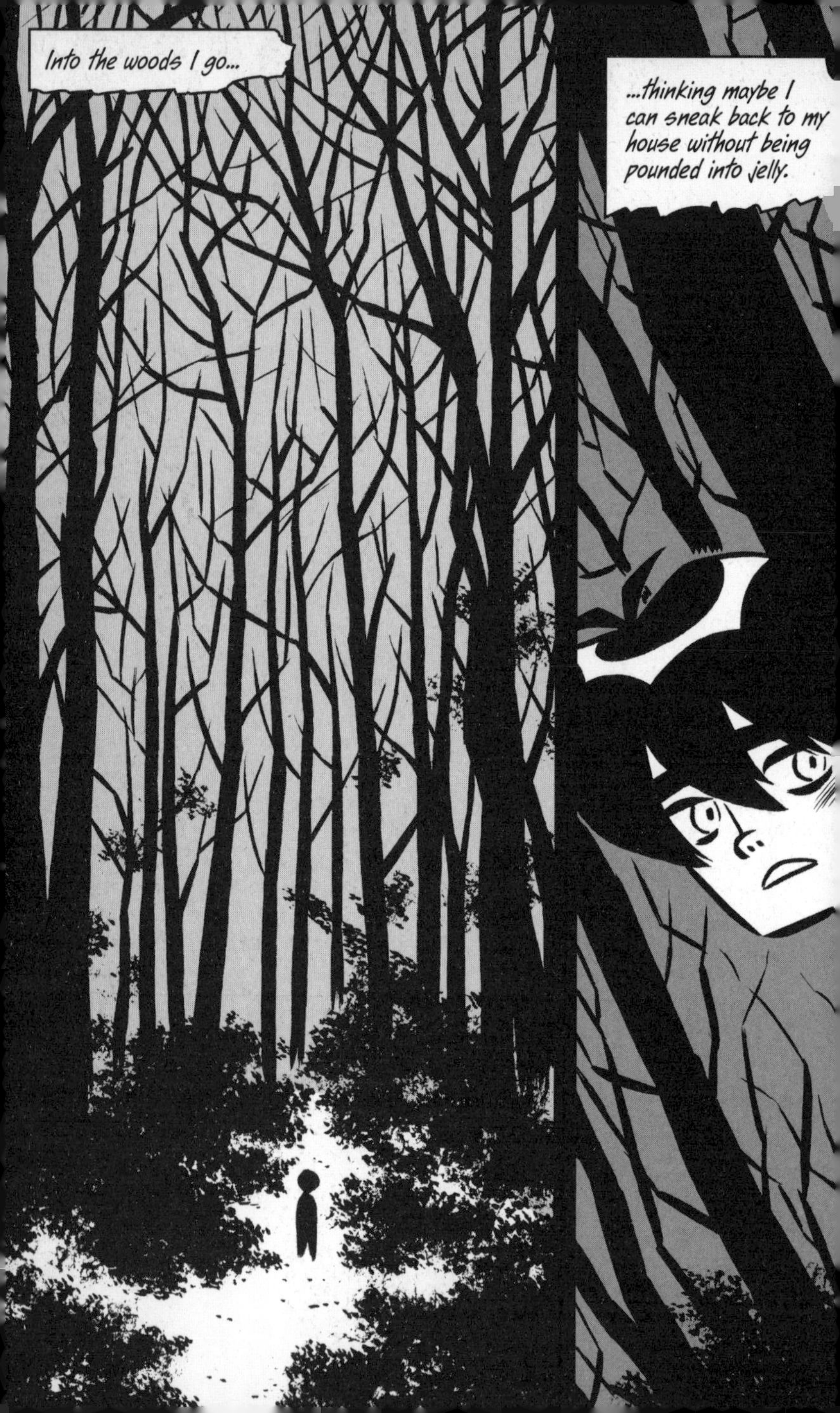

Into the woods I go...
...thinking maybe I can sneak back to my house without being pounded into jelly.

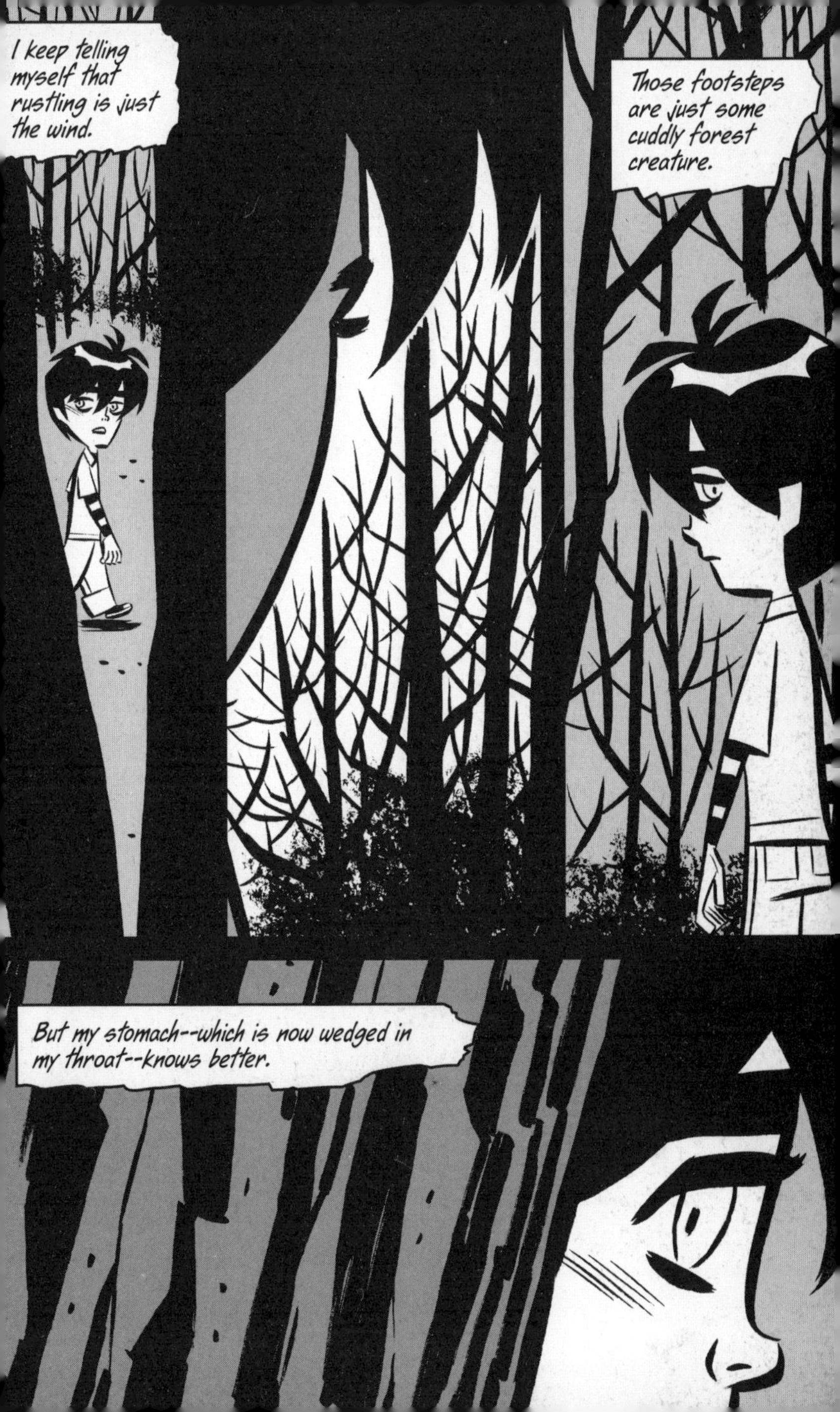
I keep telling myself that rustling is just the wind.
Those footsteps are just some cuddly forest creature.
But my stomach--which is now wedged in my throat--knows better.

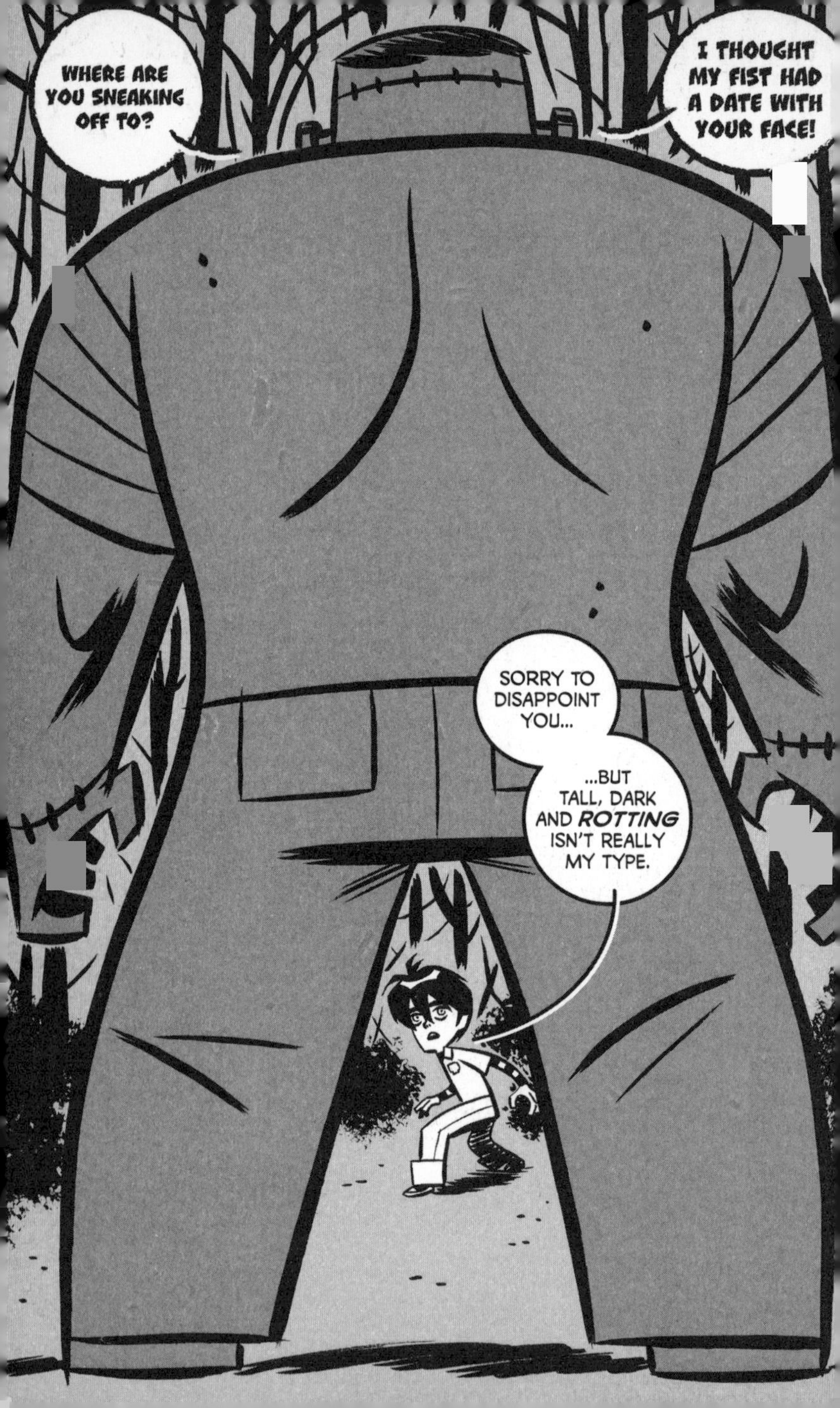
WHERE ARE YOU SNEAKING OFF TO?
I THOUGHT MY FIST HAD A DATE WITH YOUR FACE!
SORRY TO DISAPPOINT YOU...
...BUT TALL, DARK AND ROTTING ISN'T REALLY MY TYPE.

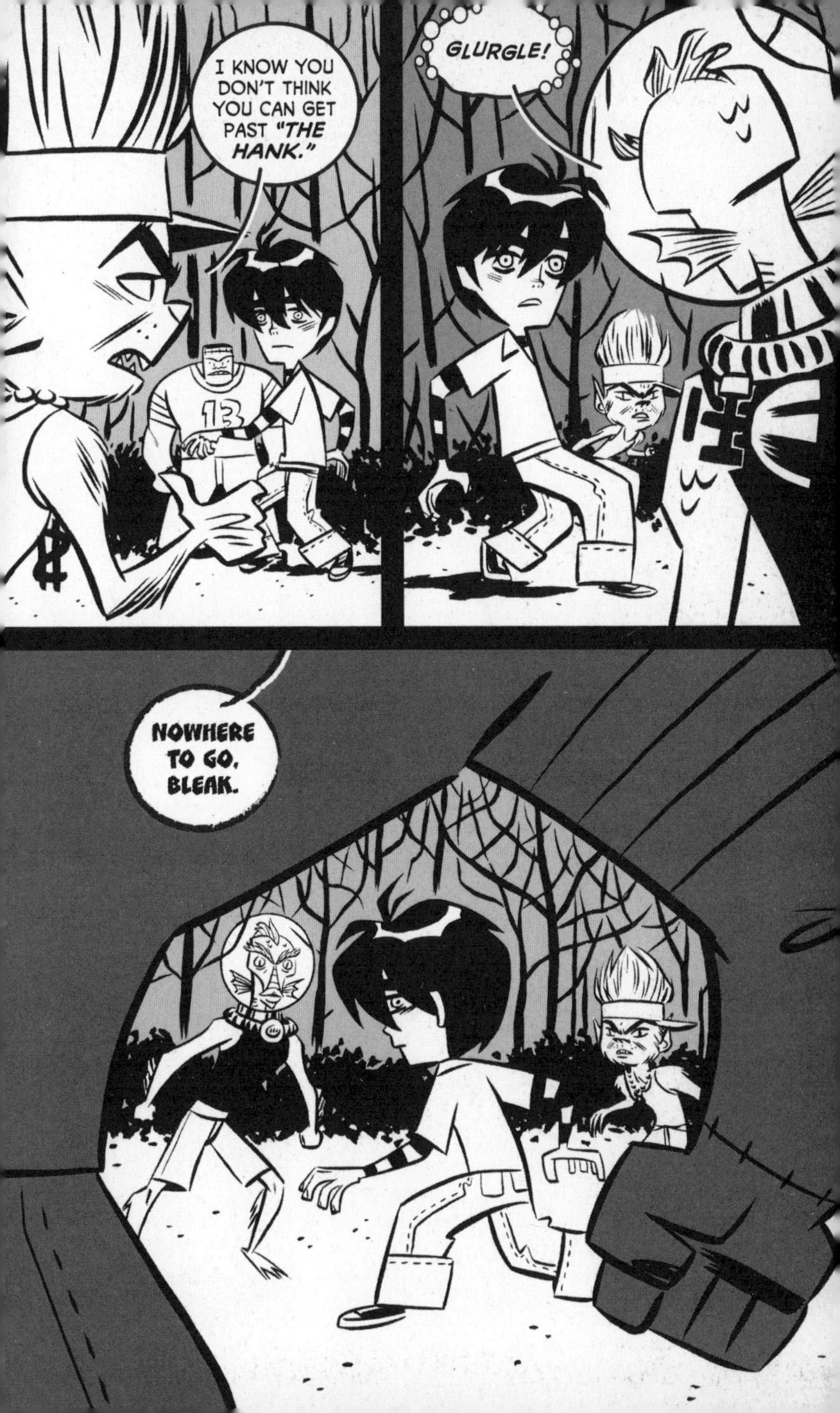
I KNOW YOU DON'T THINK YOU CAN GET PAST "THE HANK."
GLURGLE!
NOWHERE TO GO, BLEAK.

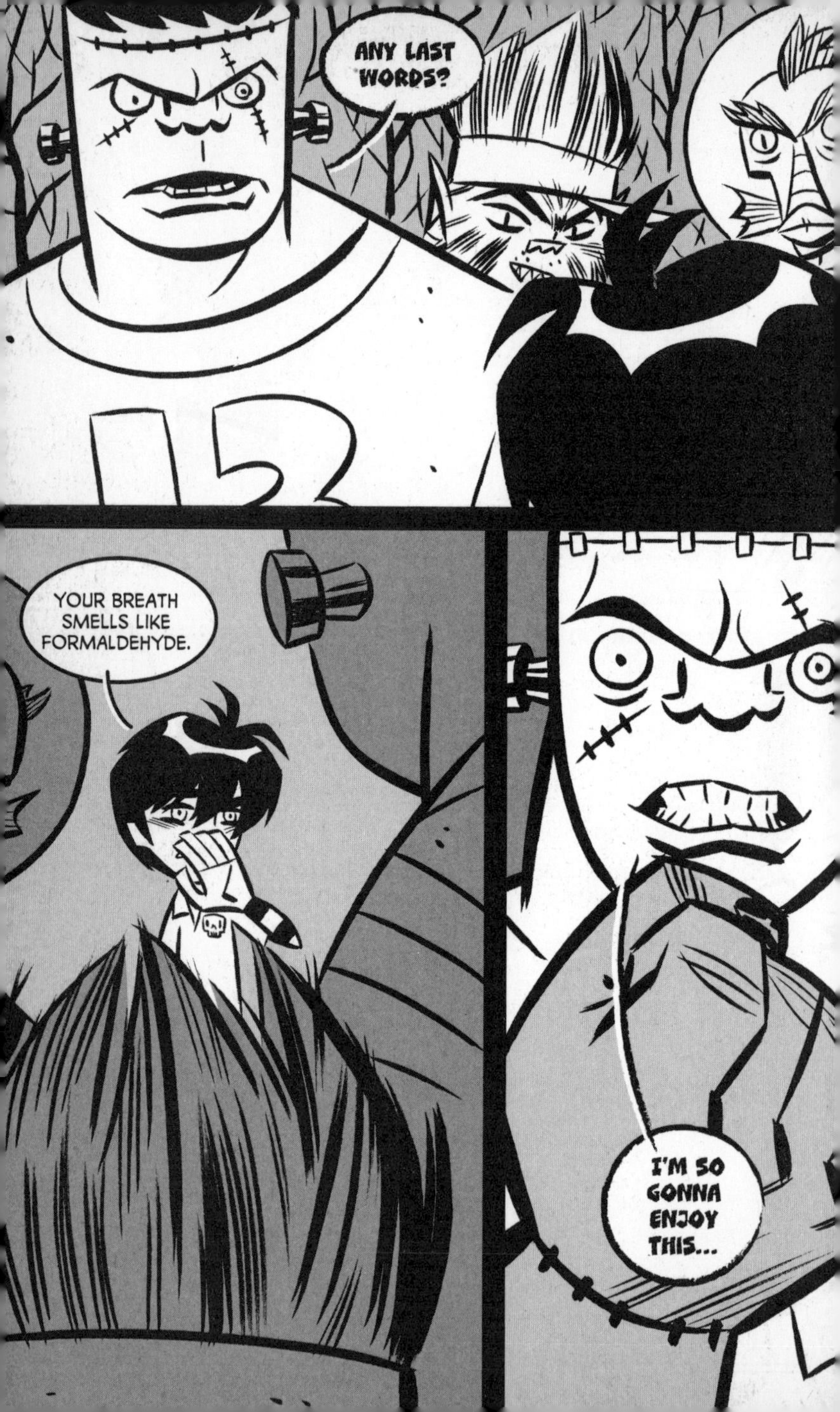
ANY LAST WORDS?
YOUR BREATH SMELLS LIKE FORMALDEHYDE.
I'M SO GONNA ENJOY THIS...

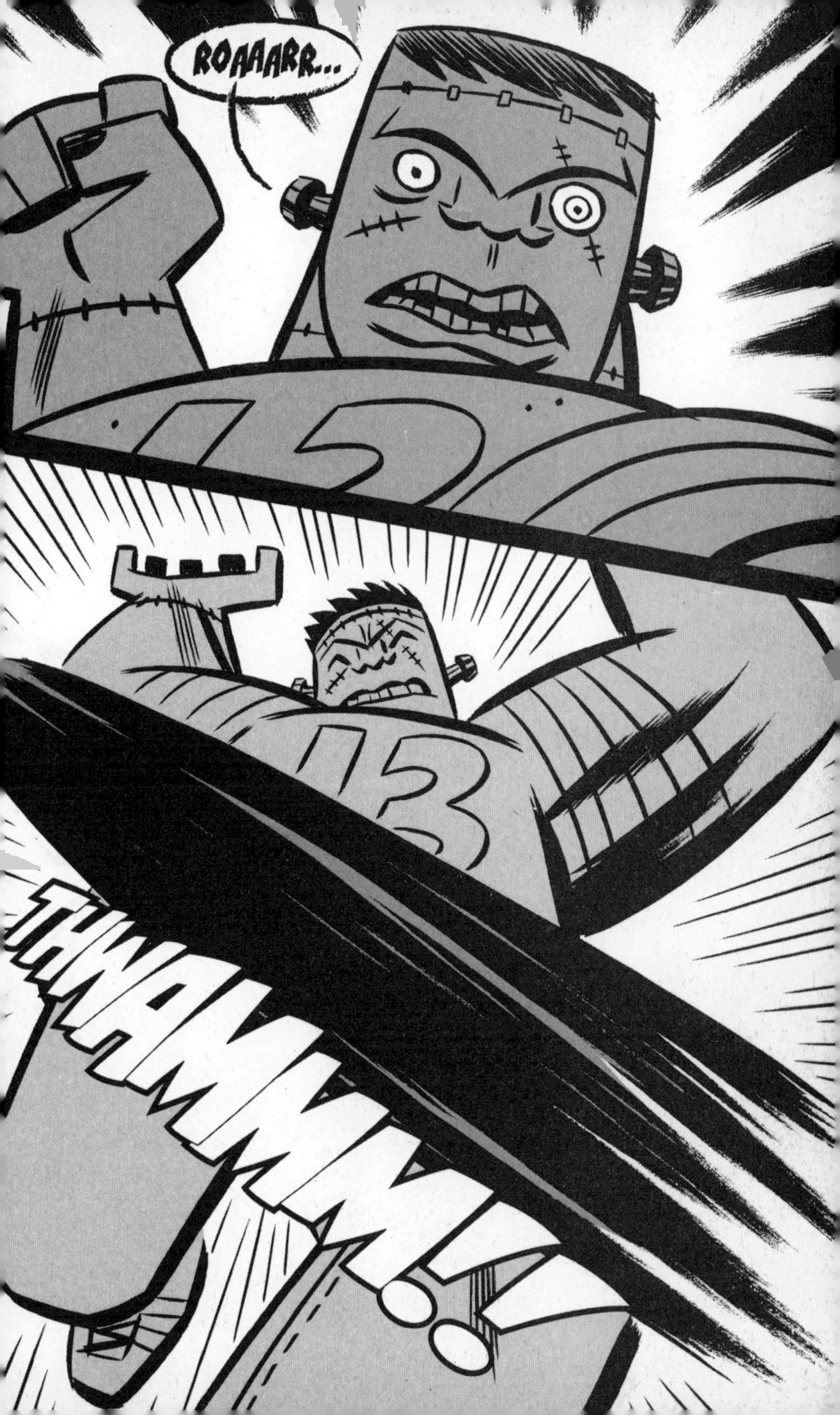
ROAAARR...
THWAMMM!

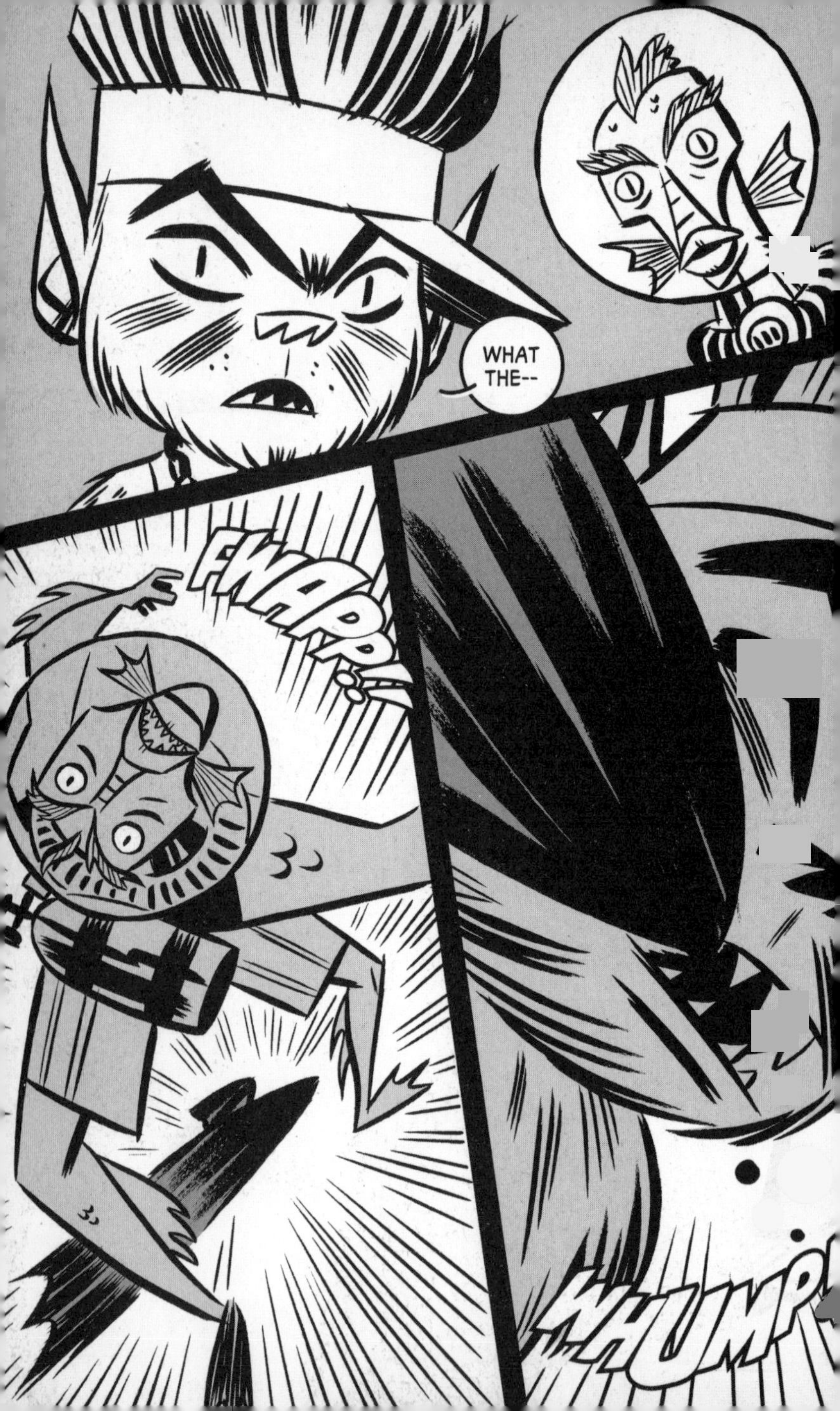
WHAT THE--
FWAPP!
WHUMP

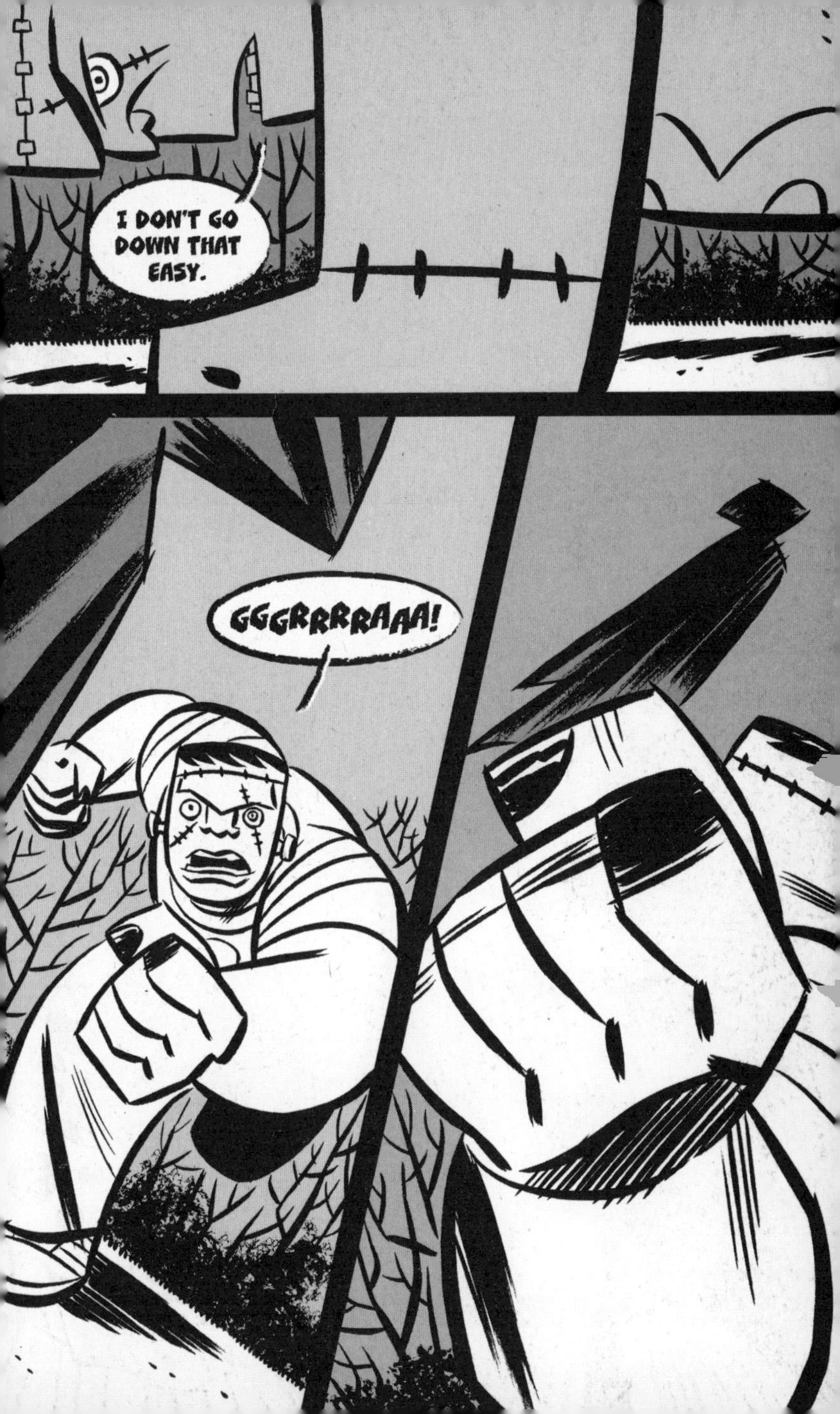
I DON'T GO DOWN THAT EASY.
GGGRRRRAAA!

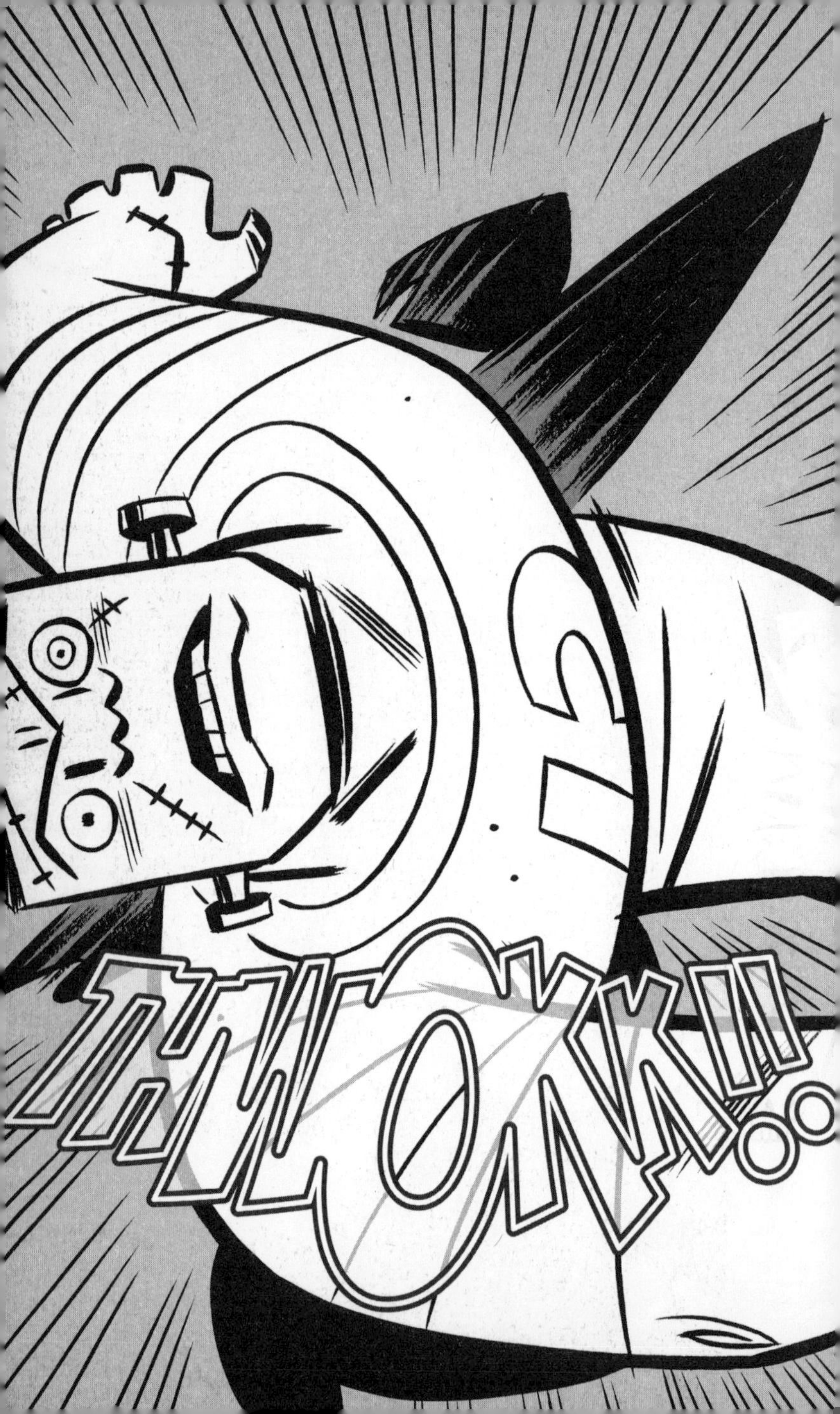
THWONK!!

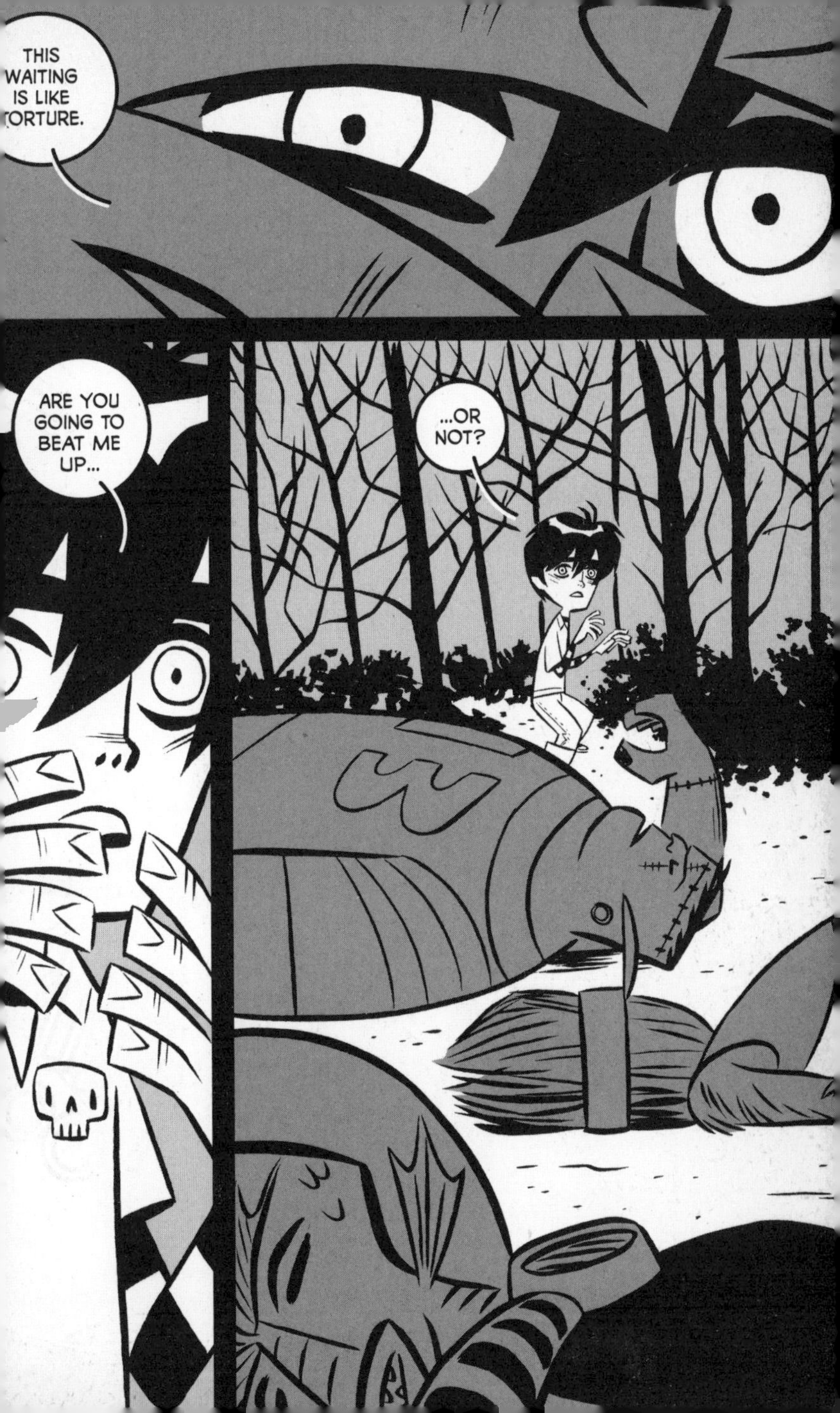
THIS WAITING IS LIKE TORTURE.
ARE YOU GOING TO BEAT ME UP...
...OR NOT?

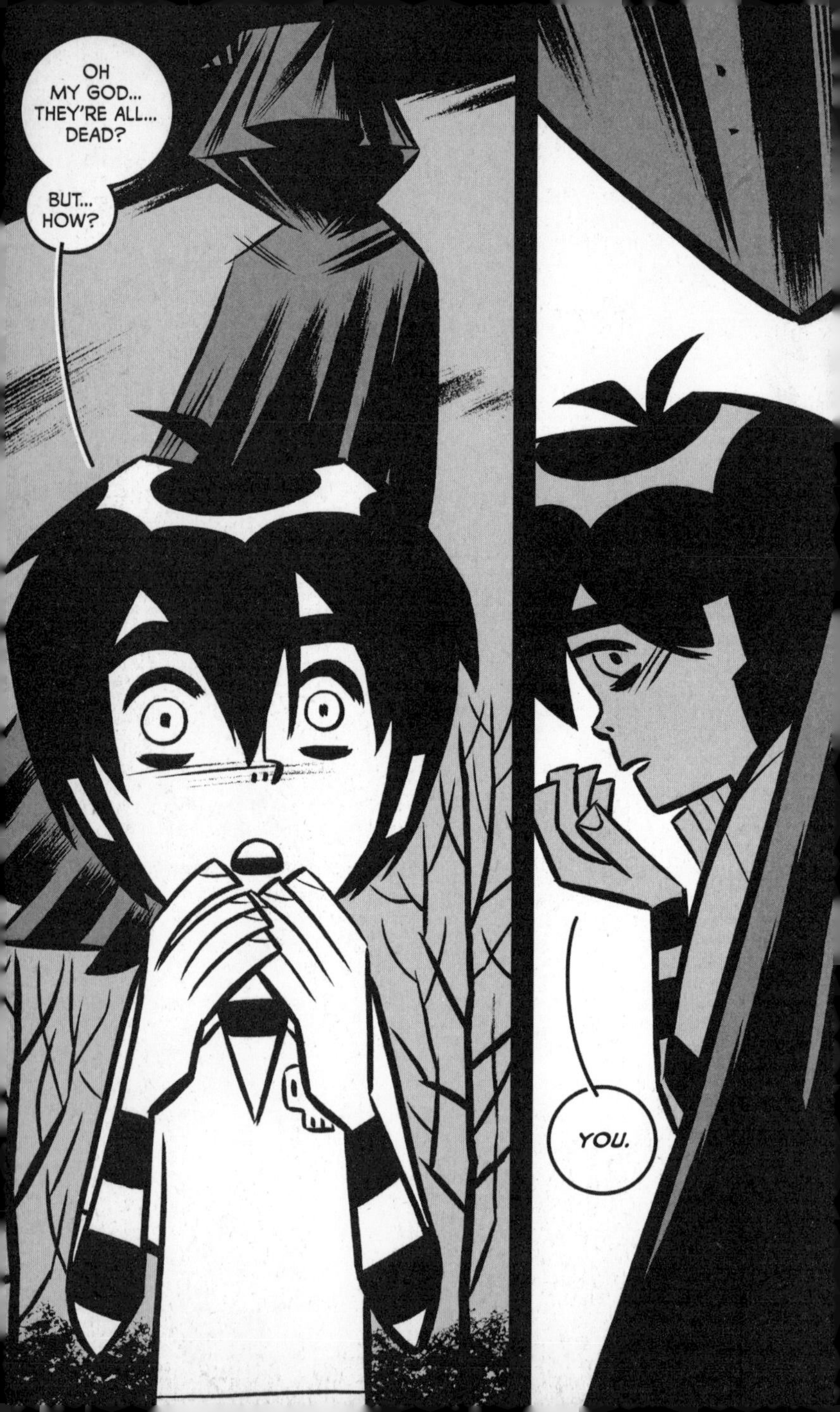
OH MY GOD... THEY'RE ALL... DEAD?
BUT... HOW?
YOU.

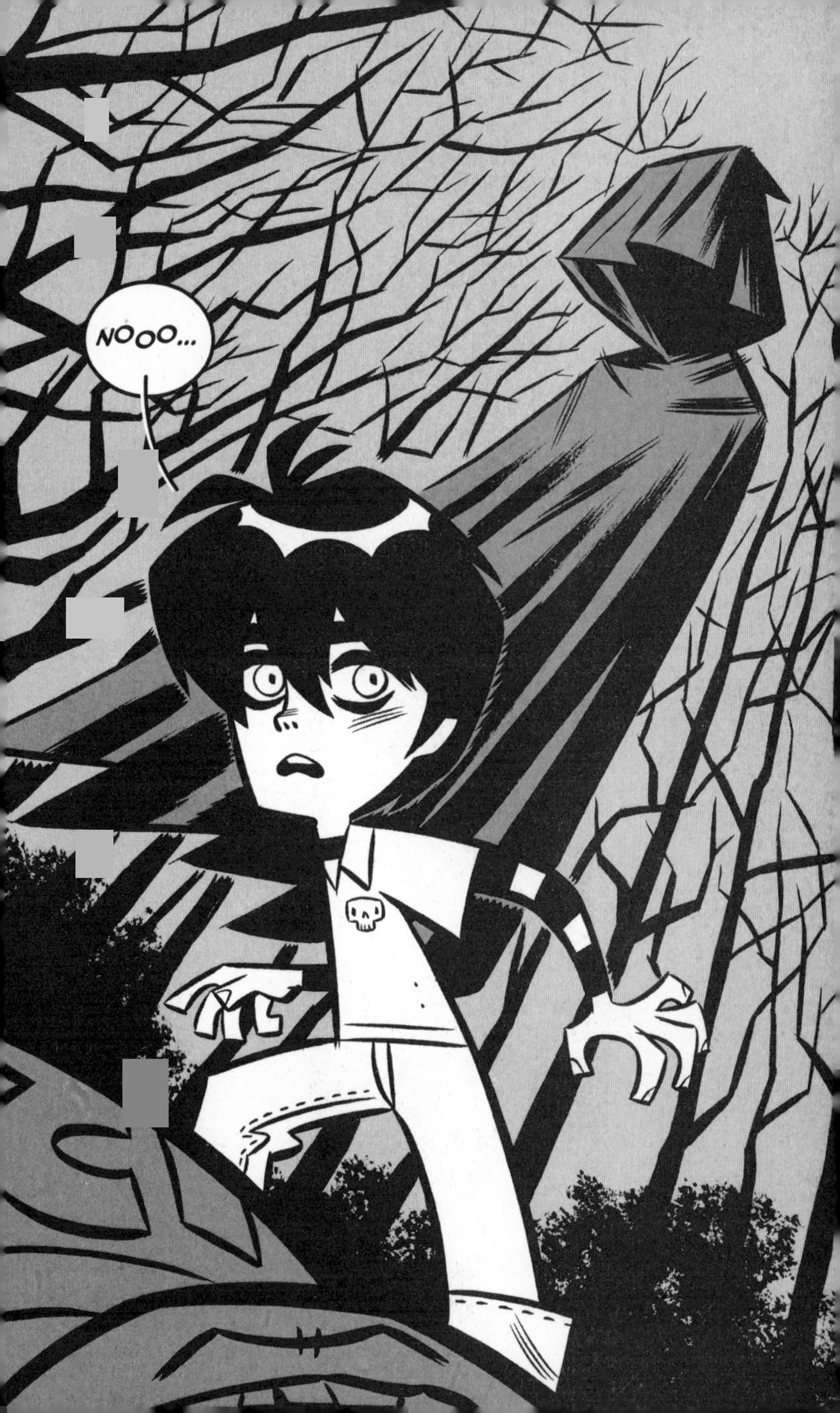
NOOO...

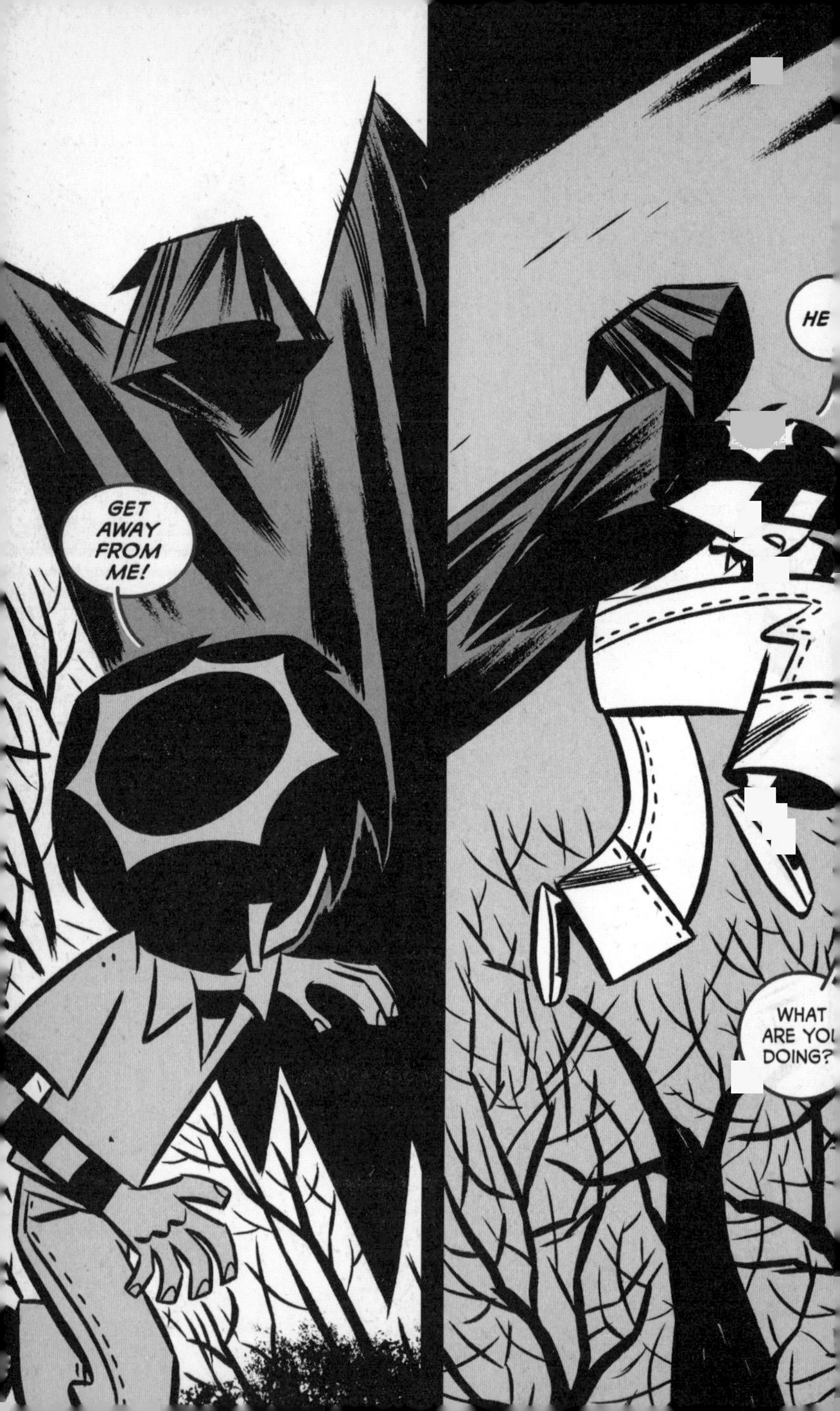
GET AWAY FROM ME!
HE
WHAT ARE YO DOING?

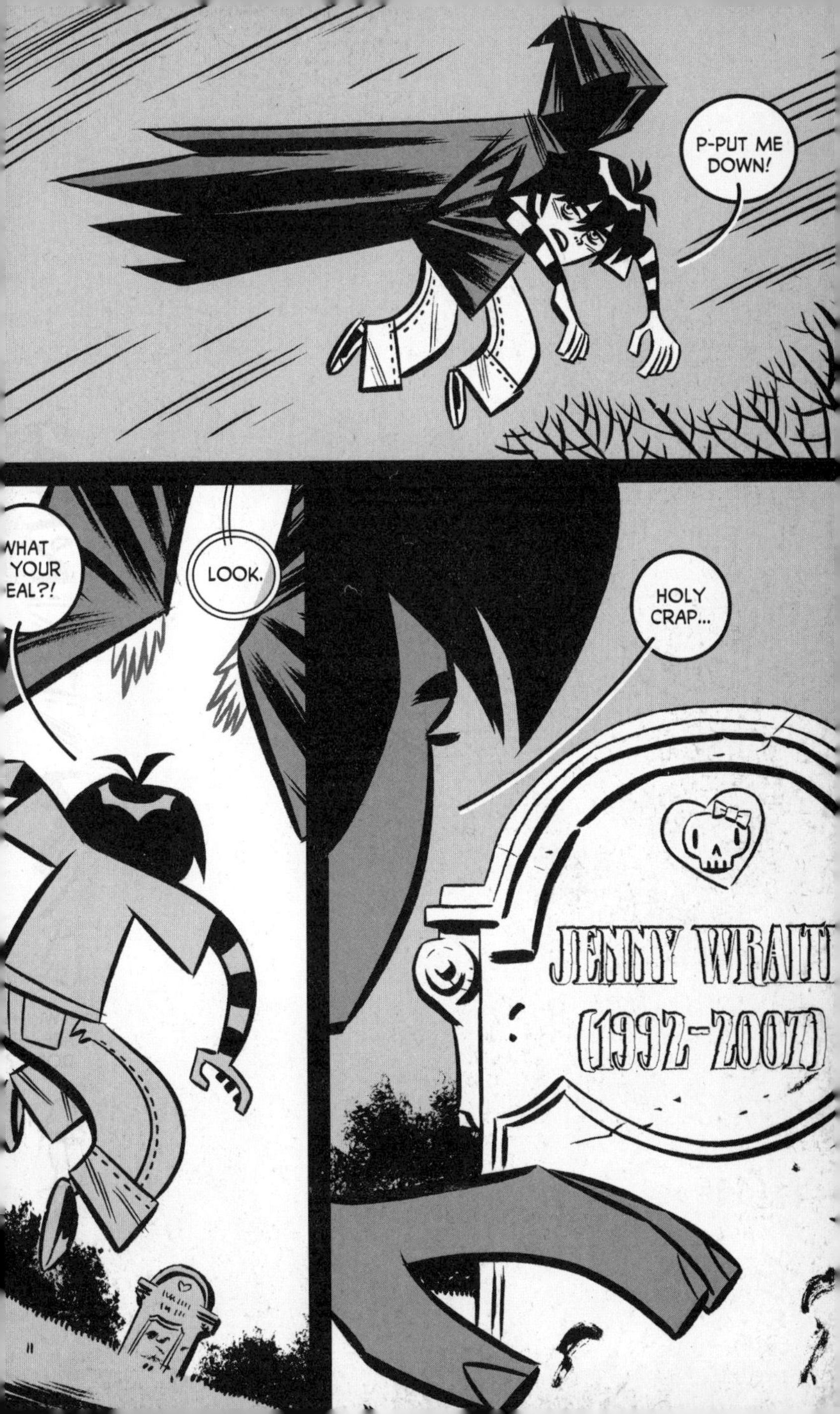

P-PUT ME DOWN!
WHAT YOUR EAL?!
LOOK.
HOLY CRAP...
JENNY WRAIT
(1992-2007)

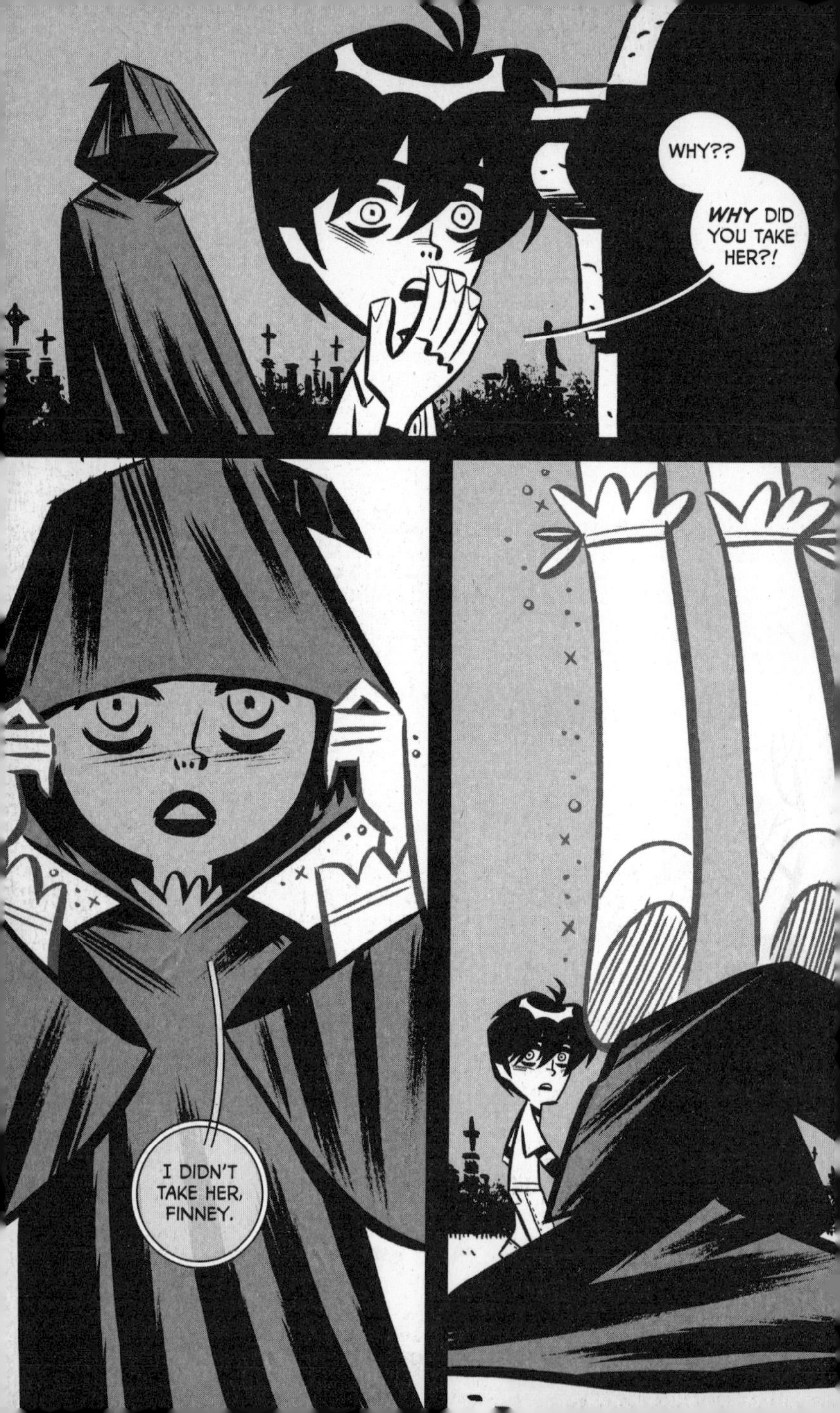
WHY??
WHY DID YOU TAKE HER?!
I DIDN'T TAKE HER, FINNEY.

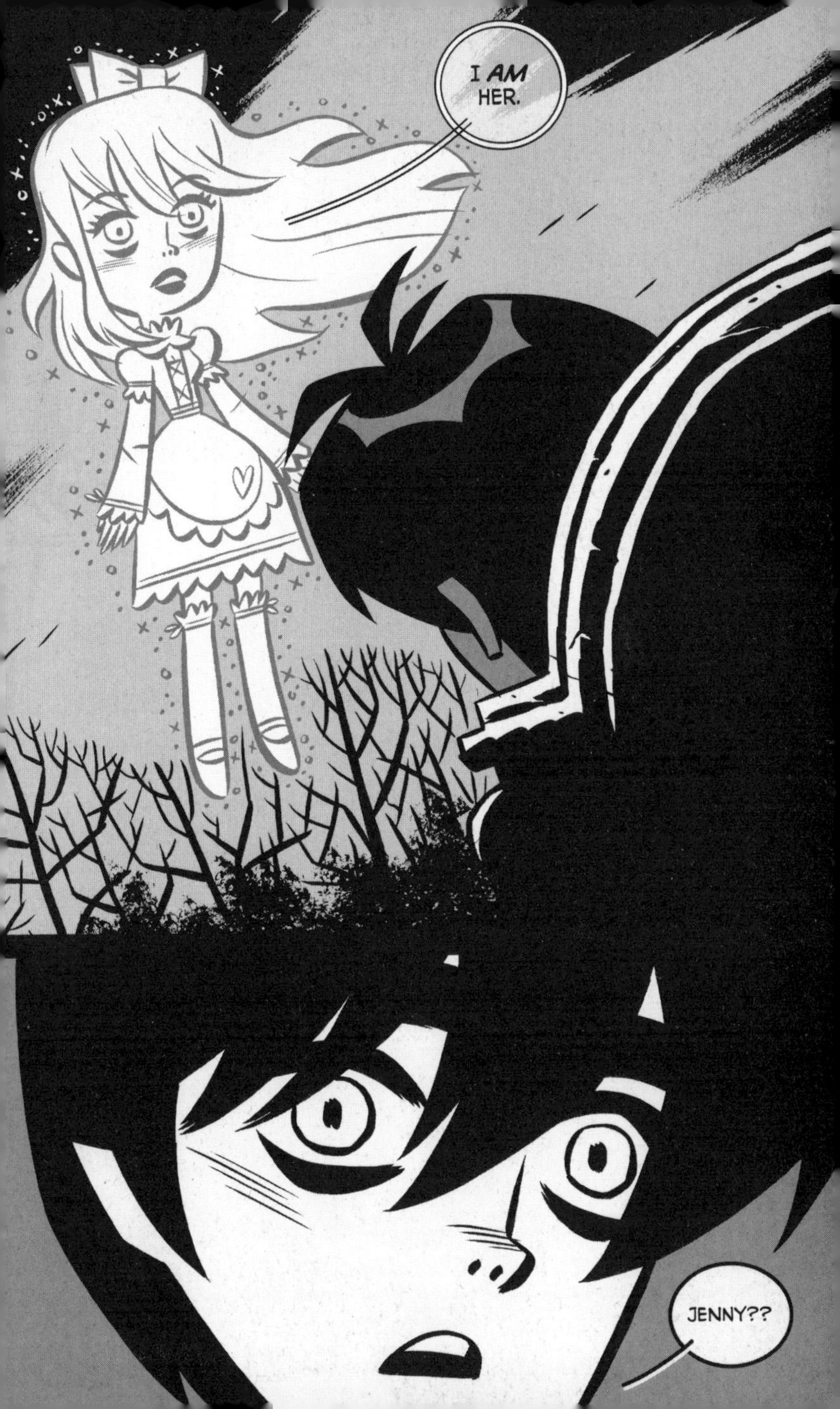
I AM HER.
JENNY??

CHAPTER SEVEN

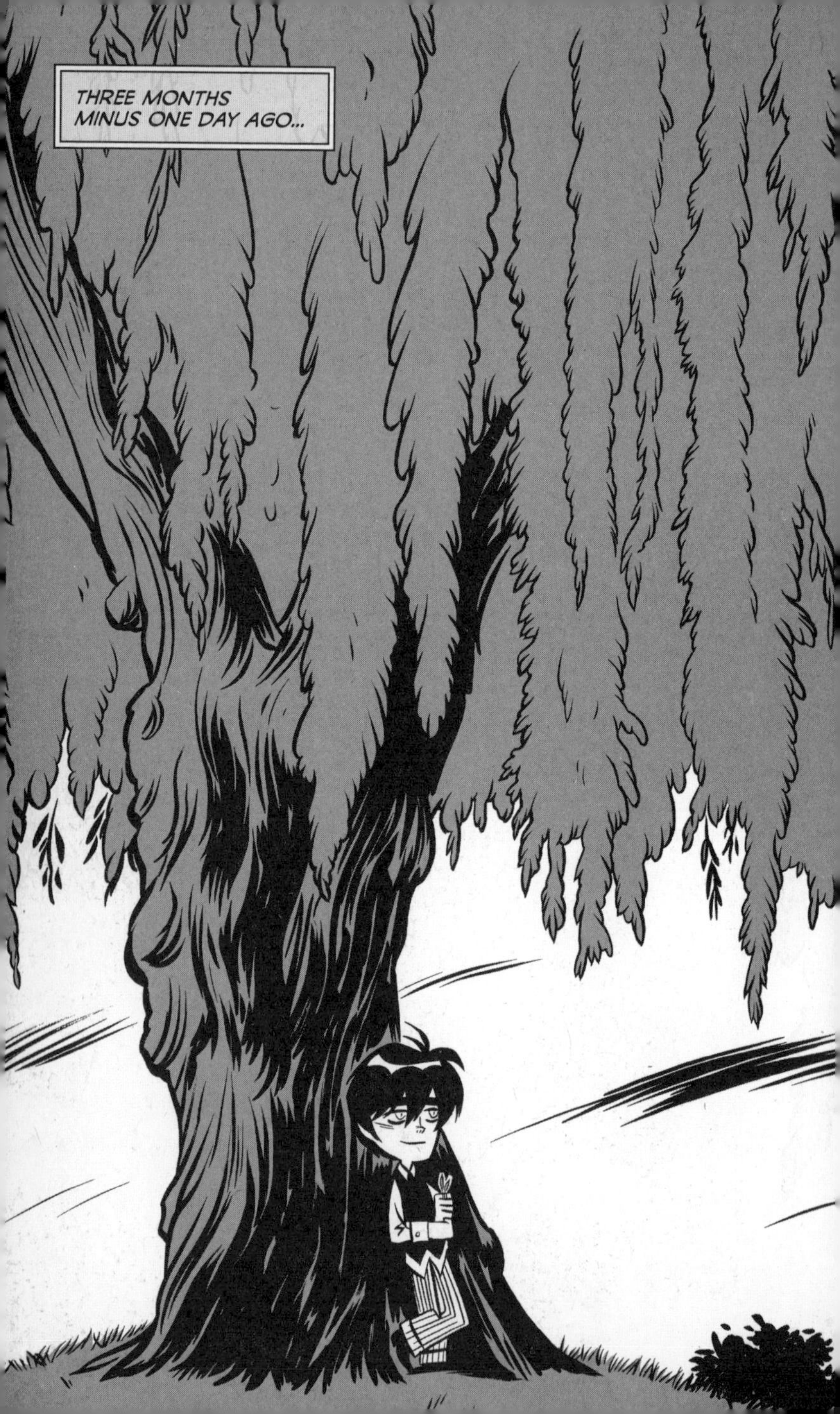
THREE MONTHS MINUS ONE DAY AGO...

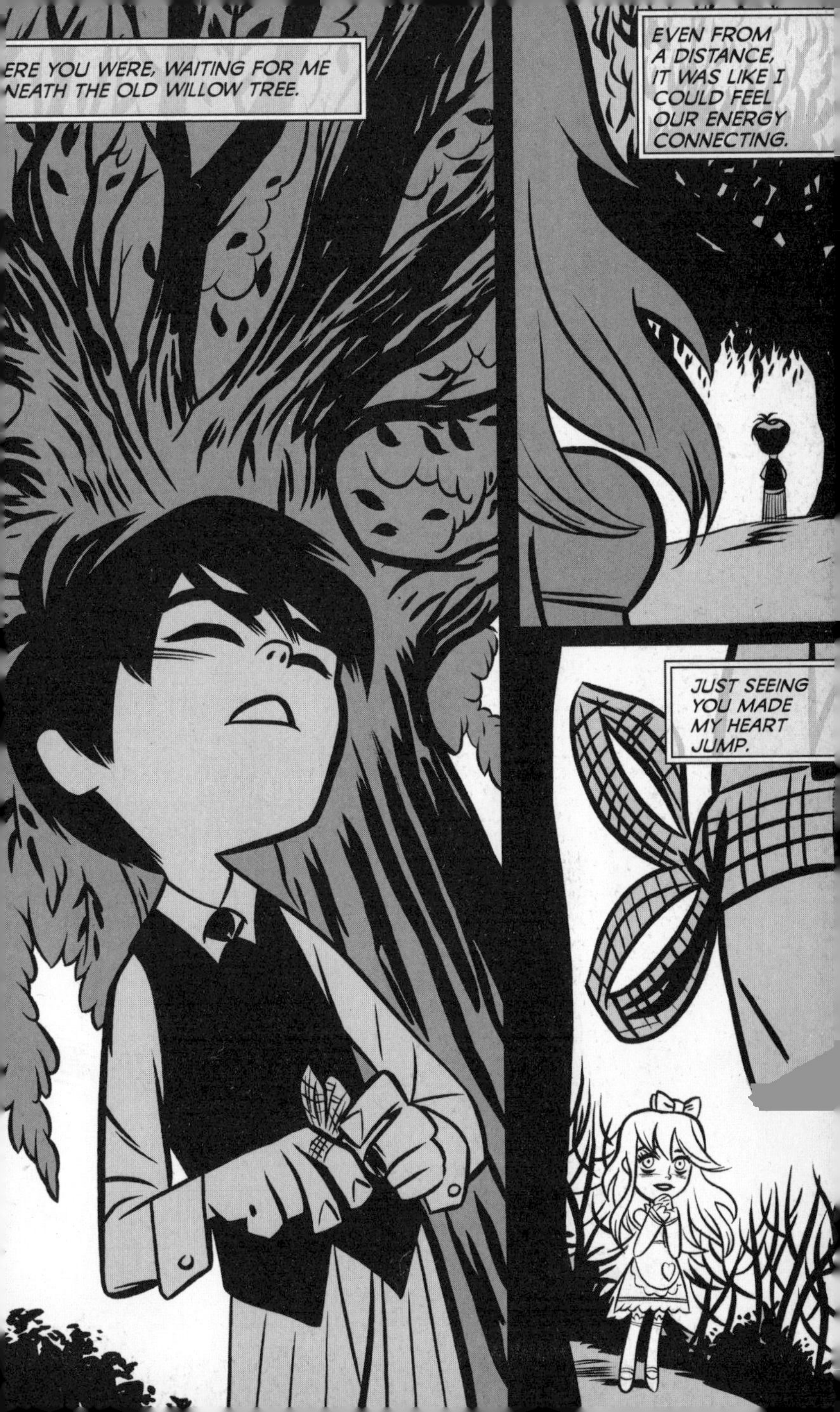
ERE YOU WERE, WAITING FOR ME
NEATH THE OLD WILLOW TREE.
EVEN FROM A DISTANCE, IT WAS LIKE I COULD FEEL OUR ENERGY CONNECTING.
JUST SEEING YOU MADE MY HEART JUMP.

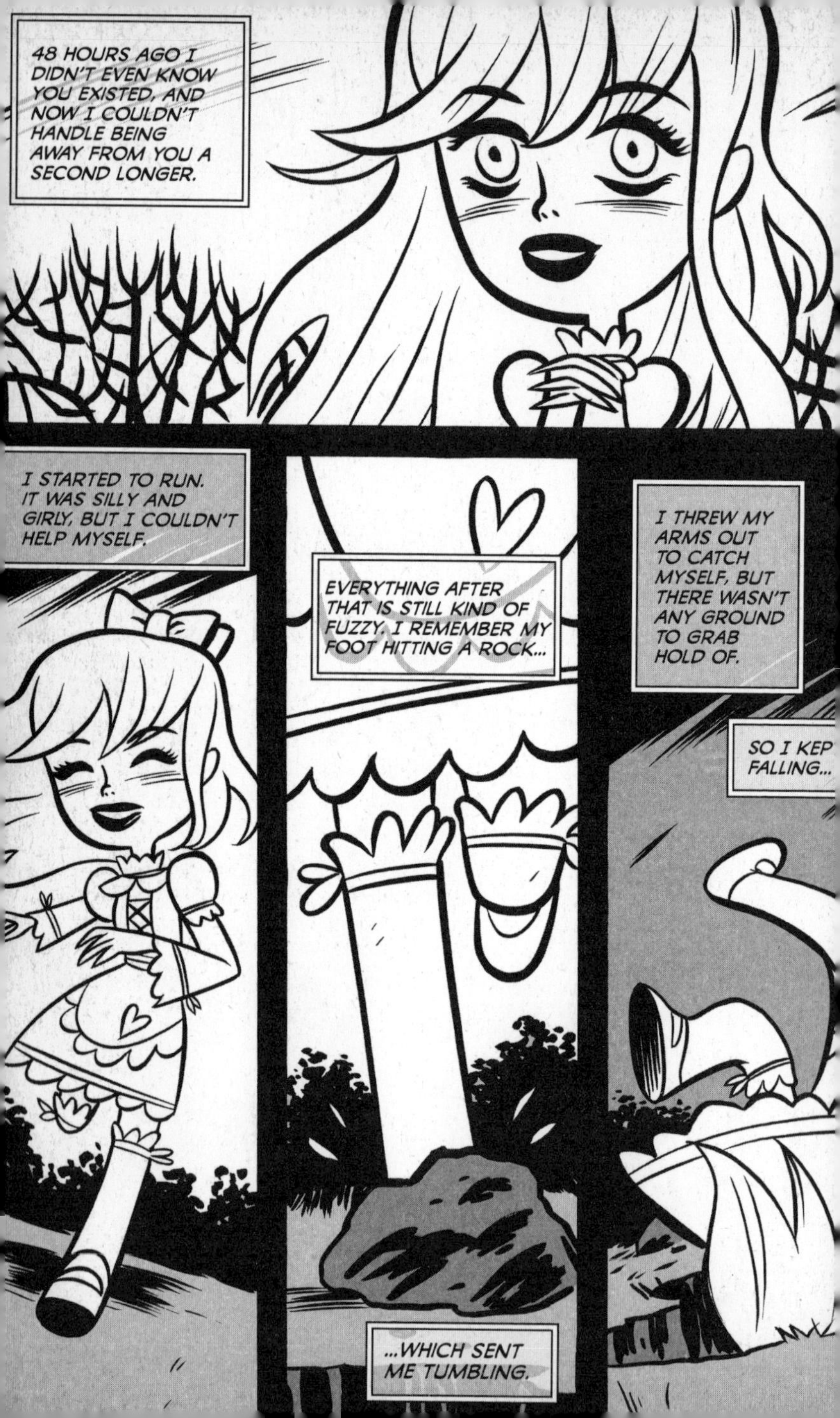
48 HOURS AGO I DIDN'T EVEN KNOW YOU EXISTED, AND NOW I COULDN'T HANDLE BEING AWAY FROM YOU A SECOND LONGER.
I STARTED TO RUN. IT WAS SILLY AND GIRLY, BUT I COULDN'T HELP MYSELF.
EVERYTHING AFTER THAT IS STILL KIND OF FUZZY. I REMEMBER MY FOOT HITTING A ROCK...
...WHICH SENT ME TUMBLING.
I THREW MY ARMS OUT TO CATCH MYSELF, BUT THERE WASN'T ANY GROUND TO GRAB HOLD OF.
SO I KEP FALLING...

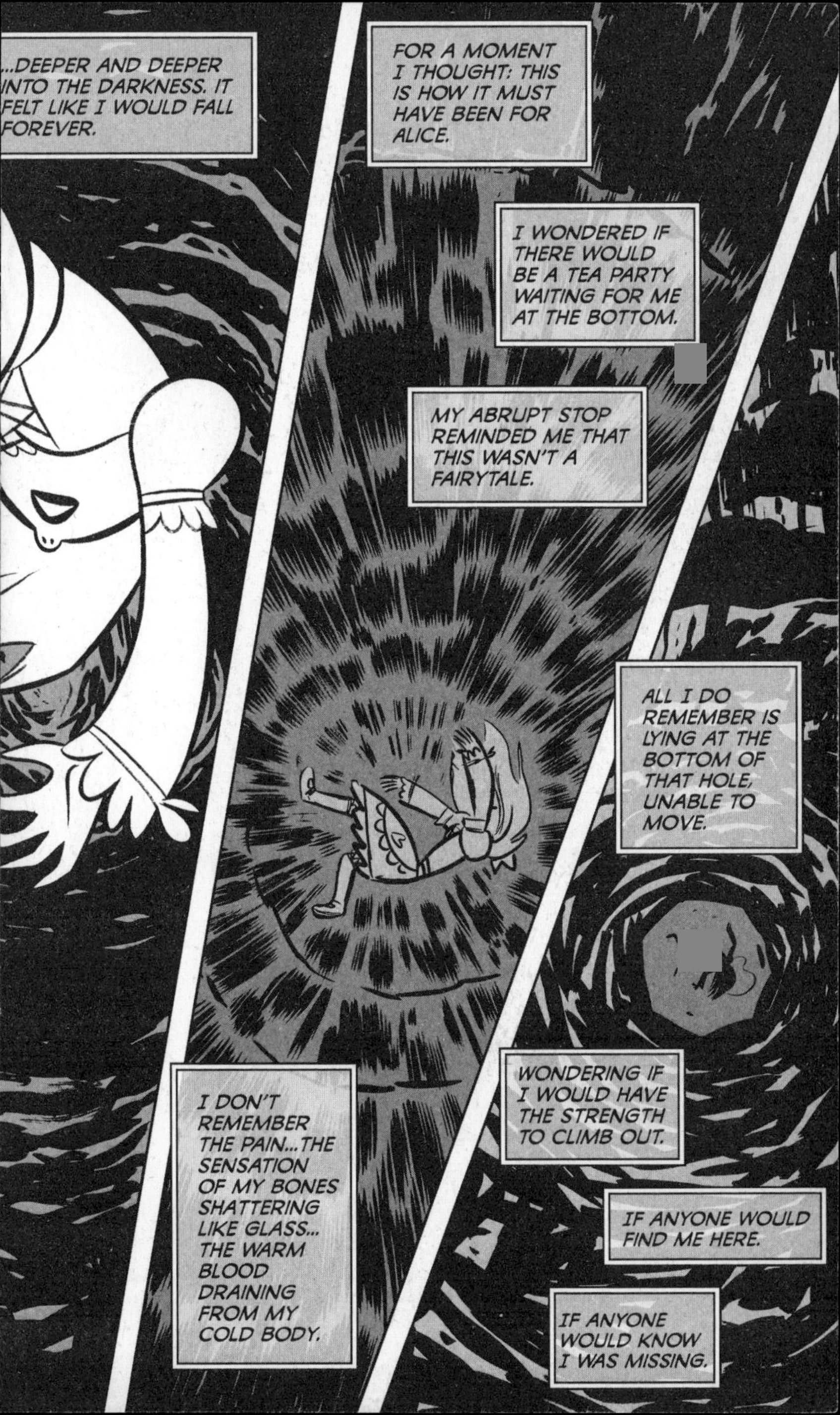
...DEEPER AND DEEPER INTO THE DARKNESS. IT FELT LIKE I WOULD FALL FOREVER.
FOR A MOMENT I THOUGHT: THIS IS HOW IT MUST HAVE BEEN FOR ALICE.
I WONDERED IF THERE WOULD BE A TEA PARTY WAITING FOR ME AT THE BOTTOM.
MY ABRUPT STOP REMINDED ME THAT THIS WASN'T A FAIRYTALE.
I DON'T REMEMBER THE PAIN...THE SENSATION OF MY BONES SHATTERING LIKE GLASS... THE WARM BLOOD DRAINING FROM MY COLD BODY.
ALL I DO REMEMBER IS LYING AT THE BOTTOM OF THAT HOLE, UNABLE TO MOVE.
WONDERING IF I WOULD HAVE THE STRENGTH TO CLIMB OUT.
IF ANYONE WOULD FIND ME HERE.
IF ANYONE WOULD KNOW I WAS MISSING.

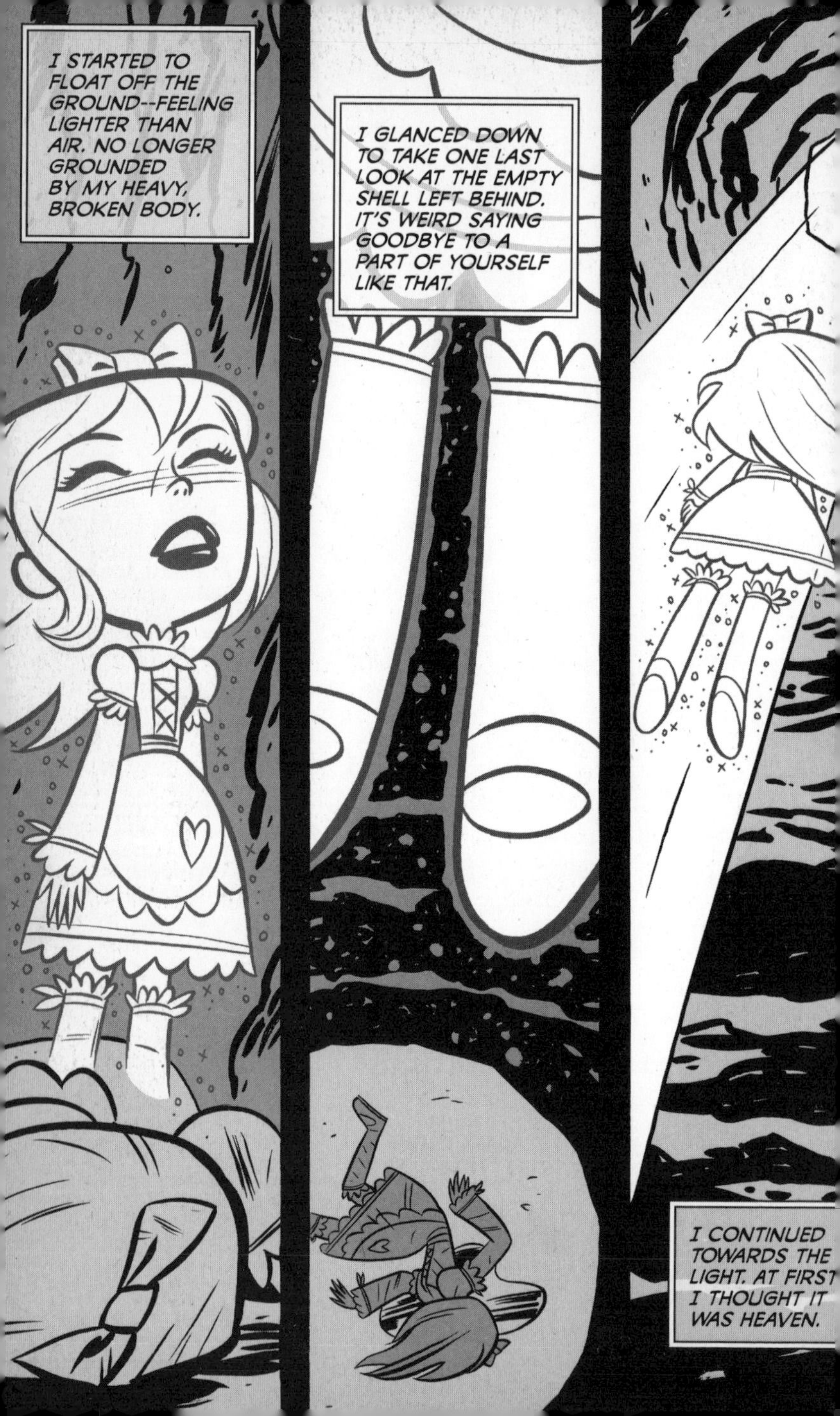
I STARTED TO FLOAT OFF THE GROUND--FEELING LIGHTER THAN AIR. NO LONGER GROUNDED BY MY HEAVY, BROKEN BODY.
I GLANCED DOWN TO TAKE ONE LAST LOOK AT THE EMPTY SHELL LEFT BEHIND. IT'S WEIRD SAYING GOODBYE TO A PART OF YOURSELF LIKE THAT.
I CONTINUED TOWARDS THE LIGHT. AT FIRST I THOUGHT IT WAS HEAVEN.

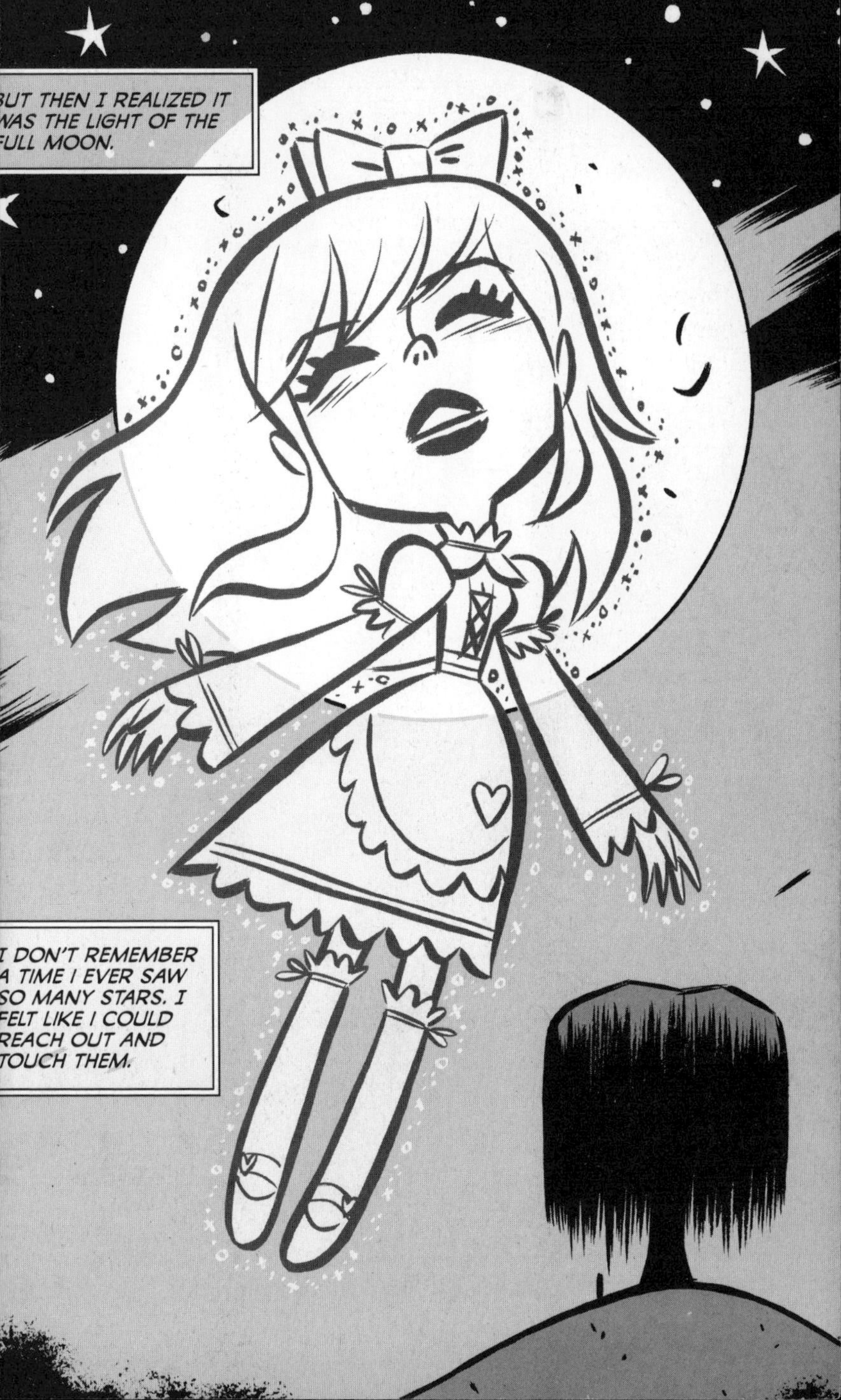
BUT THEN I REALIZED IT WAS THE LIGHT OF THE FULL MOON.
I DON'T REMEMBER A TIME I EVER SAW SO MANY STARS. I FELT LIKE I COULD REACH OUT AND TOUCH THEM.

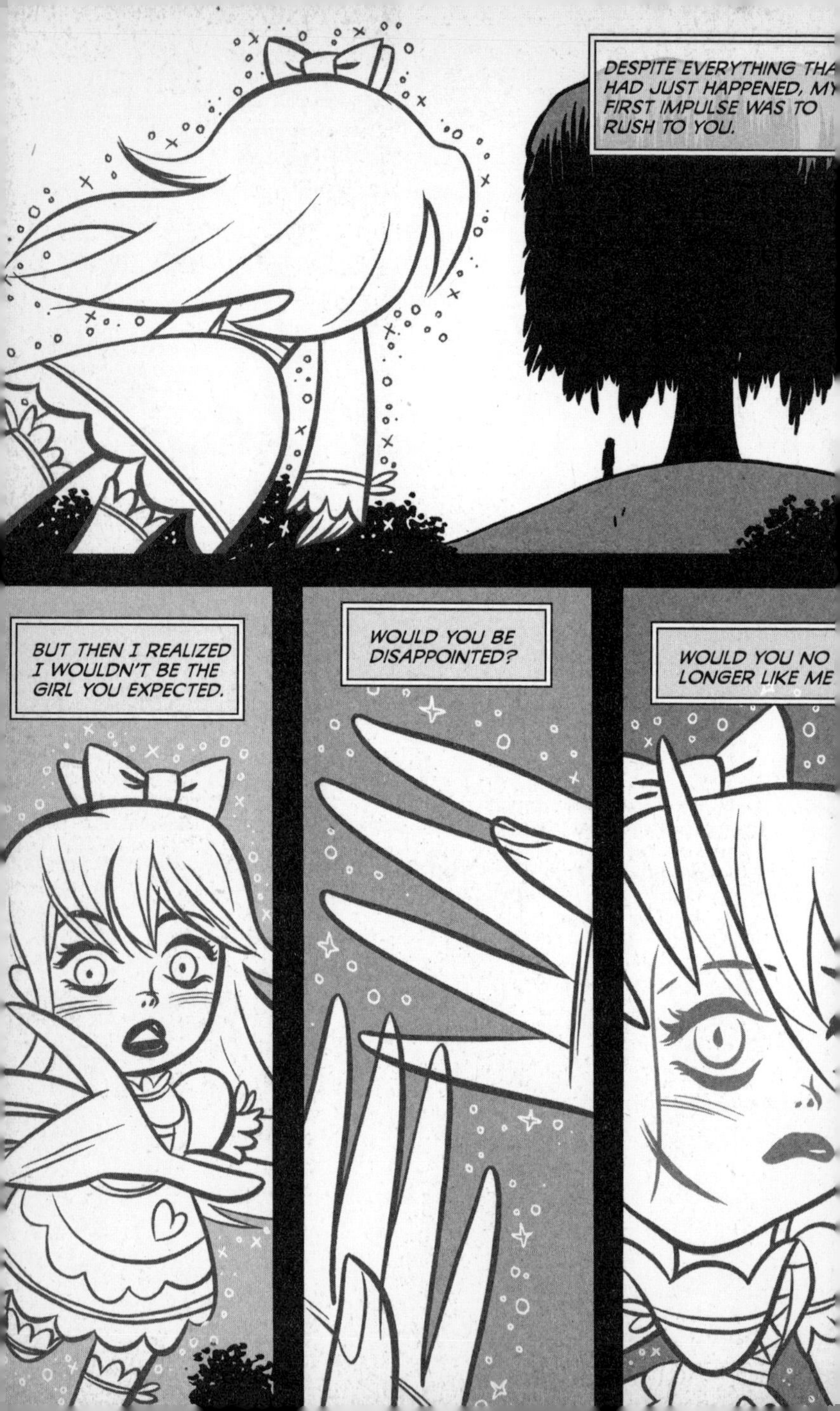
DESPITE EVERYTHING THA
HAD JUST HAPPENED, MY
FIRST IMPULSE WAS TO
RUSH TO YOU.
BUT THEN I REALIZED
I WOULDN'T BE THE
GIRL YOU EXPECTED.
WOULD YOU BE
DISAPPOINTED?
WOULD YOU NO
LONGER LIKE ME

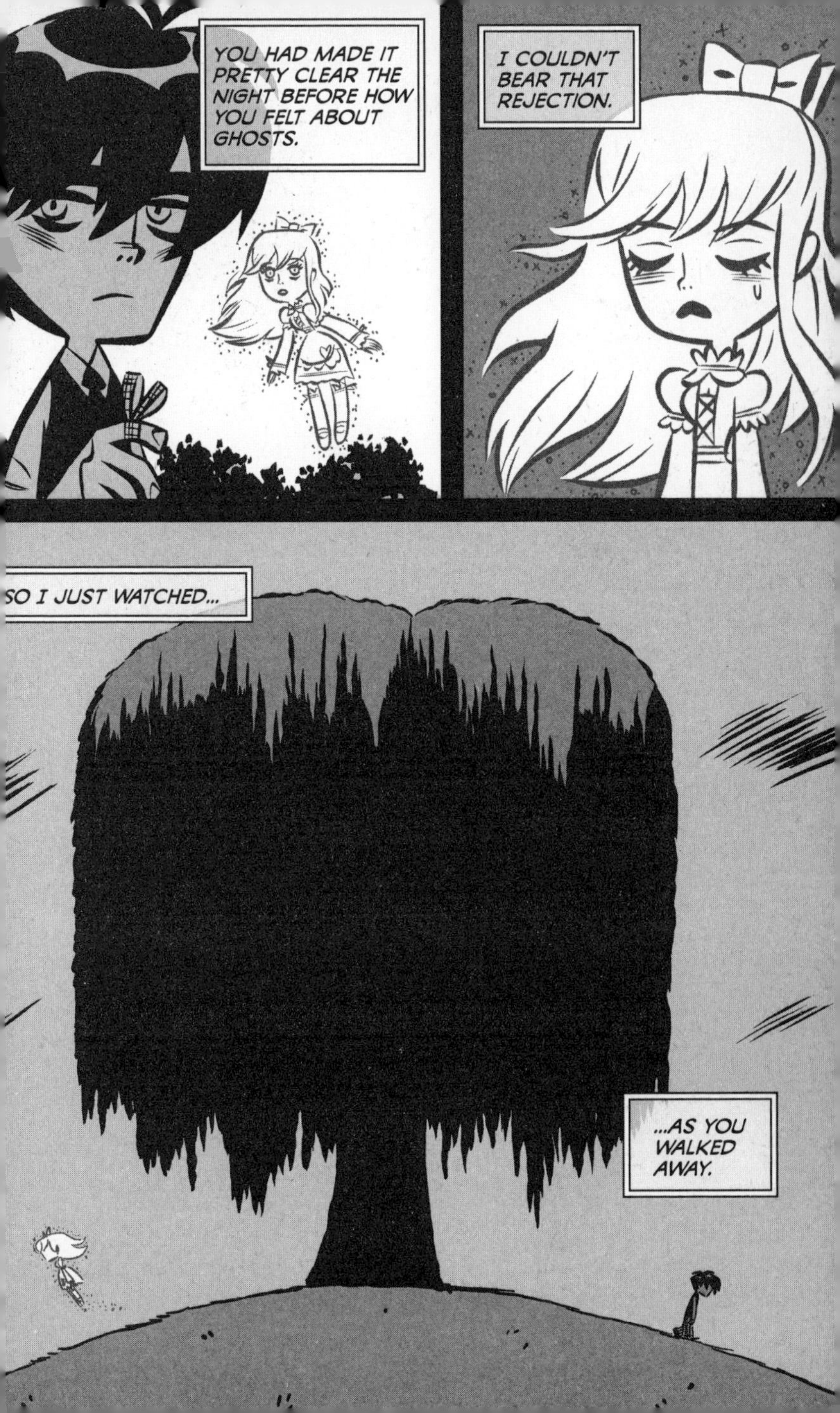
YOU HAD MADE IT PRETTY CLEAR THE NIGHT BEFORE HOW YOU FELT ABOUT GHOSTS.
I COULDN'T BEAR THAT REJECTION.
SO I JUST WATCHED...
...AS YOU WALKED AWAY.

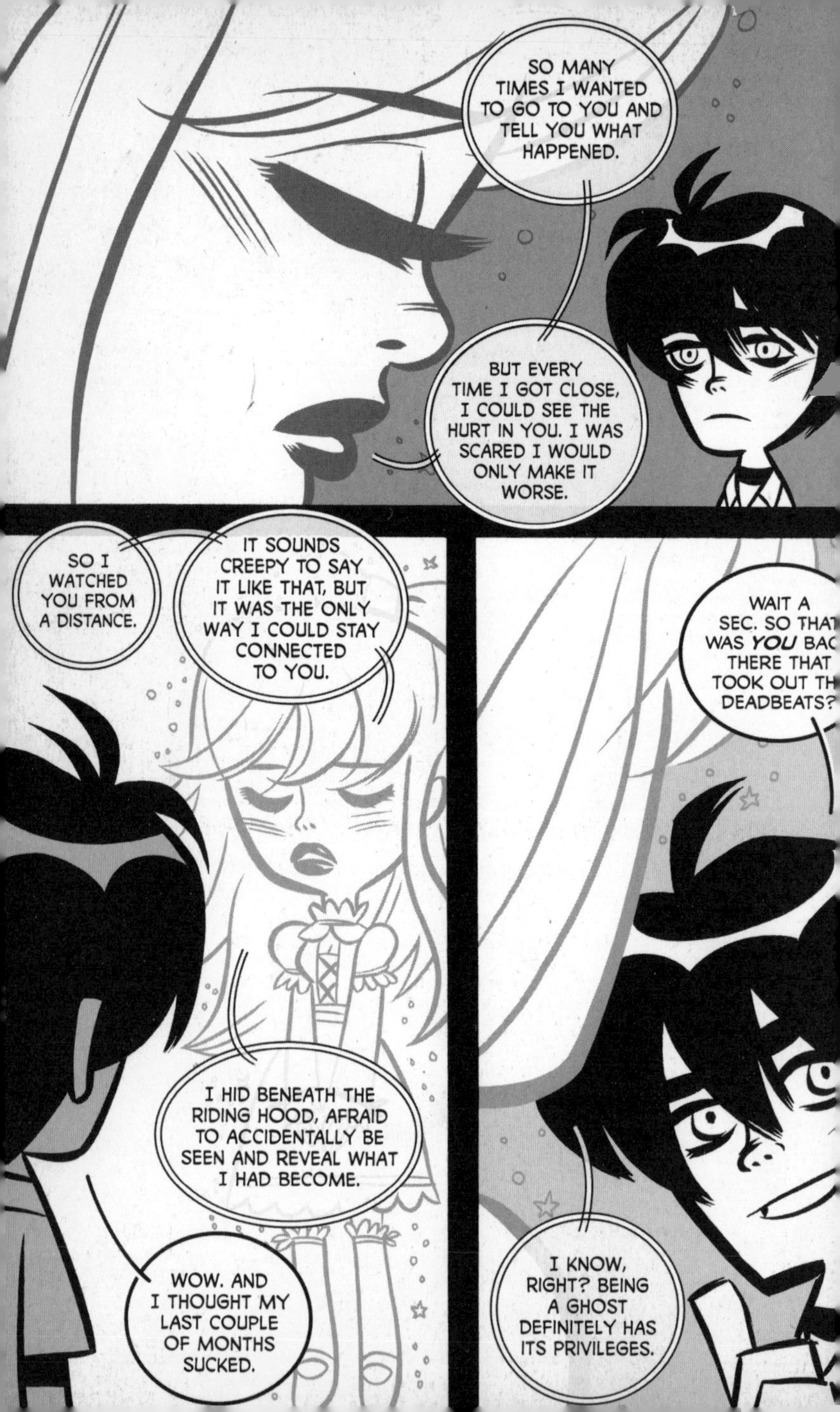

SO MANY TIMES I WANTED TO GO TO YOU AND TELL YOU WHAT HAPPENED.
BUT EVERY TIME I GOT CLOSE, I COULD SEE THE HURT IN YOU. I WAS SCARED I WOULD ONLY MAKE IT WORSE.
SO I WATCHED YOU FROM A DISTANCE.
IT SOUNDS CREEPY TO SAY IT LIKE THAT, BUT IT WAS THE ONLY WAY I COULD STAY CONNECTED TO YOU.
I HID BENEATH THE RIDING HOOD, AFRAID TO ACCIDENTALLY BE SEEN AND REVEAL WHAT I HAD BECOME.
WOW. AND I THOUGHT MY LAST COUPLE OF MONTHS SUCKED.
WAIT A SEC. SO THAT WAS *YOU* BAC THERE THAT TOOK OUT TH DEADBEATS?
I KNOW, RIGHT? BEING A GHOST DEFINITELY HAS ITS PRIVILEGES.

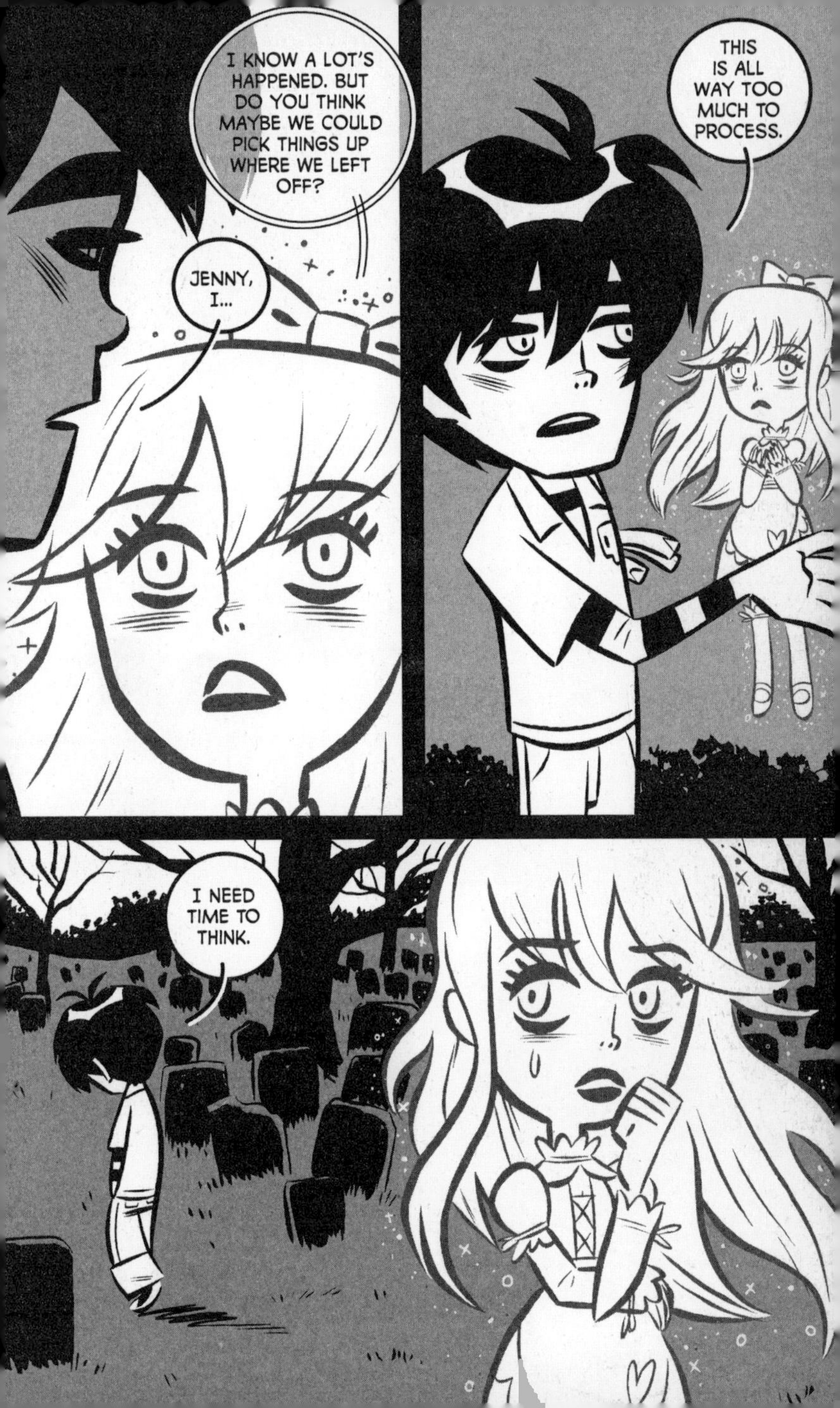
I KNOW A LOT'S HAPPENED. BUT DO YOU THINK MAYBE WE COULD PICK THINGS UP WHERE WE LEFT OFF?
JENNY, I...
THIS IS ALL WAY TOO MUCH TO PROCESS.
I NEED TIME TO THINK.

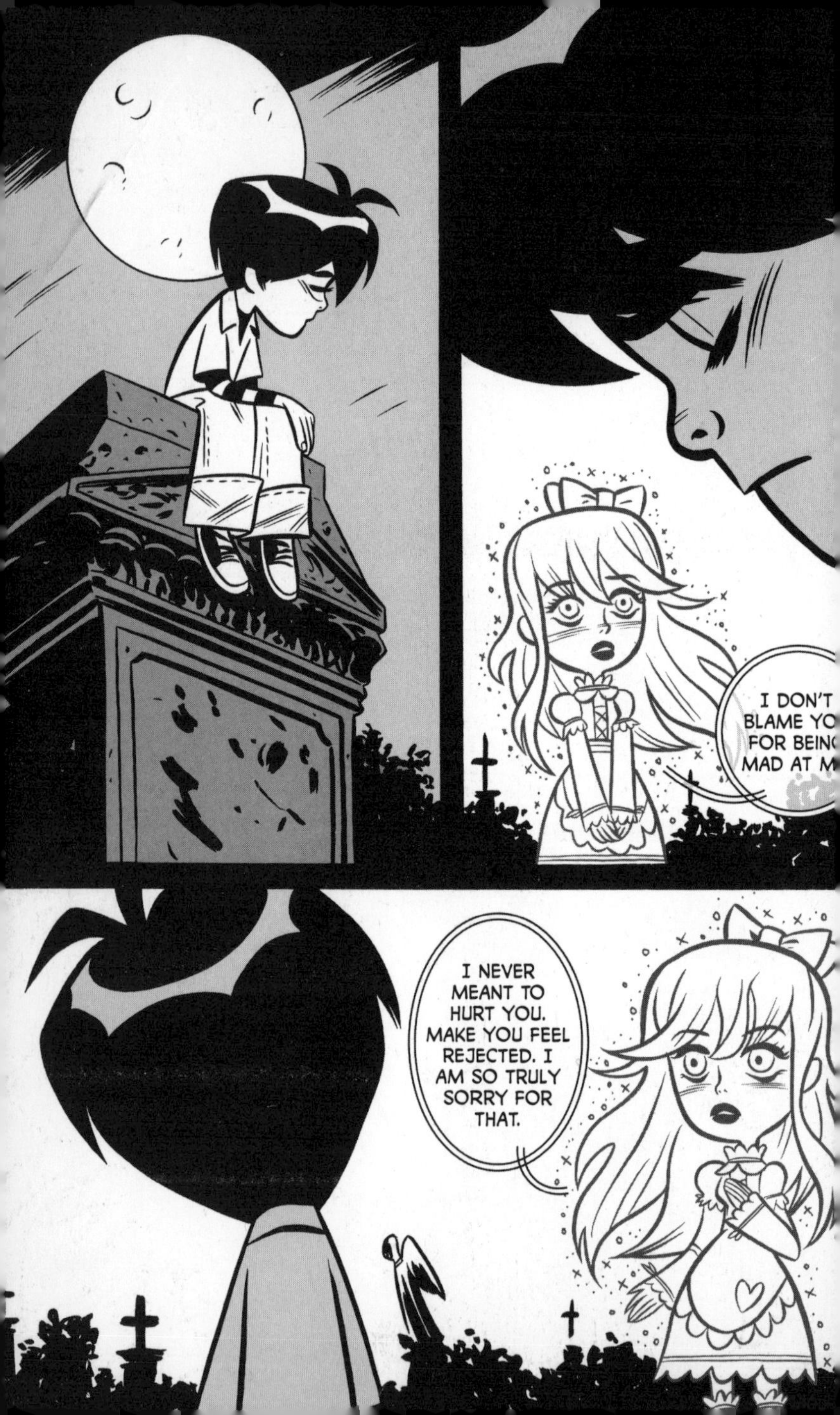
I DON'T BLAME YO FOR BEIN MAD AT M
I NEVER MEANT TO HURT YOU. MAKE YOU FEEL REJECTED. I AM SO TRULY SORRY FOR THAT.

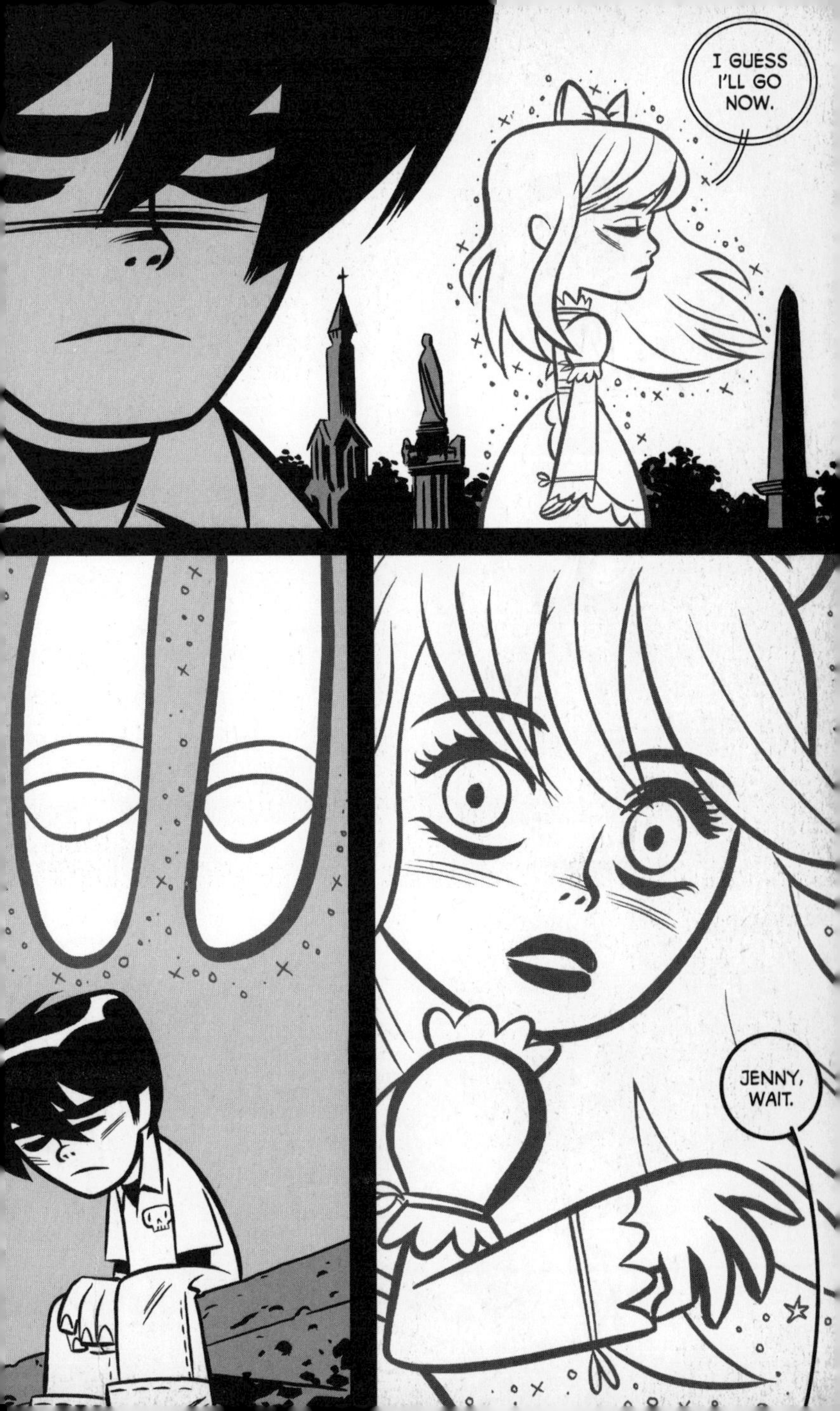
I GUESS I'LL GO NOW.
JENNY, WAIT.

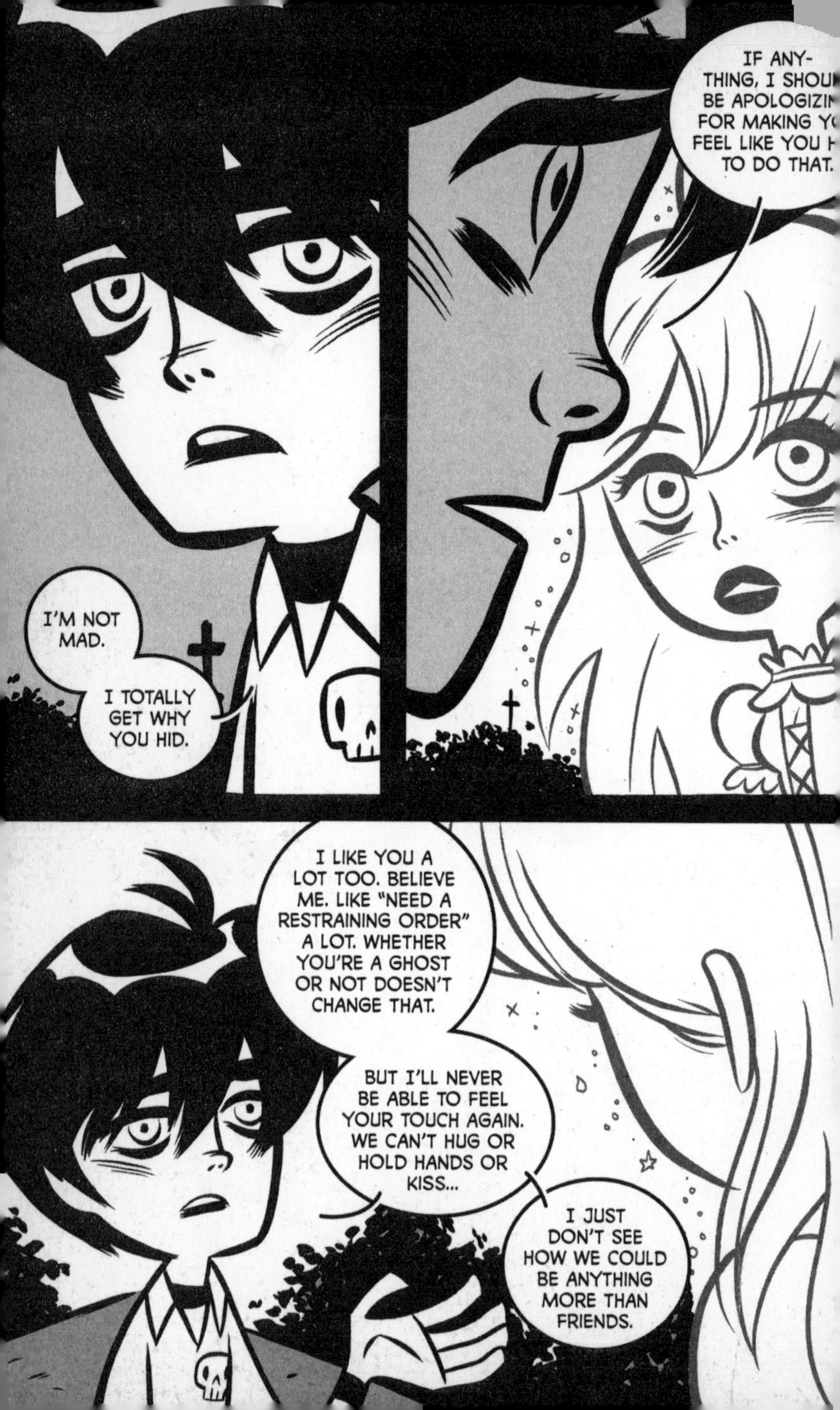
I'M NOT MAD.
I TOTALLY GET WHY YOU HID.
IF ANY-THING, I SHOU BE APOLOGIZIN FOR MAKING Y FEEL LIKE YOU TO DO THAT.
I LIKE YOU A LOT TOO. BELIEVE ME. LIKE "NEED A RESTRAINING ORDER" A LOT. WHETHER YOU'RE A GHOST OR NOT DOESN'T CHANGE THAT.
BUT I'LL NEVER BE ABLE TO FEEL YOUR TOUCH AGAIN. WE CAN'T HUG OR HOLD HANDS OR KISS...
I JUST DON'T SEE HOW WE COULD BE ANYTHING MORE THAN FRIENDS.

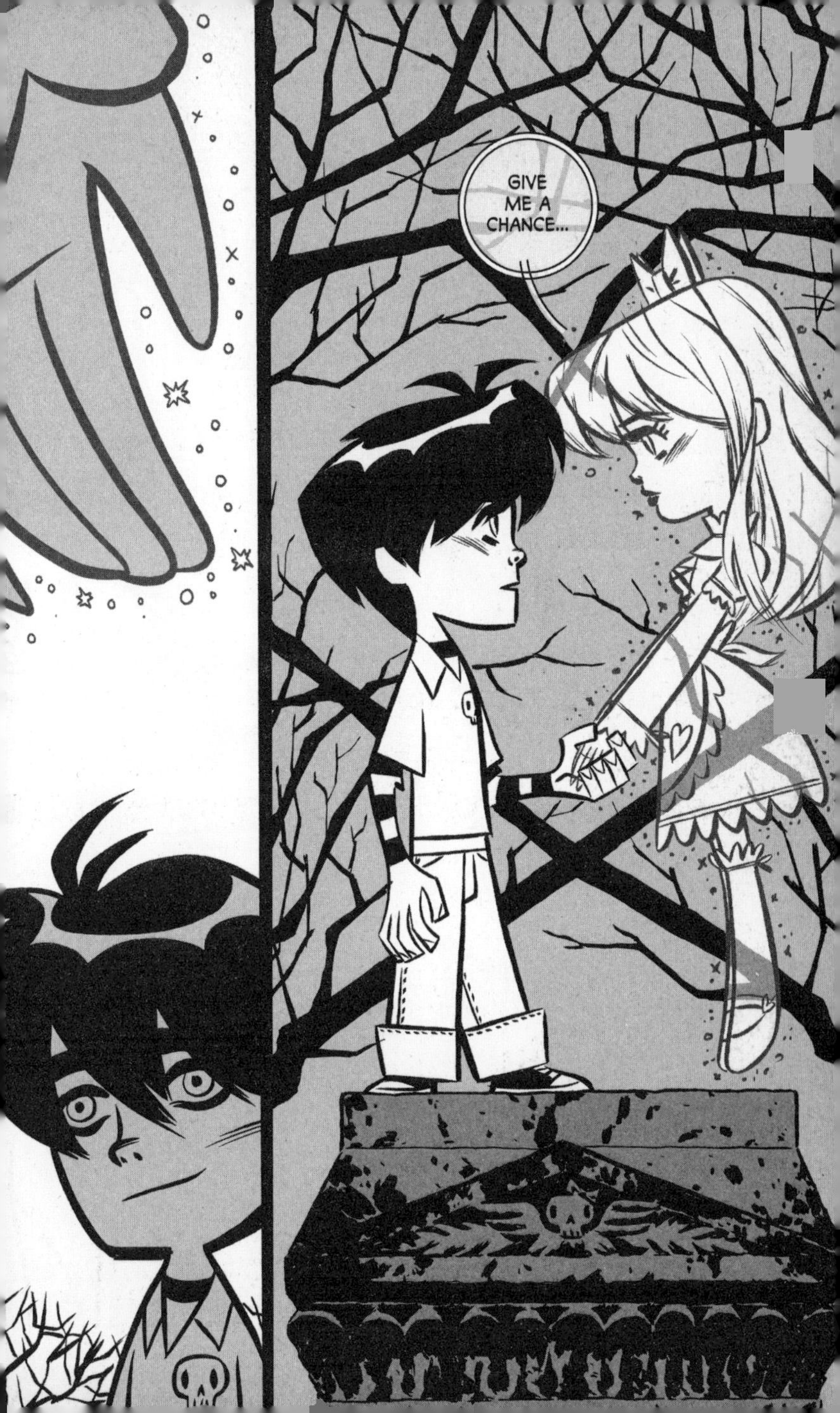
GIVE ME A CHANCE...

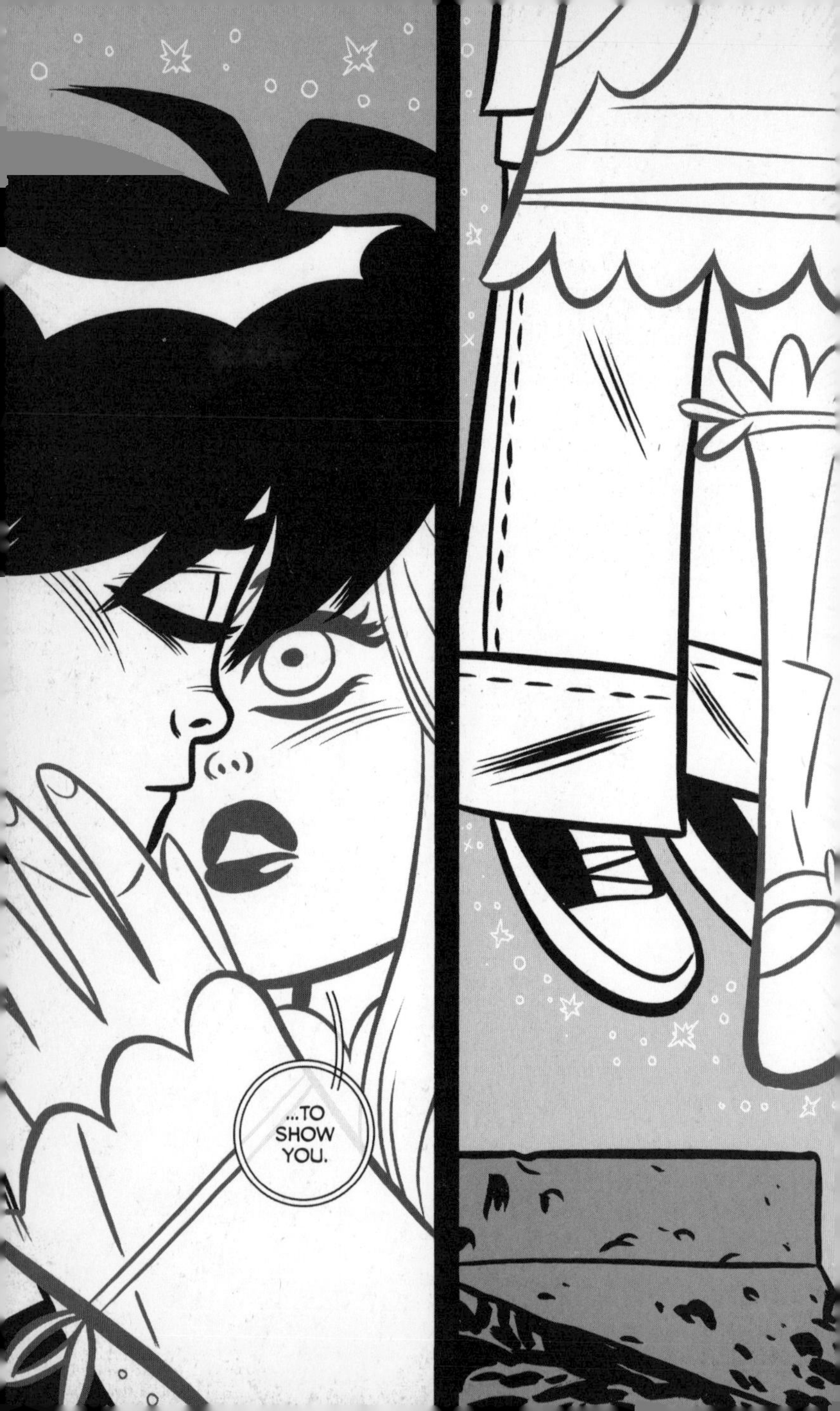
...TO SHOW YOU.

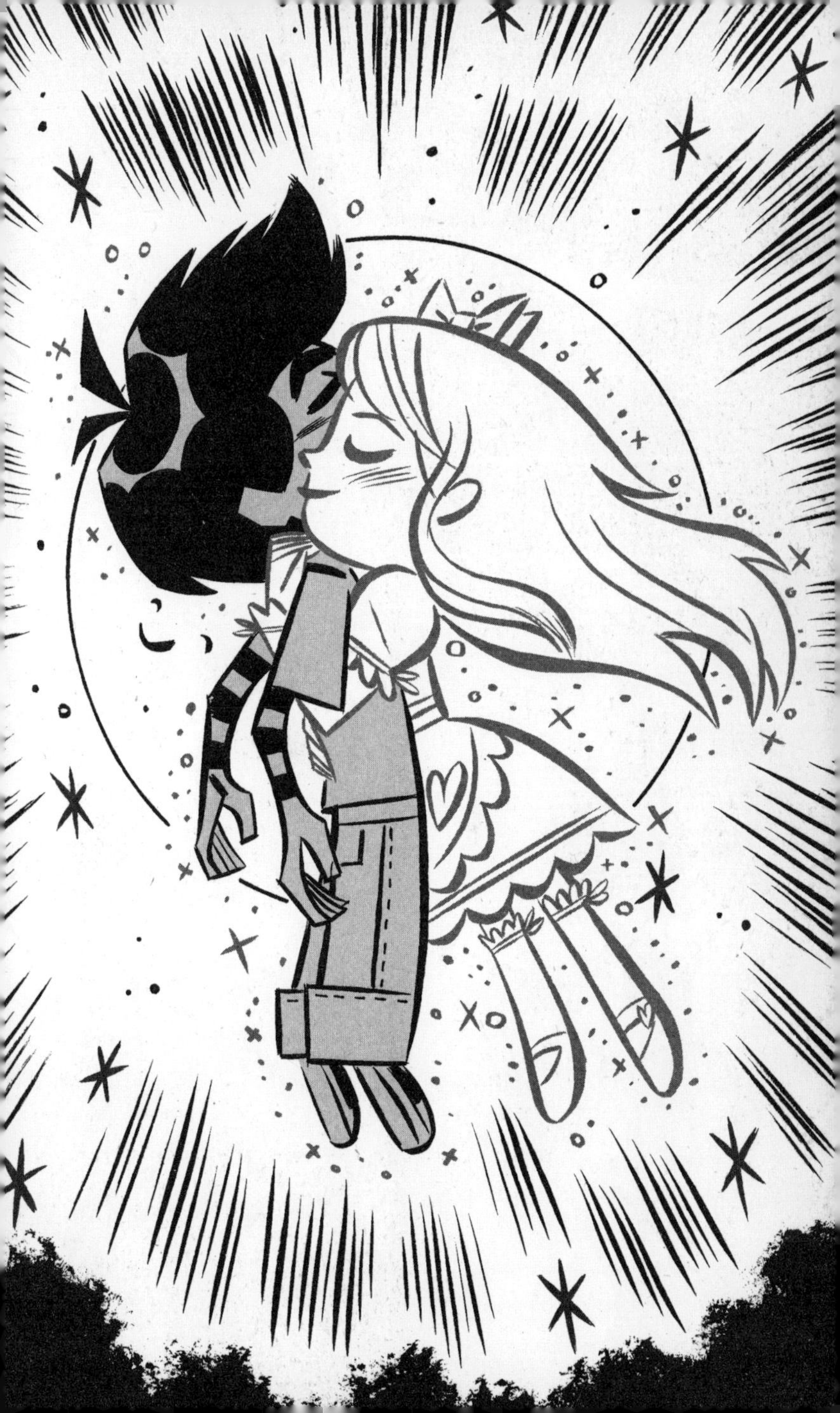

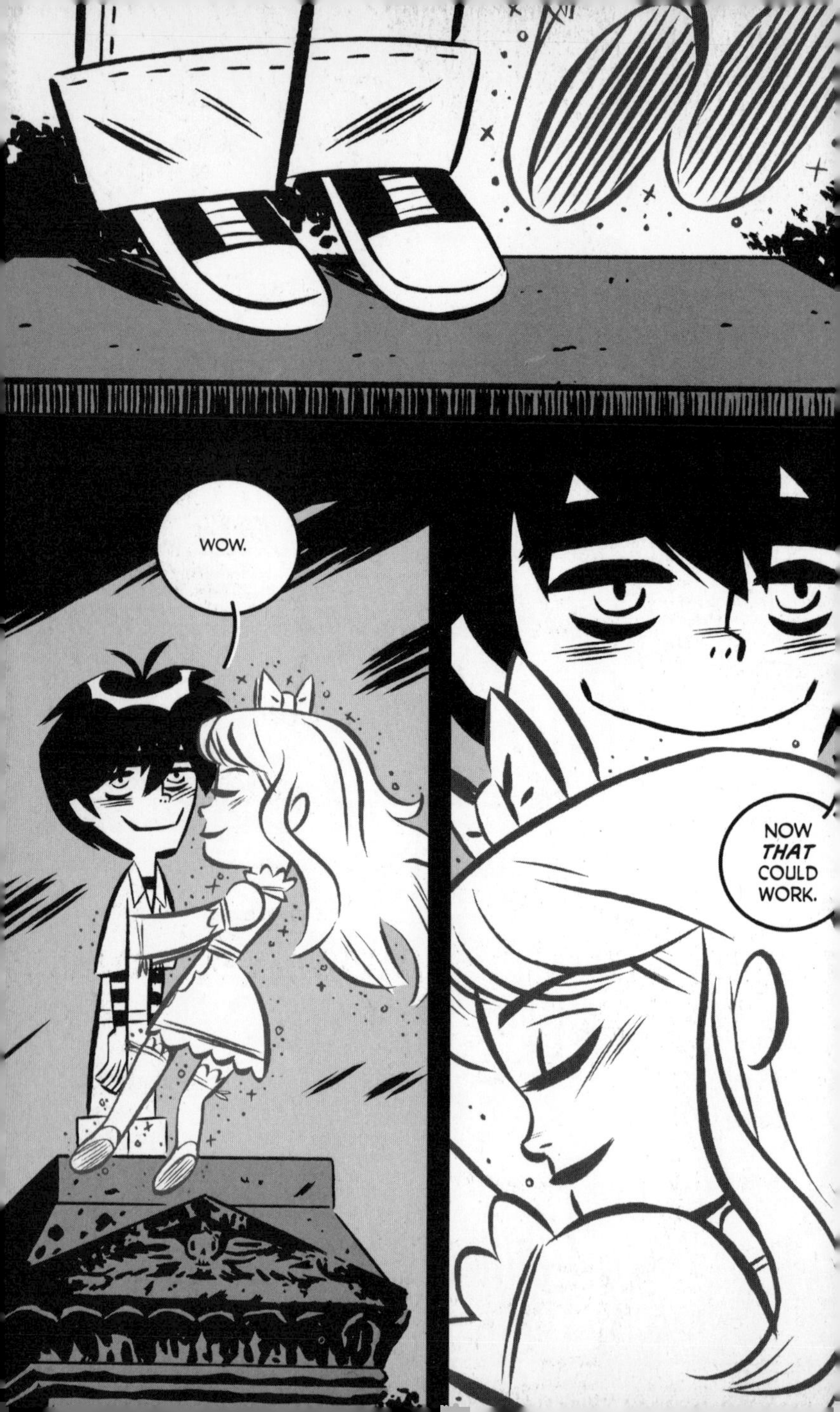
WOW.
NOW *THAT* COULD WORK.

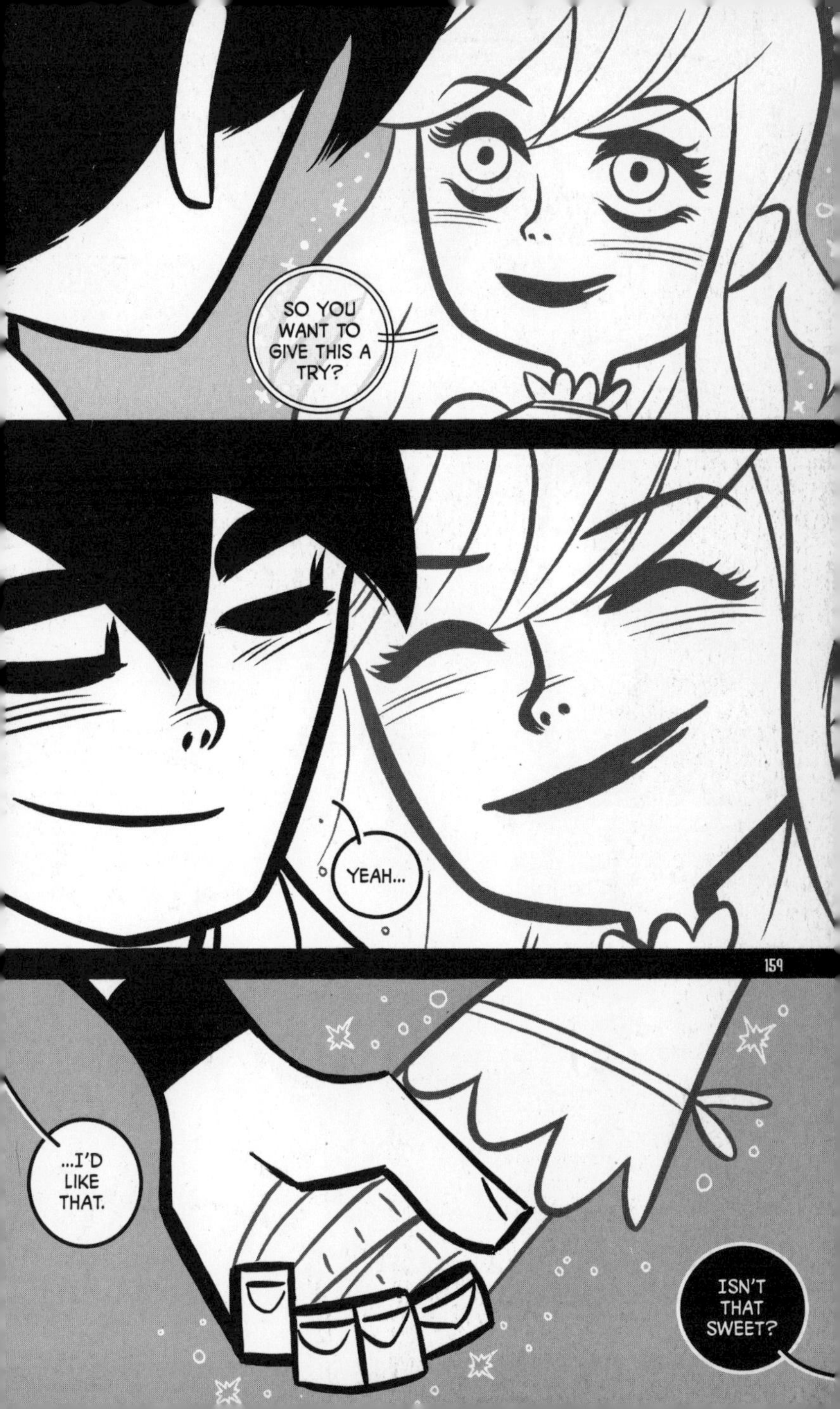
SO YOU WANT TO GIVE THIS A TRY?
YEAH...
...I'D LIKE THAT.
ISN'T THAT SWEET?

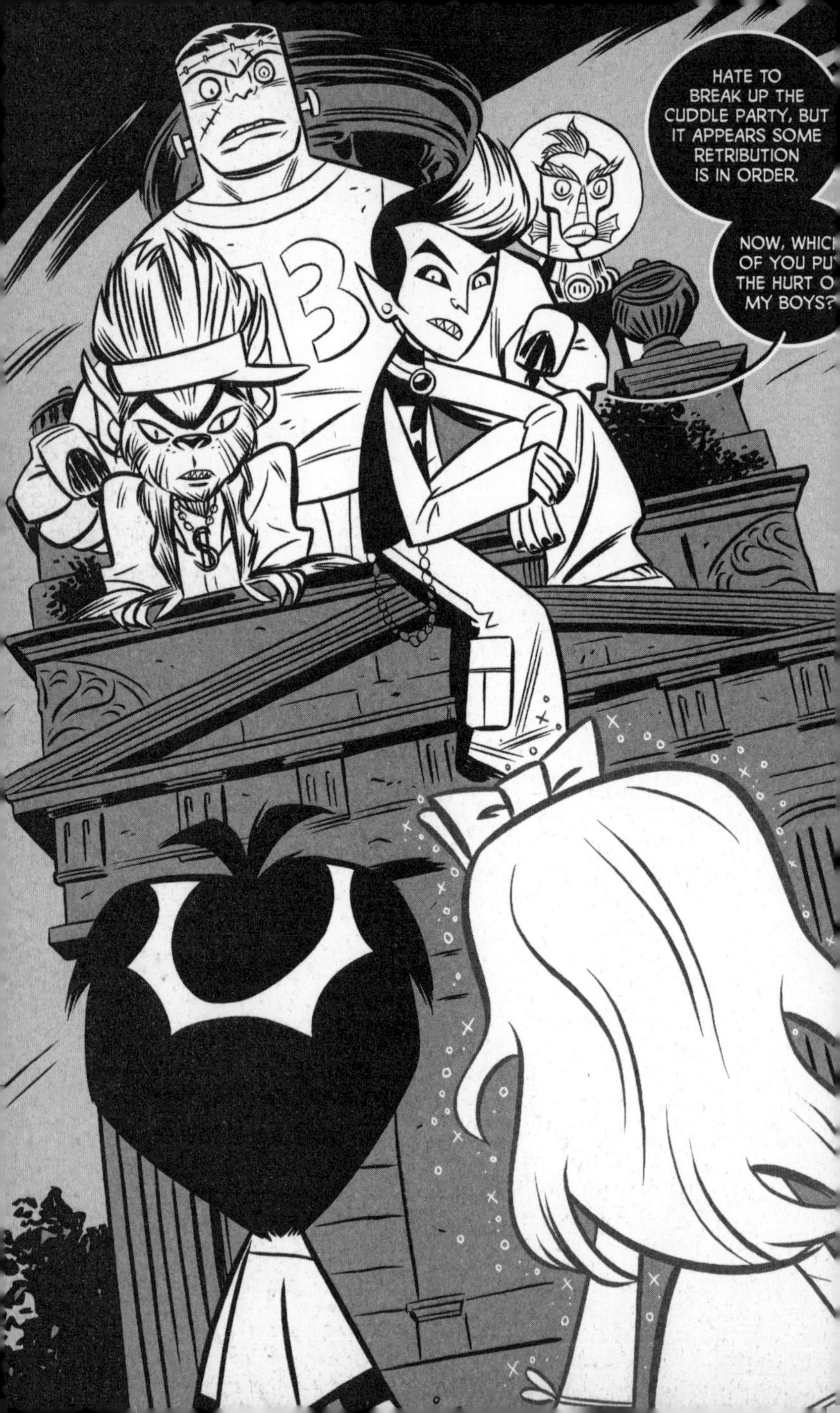
HATE TO BREAK UP THE CUDDLE PARTY, BUT IT APPEARS SOME RETRIBUTION IS IN ORDER.
NOW, WHIC OF YOU PU THE HURT O MY BOYS?

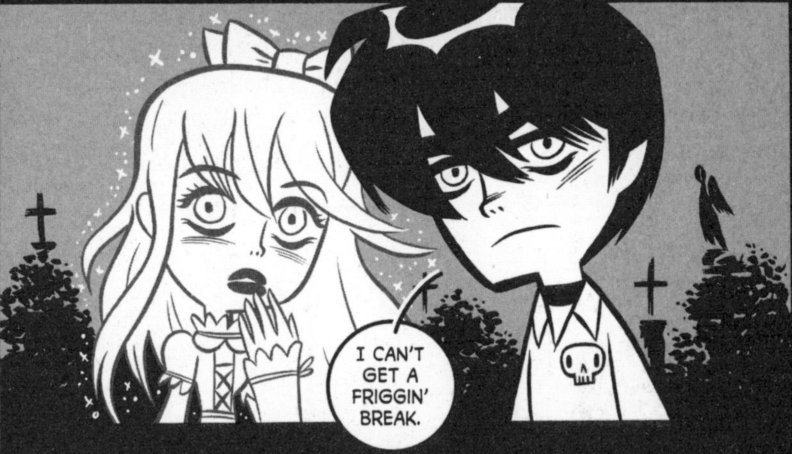
I CAN'T GET A FRIGGIN' BREAK.

TO BE CONTINUED...

IN THE NEXT

My Dead Girlfriend ™

Finney, Jenny, and the Deadbeats
resolve their unfinished business,
but in a way that no one -- especially
Finney -- will ever suspect.

And what will Dahlia think
of Finney's new girlfriend?

Finney's life is about to get
a whole lot MORE complicated!

THE ARCADE

Featuring the work of
MICHAEL ALLRED
J. BONE
NICK DERINGTON
SEAN PHILLIPS
ALAN LAU
ROQUE BALLESTEROS
BRAD RAU
ANDI WATSON
COLLEEN COOVER
DEAN HASPIEL
DAN BRERETON

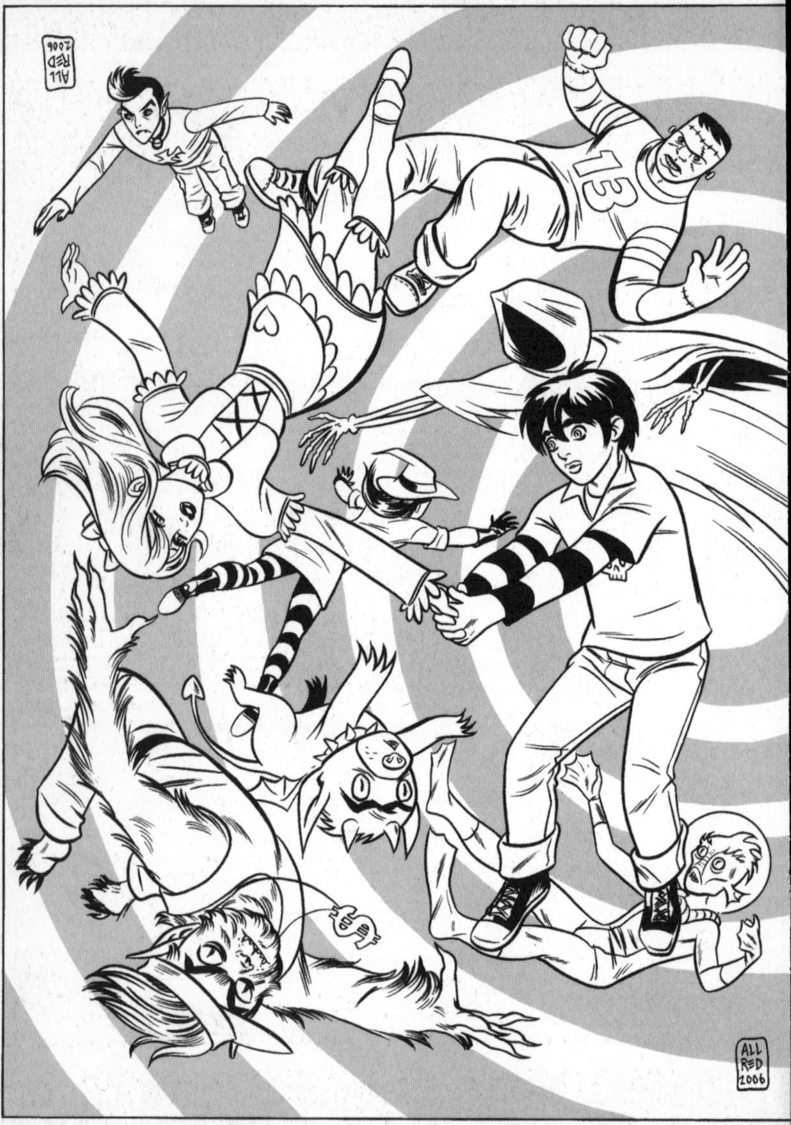
ALL RED 2006

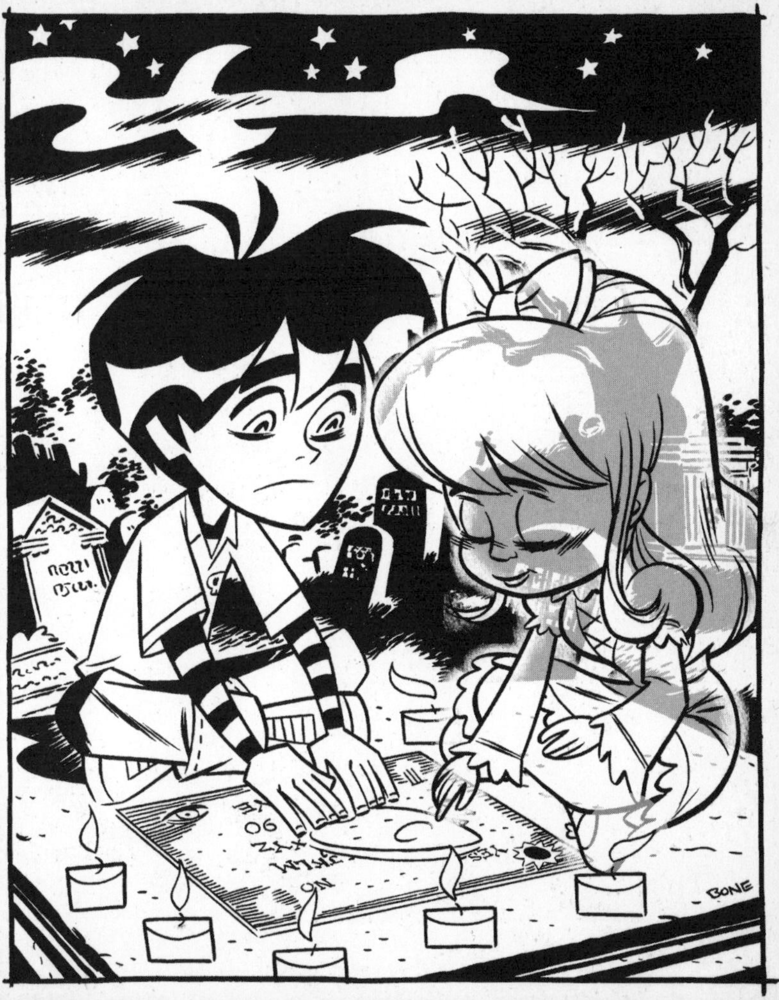
BONE

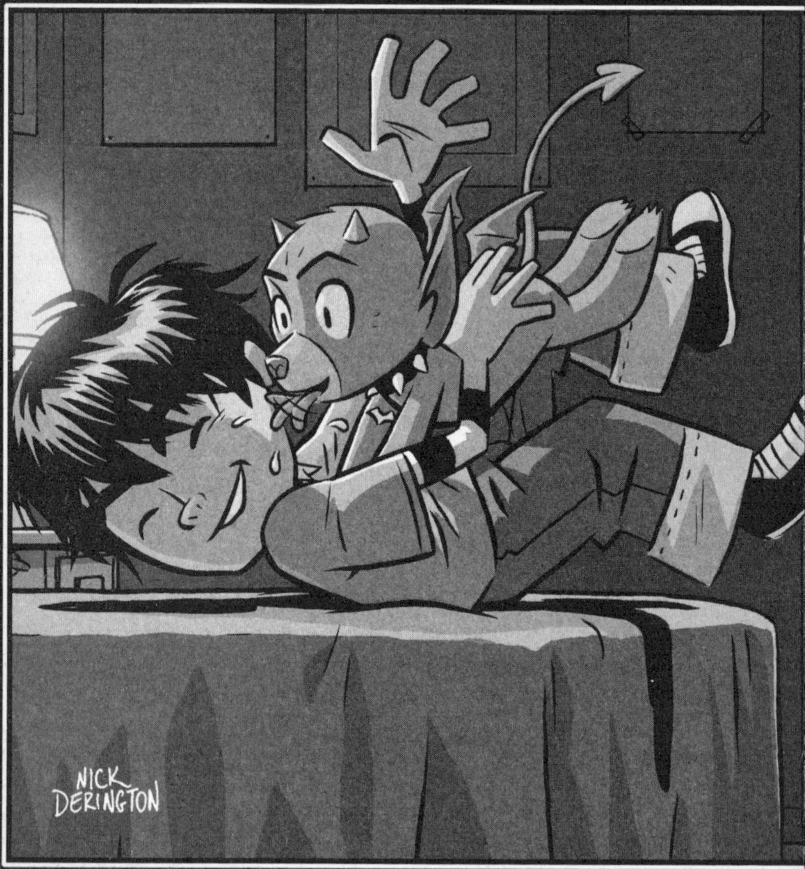
NICK
DERINGTON

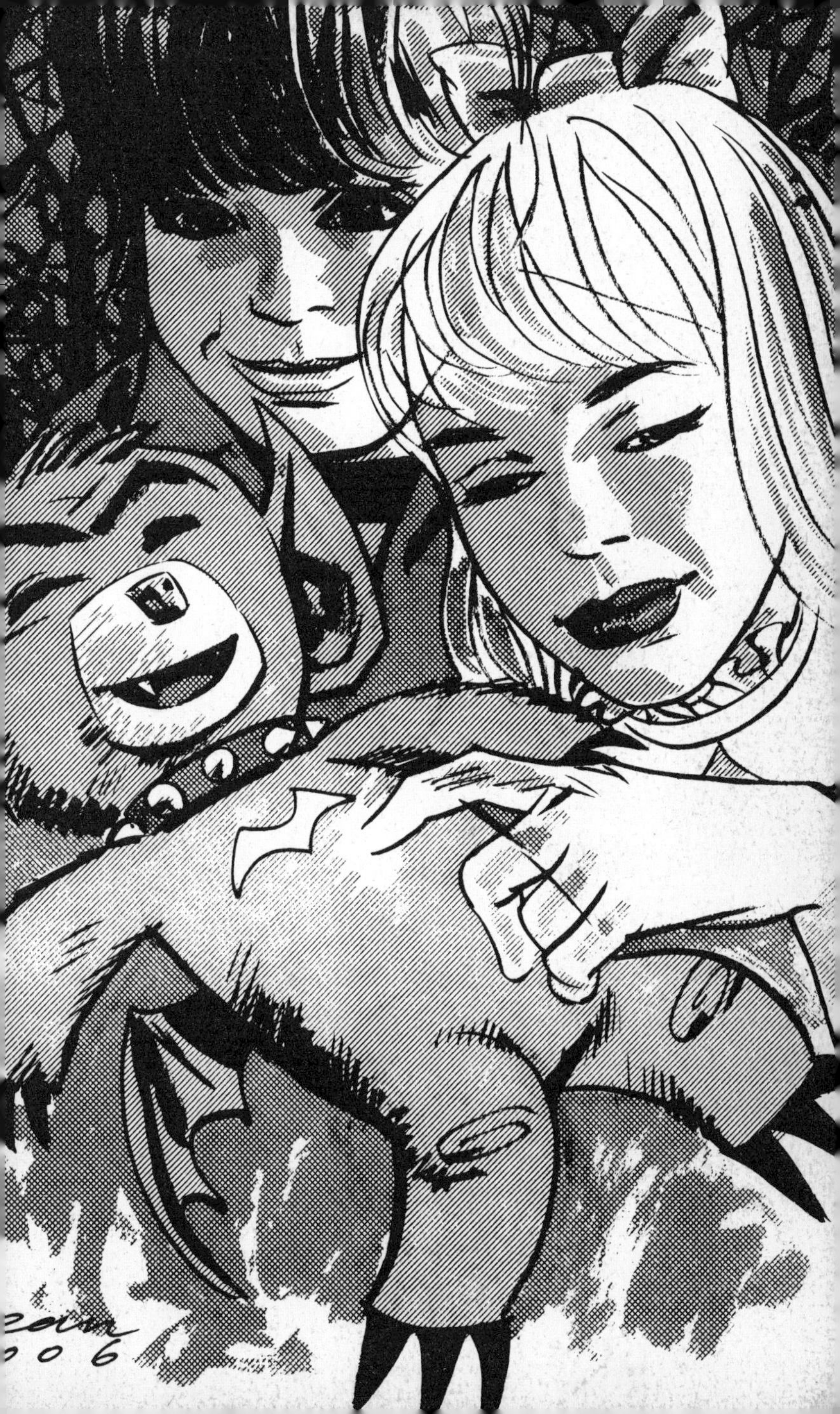

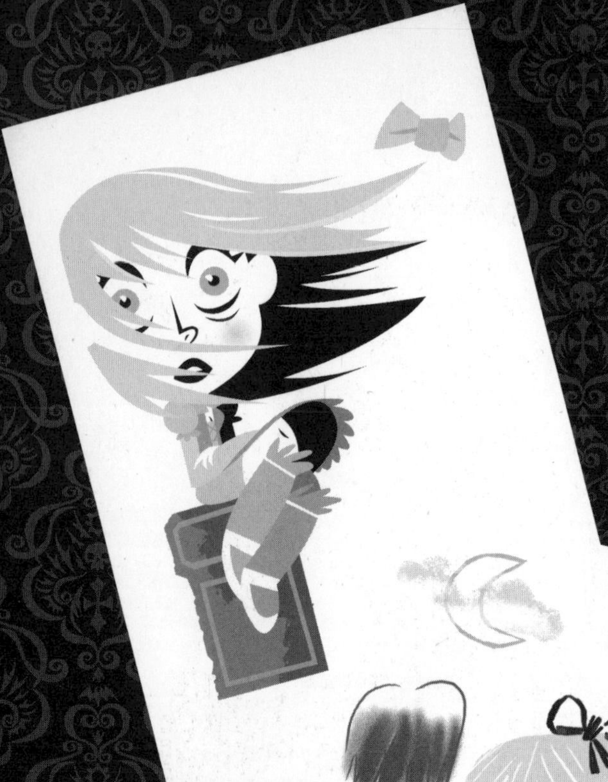

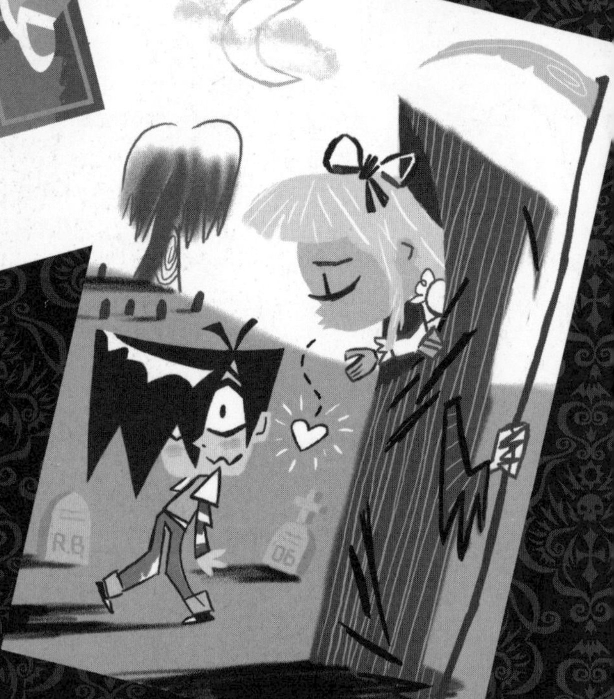
R.B

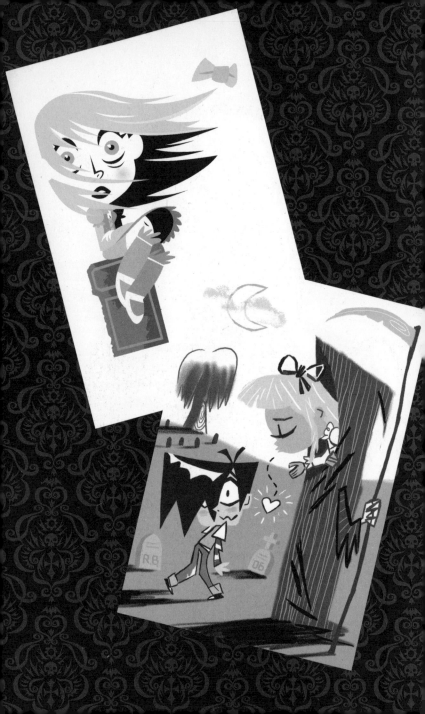

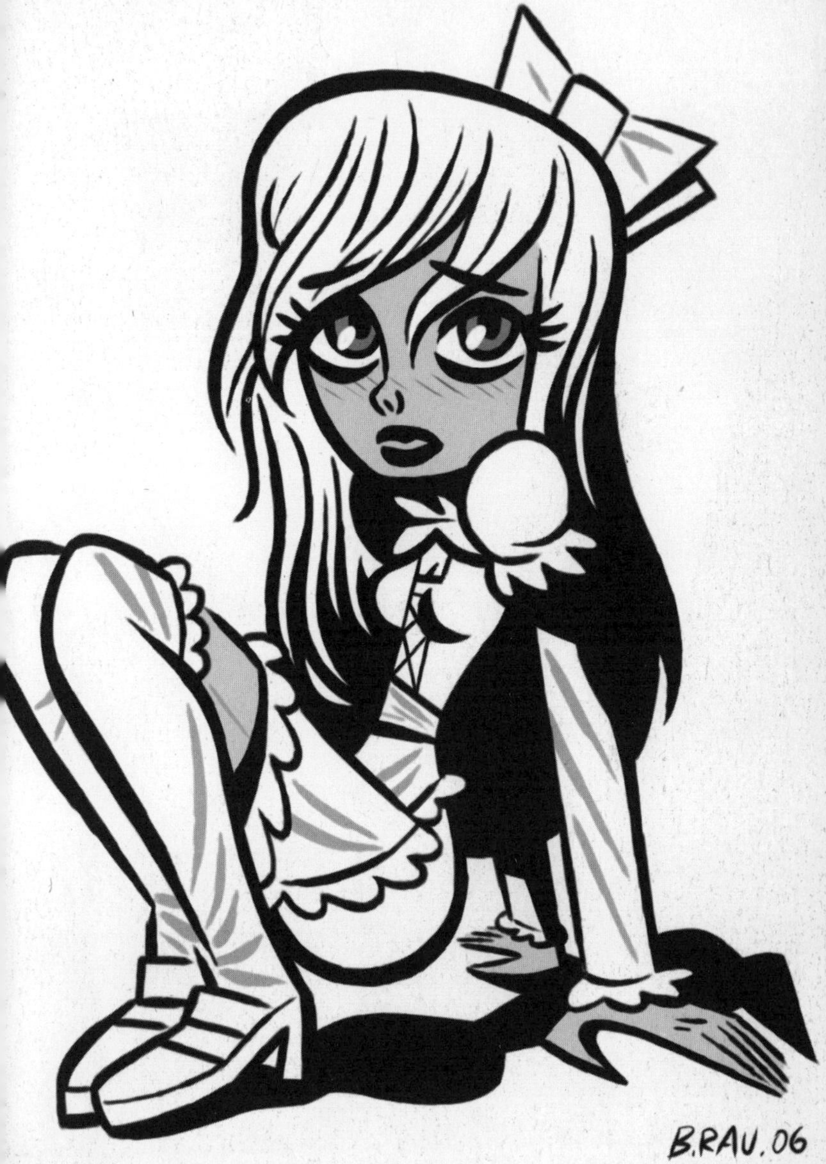
B.RAU.06

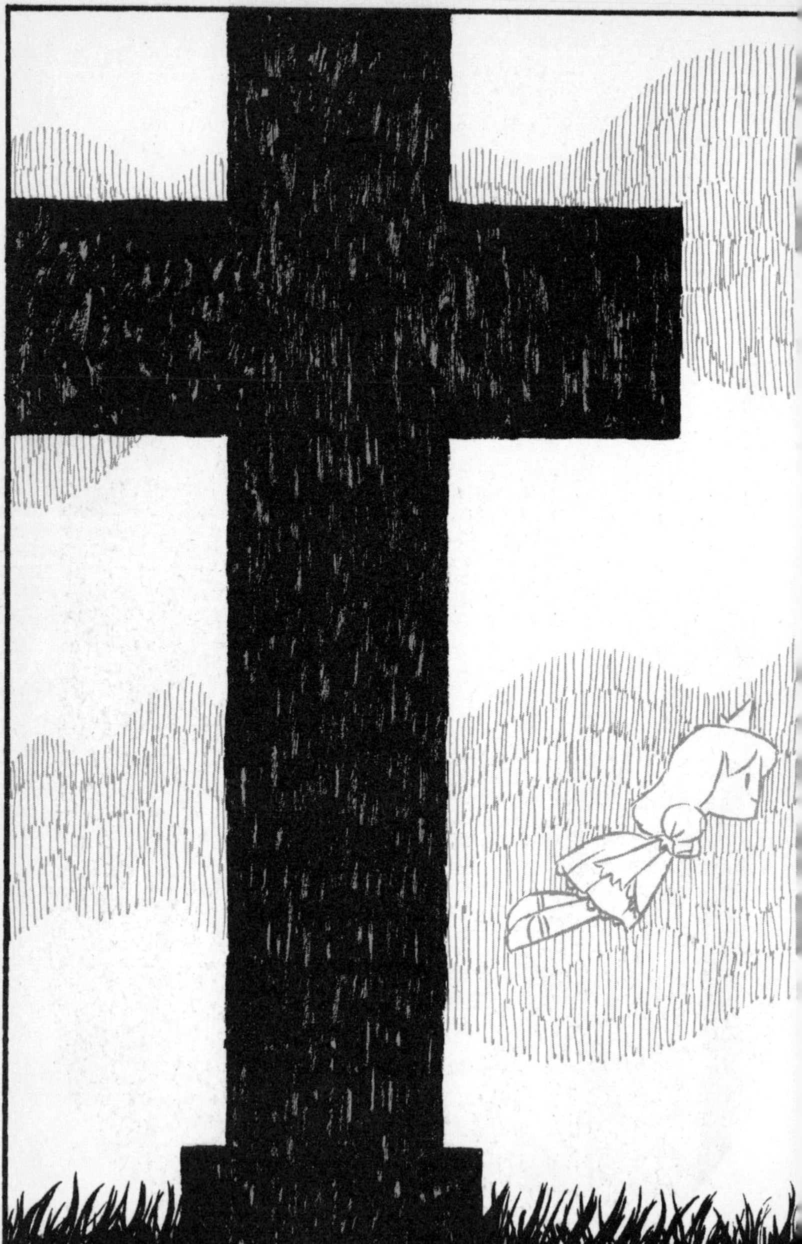

andi

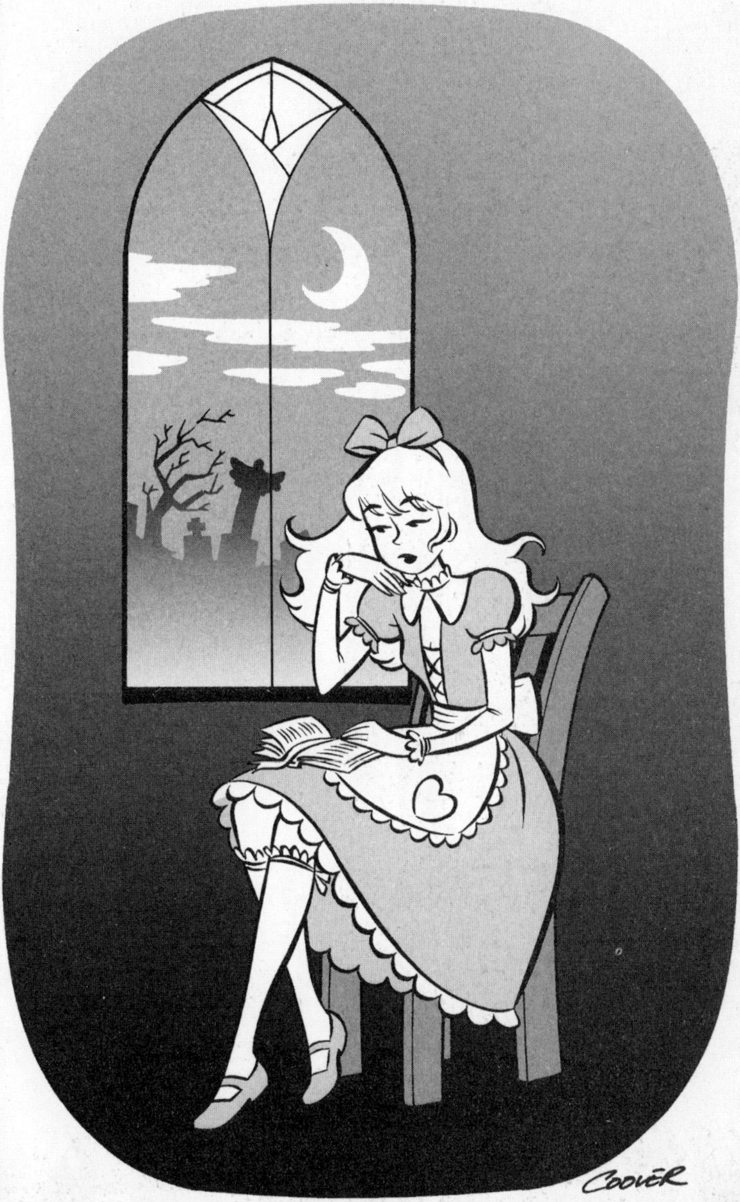
COOVER

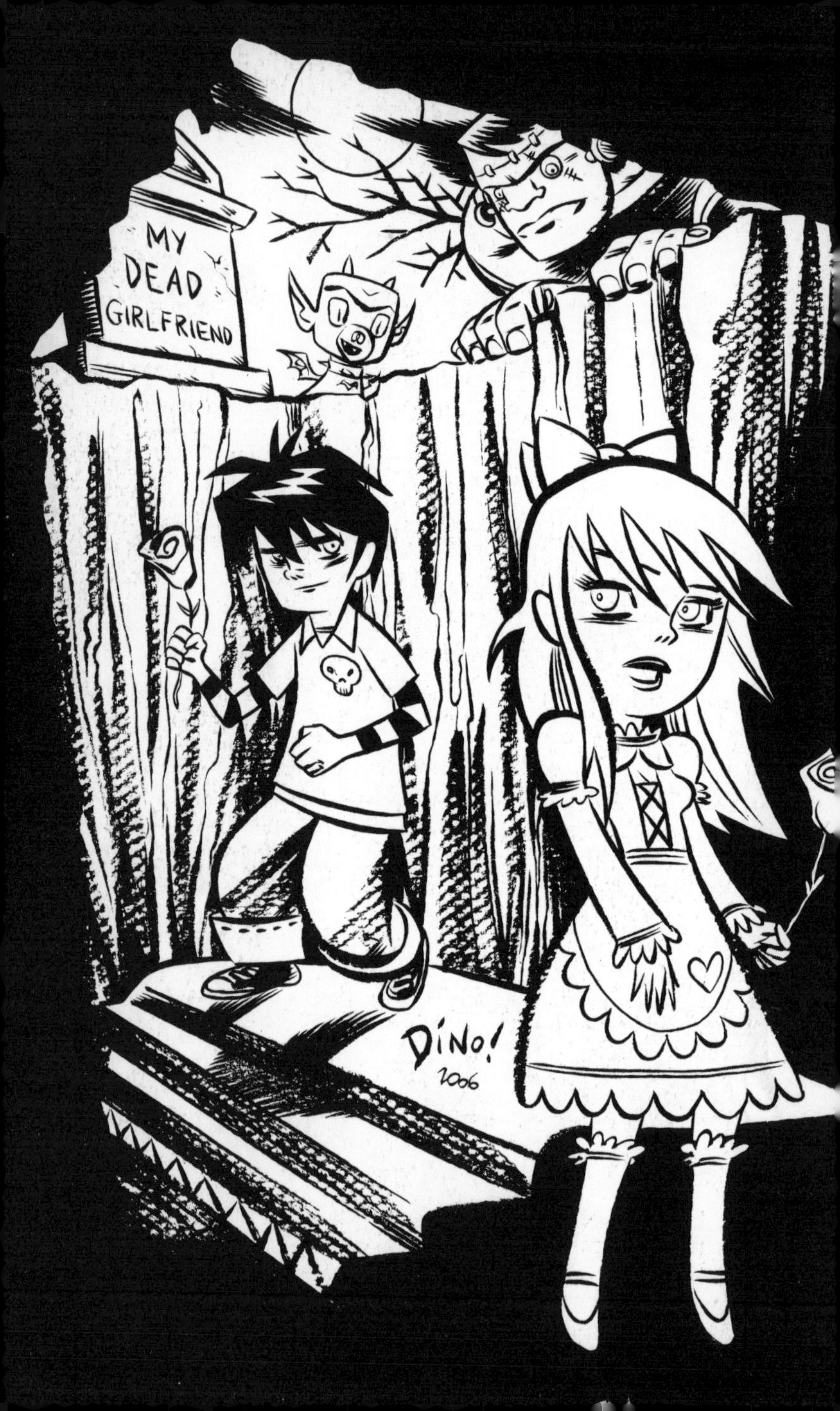
MY DEAD GIRLFRIEND
DINO! 2006

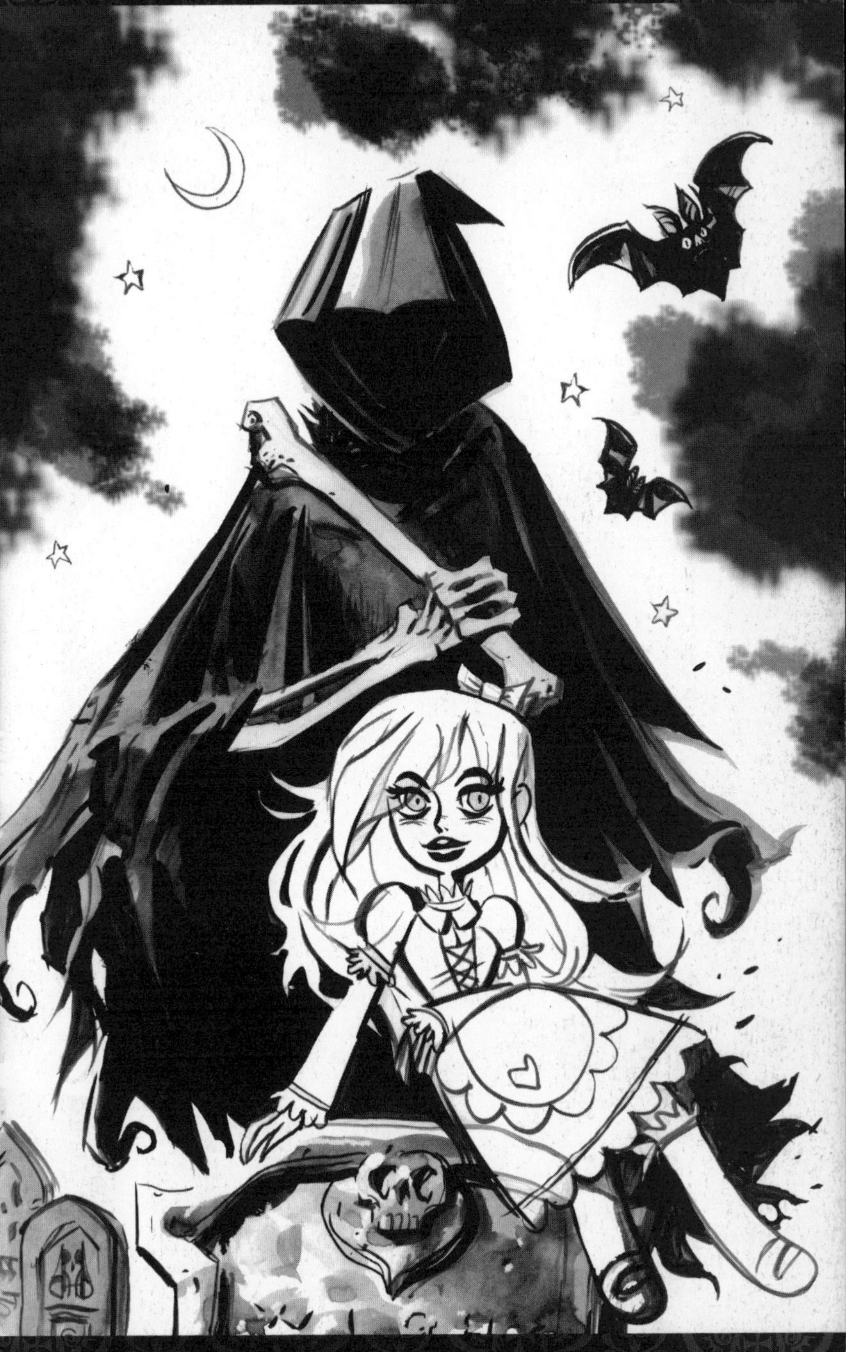

THE VAULT

THIS PAGE:
The first and final character design of Finney Bleak

OPPOSITE:
Promotional illustration of Finney

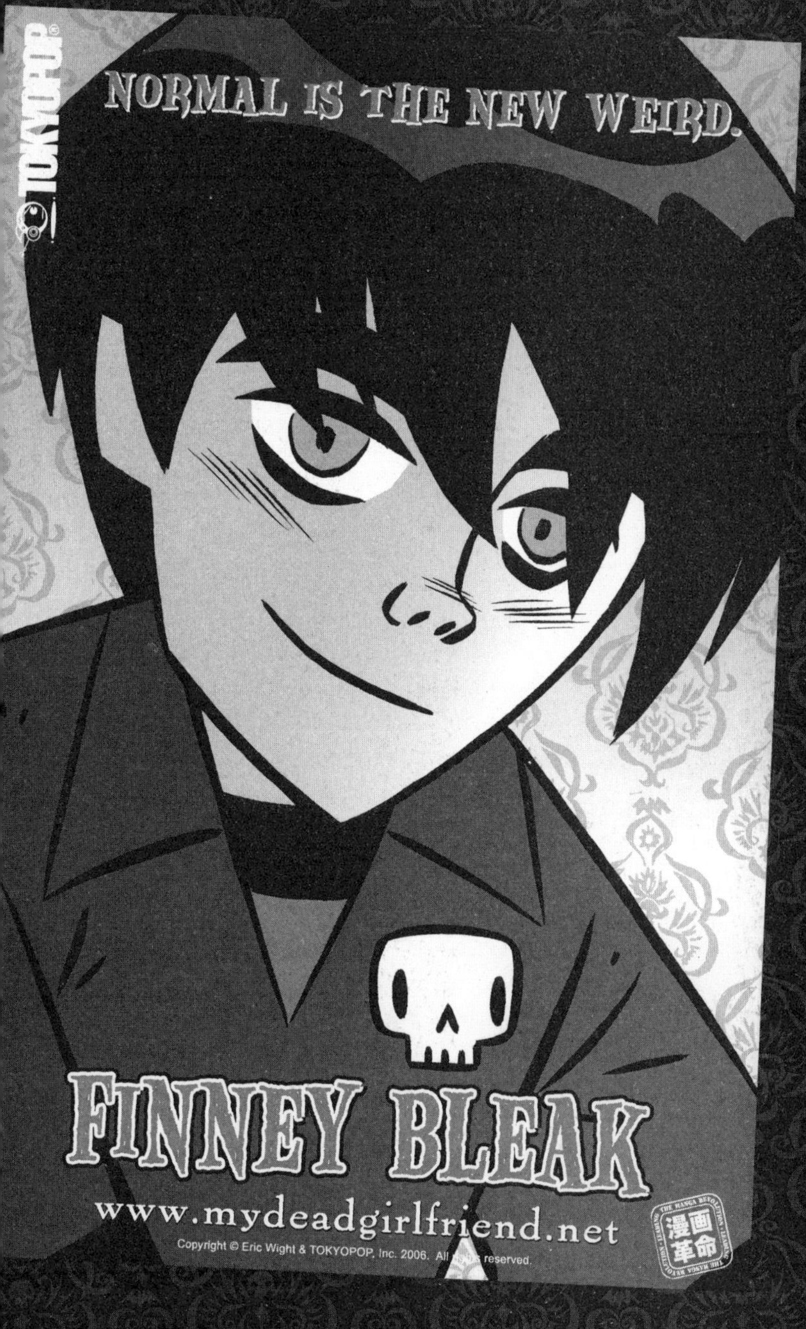
TOKYOPOP
NORMAL IS THE NEW WEIRD.
FINNEY BLEAK
www.mydeadgirlfriend.net
Copyright © Eric Wight & TOKYOPOP, Inc. 2006. All rights reserved.
漫画革命
THE MANGA REVOLUTION

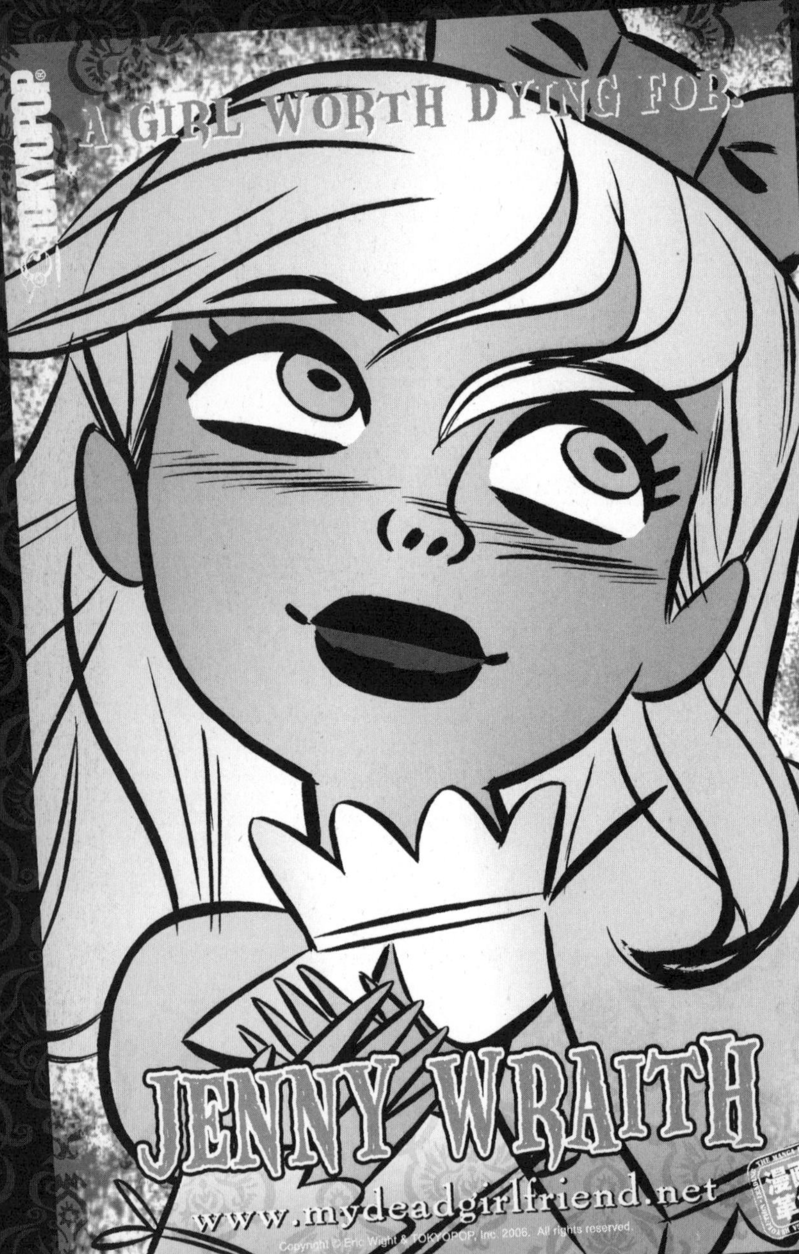
TOKYOPOP
A GIRL WORTH DYING FOR.
JENNY WRAITH
www.mydeadgirlfriend.net
Copyright © Eric Wight & TOKYOPOP, Inc. 2006. All rights reserved.
漫画革命

THIS PAGE:
Character design for
Jenny Wraith

OPPOSITE:
Promotional
illustration of
Jenny

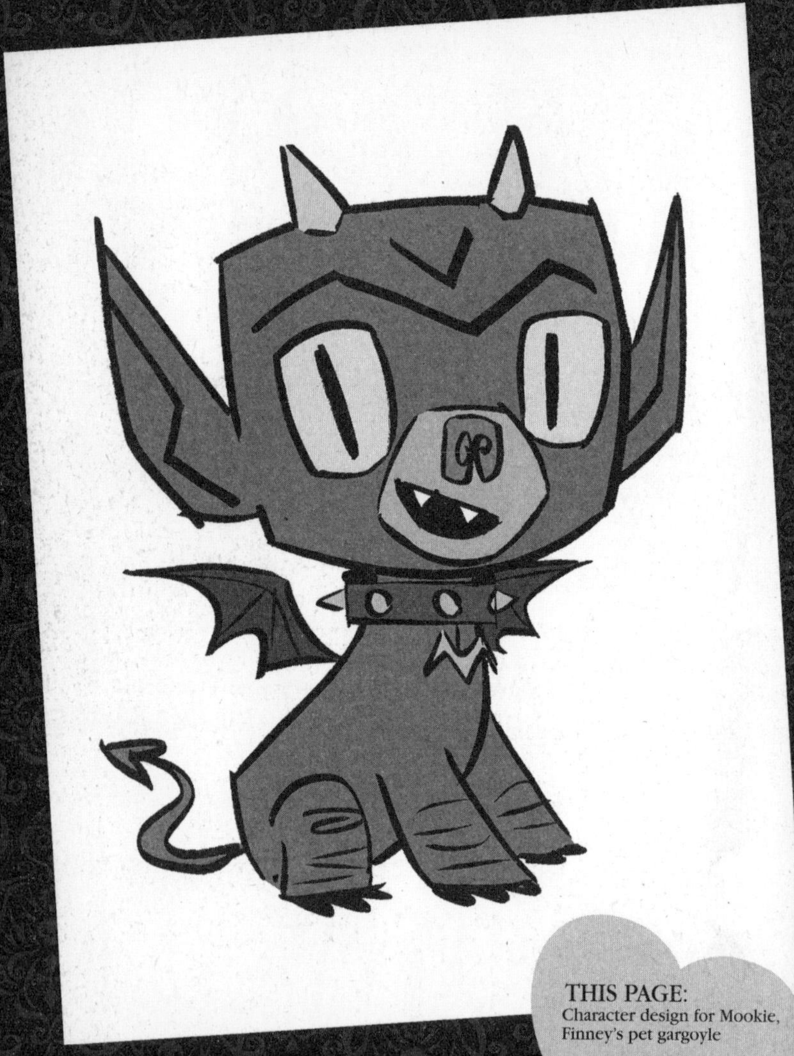

THIS PAGE:
Character design for Mookie, Finney's pet gargoyle

OPPOSITE:
Promotional illustration of Mookie

MAN'S BEST FIEND.

MOOKIE

www.mydeadgirlfriend.net

THIS PAGE &
OPPOSITE:
Unused cover thumbnail sketches

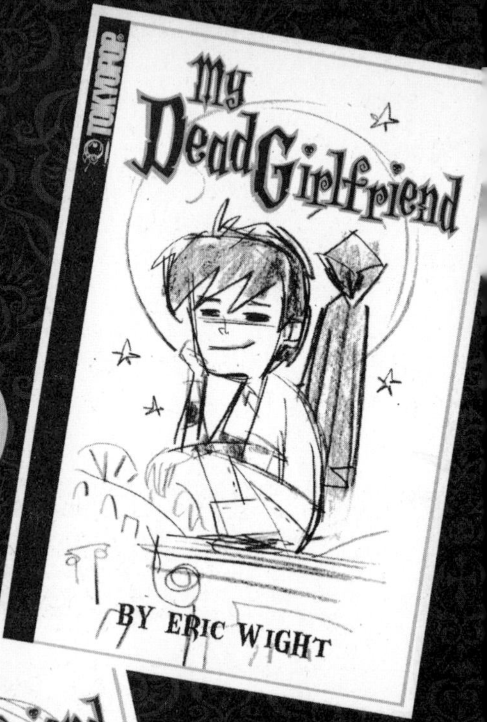
TOKYOPOP
My Dead Girlfriend
BY ERIC WIGHT

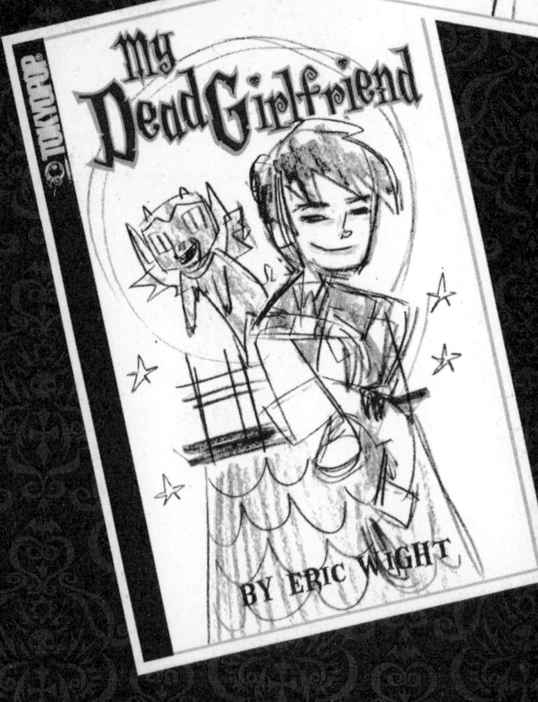
TOKYOPOP
My Dead Girlfriend
BY ERIC WIGHT

My Dead Girlfriend
BY ERIC WIGHT

My Dead Girlfriend
BY ERIC WIGHT

THIS PAGE:
Character design sketches for Salamander Mugwort and Drake Rippington

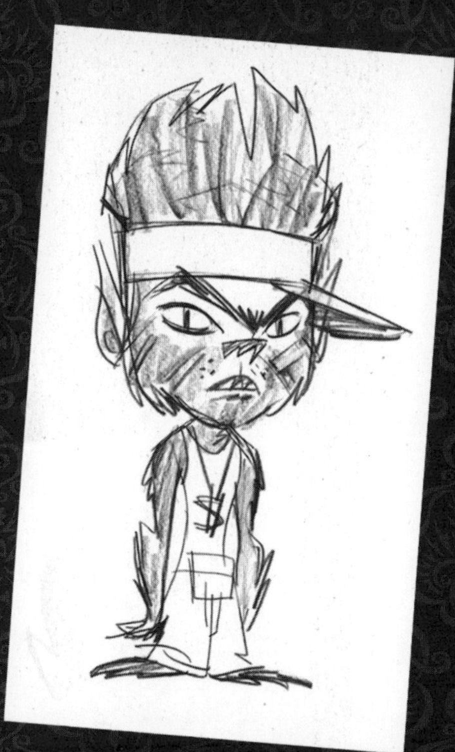

LEFT:
Character design sketch for Hank Palmer.

BELOW:
Thumbnail sketches for a promotional trading card series

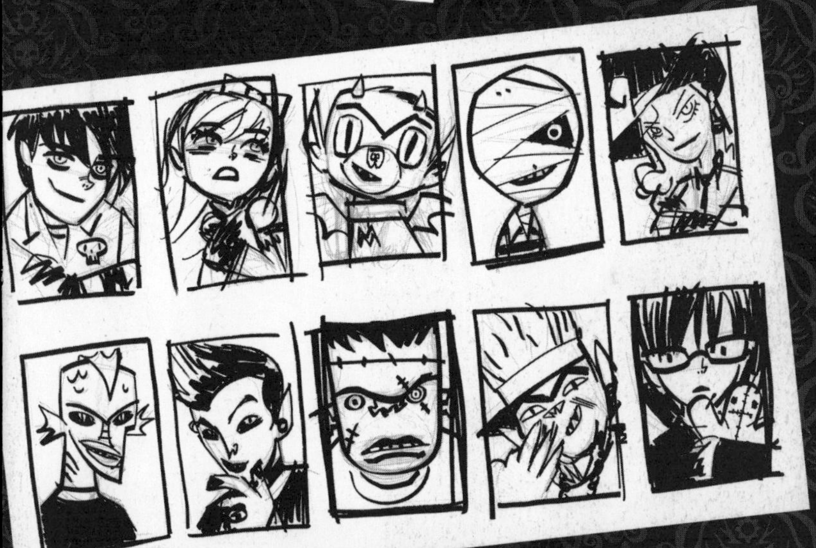

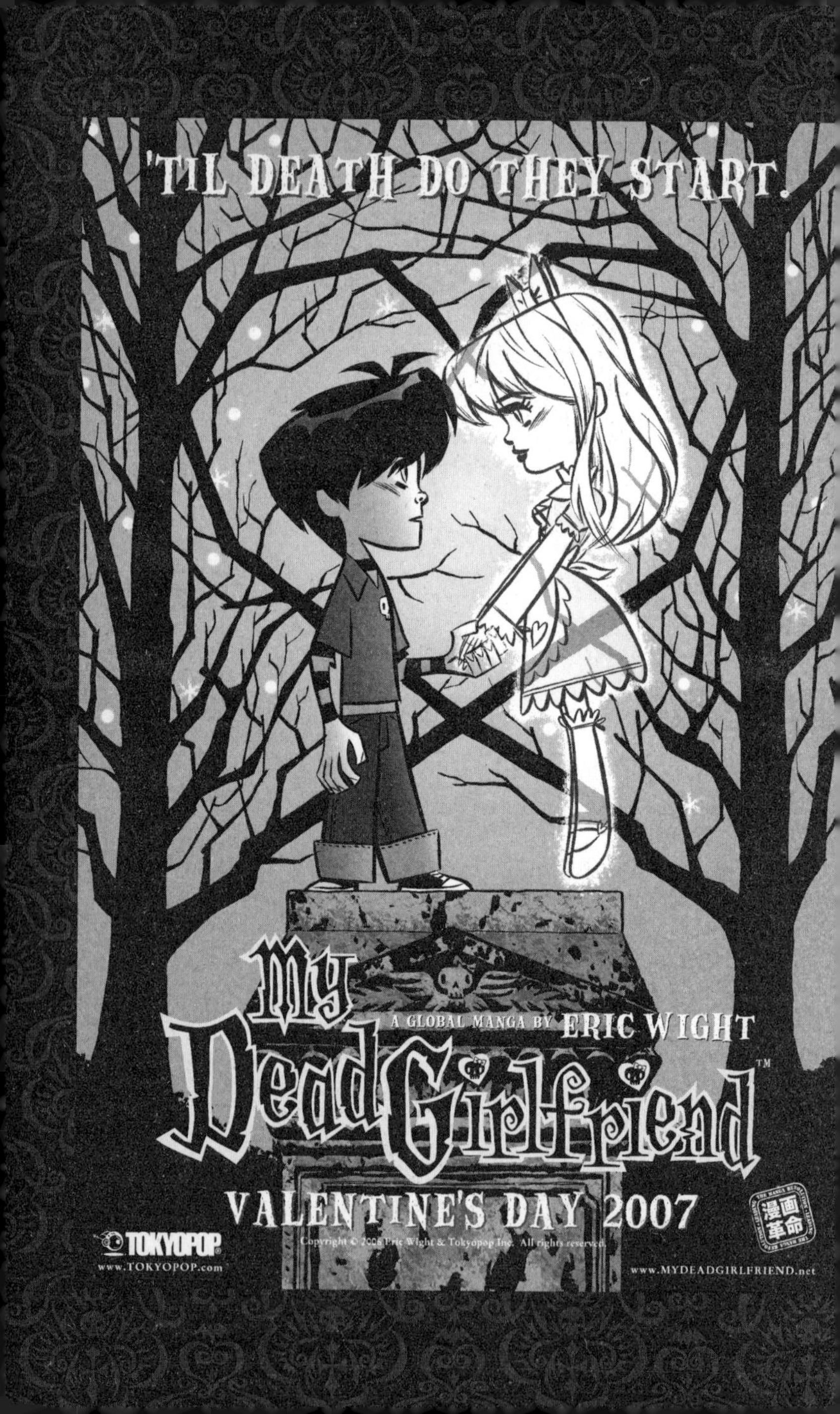

'TIL DEATH DO THEY START.
My Dead Girlfriend™
A GLOBAL MANGA BY ERIC WIGHT
VALENTINE'S DAY 2007
TOKYOPOP
www.TOKYOPOP.com
Copyright © 2006 Eric Wight & Tokyopop Inc. All rights reserved.
漫画革命
www.MYDEADGIRLFRIEND.net

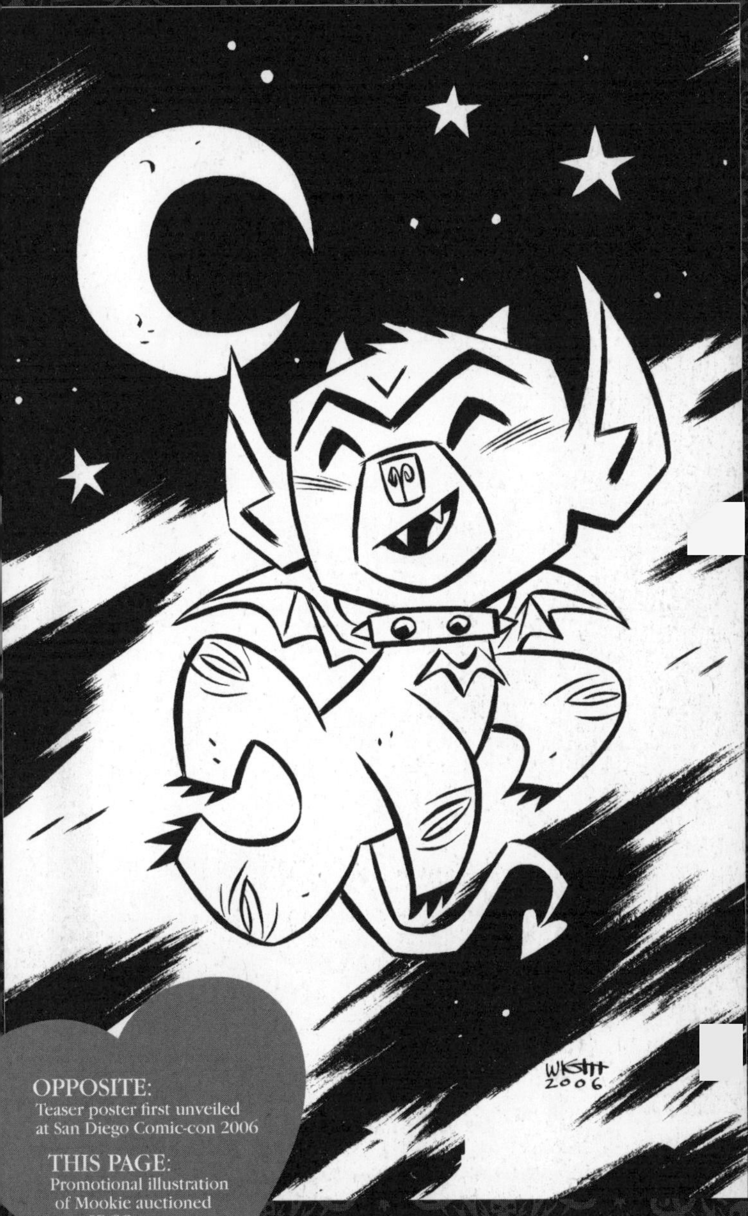

OPPOSITE:
Teaser poster first unveiled at San Diego Comic-con 2006

THIS PAGE:
Promotional illustration of Mookie auctioned at SDCC

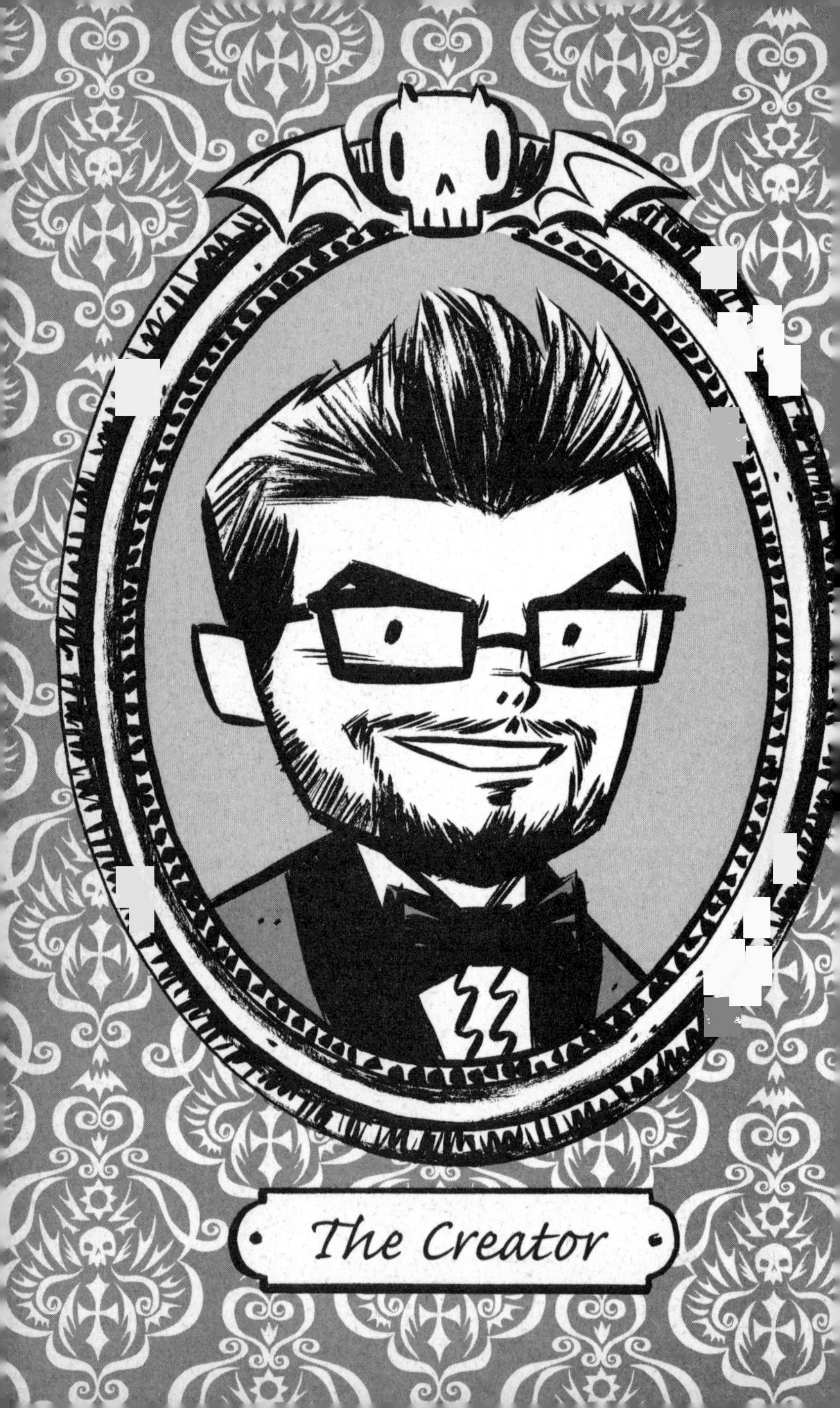
The Creator

ABOUT THE CREATOR

After spending most of his childhood wishing for superpowers, Eric Wight conceded that while he may never fly or have x-ray vision, being able to draw pretty pictures and make people laugh is pretty cool too. Getting paid for it doesn't suck either.

He even has a website to show off how much fun he's having: www.ericwight.com.